LAID BACK CAMP

Afro

1

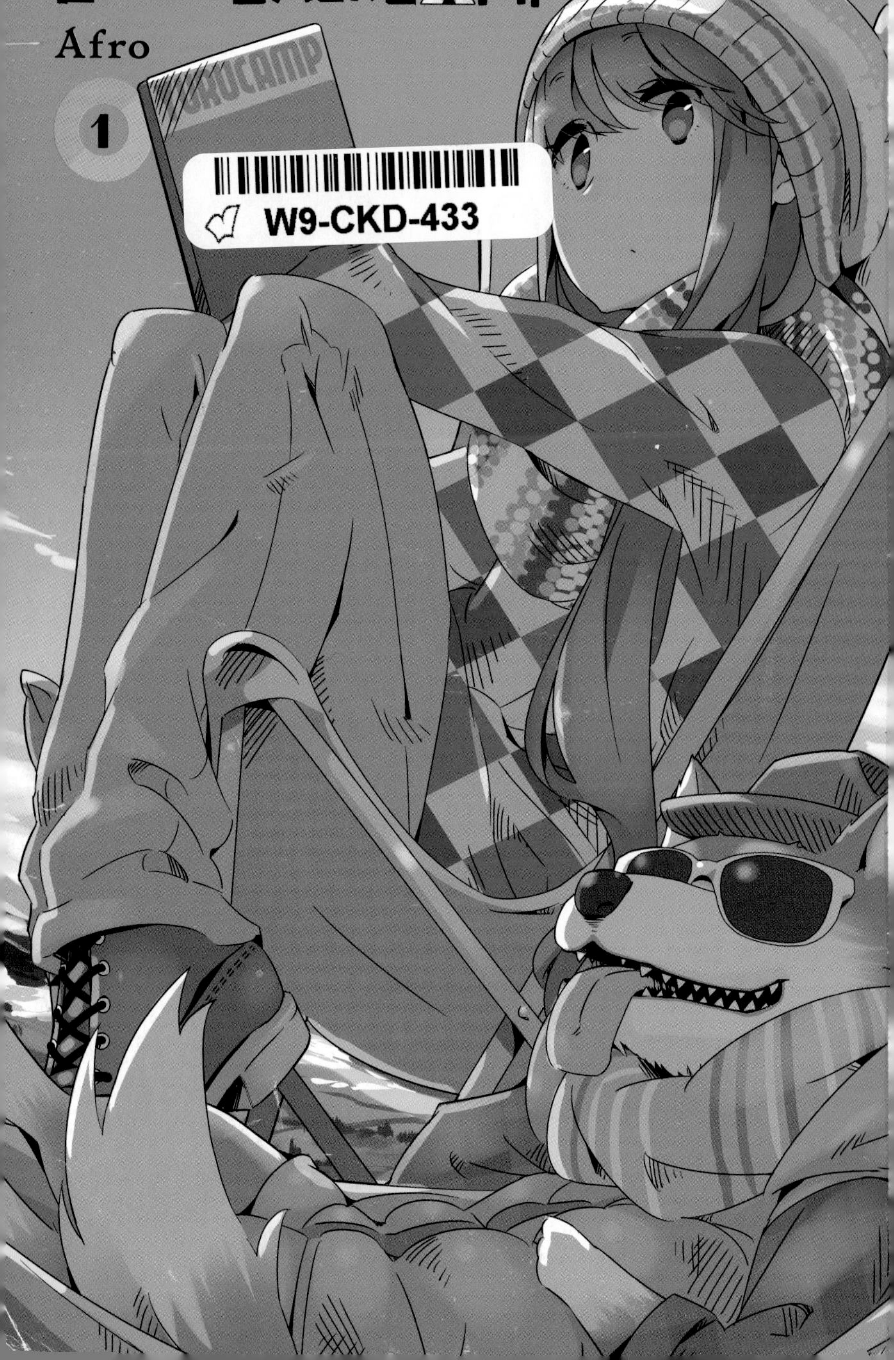

1

LAID-BACK CAMP

contents

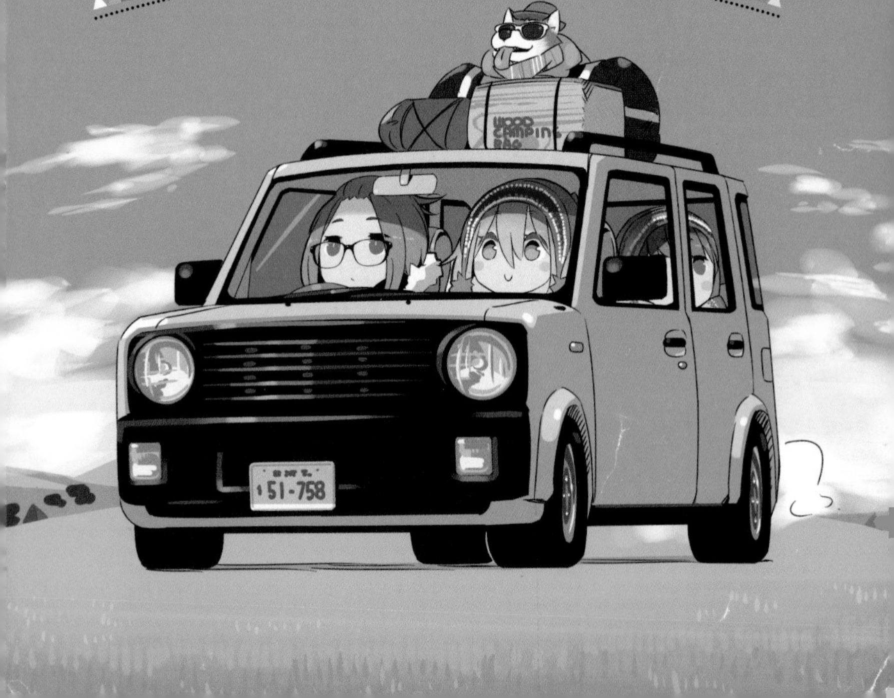

WOOD CAMPING BAG
51-758

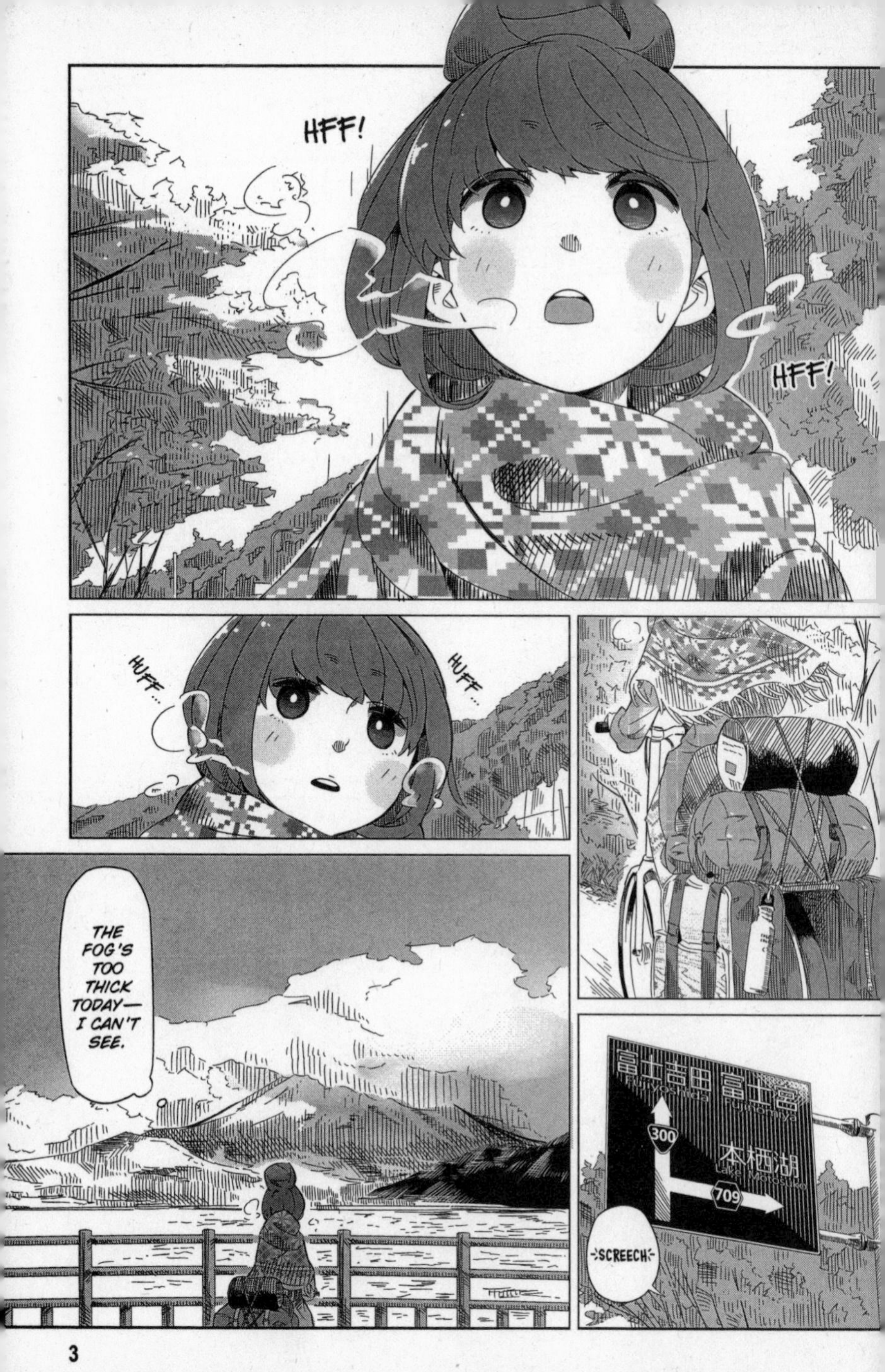
HFF!
HFF!
HUFF...
HUFF...
富士吉田
富士宮
300
本栖湖
709
SCREECH
THE FOG'S TOO THICK TODAY— I CAN'T SEE.

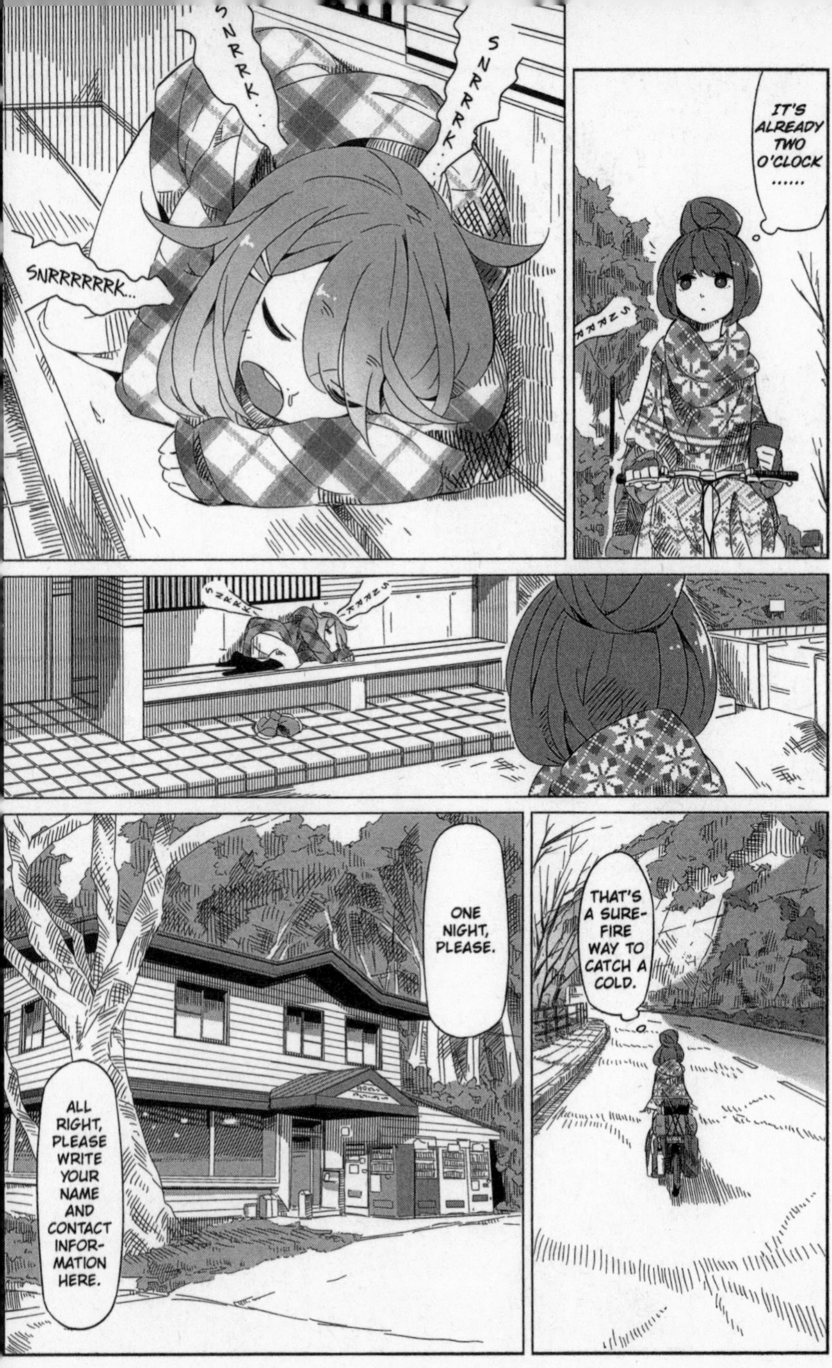
IT'S ALREADY TWO O'CLOCK......
SNRRK
SNRRRK...
SNRRK...
SNRRRRRRK...
THAT'S A SURE-FIRE WAY TO CATCH A COLD.
ONE NIGHT, PLEASE.
ALL RIGHT, PLEASE WRITE YOUR NAME AND CONTACT INFORMATION HERE.

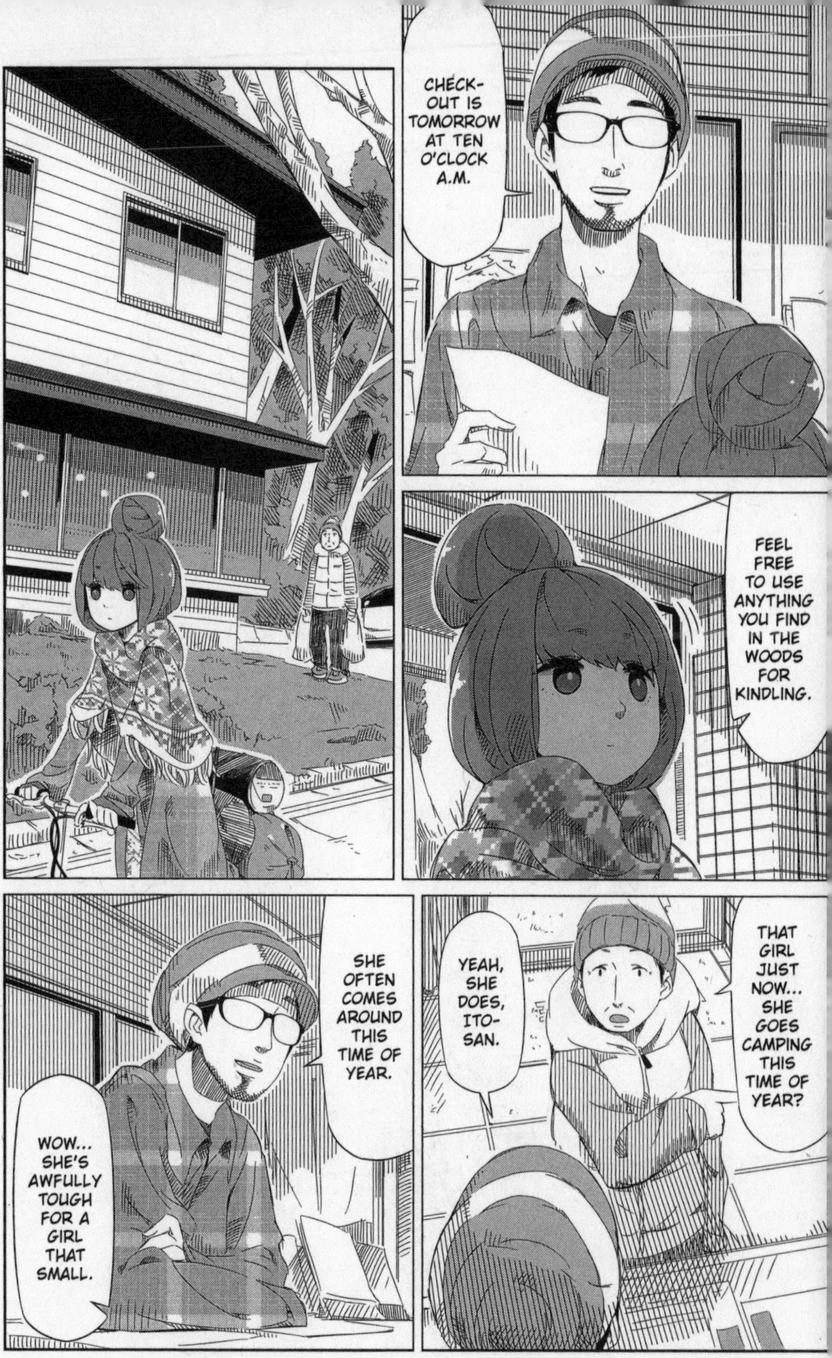
CHECK-OUT IS TOMORROW AT TEN O'CLOCK A.M.
FEEL FREE TO USE ANYTHING YOU FIND IN THE WOODS FOR KINDLING.
THAT GIRL JUST NOW... SHE GOES CAMPING THIS TIME OF YEAR?
YEAH, SHE DOES, ITO-SAN.
SHE OFTEN COMES AROUND THIS TIME OF YEAR.
WOW... SHE'S AWFULLY TOUGH FOR A GIRL THAT SMALL.

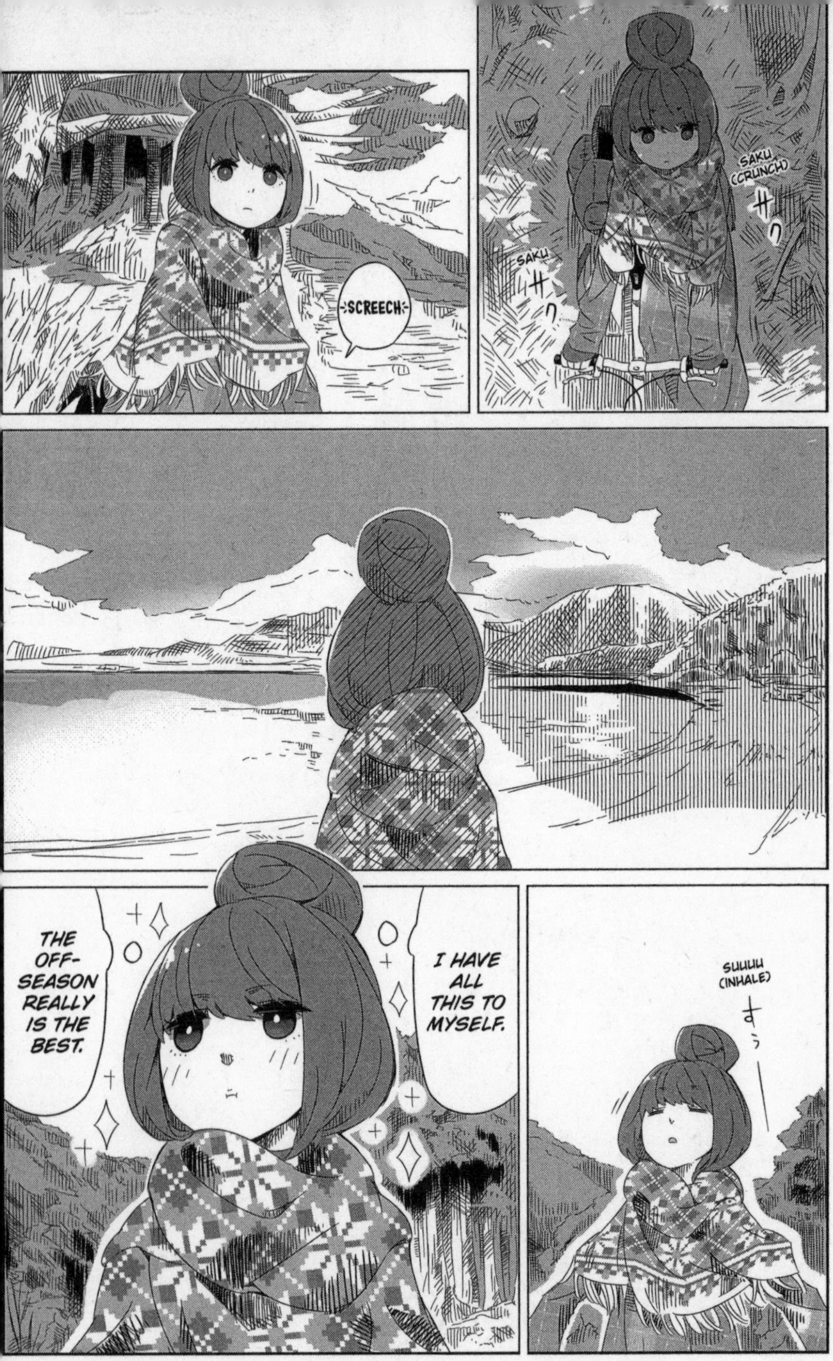
SAKU (CRUNCH)
サク
SAKU
サク
SCREECH
SUUUU (INHALE)
すぅ―
I HAVE ALL THIS TO MYSELF.
THE OFF-SEASON REALLY IS THE BEST.

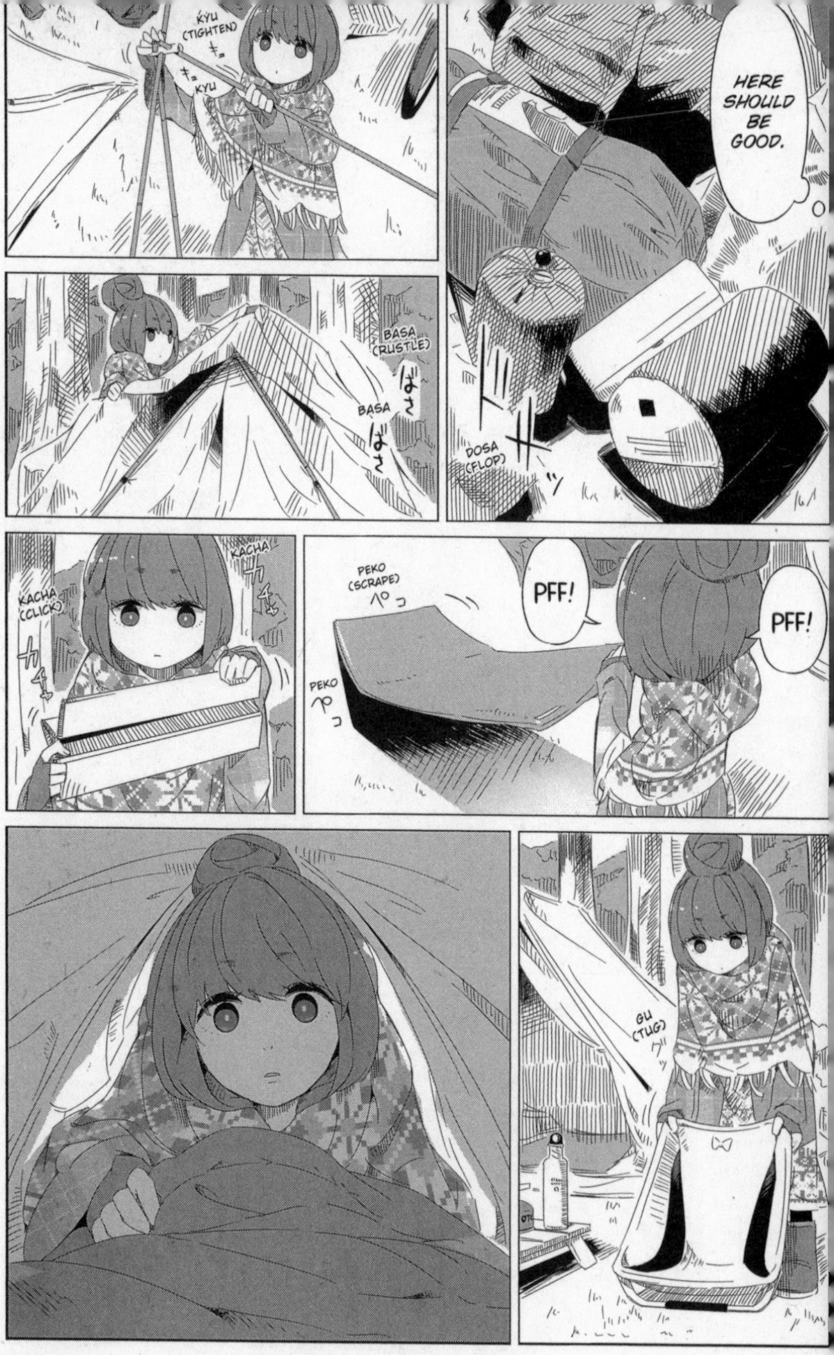
HERE SHOULD BE GOOD.
DOSA (FLOP)
ドサッ
KYU (TIGHTEN)
キュ
キュ
KYU
BASA (RUSTLE)
ばさ
BASA
ばさ
PFF!
PFF!
PEKO (SCRAPE)
ペコ
PEKO
ペコ
KACHA
カチャ
KACHA (CLICK)
カチャ
GU (TUG)
グッ

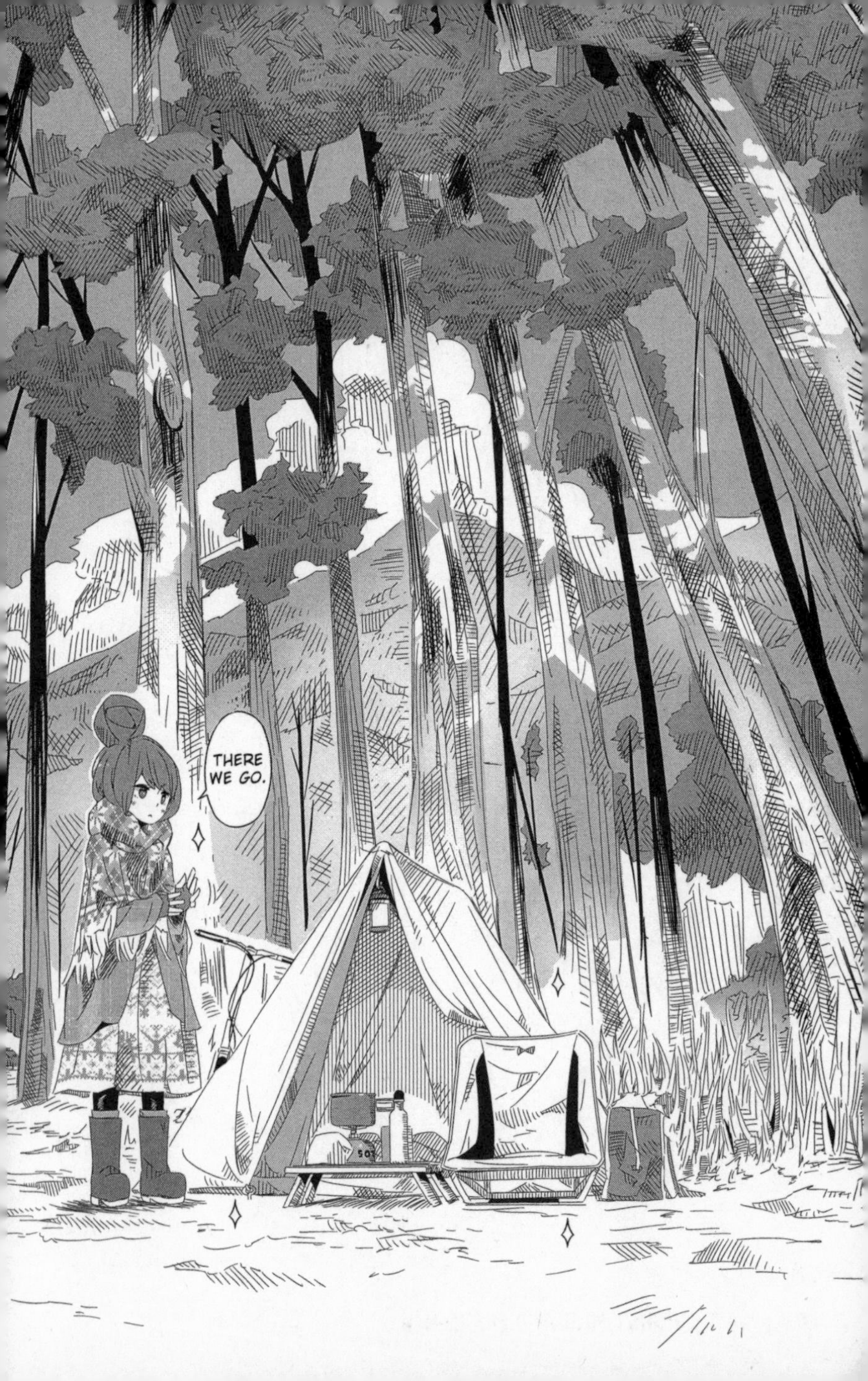
THERE WE GO.

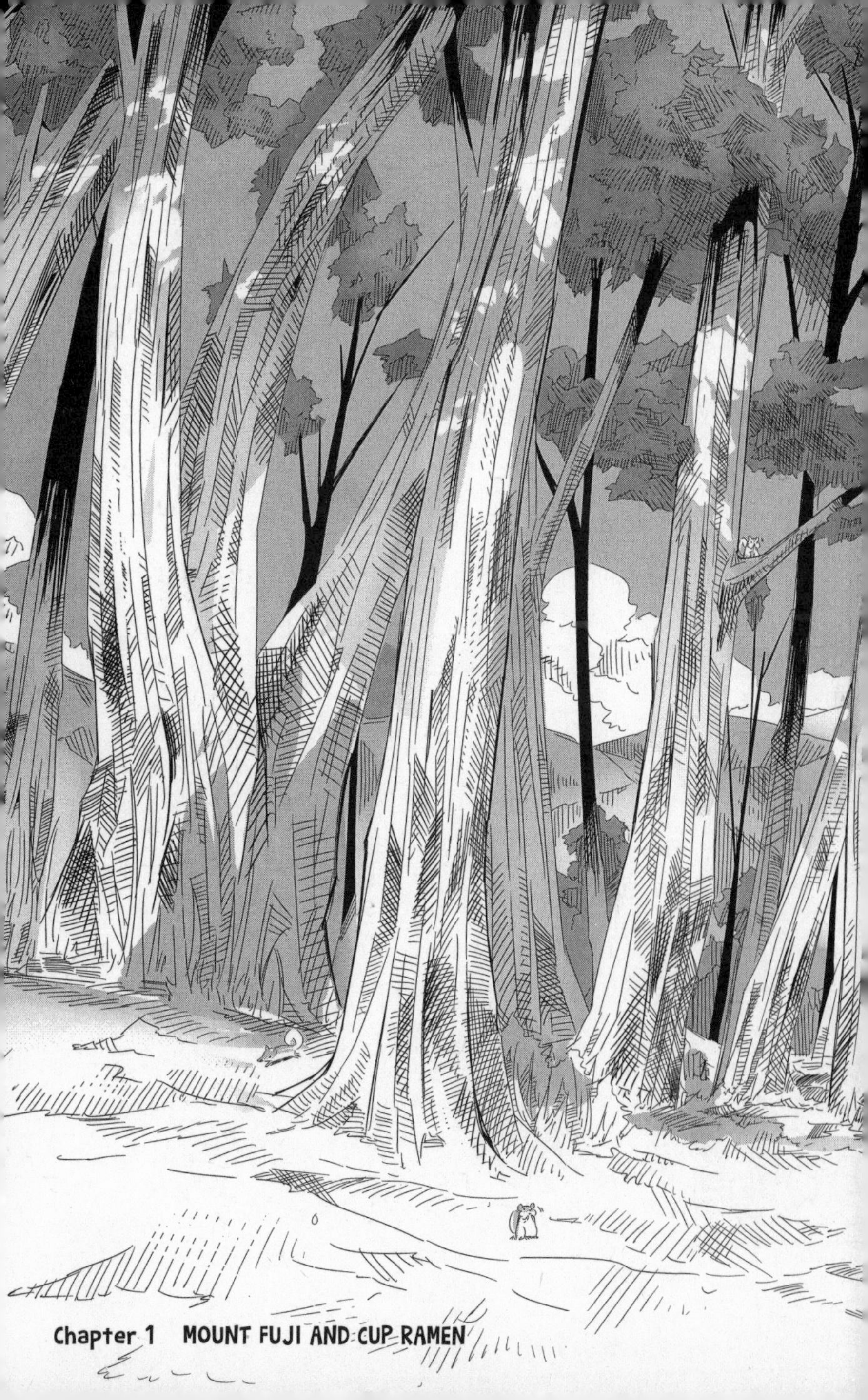

Chapter 1 MOUNT FUJI AND CUP RAMEN

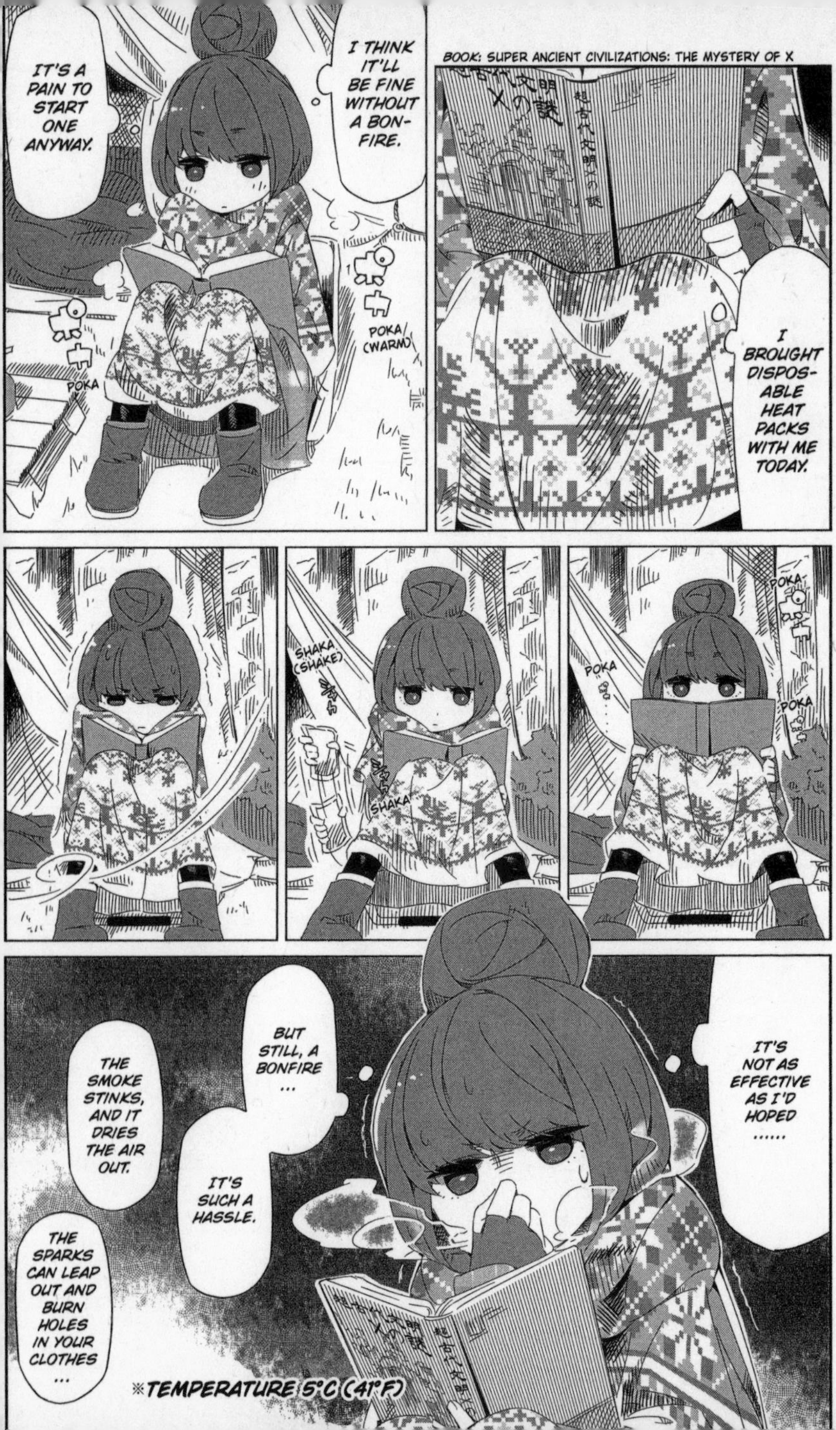
BOOK: SUPER ANCIENT CIVILIZATIONS: THE MYSTERY OF X
超古代文明Xの謎
I BROUGHT DISPOSABLE HEAT PACKS WITH ME TODAY.
I THINK IT'LL BE FINE WITHOUT A BONFIRE.
IT'S A PAIN TO START ONE ANYWAY.
POKA (WARM)
POKA
POKA
POKA
POKA
SHAKA (SHAKE)
SHAKA
IT'S NOT AS EFFECTIVE AS I'D HOPED......
BUT STILL, A BONFIRE...
THE SMOKE STINKS, AND IT DRIES THE AIR OUT.
IT'S SUCH A HASSLE.
THE SPARKS CAN LEAP OUT AND BURN HOLES IN YOUR CLOTHES...
※TEMPERATURE 5°C (41°F)

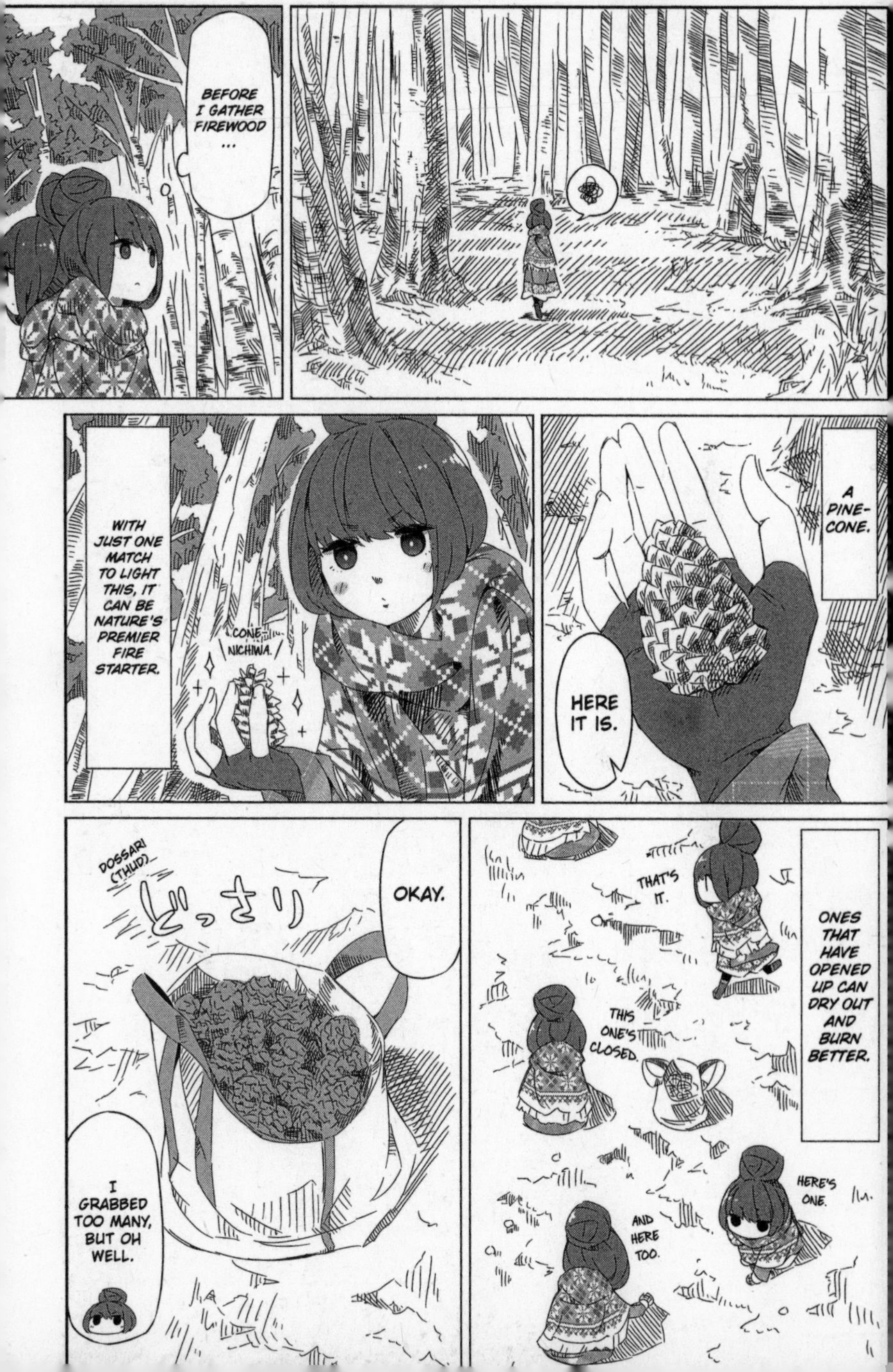
BEFORE I GATHER FIREWOOD ...
A PINE-CONE.
HERE IT IS.
WITH JUST ONE MATCH TO LIGHT THIS, IT CAN BE NATURE'S PREMIER FIRE STARTER.
CONE NICHIWA.
ONES THAT HAVE OPENED UP CAN DRY OUT AND BURN BETTER.
THAT'S IT.
THIS ONE'S CLOSED.
HERE'S ONE.
AND HERE TOO.
OKAY.
DOSSARI (THUD)
どっさり
I GRABBED TOO MANY, BUT OH WELL.

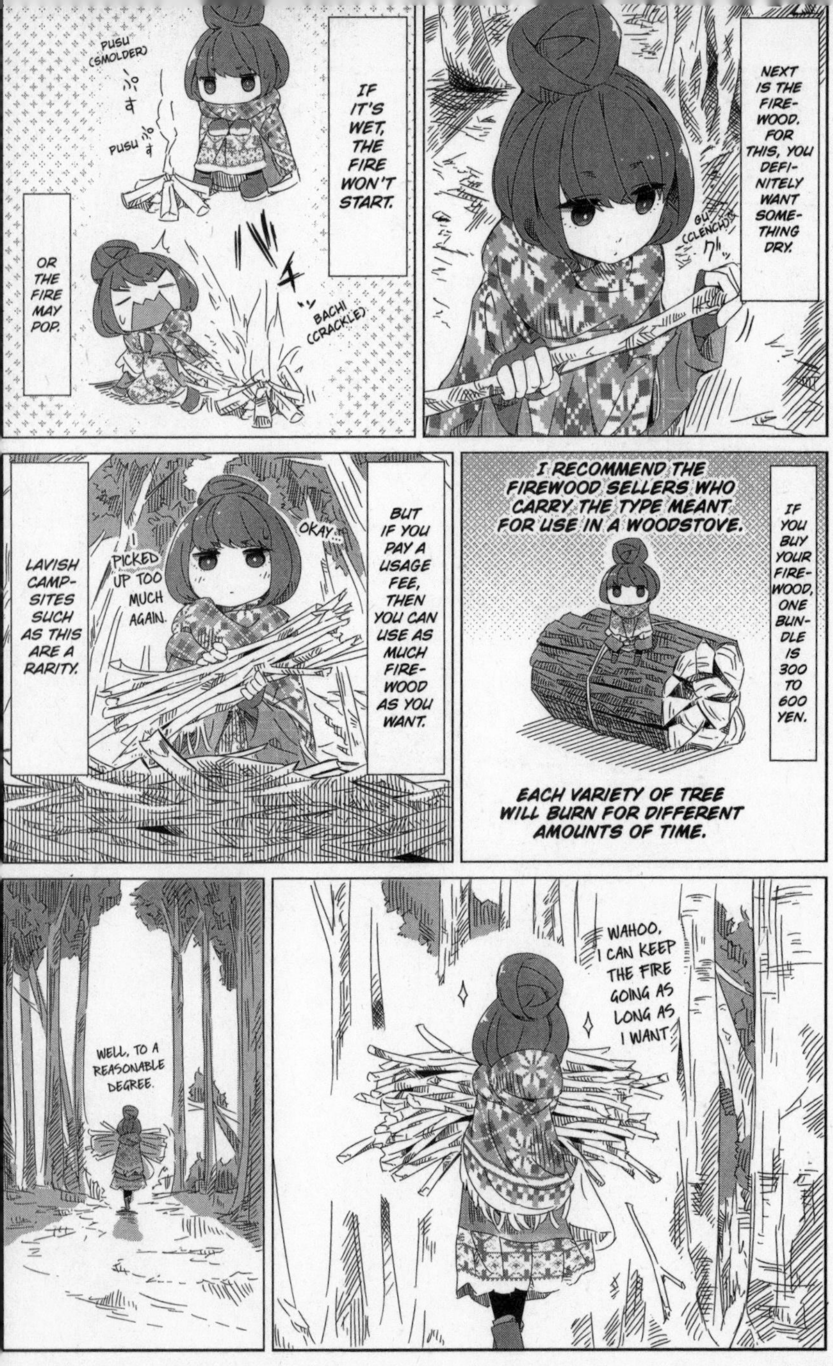
NEXT IS THE FIRE-WOOD. FOR THIS, YOU DEFI-NITELY WANT SOME-THING DRY.
GU (CLENCH)
グッ
IF IT'S WET, THE FIRE WON'T START.
PUSU (SMOLDER)
ぷす
PUSU
ぷす
OR THE FIRE MAY POP.
BACHI (CRACKLE)
IF YOU BUY YOUR FIRE-WOOD, ONE BUN-DLE IS 300 TO 600 YEN.
I RECOMMEND THE FIREWOOD SELLERS WHO CARRY THE TYPE MEANT FOR USE IN A WOODSTOVE.
EACH VARIETY OF TREE WILL BURN FOR DIFFERENT AMOUNTS OF TIME.
BUT IF YOU PAY A USAGE FEE, THEN YOU CAN USE AS MUCH FIRE-WOOD AS YOU WANT.
OKAY...
PICKED UP TOO MUCH AGAIN.
LAVISH CAMP-SITES SUCH AS THIS ARE A RARITY.
WAHOO, I CAN KEEP THE FIRE GOING AS LONG AS I WANT.
WELL, TO A REASONABLE DEGREE.

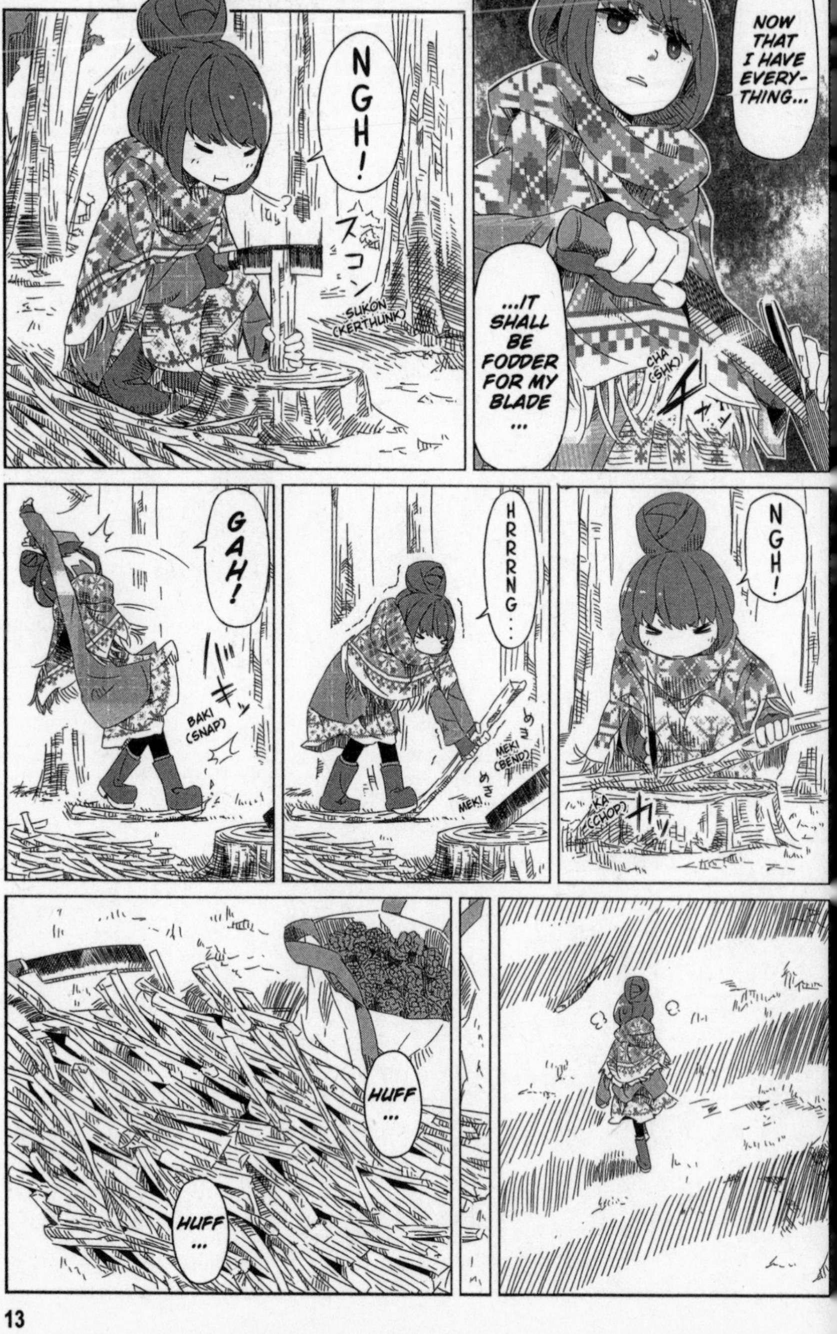
NOW THAT I HAVE EVERYTHING...
...IT SHALL BE FODDER FOR MY BLADE...
CHA (SHK)
NGH!
SUKON (KERTHUNK)
NGH!
KA (CHOP)
HRRRNG...
MEKI (BEND)
MEK!
GAH!
BAKI (SNAP)
HUFF...
HUFF...

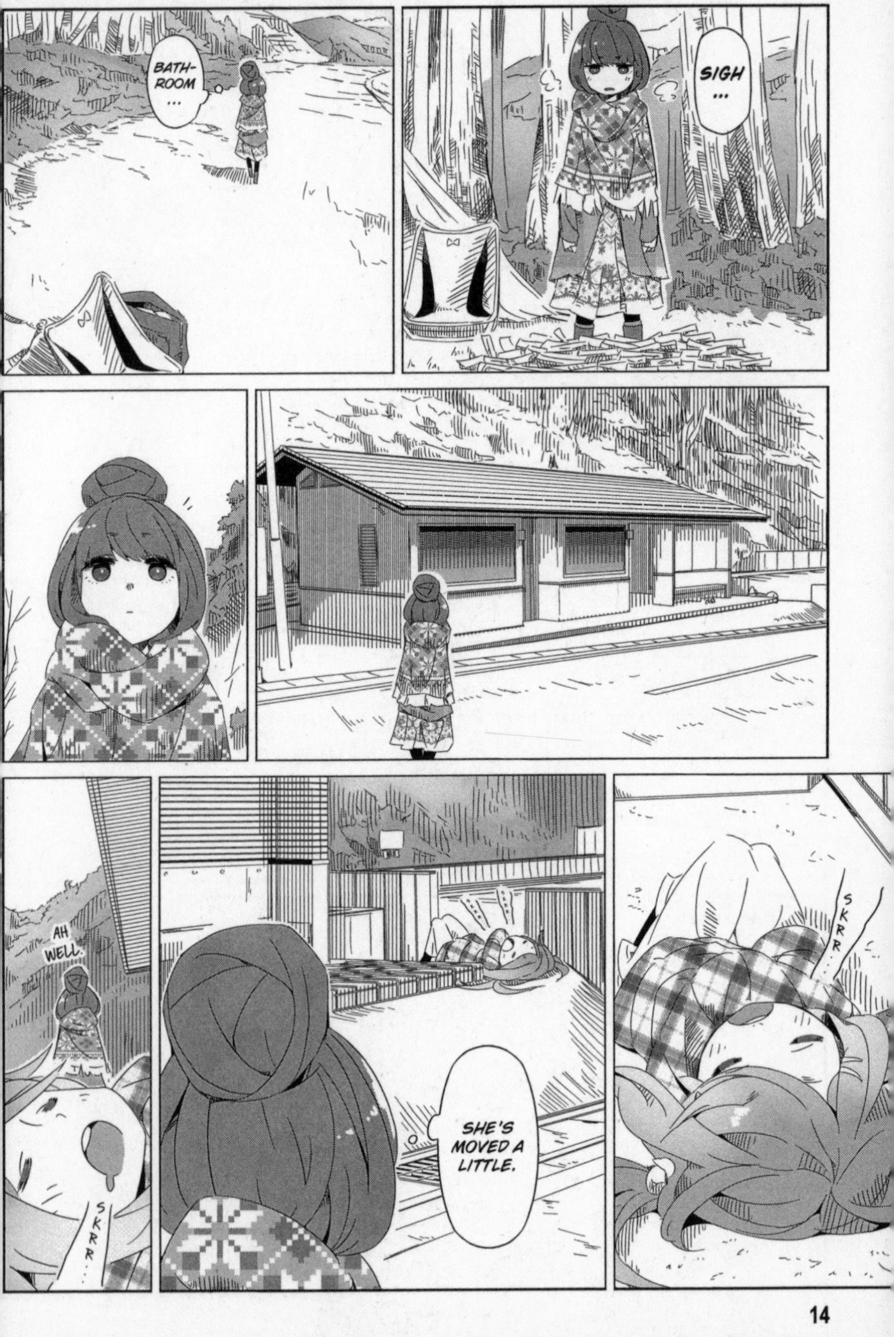
SIGH ...
BATH-ROOM ...
SKRR...
SHE'S MOVED A LITTLE.
AH WELL.
SKRR...

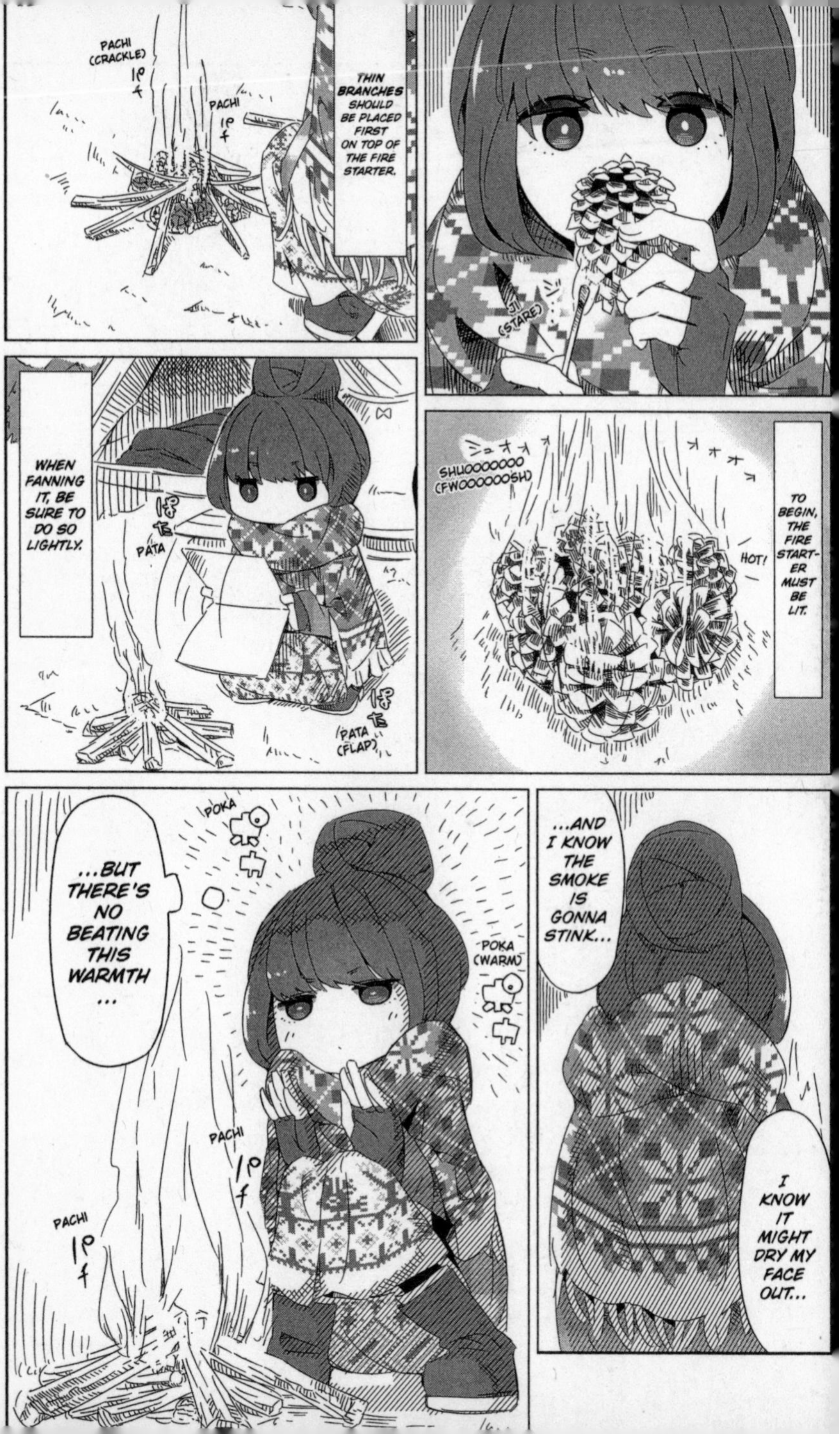
JI (STARE)
TO BEGIN, THE FIRE STARTER MUST BE LIT.
SHUOOOOOOO (FWOOOOOOSH)
HOT!
THIN BRANCHES SHOULD BE PLACED FIRST ON TOP OF THE FIRE STARTER.
PACHI (CRACKLE)
PACHI
WHEN FANNING IT, BE SURE TO DO SO LIGHTLY.
PATA
PATA (FLAP)
I KNOW IT MIGHT DRY MY FACE OUT...
...AND I KNOW THE SMOKE IS GONNA STINK...
...BUT THERE'S NO BEATING THIS WARMTH...
POKA
POKA (WARM)
PACHI
PACHI

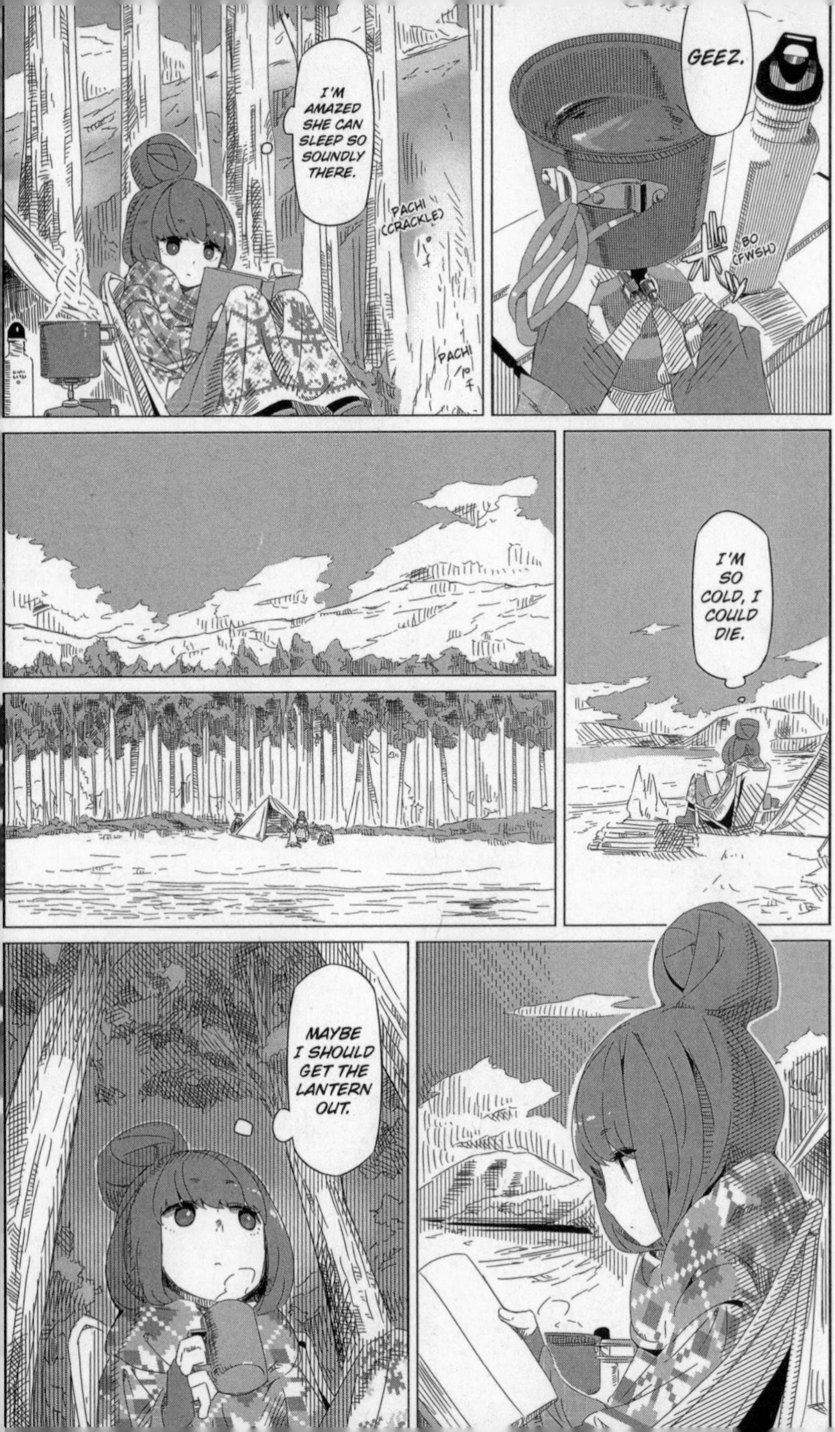
GEEZ.
BO (FWSH)
I'M AMAZED SHE CAN SLEEP SO SOUNDLY THERE.
PACHI (CRACKLE)
PACHI
I'M SO COLD, I COULD DIE.
MAYBE I SHOULD GET THE LANTERN OUT.

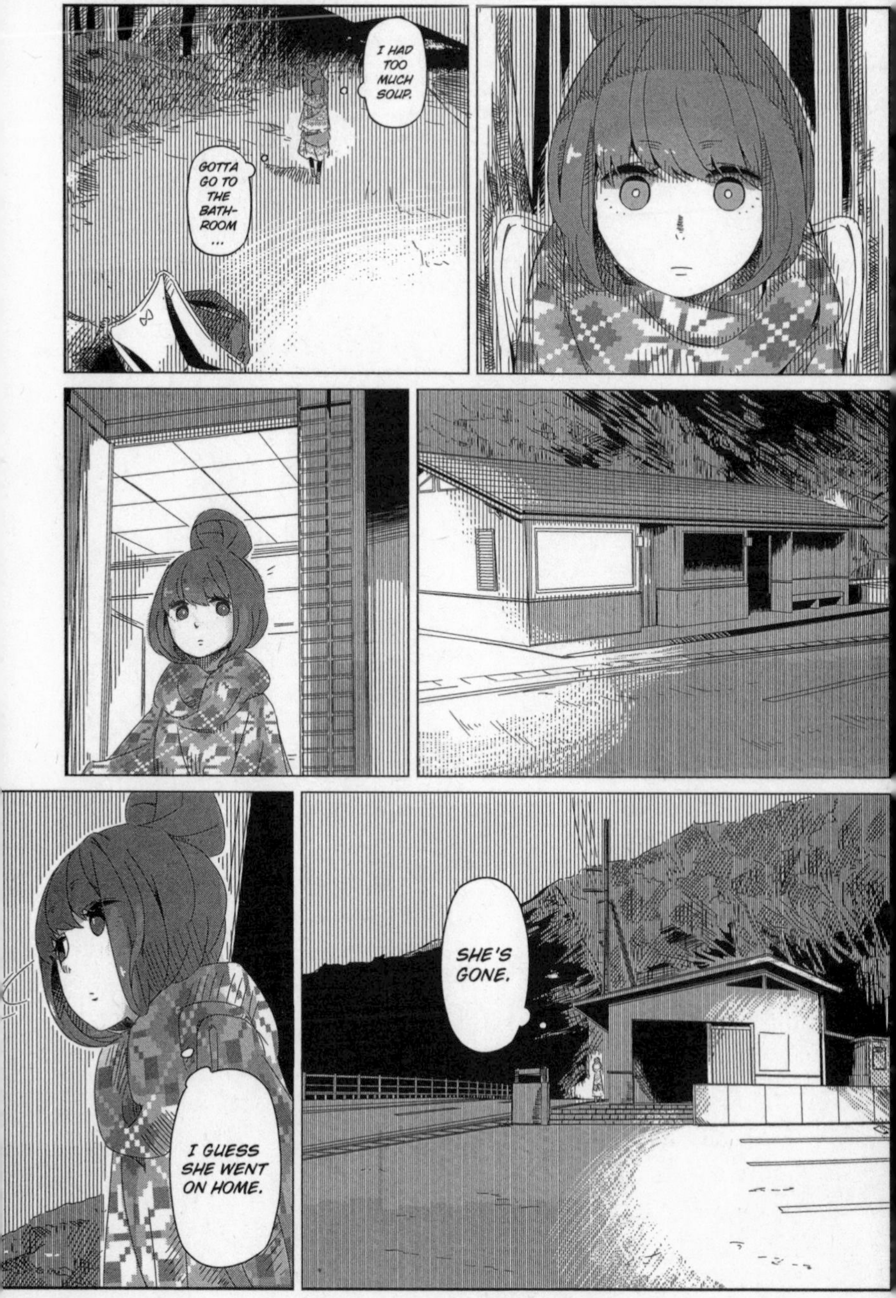
I HAD TOO MUCH SOUP.
GOTTA GO TO THE BATH-ROOM ...
SHE'S GONE.
I GUESS SHE WENT ON HOME.

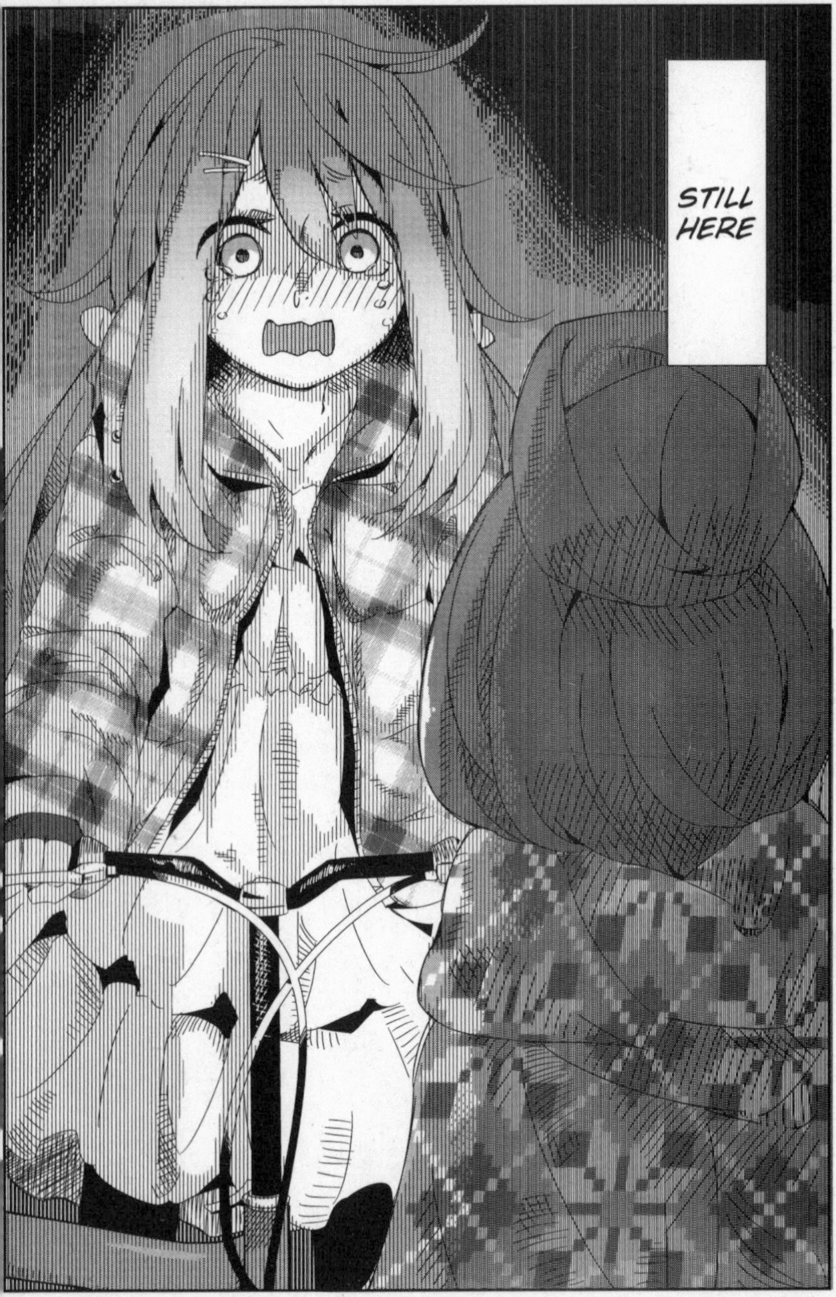
STILL HERE

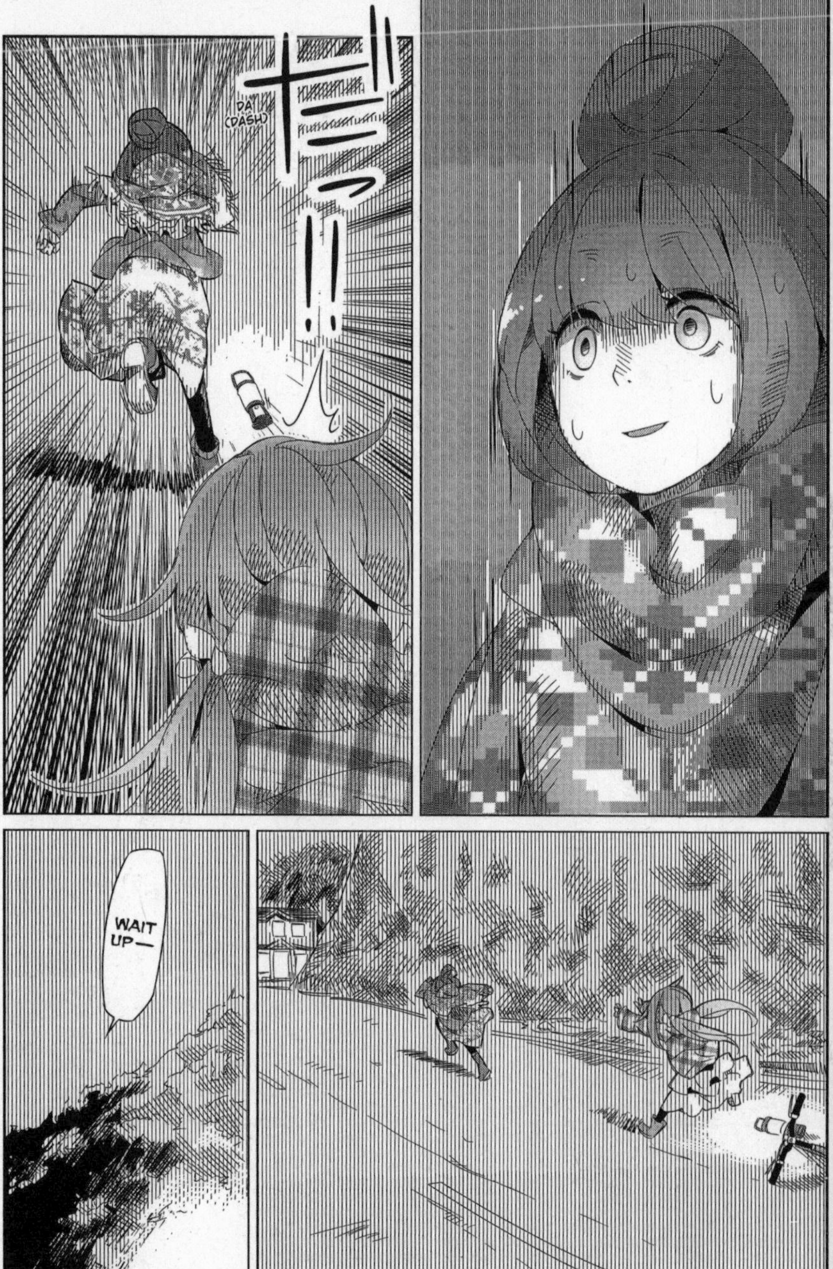
だっ!!
DA (DASH)
WAIT UP—

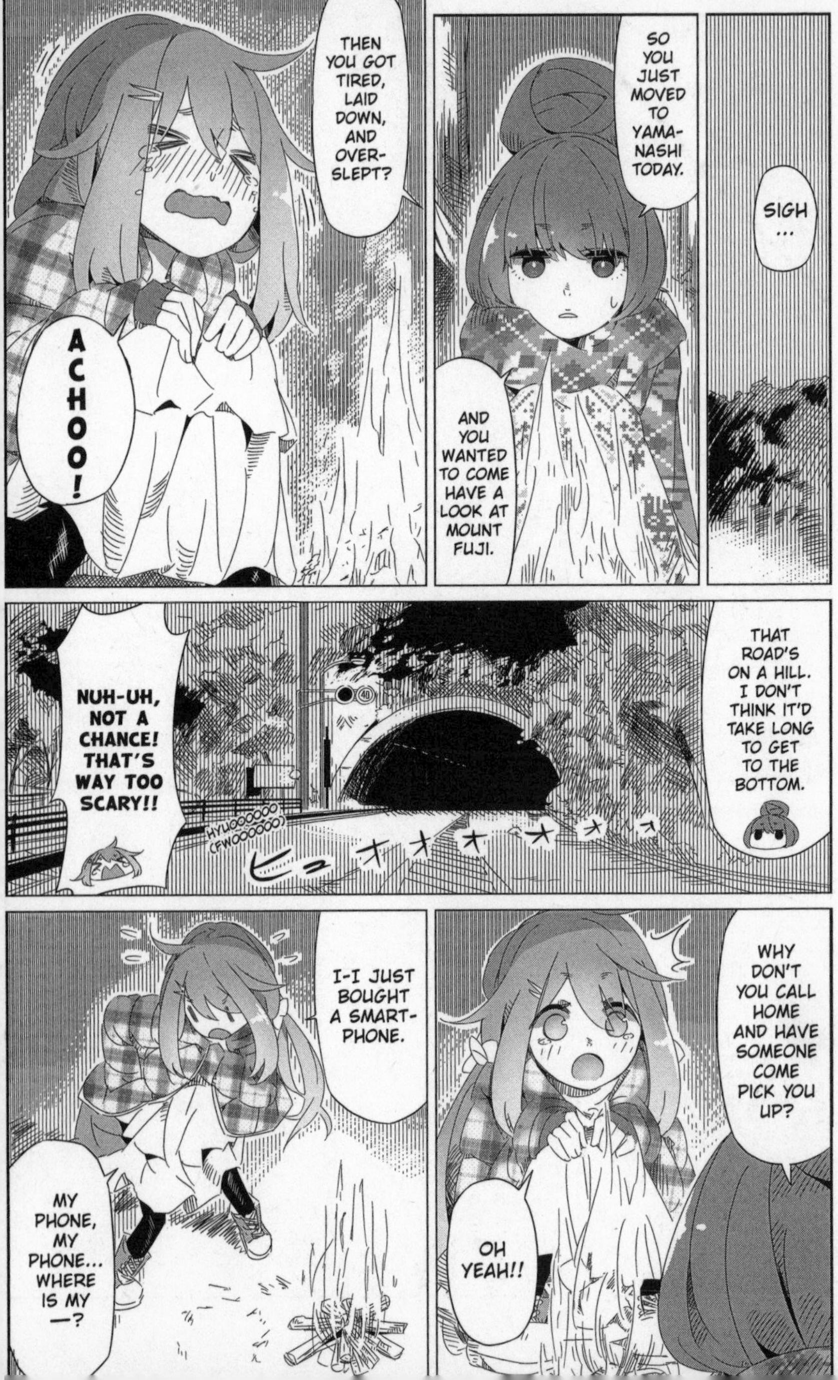
SIGH...
SO YOU JUST MOVED TO YAMANASHI TODAY.
AND YOU WANTED TO COME HAVE A LOOK AT MOUNT FUJI.
THEN YOU GOT TIRED, LAID DOWN, AND OVERSLEPT?
ACHOO!
THAT ROAD'S ON A HILL. I DON'T THINK IT'D TAKE LONG TO GET TO THE BOTTOM.
HYUOOOOOO (FWOOOOOO)
NUH-UH, NOT A CHANCE! THAT'S WAY TOO SCARY!!
WHY DON'T YOU CALL HOME AND HAVE SOMEONE COME PICK YOU UP?
OH YEAH!!
I-I JUST BOUGHT A SMARTPHONE.
MY PHONE, MY PHONE... WHERE IS MY—?

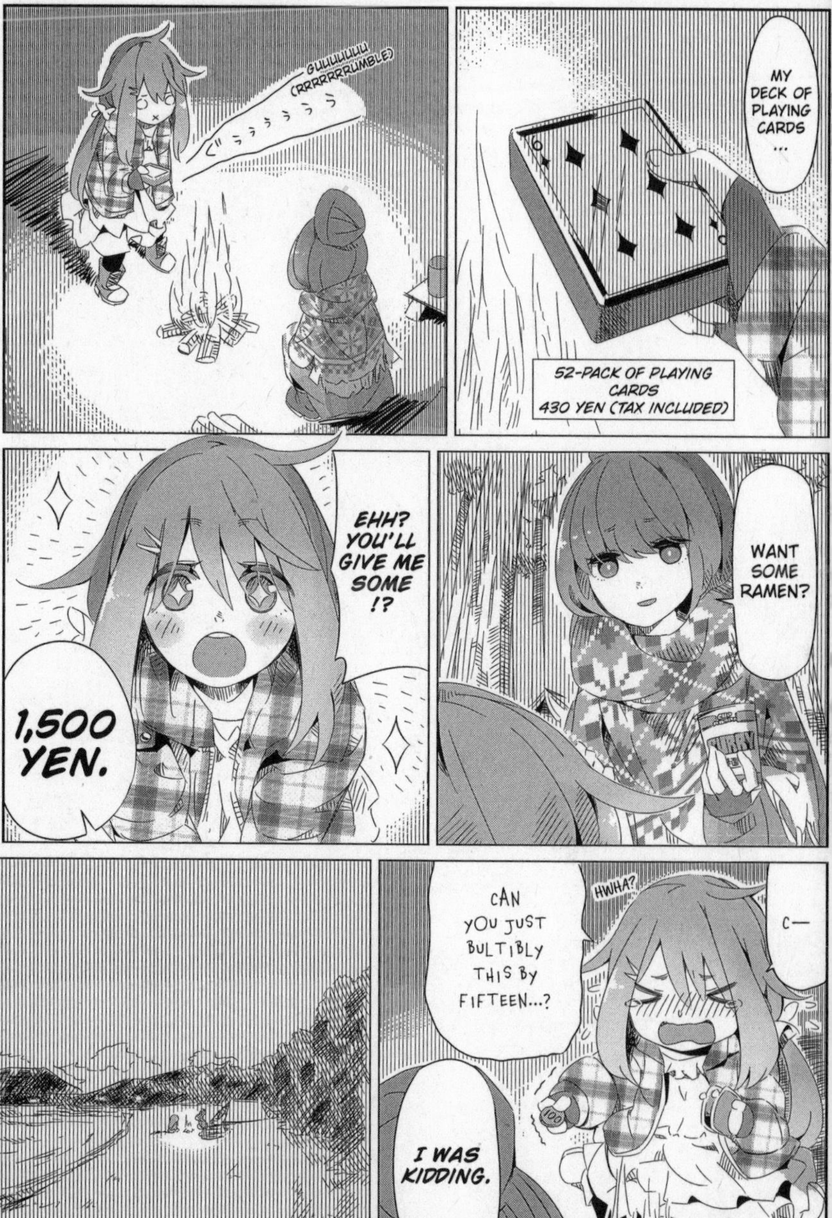
MY DECK OF PLAYING CARDS...
52-PACK OF PLAYING CARDS
430 YEN (TAX INCLUDED)
ぐぅぅぅぅぅぅ
GUUUUUUU
(RRRRRRRUMBLE)
WANT SOME RAMEN?
EHH? YOU'LL GIVE ME SOME!?
1,500 YEN.
HWHA?
C—
CAN YOU JUST BULTIBLY THIS BY FIFTEEN...?
I WAS KIDDING.

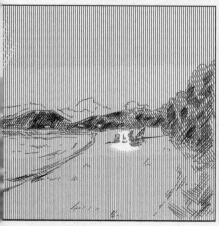

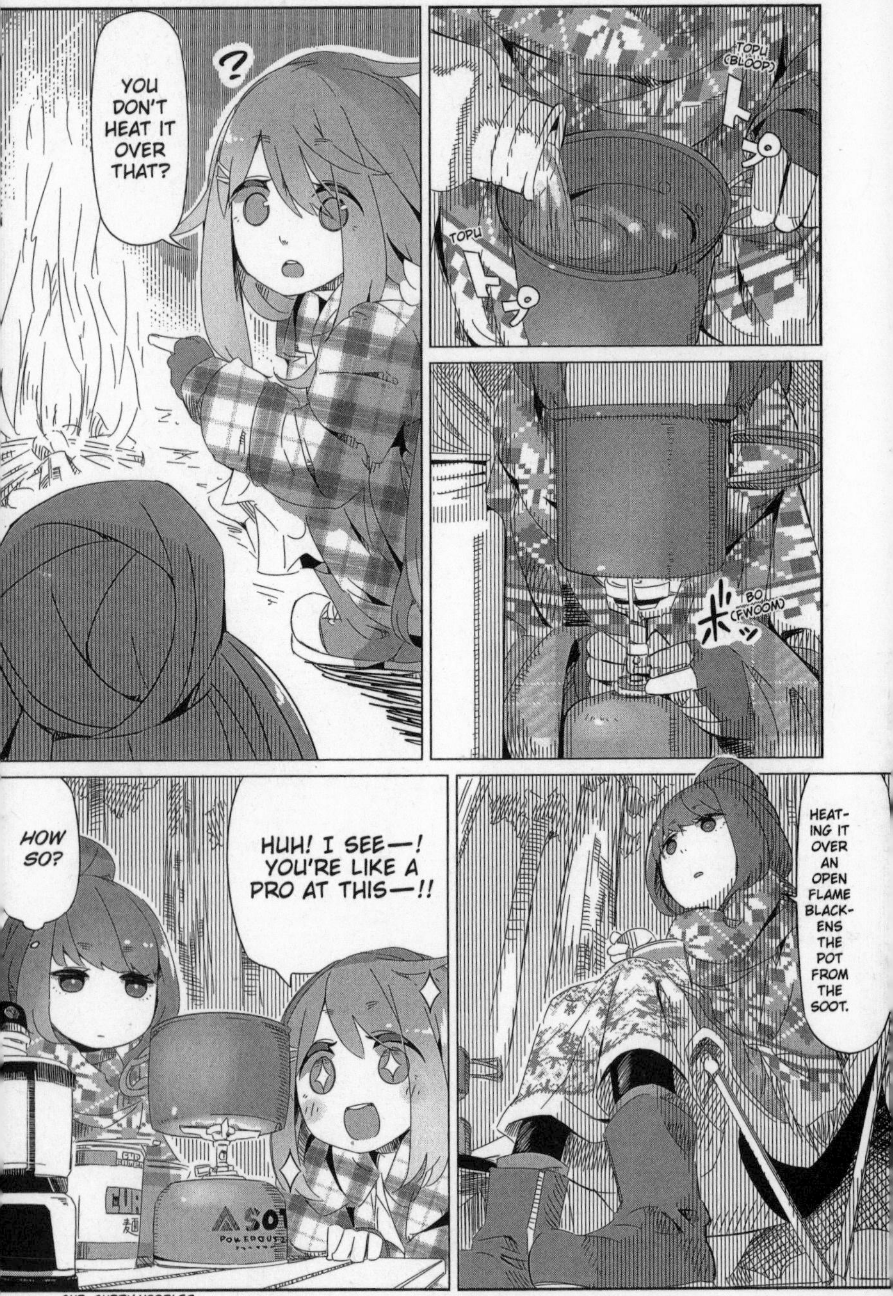
TOPU (BLOOP)
トプ
TOPU
トプ
BO (FWOOM)
ボッ
YOU DON'T HEAT IT OVER THAT?
?
HEAT-ING IT OVER AN OPEN FLAME BLACK-ENS THE POT FROM THE SOOT.
HUH! I SEE—! YOU'RE LIKE A PRO AT THIS—!!
HOW SO?

CUP: CURRY NOODLES

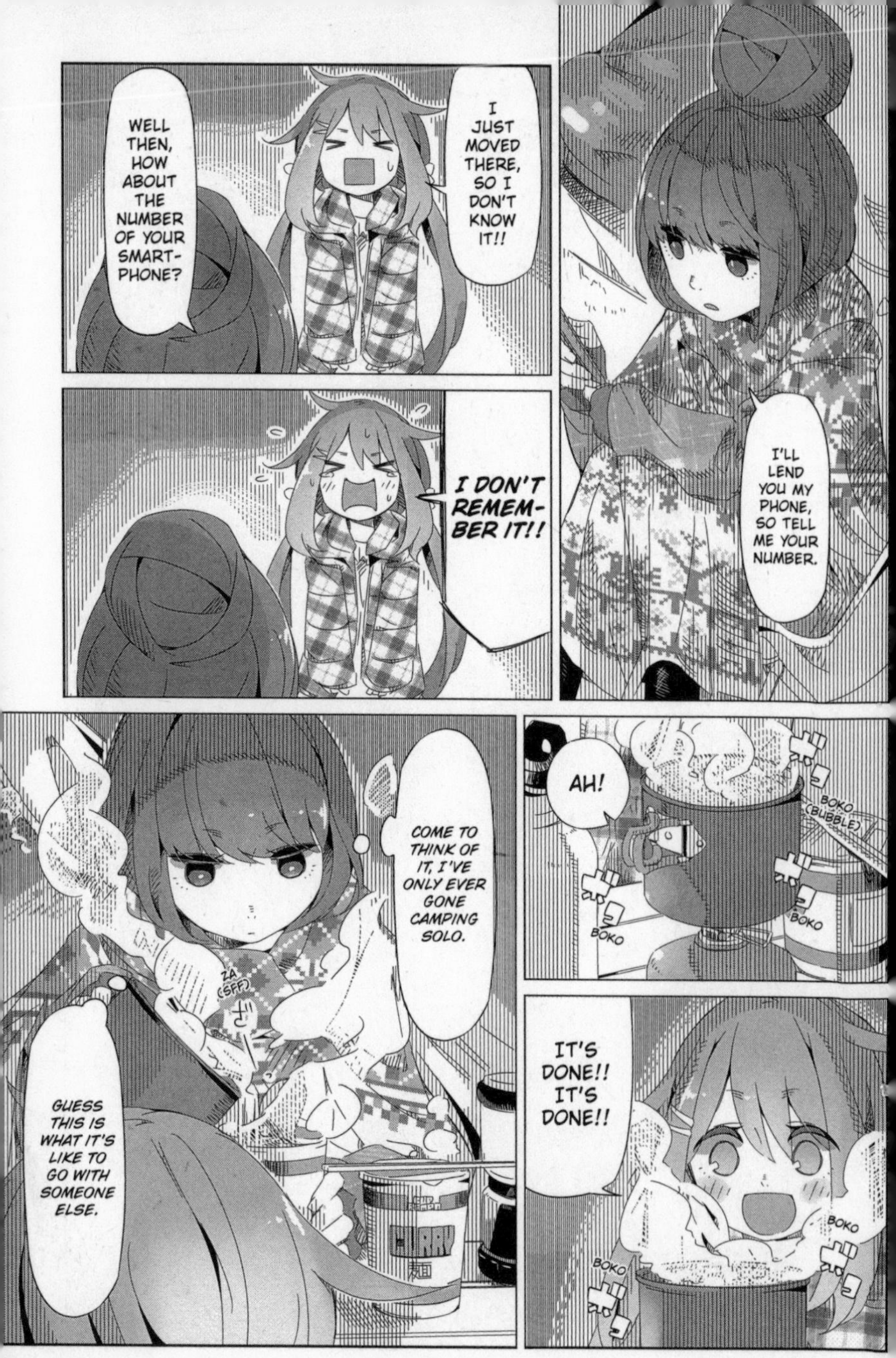
I'LL LEND YOU MY PHONE, SO TELL ME YOUR NUMBER.
I JUST MOVED THERE, SO I DON'T KNOW IT!!
WELL THEN, HOW ABOUT THE NUMBER OF YOUR SMART-PHONE?
I DON'T REMEMBER IT!!
AH!
BOKO (BUBBLE)
BOKO
BOKO
IT'S DONE!! IT'S DONE!!
BOKO
BOKO
COME TO THINK OF IT, I'VE ONLY EVER GONE CAMPING SOLO.
ZA (SFF)
GUESS THIS IS WHAT IT'S LIKE TO GO WITH SOMEONE ELSE.
CURRY

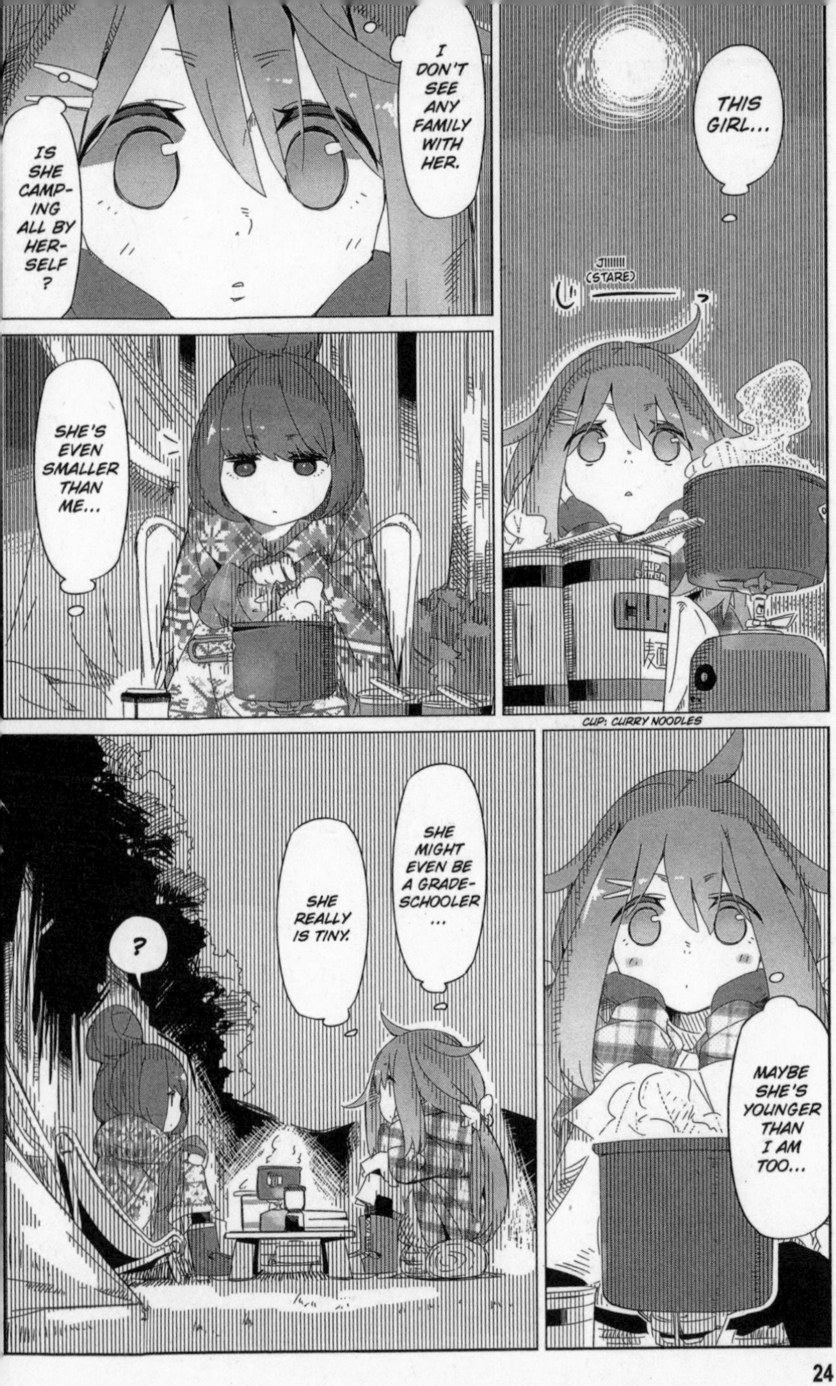
THIS GIRL...
JIIIIII (STARE)
CUP: CURRY NOODLES
I DON'T SEE ANY FAMILY WITH HER.
IS SHE CAMPING ALL BY HERSELF?
SHE'S EVEN SMALLER THAN ME...
MAYBE SHE'S YOUNGER THAN I AM TOO...
SHE MIGHT EVEN BE A GRADE-SCHOOLER...
SHE REALLY IS TINY.
?

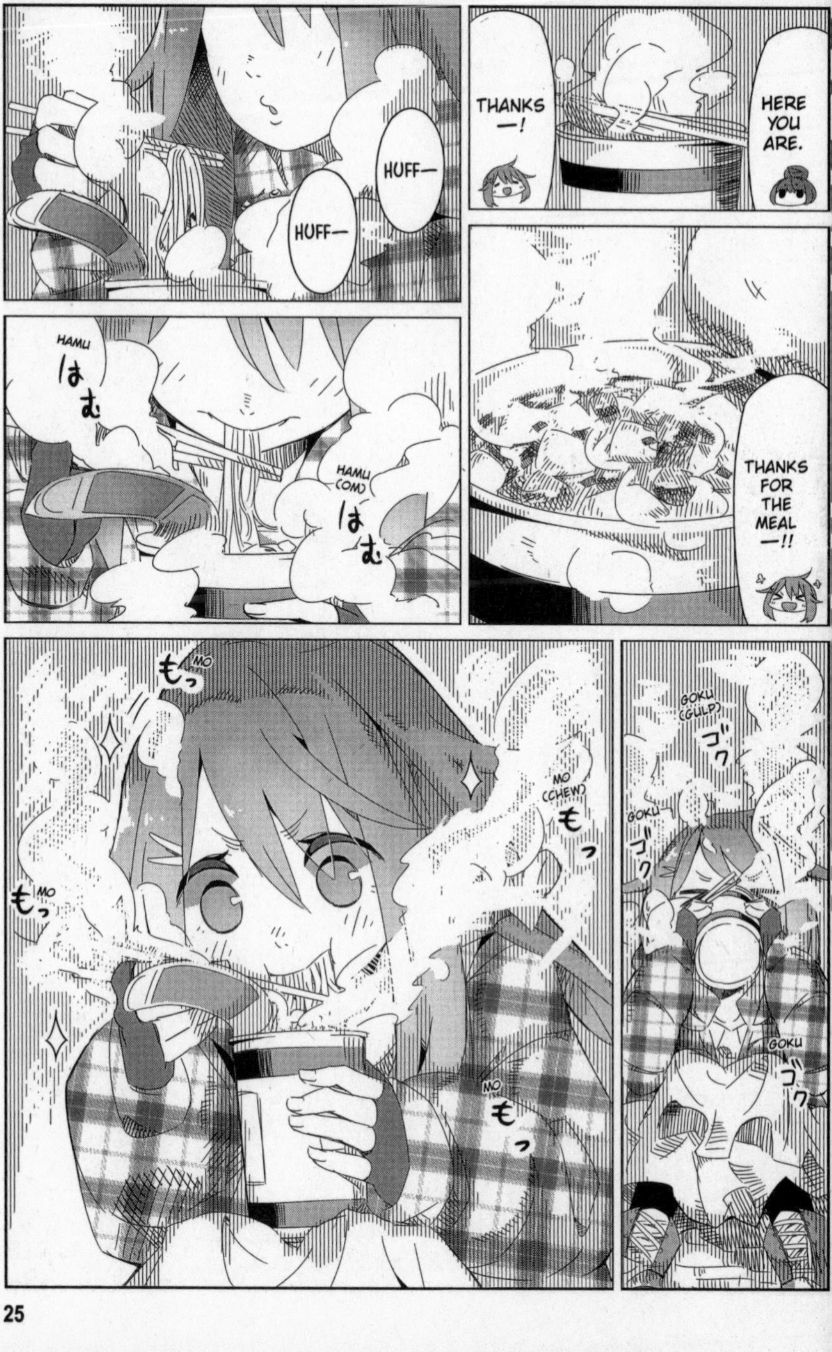
HERE YOU ARE.
THANKS—!
HUFF—
HUFF—
THANKS FOR THE MEAL—!!
HAMU
はむ
HAMU (OM)
はむ
GOKU (GULP)
ゴク
GOKU
ゴク
GOKU
ゴク
MO
もっ
MO (CHEW)
もっ
MO
もっ
MO
もっ

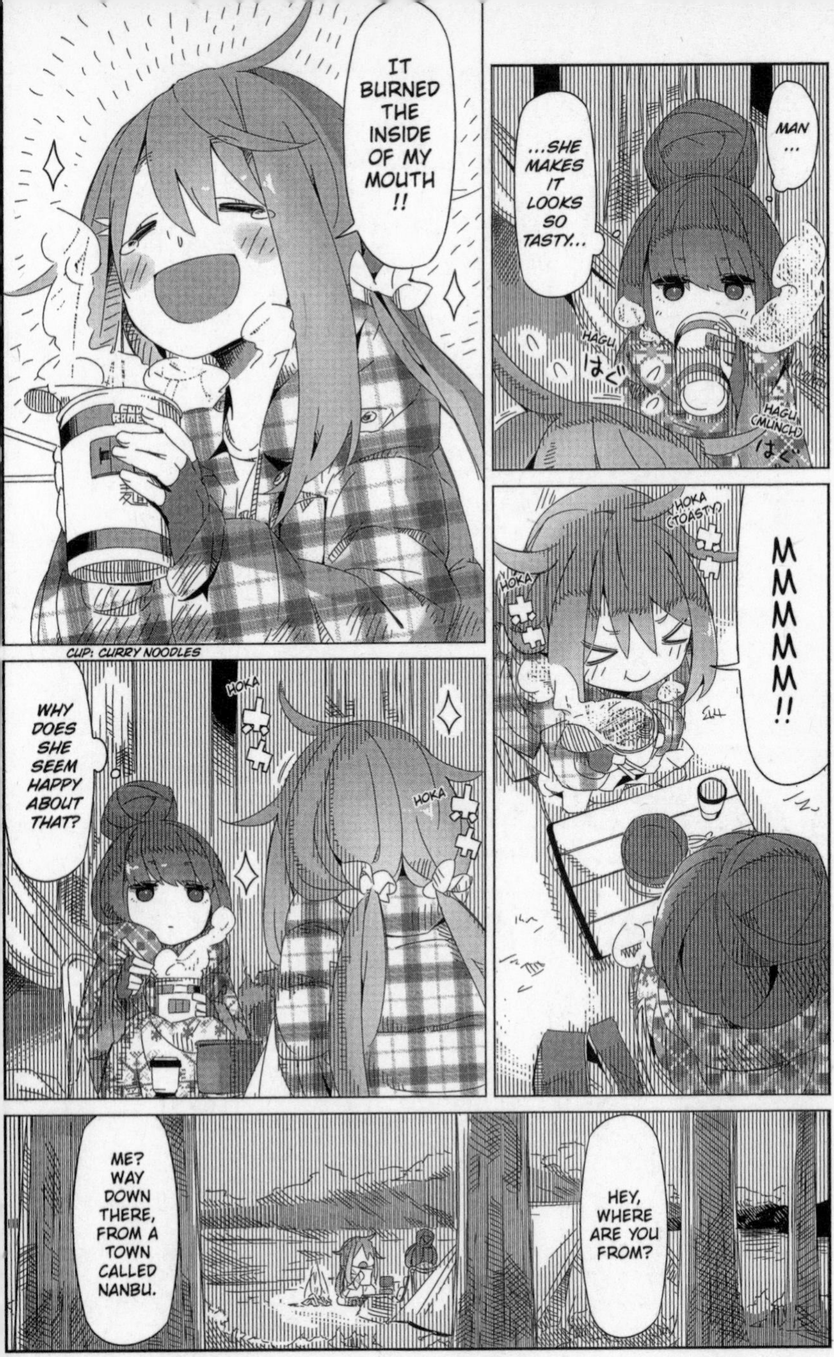
MAN...
...SHE MAKES IT LOOKS SO TASTY...
HAGU
はぐ
HAGU (MUNCH)
はぐ
IT BURNED THE INSIDE OF MY MOUTH!!
CUP: CURRY NOODLES
HOKA (TOASTY)
HOKA
MMMMMM!!
WHY DOES SHE SEEM HAPPY ABOUT THAT?
HOKA
HOKA
HEY, WHERE ARE YOU FROM?
ME? WAY DOWN THERE, FROM A TOWN CALLED NANBU.

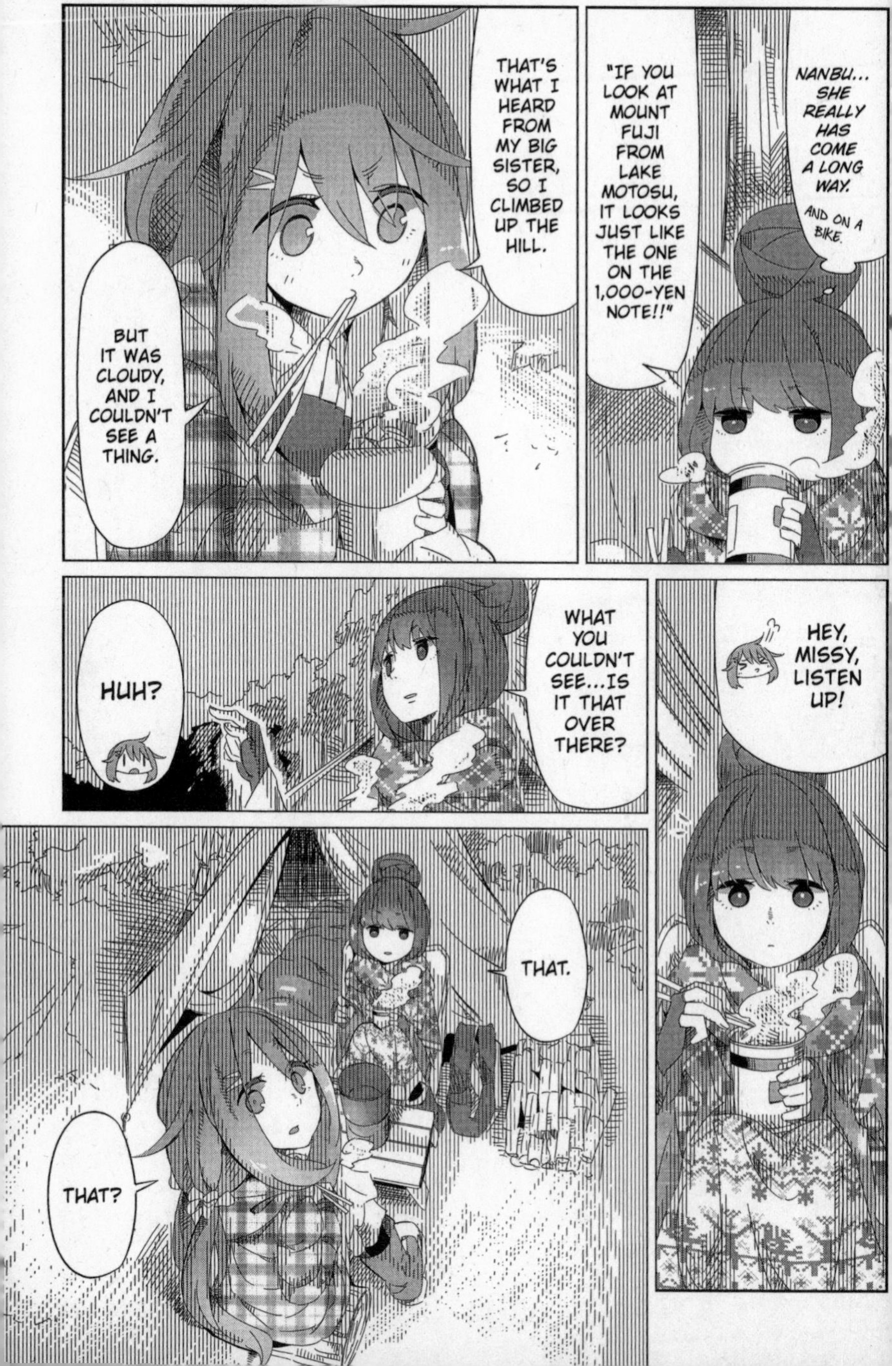
NANBU... SHE REALLY HAS COME A LONG WAY.
AND ON A BIKE.
"IF YOU LOOK AT MOUNT FUJI FROM LAKE MOTOSU, IT LOOKS JUST LIKE THE ONE ON THE 1,000-YEN NOTE!!"
THAT'S WHAT I HEARD FROM MY BIG SISTER, SO I CLIMBED UP THE HILL.
BUT IT WAS CLOUDY, AND I COULDN'T SEE A THING.
HEY, MISSY, LISTEN UP!
WHAT YOU COULDN'T SEE...IS IT THAT OVER THERE?
HUH?
THAT.
THAT?

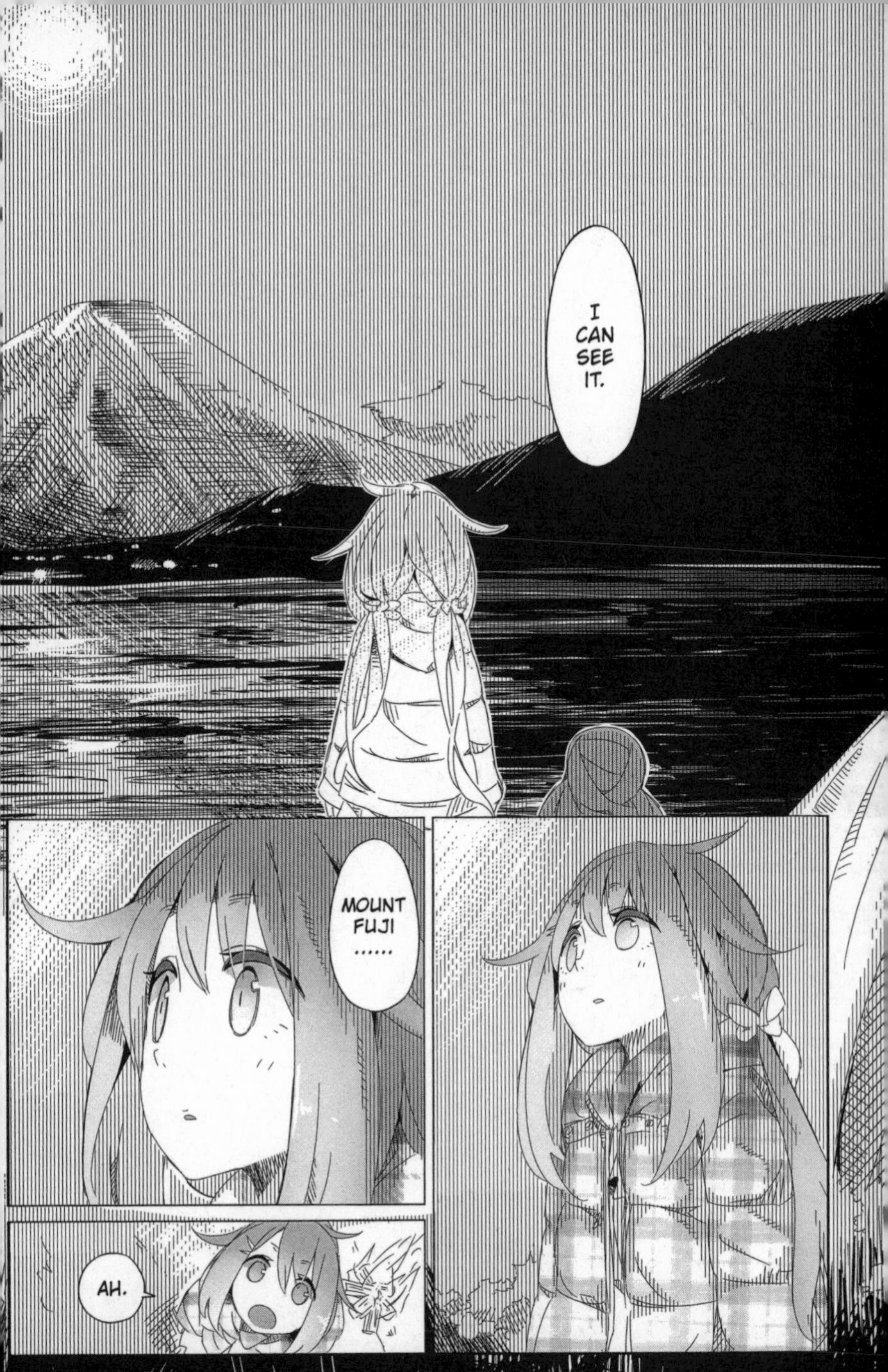
I CAN SEE IT.
MOUNT FUJI ......
AH.

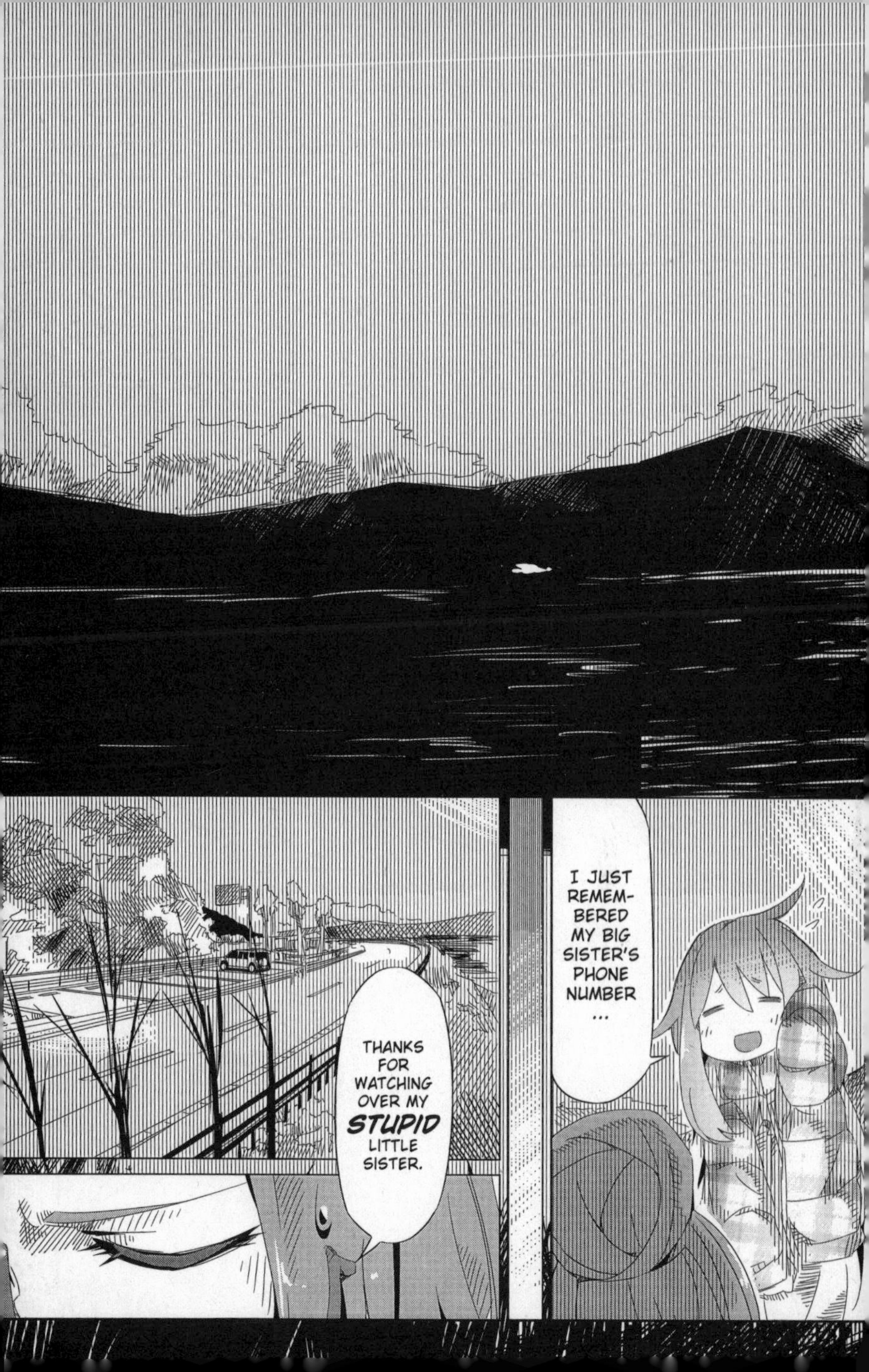
I JUST REMEMBERED MY BIG SISTER'S PHONE NUMBER...
THANKS FOR WATCHING OVER MY STUPID LITTLE SISTER.

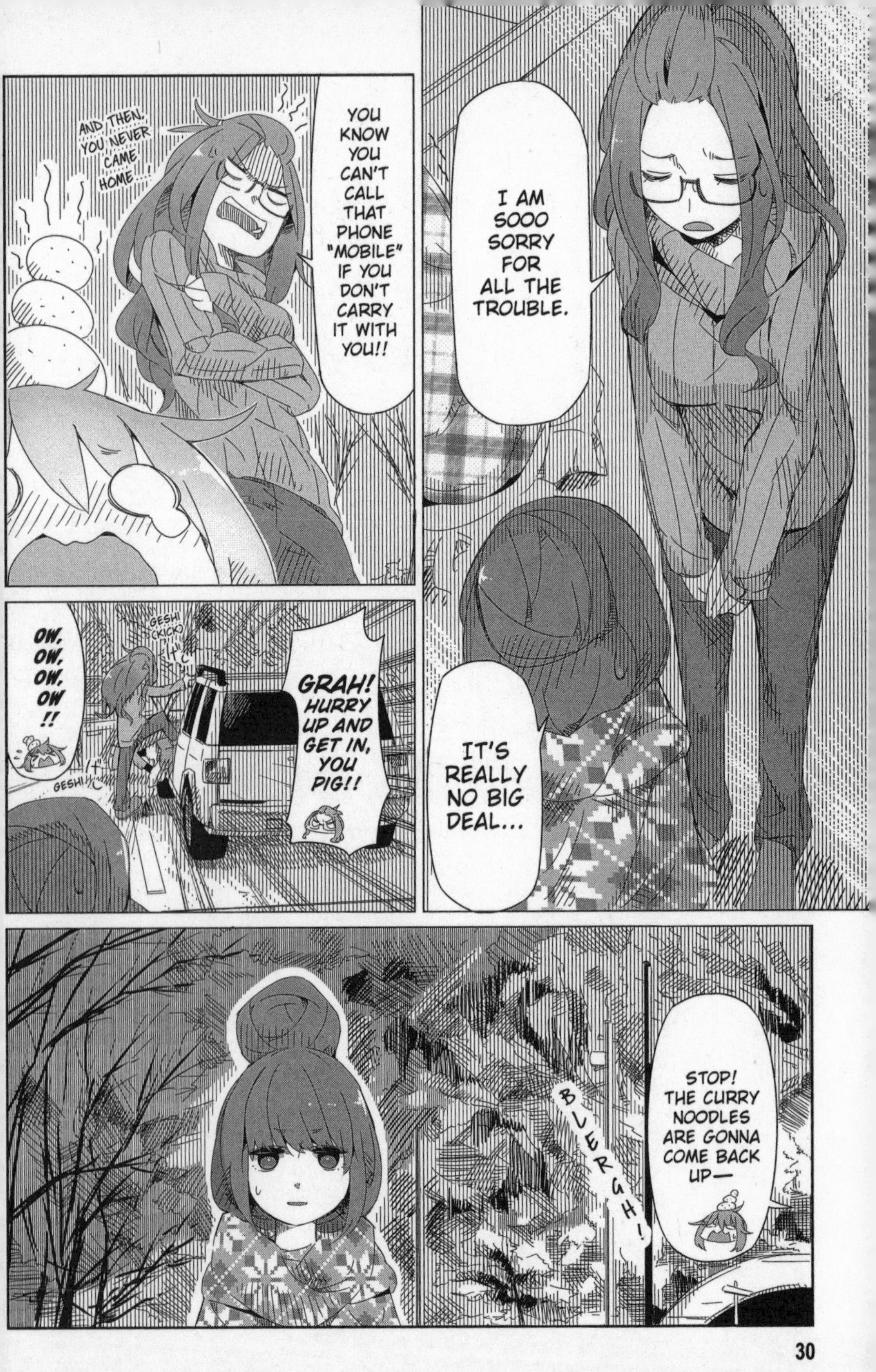
I AM SOOO SORRY FOR ALL THE TROUBLE.
IT'S REALLY NO BIG DEAL...
YOU KNOW YOU CAN'T CALL THAT PHONE "MOBILE" IF YOU DON'T CARRY IT WITH YOU!!
AND THEN, YOU NEVER CAME HOME...!
GRAH! HURRY UP AND GET IN, YOU PIG!!
GESHI (KICK)
OW, OW, OW, OW!!
GESHI
STOP! THE CURRY NOODLES ARE GONNA COME BACK UP—
BLERGH!

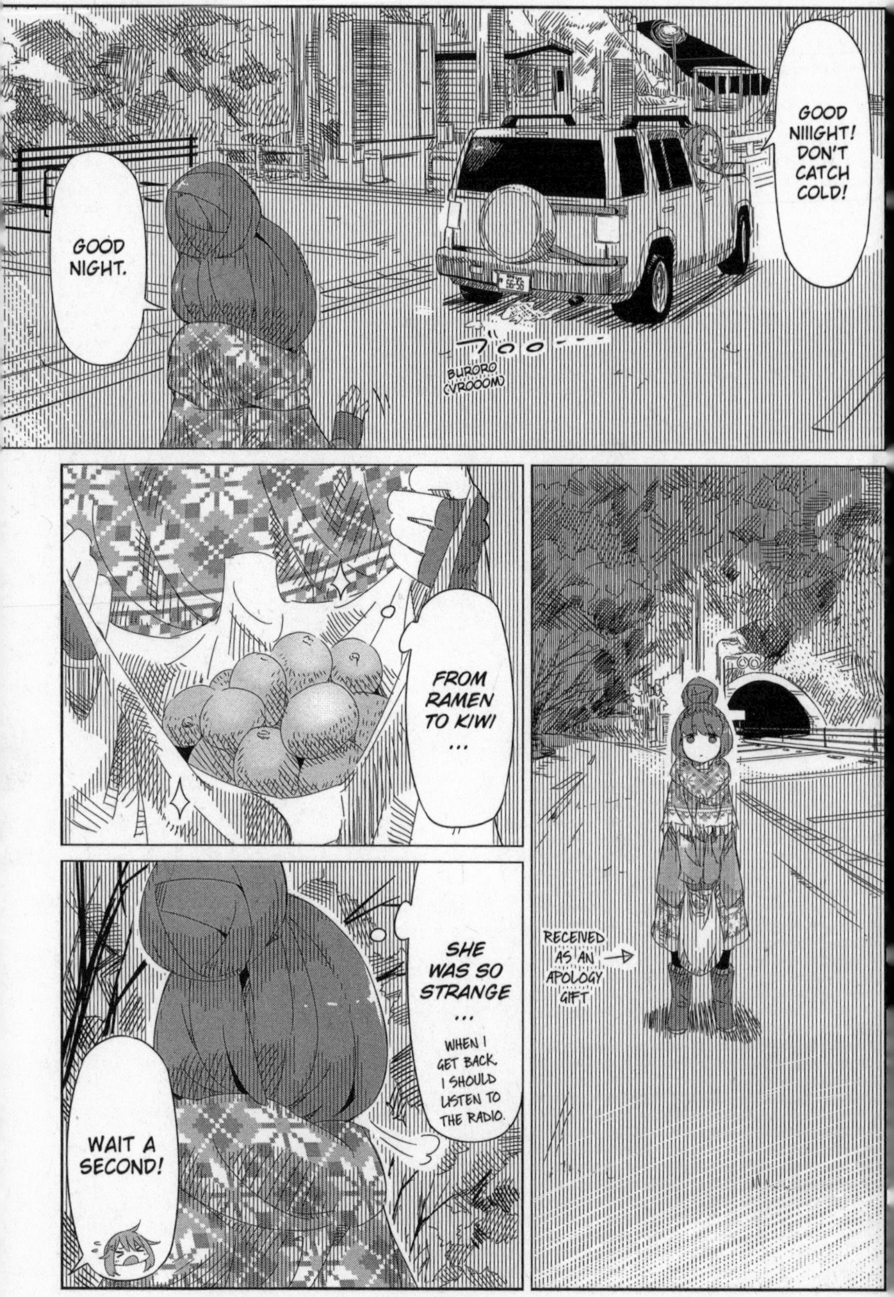
GOOD NIIIGHT! DON'T CATCH COLD!
BURORO (VROOOM)
GOOD NIGHT.
RECEIVED AS AN APOLOGY GIFT
FROM RAMEN TO KIWI ...
SHE WAS SO STRANGE ...
WHEN I GET BACK, I SHOULD LISTEN TO THE RADIO.
WAIT A SECOND!

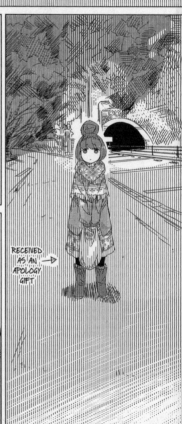

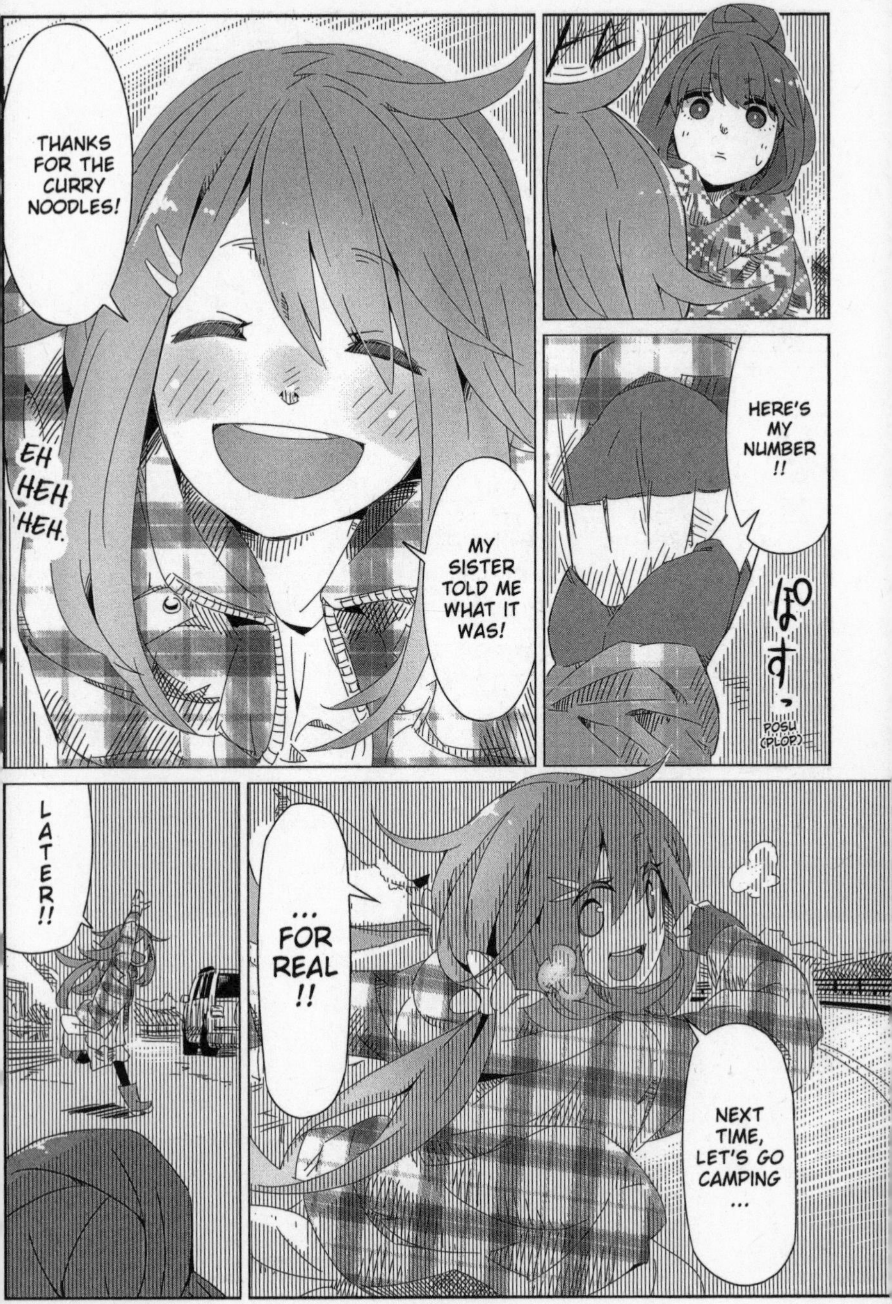
HERE'S MY NUMBER !!
ぽすっ
POSU (PLOP)
THANKS FOR THE CURRY NOODLES!
MY SISTER TOLD ME WHAT IT WAS!
EH HEH HEH.
NEXT TIME, LET'S GO CAMPING ...
... FOR REAL !!
LATER!!

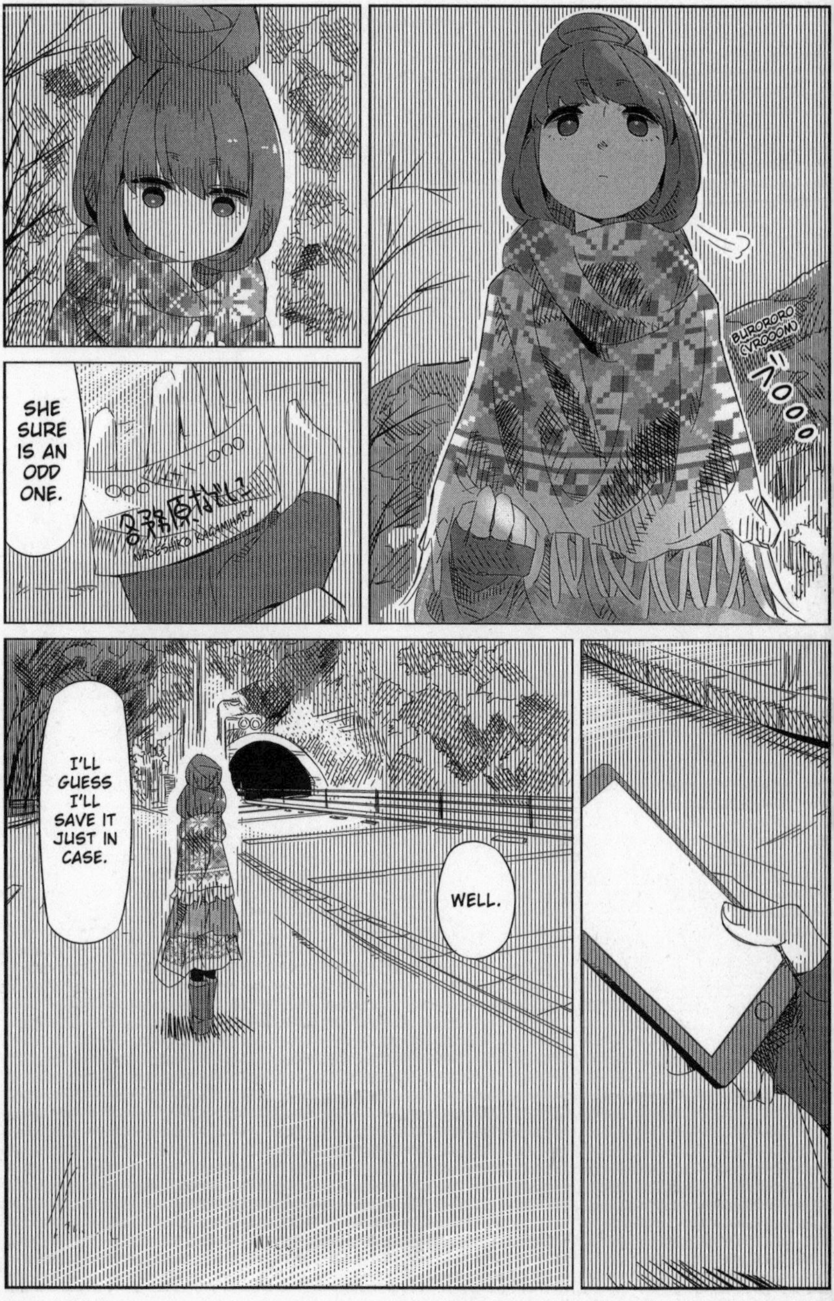
BURORORO (VROOOM)
各務原なでしこ
NADESHIKO KAGAMIHARA
SHE SURE IS AN ODD ONE.
WELL.
I'LL GUESS I'LL SAVE IT JUST IN CASE.

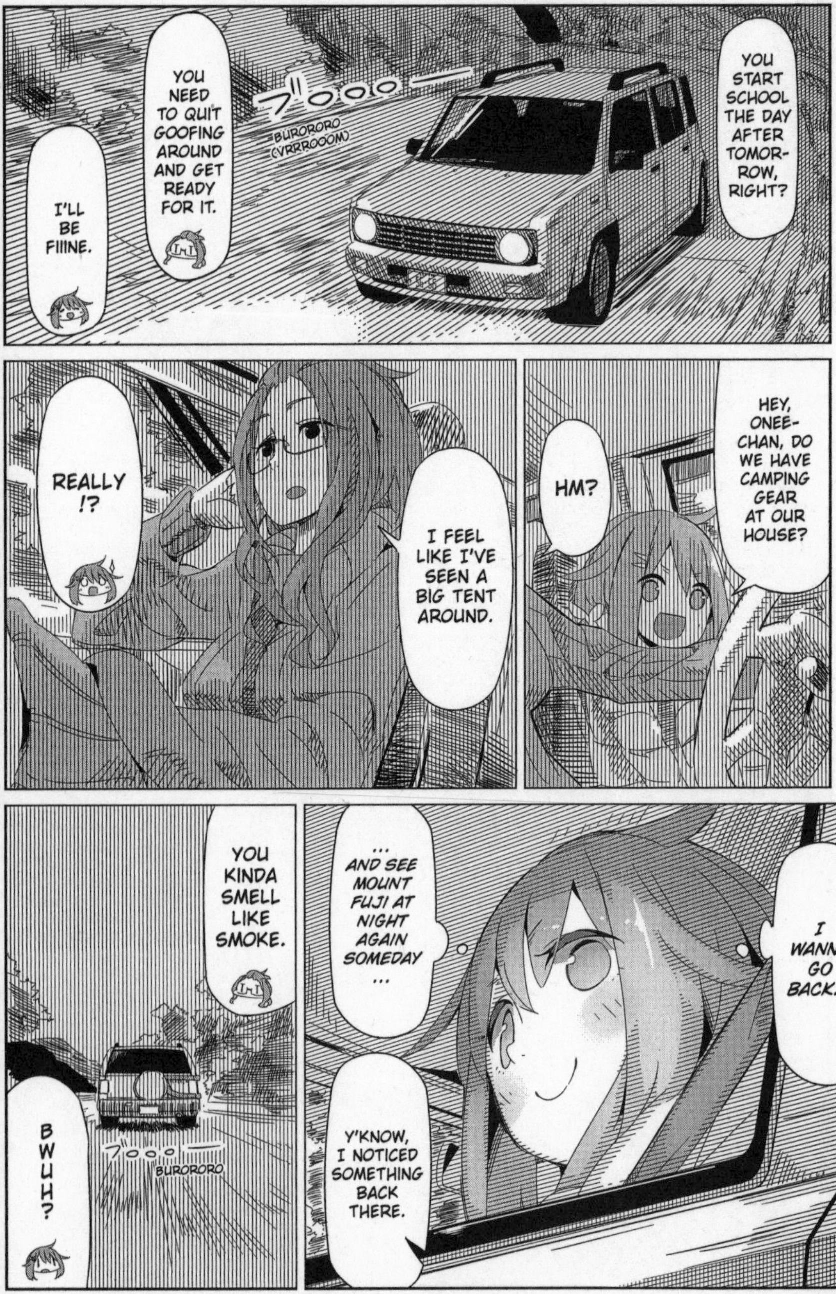
YOU START SCHOOL THE DAY AFTER TOMORROW, RIGHT?
ブロロロ——
BURORORO (VRRROOOM)
YOU NEED TO QUIT GOOFING AROUND AND GET READY FOR IT.
I'LL BE FIIINE.
HEY, ONEE-CHAN, DO WE HAVE CAMPING GEAR AT OUR HOUSE?
HM?
I FEEL LIKE I'VE SEEN A BIG TENT AROUND.
REALLY!?
I WANNA GO BACK...
...AND SEE MOUNT FUJI AT NIGHT AGAIN SOMEDAY...
Y'KNOW, I NOTICED SOMETHING BACK THERE.
YOU KINDA SMELL LIKE SMOKE.
ブロロ—
BURORORO
BWUH?

WOW, THERE'S EVEN MORE GOOD FIREWOOD TODAY...

IT'S BAIT.

THIS CAMPSITE REALLY IS NICE.

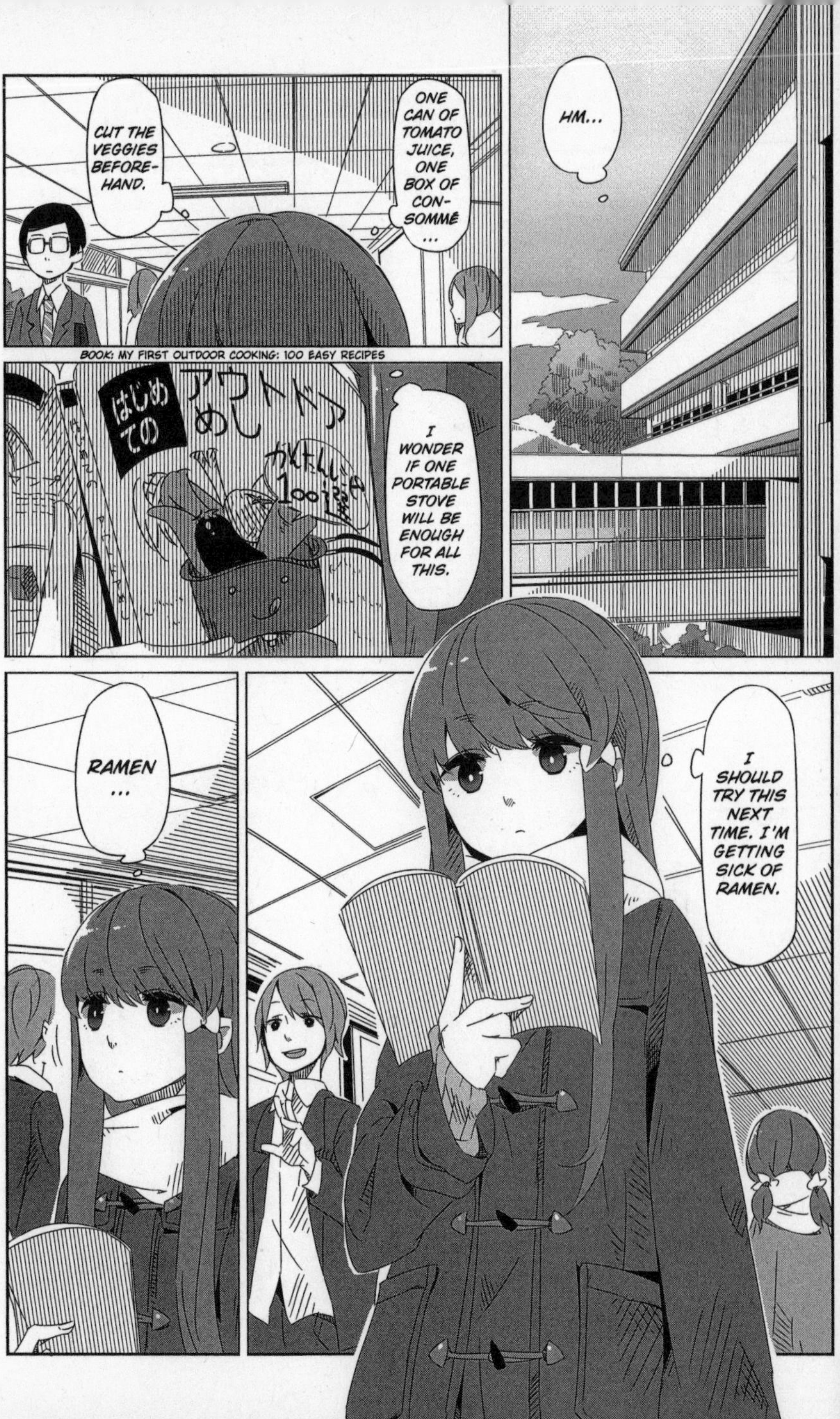
HM...
ONE CAN OF TOMATO JUICE, ONE BOX OF CON-SOMMÉ...
CUT THE VEGGIES BEFORE-HAND.
BOOK: MY FIRST OUTDOOR COOKING: 100 EASY RECIPES
はじめての
アウトドアめし
I WONDER IF ONE PORTABLE STOVE WILL BE ENOUGH FOR ALL THIS.
I SHOULD TRY THIS NEXT TIME. I'M GETTING SICK OF RAMEN.
RAMEN...

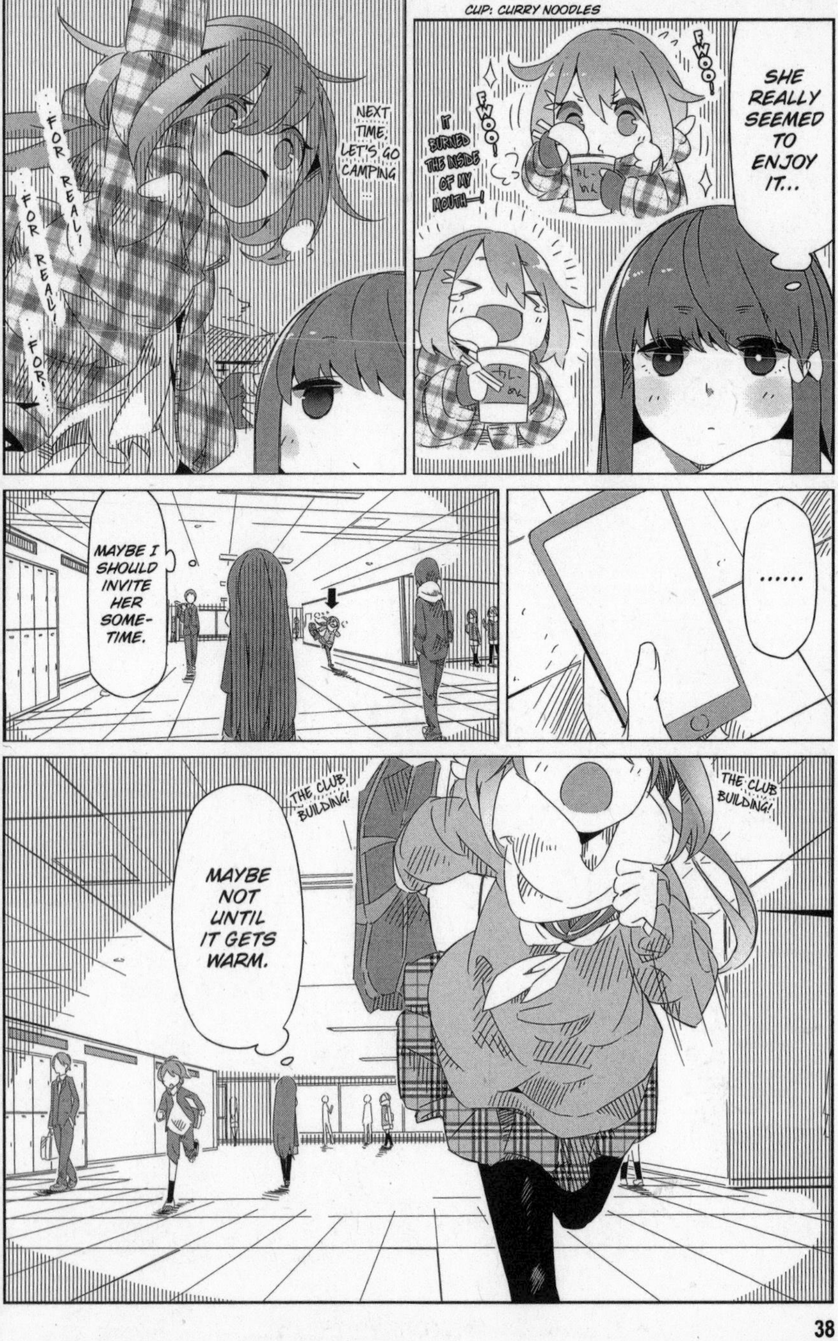
CUP: CURRY NOODLES
SHE REALLY SEEMED TO ENJOY IT...
FWOO!
FWOO!
IT BURNED THE INSIDE OF MY MOUTH—!
NEXT TIME, LET'S GO CAMPING...!
...FOR REAL!
...FOR REAL!
...FOR...
......
MAYBE I SHOULD INVITE HER SOME-TIME.
THE CLUB BUILDING!
THE CLUB BUILDING!
MAYBE NOT UNTIL IT GETS WARM.

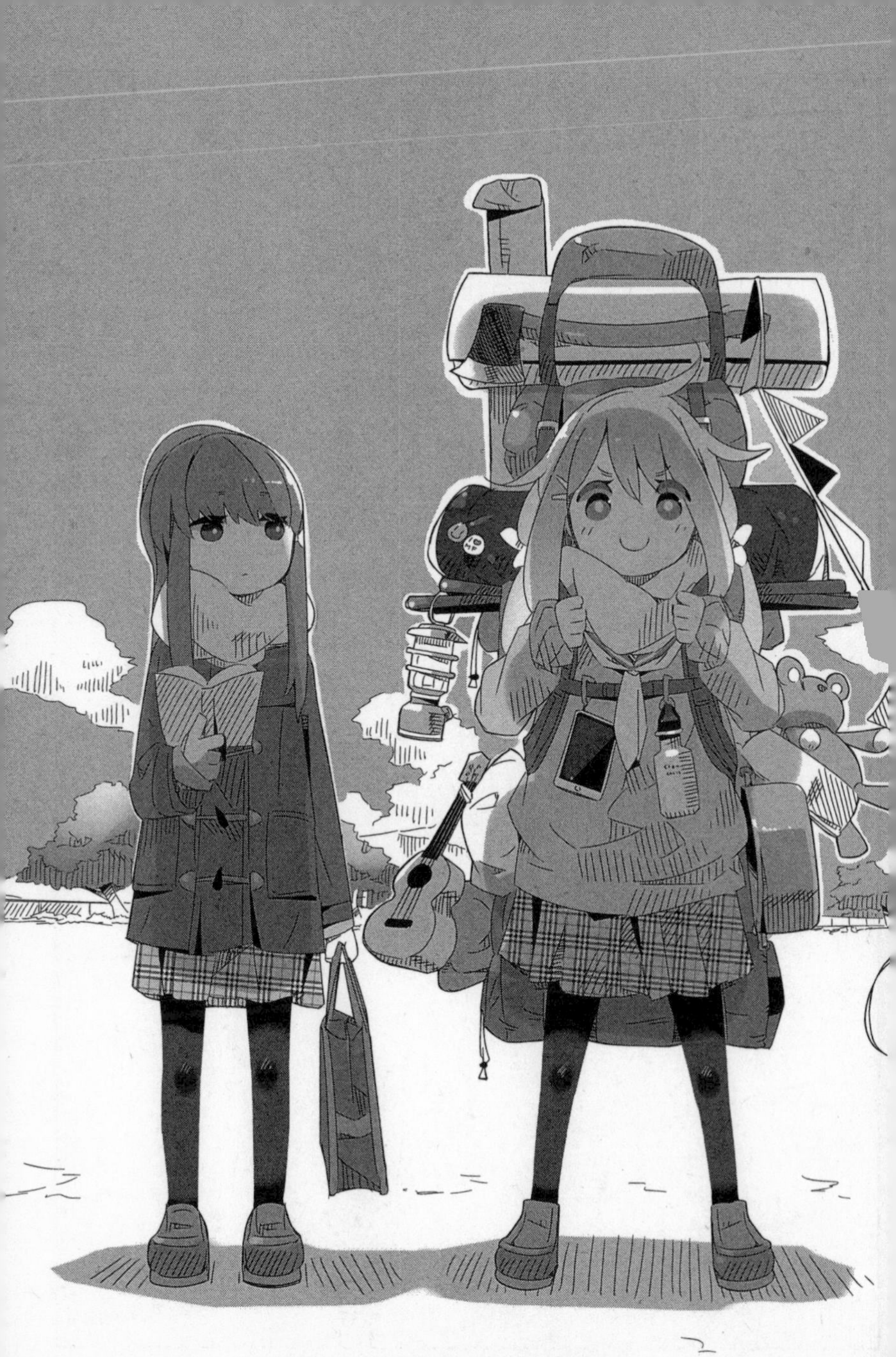

Chapter 2 WELCOME TO THE OEC!

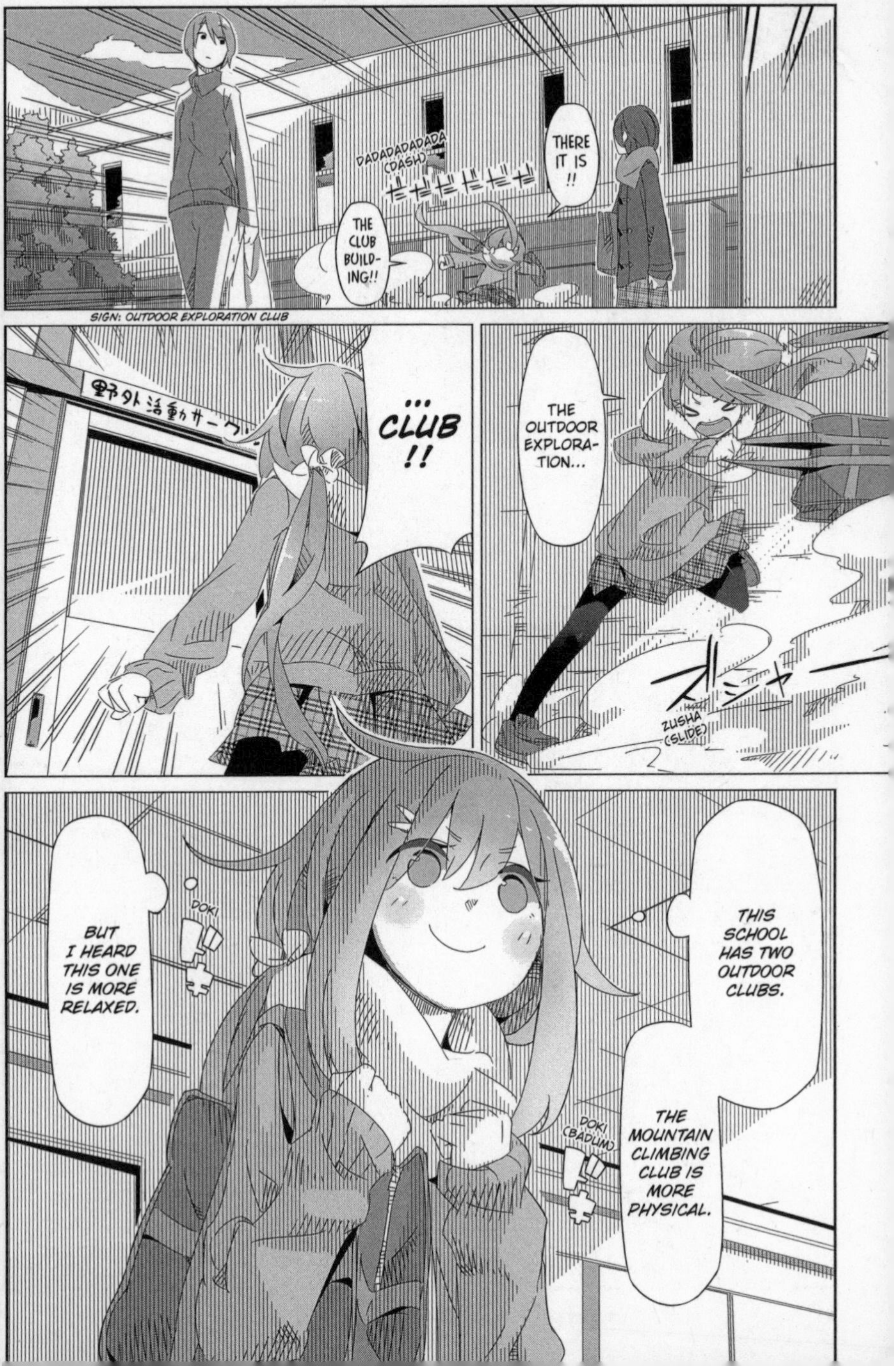
THERE IT IS !!
DADADADADADA (DASH)
THE CLUB BUILDING!!
SIGN: OUTDOOR EXPLORATION CLUB
THE OUTDOOR EXPLORATION...
ZUSHA (SLIDE)
... CLUB !!
THIS SCHOOL HAS TWO OUTDOOR CLUBS.
THE MOUNTAIN CLIMBING CLUB IS MORE PHYSICAL.
DOKI (BADUM)
DOKI
BUT I HEARD THIS ONE IS MORE RELAXED.

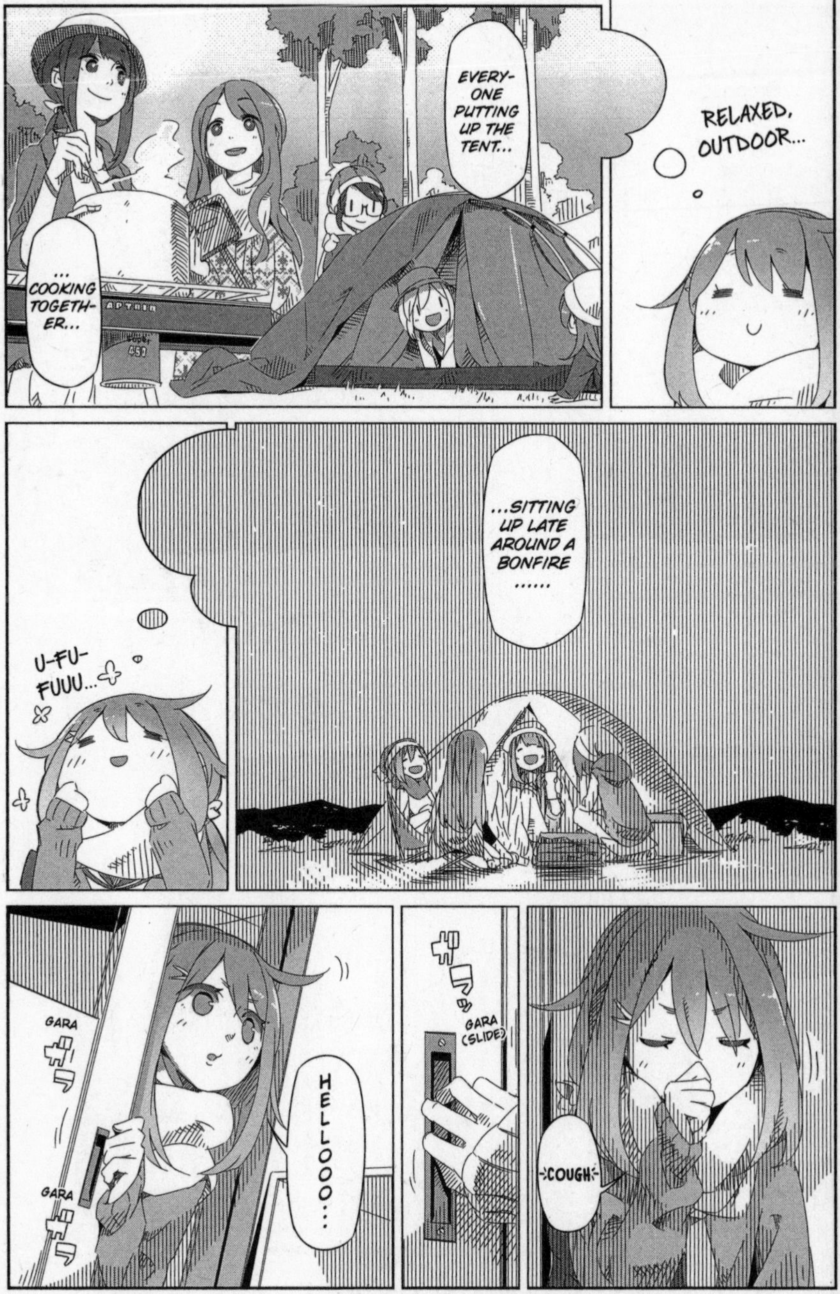
RELAXED, OUTDOOR...
EVERY-ONE PUTTING UP THE TENT...
...COOKING TOGETH-ER...
...SITTING UP LATE AROUND A BONFIRE ......
U-FU-FUUU...
-COUGH-
GARA (SLIDE)
GARA
GARA
HELLOOO...

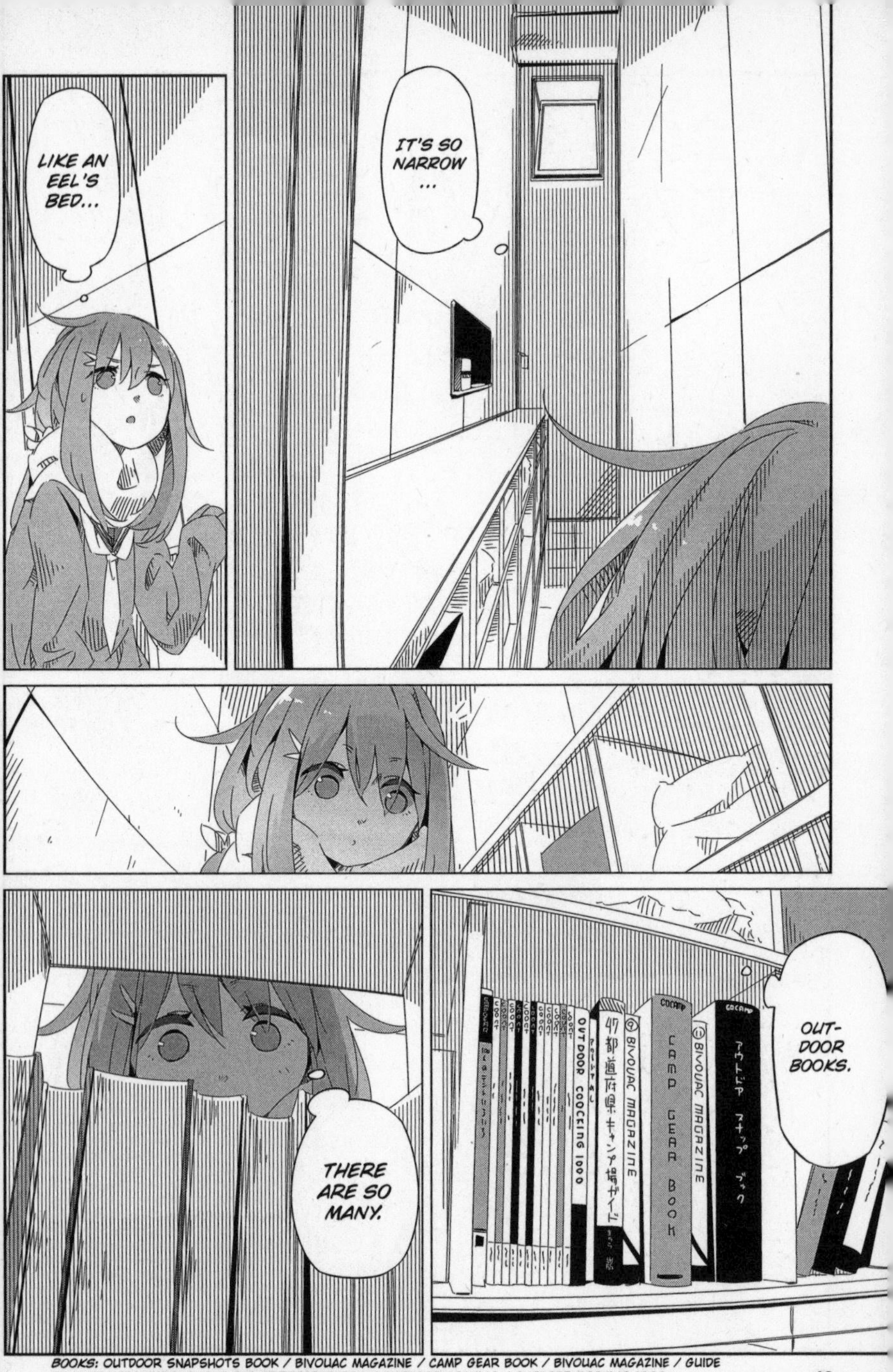
IT'S SO NARROW ...
LIKE AN EEL'S BED...
OUT-DOOR BOOKS.
BIVOUAC MAGAZINE
アウトドア スナップ ブック
CAMP GEAR BOOK
BIVOUAC MAGAZINE
47都道府県キャンプ場ガイド
OUTDOOR COOKING 1000
THERE ARE SO MANY.

BOOKS: OUTDOOR SNAPSHOTS BOOK / BIVOUAC MAGAZINE / CAMP GEAR BOOK / BIVOUAC MAGAZINE / GUIDE TO CAMPSITES THROUGHOUT THE 47 PREFECTURES / OUTDOOR COOKING / OUTDOOR COOKING 1000

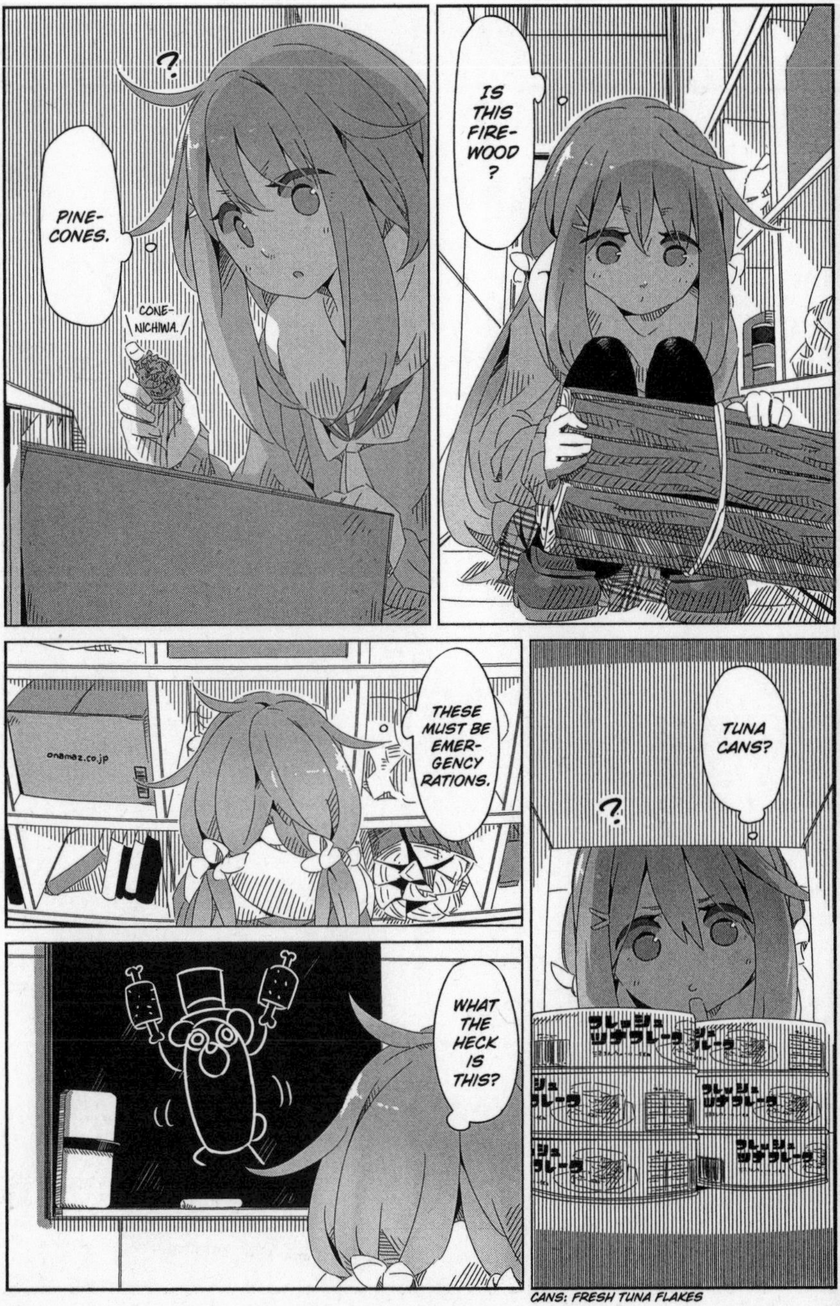
IS THIS FIRE-WOOD?
?
PINE-CONES.
CONE-NICHIWA.
TUNA CANS?
?
THESE MUST BE EMER-GENCY RATIONS.
onamaz.co.jp
WHAT THE HECK IS THIS?
CANS: FRESH TUNA FLAKES

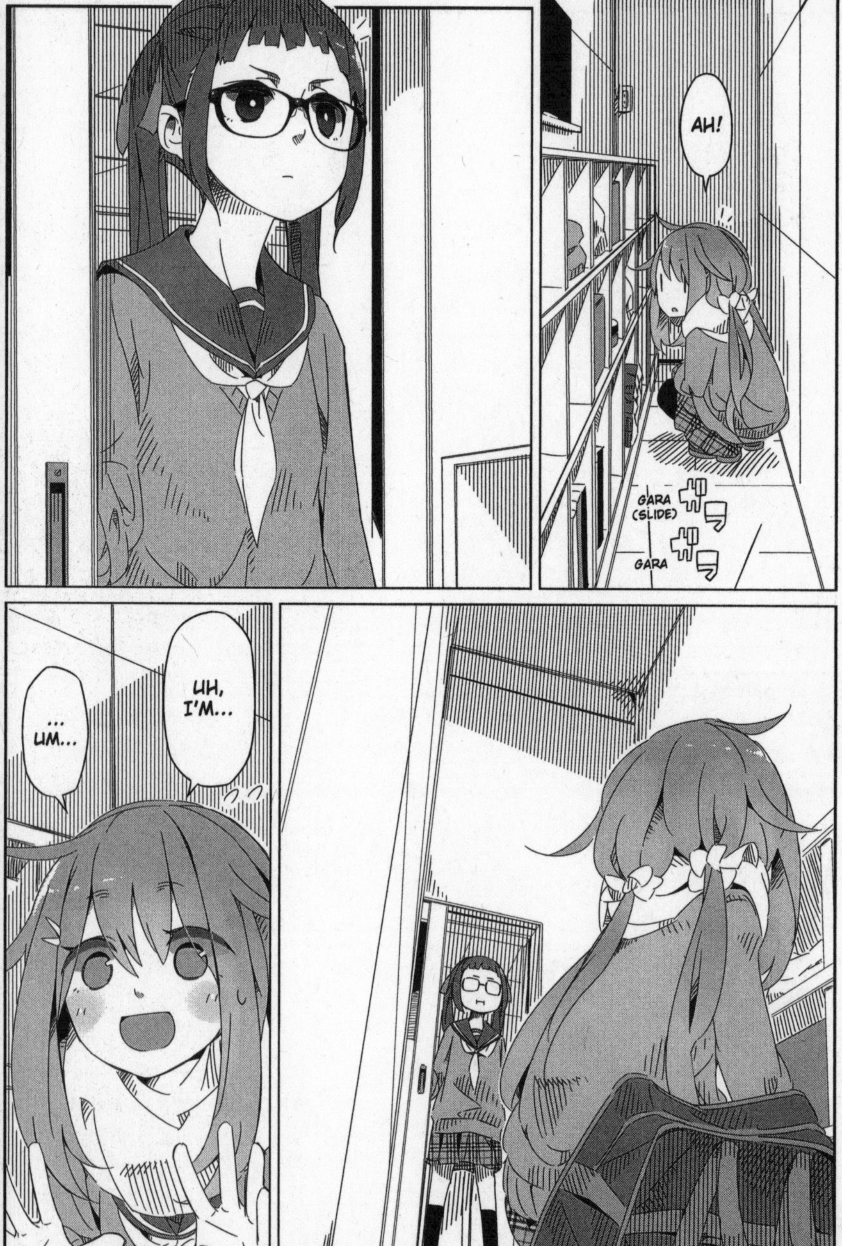
AH!
GARA (SLIDE)
GARA
UH, I'M...
... UM...

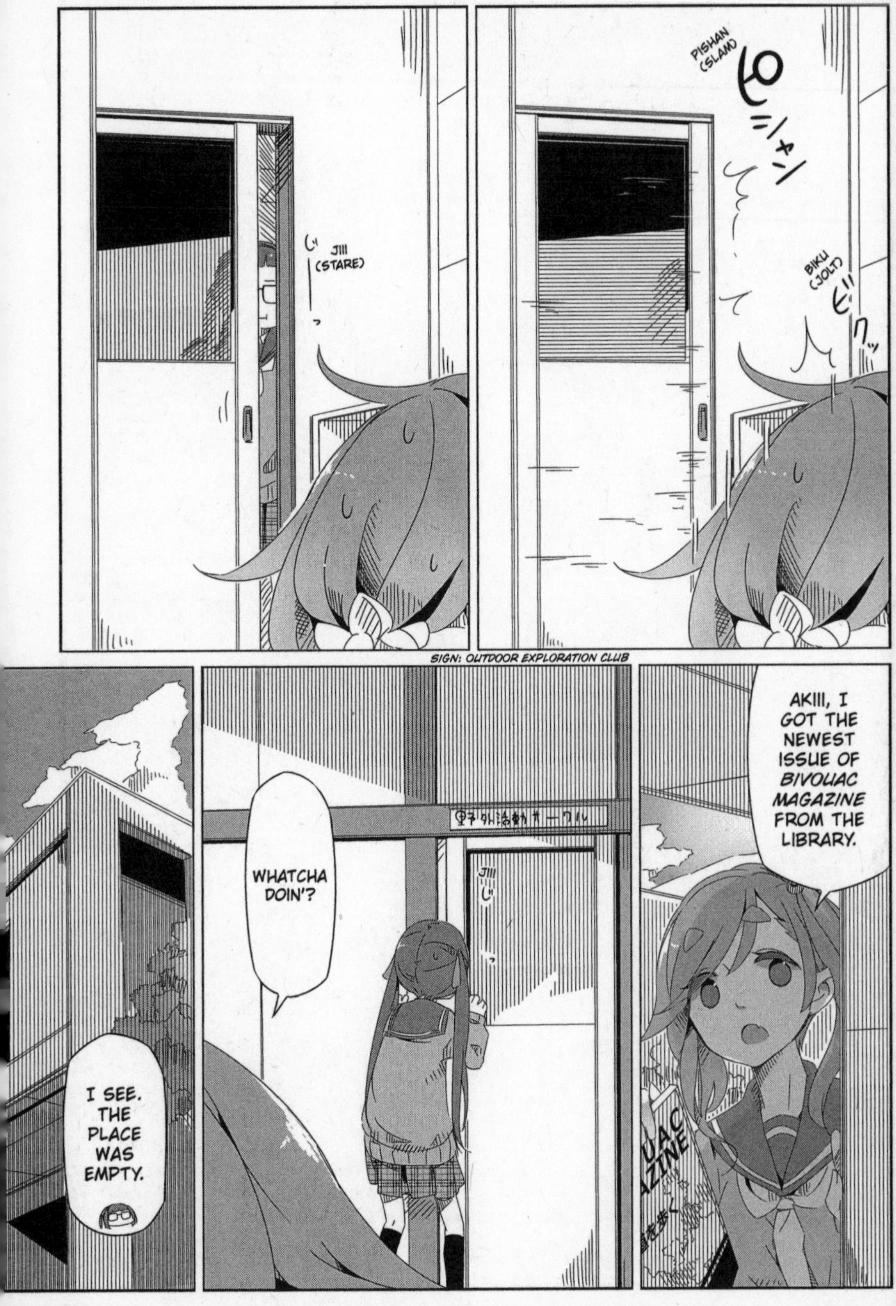
ピシャン
PISHAN (SLAM)
ビクッ
BIKU (JOLT)
じー
JIII (STARE)
SIGN: OUTDOOR EXPLORATION CLUB
AKIII, I GOT THE NEWEST ISSUE OF *BIVOUAC MAGAZINE* FROM THE LIBRARY.
WHATCHA DOIN'?
野外活動サークル
じー
JIII
I SEE. THE PLACE WAS EMPTY.

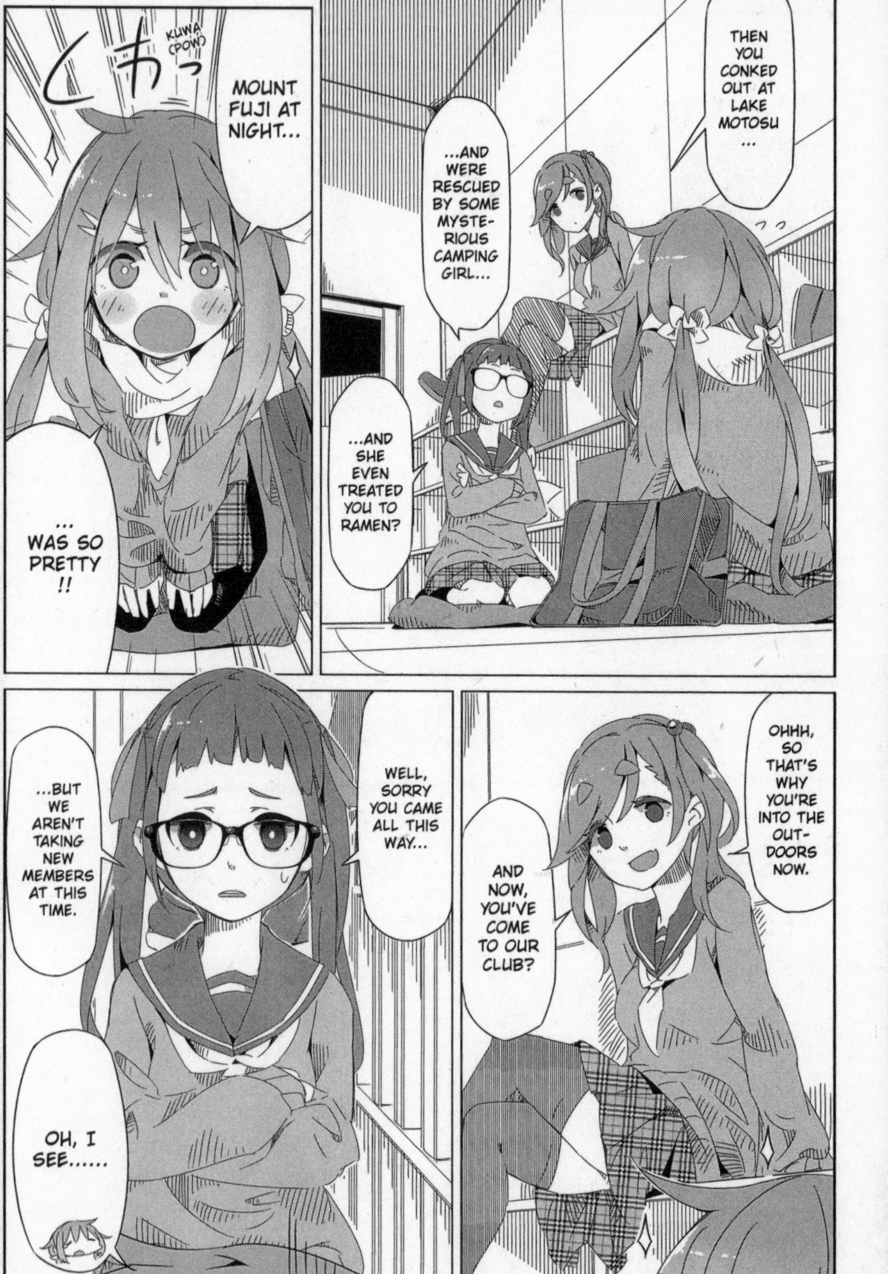
THEN YOU CONKED OUT AT LAKE MOTOSU ...
...AND WERE RESCUED BY SOME MYSTE-RIOUS CAMPING GIRL...
...AND SHE EVEN TREATED YOU TO RAMEN?
くわっ
KUWA (POW)
MOUNT FUJI AT NIGHT...
... WAS SO PRETTY !!
OHHH, SO THAT'S WHY YOU'RE INTO THE OUT-DOORS NOW.
AND NOW, YOU'VE COME TO OUR CLUB?
WELL, SORRY YOU CAME ALL THIS WAY...
...BUT WE AREN'T TAKING NEW MEMBERS AT THIS TIME.
OH, I SEE......

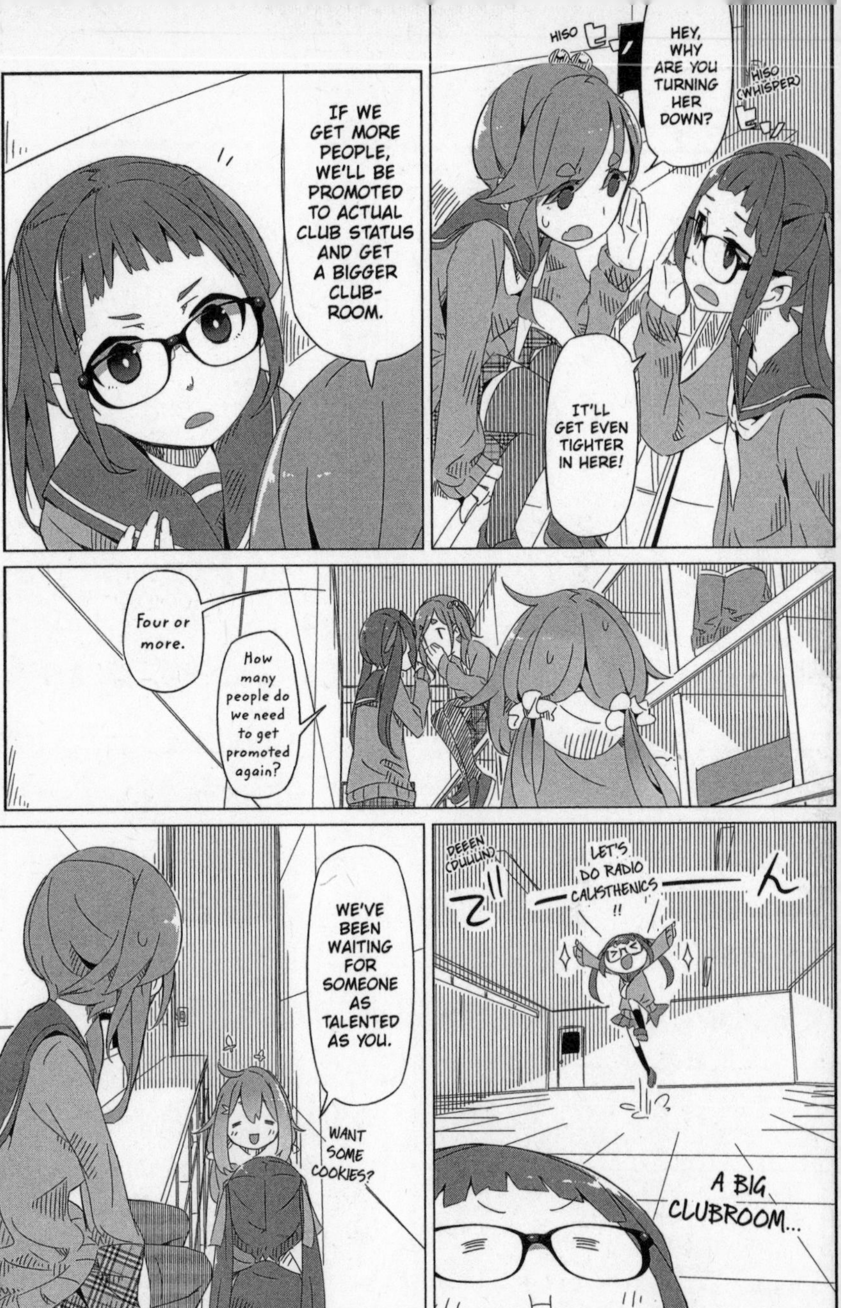
HISO
HEY, WHY ARE YOU TURNING HER DOWN?
HISO (WHISPER)
IT'LL GET EVEN TIGHTER IN HERE!
IF WE GET MORE PEOPLE, WE'LL BE PROMOTED TO ACTUAL CLUB STATUS AND GET A BIGGER CLUB-ROOM.
How many people do we need to get promoted again?
Four or more.
DEEEN (DUUUN)
LET'S DO RADIO CALISTHENICS!!
A BIG CLUBROOM...
WE'VE BEEN WAITING FOR SOMEONE AS TALENTED AS YOU.
WANT SOME COOKIES?

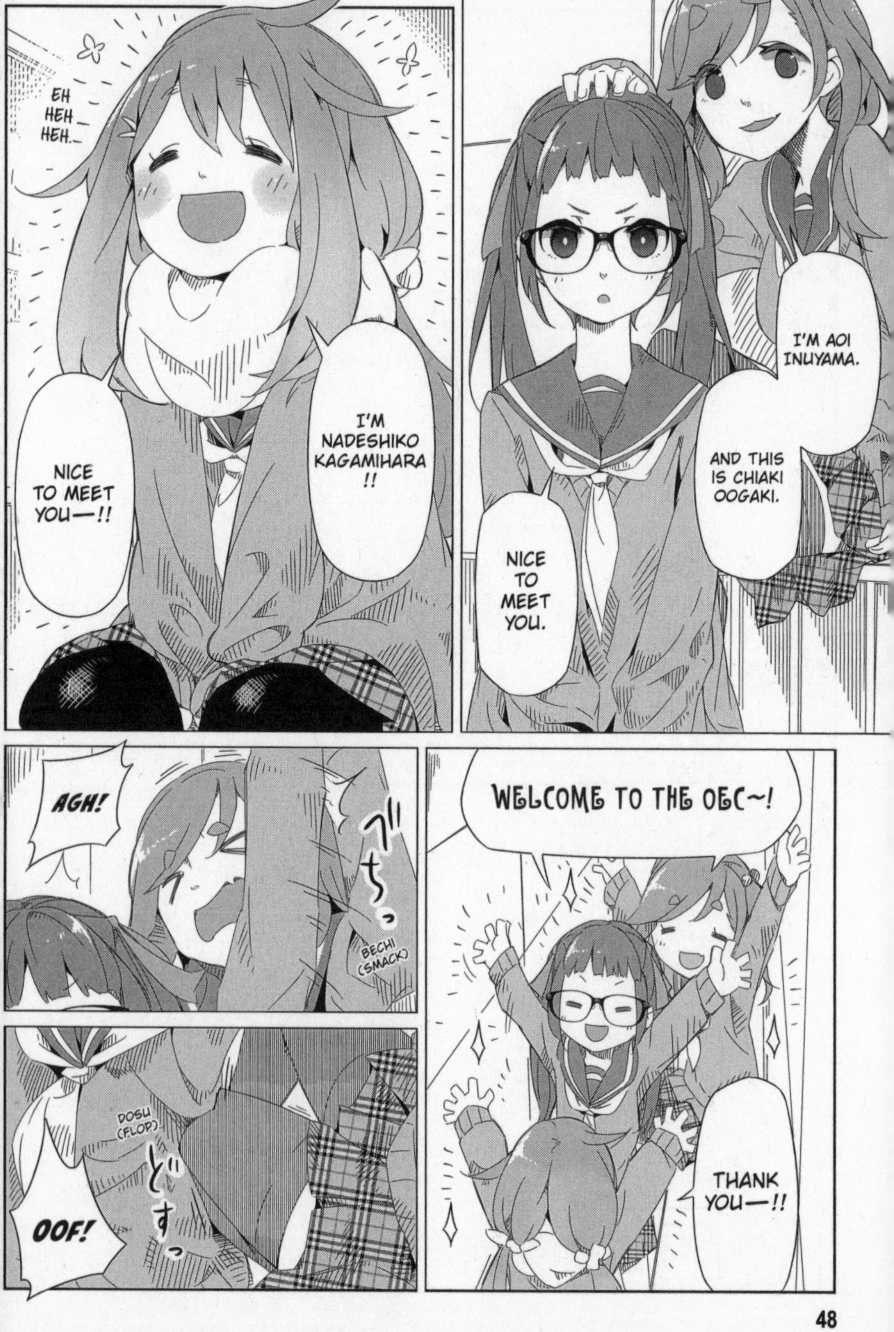
I'M AOI INUYAMA.
AND THIS IS CHIAKI OOGAKI.
NICE TO MEET YOU.
EH HEH HEH.
I'M NADESHIKO KAGAMIHARA !!
NICE TO MEET YOU—!!
WELCOME TO THE OEC~!
THANK YOU—!!
AGH!
べちっ
BECHI (SMACK)
DOSU (FLOP)
どすっ
OOF!

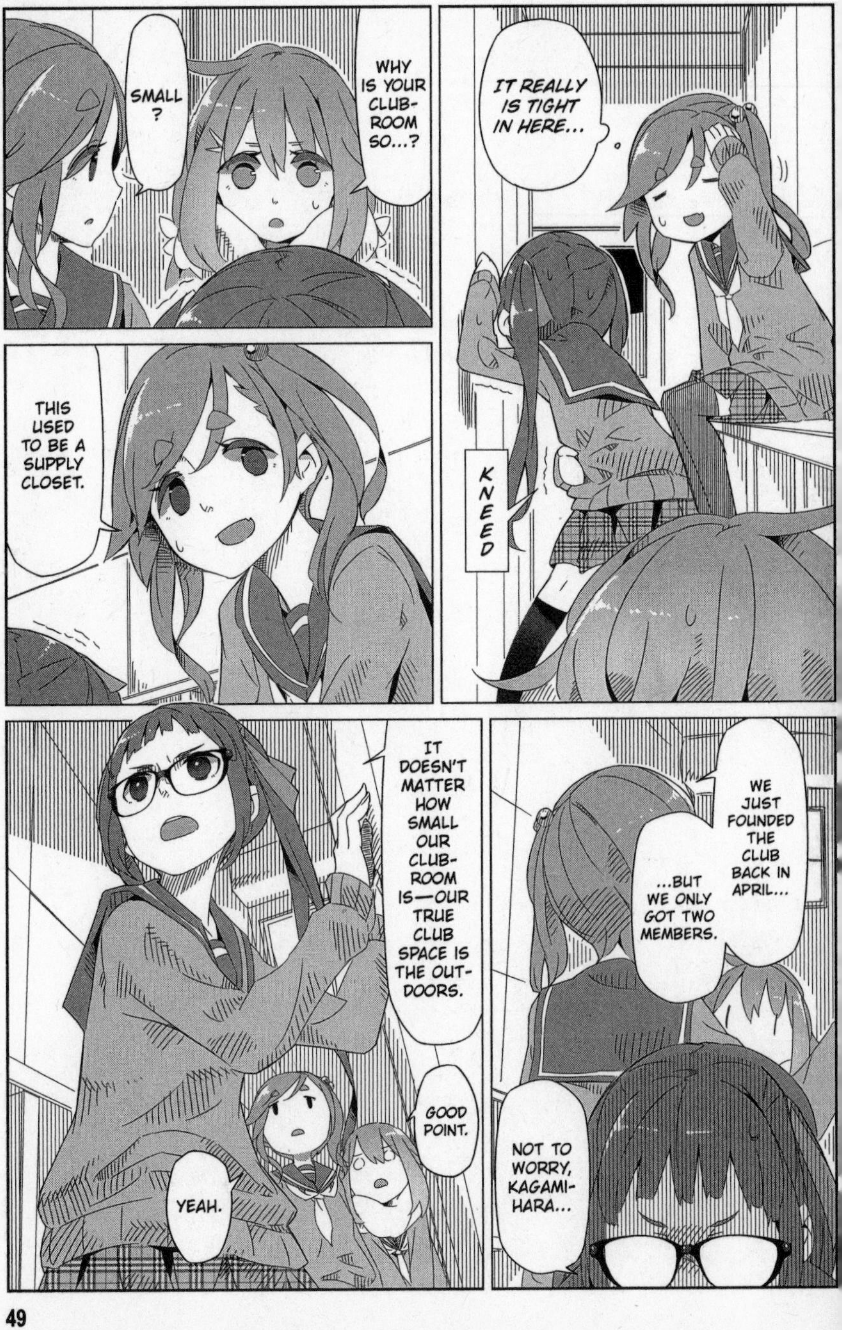
IT REALLY IS TIGHT IN HERE...
KNEED
WHY IS YOUR CLUB-ROOM SO...?
SMALL?
THIS USED TO BE A SUPPLY CLOSET.
WE JUST FOUNDED THE CLUB BACK IN APRIL...
...BUT WE ONLY GOT TWO MEMBERS.
NOT TO WORRY, KAGAMI-HARA...
IT DOESN'T MATTER HOW SMALL OUR CLUB-ROOM IS—OUR TRUE CLUB SPACE IS THE OUT-DOORS.
GOOD POINT.
YEAH.

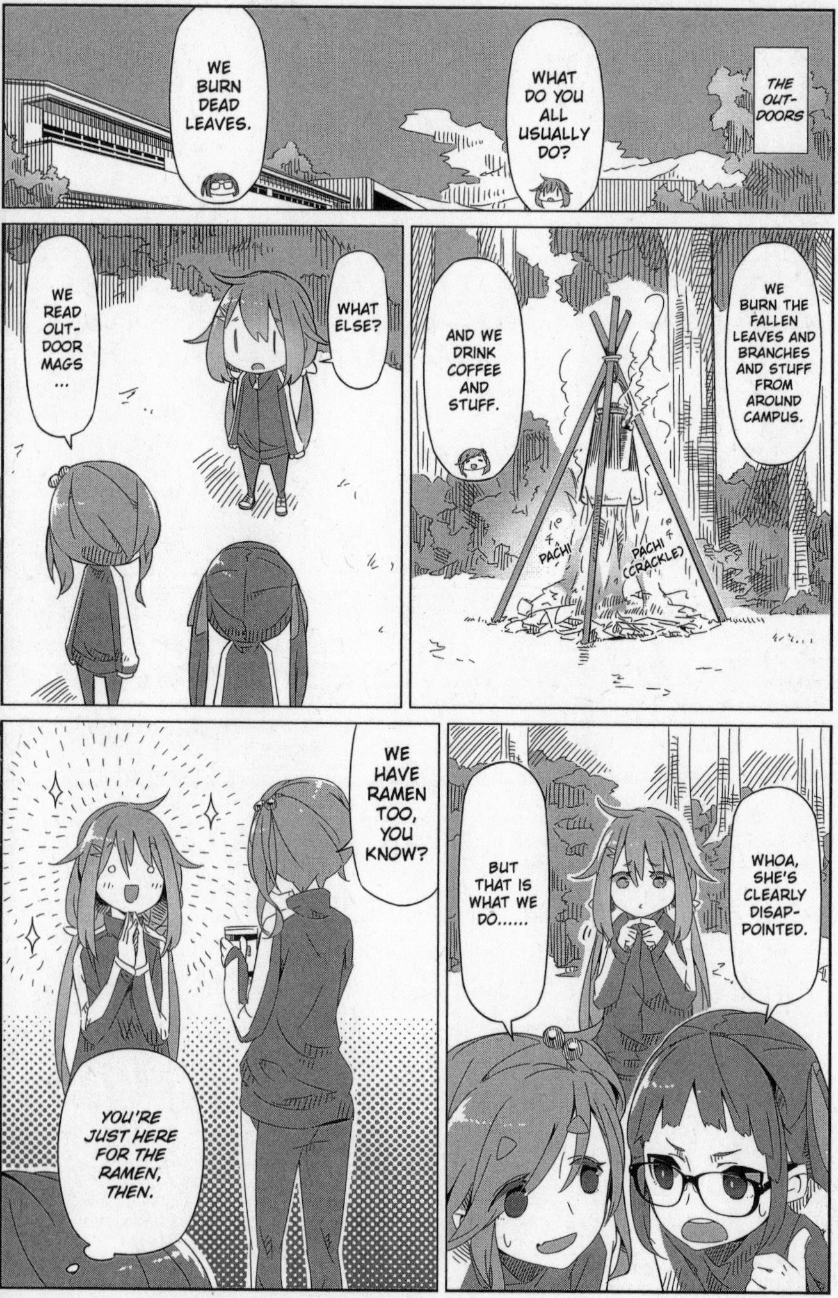
THE OUT-DOORS
WHAT DO YOU ALL USUALLY DO?
WE BURN DEAD LEAVES.
WE BURN THE FALLEN LEAVES AND BRANCHES AND STUFF FROM AROUND CAMPUS.
AND WE DRINK COFFEE AND STUFF.
PACHI (CRACKLE)
PACHI
WHAT ELSE?
WE READ OUT-DOOR MAGS ...
WHOA, SHE'S CLEARLY DISAP-POINTED.
BUT THAT IS WHAT WE DO......
WE HAVE RAMEN TOO, YOU KNOW?
YOU'RE JUST HERE FOR THE RAMEN, THEN.

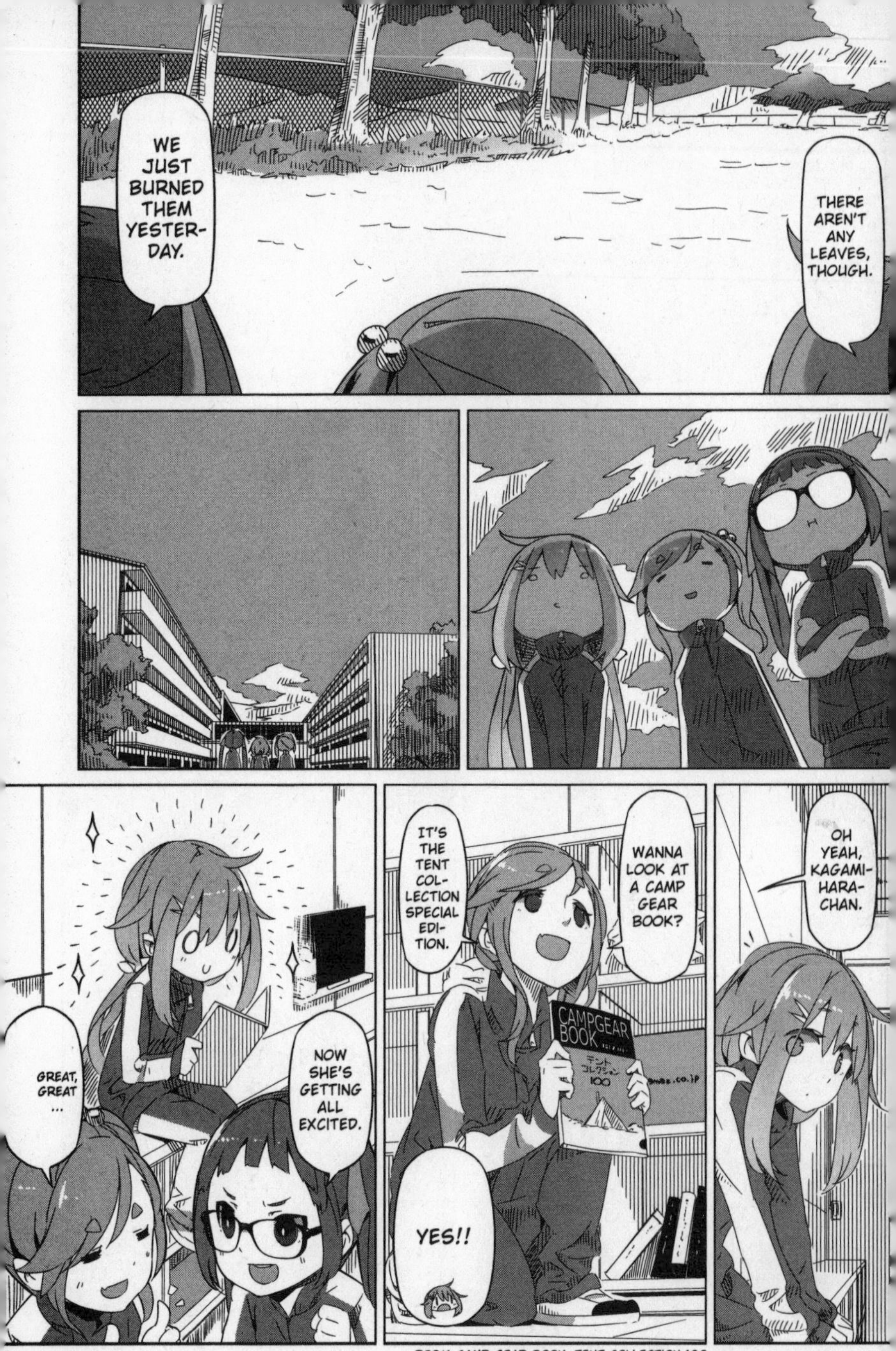
THERE AREN'T ANY LEAVES, THOUGH.
WE JUST BURNED THEM YESTER-DAY.
OH YEAH, KAGAMI-HARA-CHAN.
WANNA LOOK AT A CAMP GEAR BOOK?
IT'S THE TENT COL-LECTION SPECIAL EDI-TION.
CAMPGEAR BOOK
YES!!
NOW SHE'S GETTING ALL EXCITED.
GREAT, GREAT ...

BOOK: CAMP GEAR BOOK: TENT COLLECTION 100

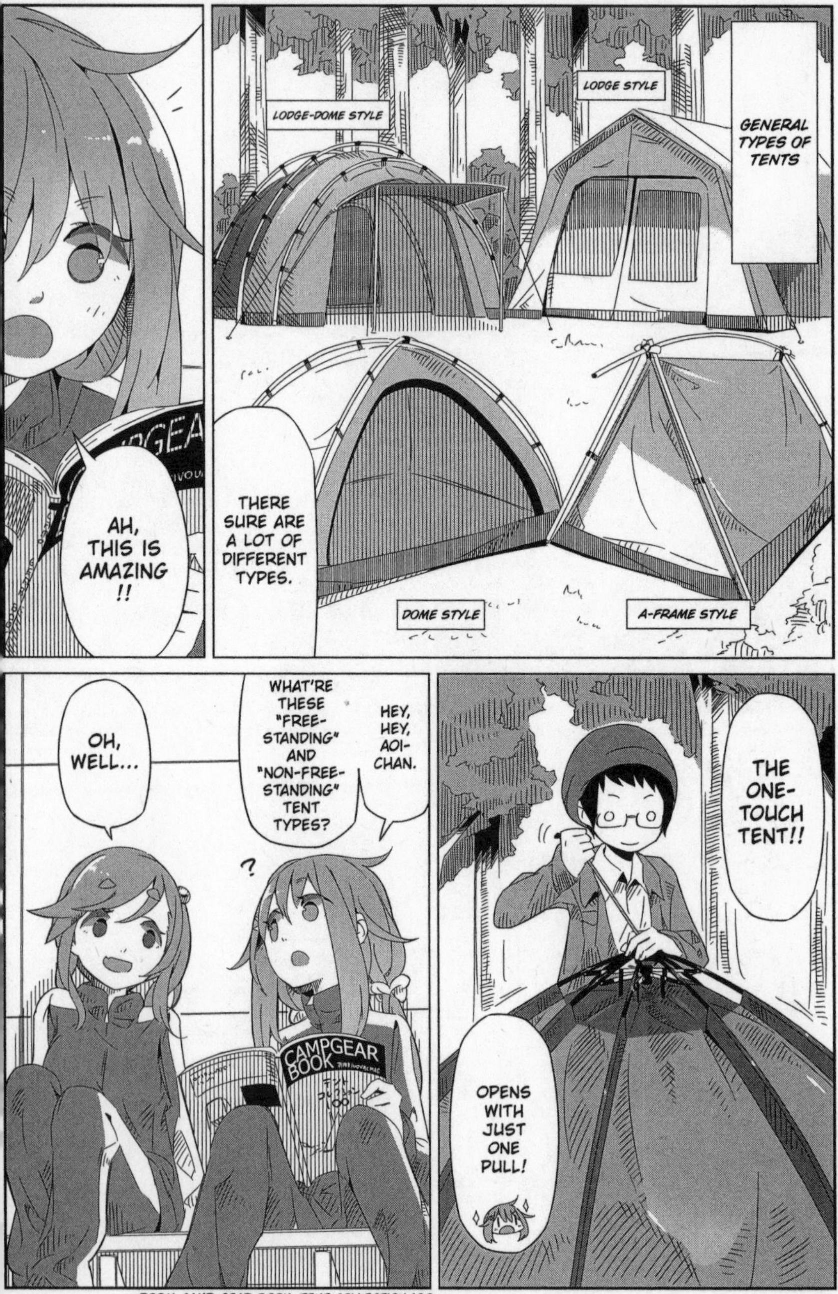
GENERAL TYPES OF TENTS
LODGE STYLE
LODGE-DOME STYLE
THERE SURE ARE A LOT OF DIFFERENT TYPES.
A-FRAME STYLE
DOME STYLE
AH, THIS IS AMAZING!!
THE ONE-TOUCH TENT!!
OPENS WITH JUST ONE PULL!
HEY, HEY, AOI-CHAN.
WHAT'RE THESE "FREE-STANDING" AND "NON-FREE-STANDING" TENT TYPES?
?
OH, WELL...
CAMPGEAR BOOK

BOOK: CAMP GEAR BOOK: TENT COLLECTION 100

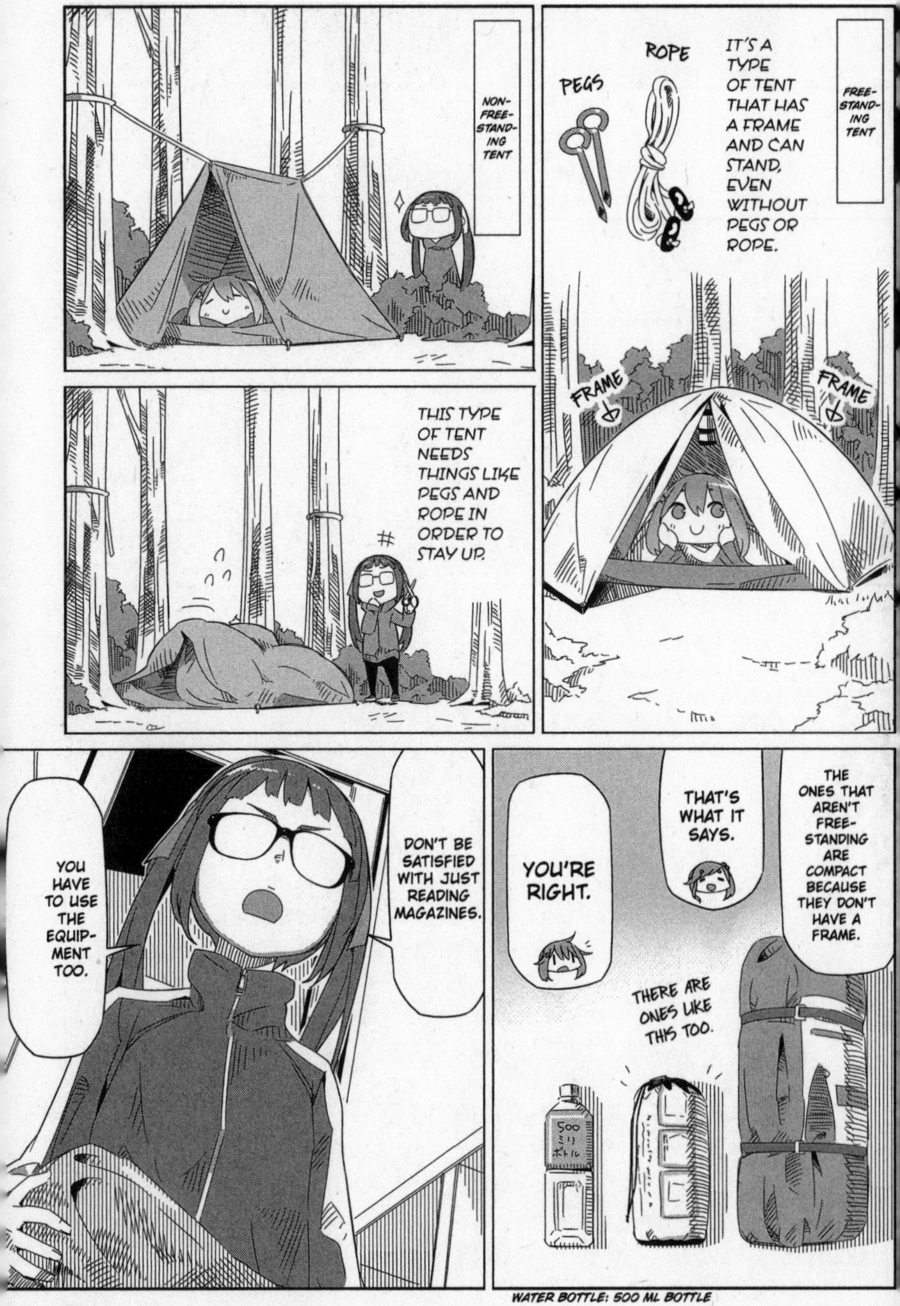
FREE-STANDING TENT
IT'S A TYPE OF TENT THAT HAS A FRAME AND CAN STAND, EVEN WITHOUT PEGS OR ROPE.
ROPE
PEGS
FRAME
FRAME
NON-FREE-STANDING TENT
THIS TYPE OF TENT NEEDS THINGS LIKE PEGS AND ROPE IN ORDER TO STAY UP.
THE ONES THAT AREN'T FREE-STANDING ARE COMPACT BECAUSE THEY DON'T HAVE A FRAME.
THAT'S WHAT IT SAYS.
YOU'RE RIGHT.
THERE ARE ONES LIKE THIS TOO.
DON'T BE SATISFIED WITH JUST READING MAGAZINES.
YOU HAVE TO USE THE EQUIPMENT TOO.
WATER BOTTLE: 500 ML BOTTLE

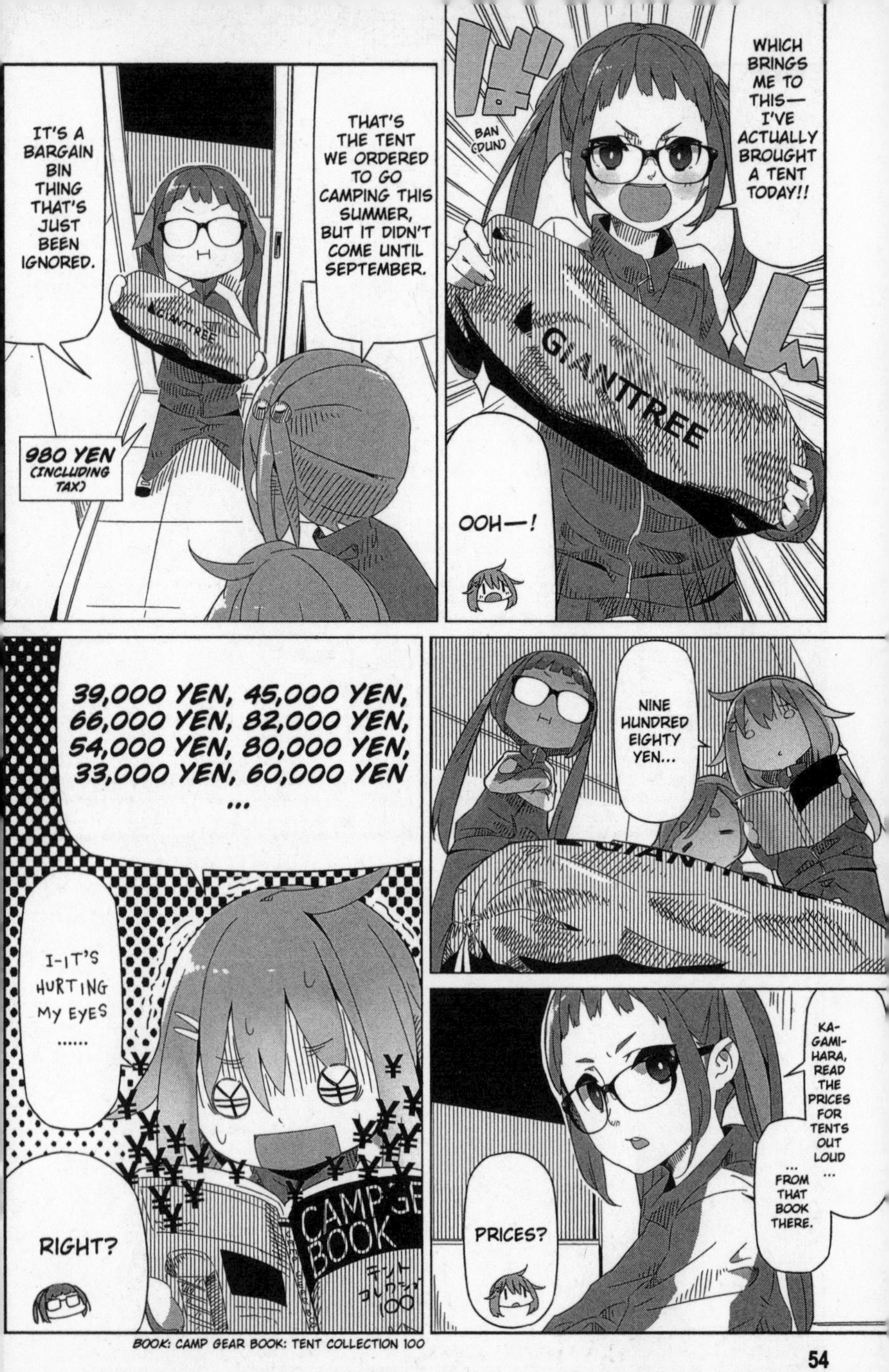
BAN (DUN)
WHICH BRINGS ME TO THIS—I'VE ACTUALLY BROUGHT A TENT TODAY!!
GIANTTREE
OOH—!
THAT'S THE TENT WE ORDERED TO GO CAMPING THIS SUMMER, BUT IT DIDN'T COME UNTIL SEPTEMBER.
IT'S A BARGAIN BIN THING THAT'S JUST BEEN IGNORED.
GIANTTREE
980 YEN (INCLUDING TAX)
NINE HUNDRED EIGHTY YEN...
KA-GAMI-HARA, READ THE PRICES FOR TENTS OUT LOUD ... FROM THAT BOOK THERE.
PRICES?
39,000 YEN, 45,000 YEN, 66,000 YEN, 82,000 YEN, 54,000 YEN, 80,000 YEN, 33,000 YEN, 60,000 YEN ...
I-IT'S HURTING MY EYES ......
RIGHT?
BOOK: CAMP GEAR BOOK: TENT COLLECTION 100

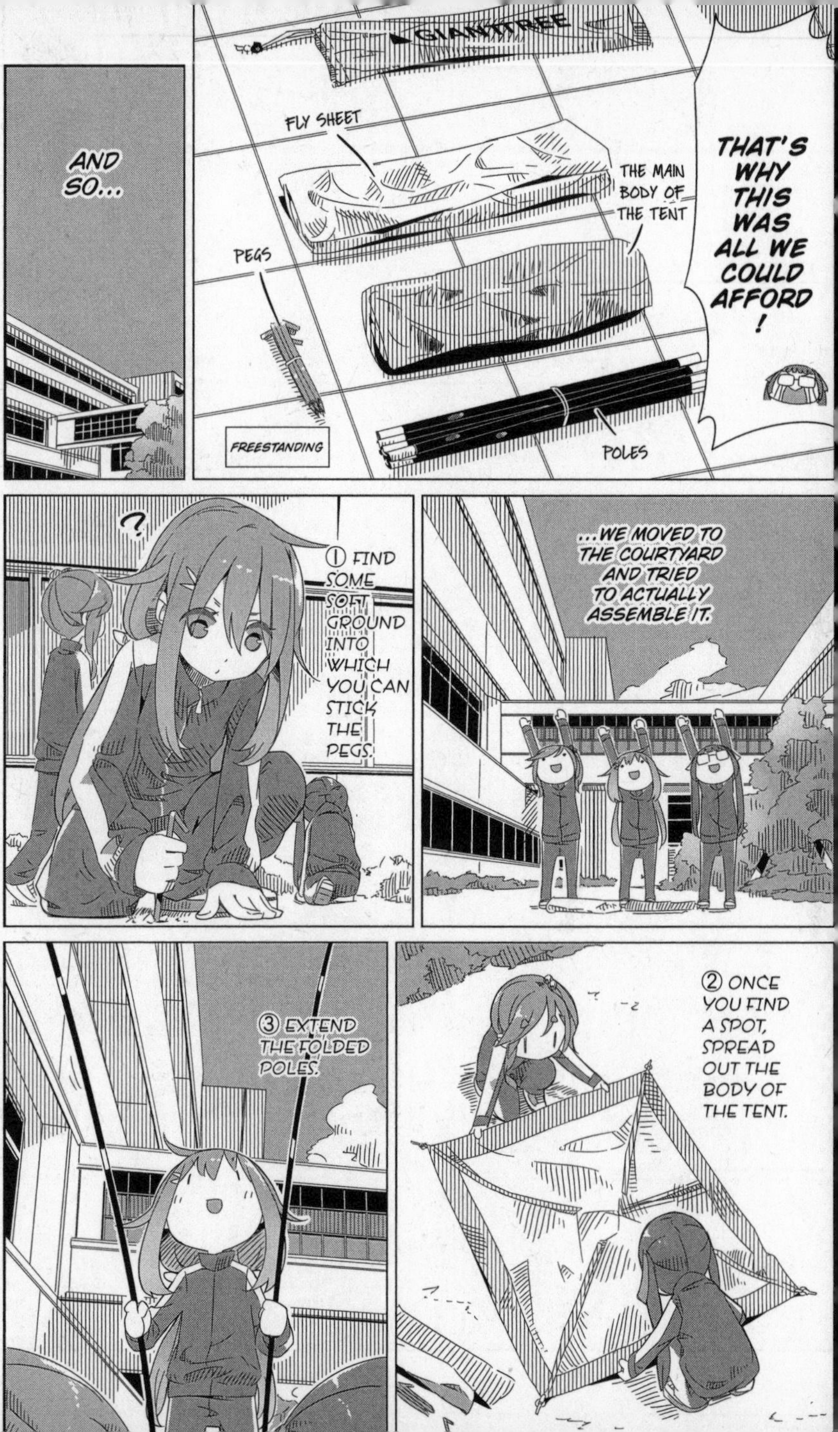
THAT'S WHY THIS WAS ALL WE COULD AFFORD!
GIANTTREE
FLY SHEET
THE MAIN BODY OF THE TENT
PEGS
POLES
FREESTANDING
AND SO...
...WE MOVED TO THE COURTYARD AND TRIED TO ACTUALLY ASSEMBLE IT.
?
① FIND SOME SOFT GROUND INTO WHICH YOU CAN STICK THE PEGS.
② ONCE YOU FIND A SPOT, SPREAD OUT THE BODY OF THE TENT.
③ EXTEND THE FOLDED POLES.

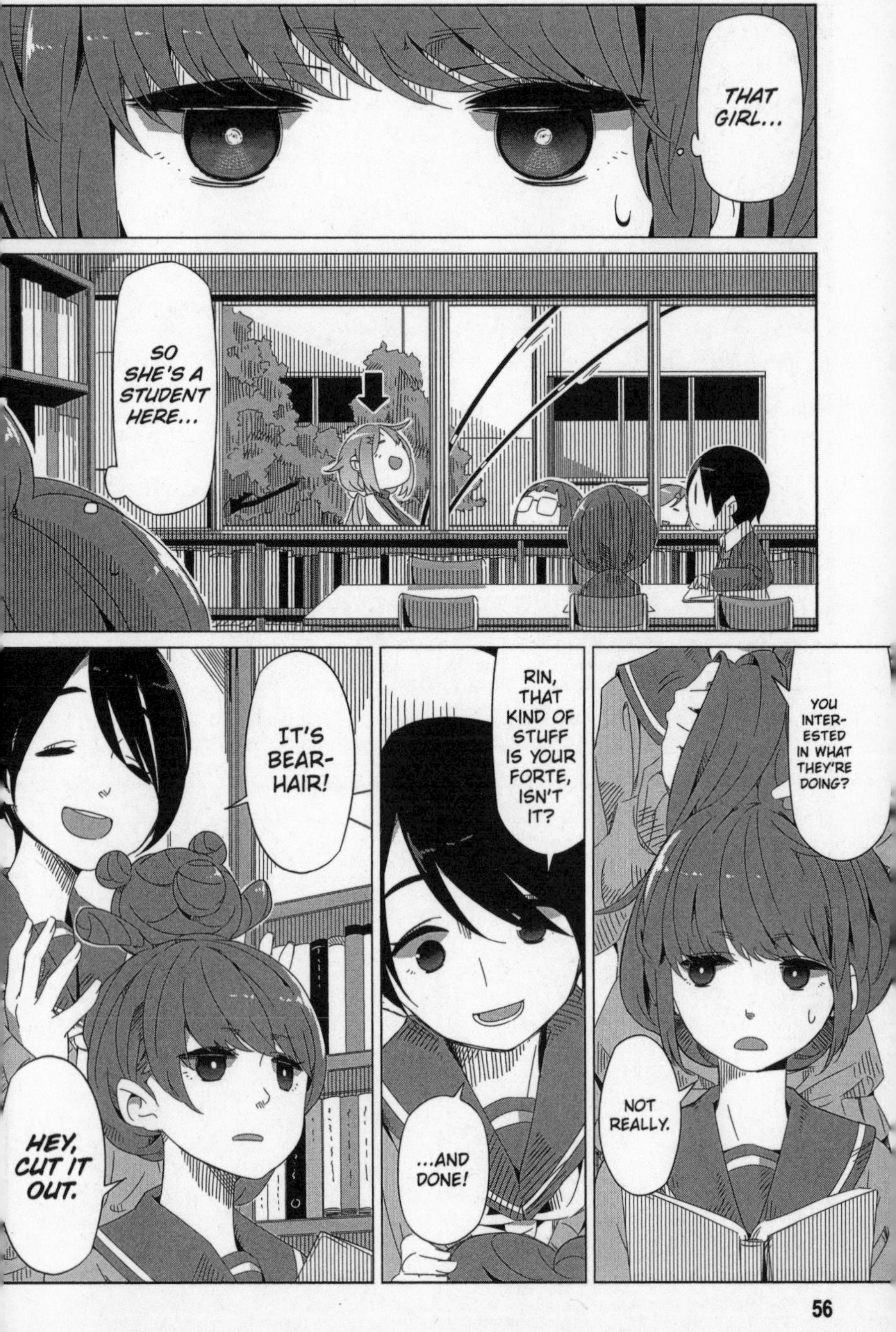
THAT GIRL...
SO SHE'S A STUDENT HERE...
YOU INTERESTED IN WHAT THEY'RE DOING?
NOT REALLY.
RIN, THAT KIND OF STUFF IS YOUR FORTE, ISN'T IT?
...AND DONE!
IT'S BEAR-HAIR!
HEY, CUT IT OUT.

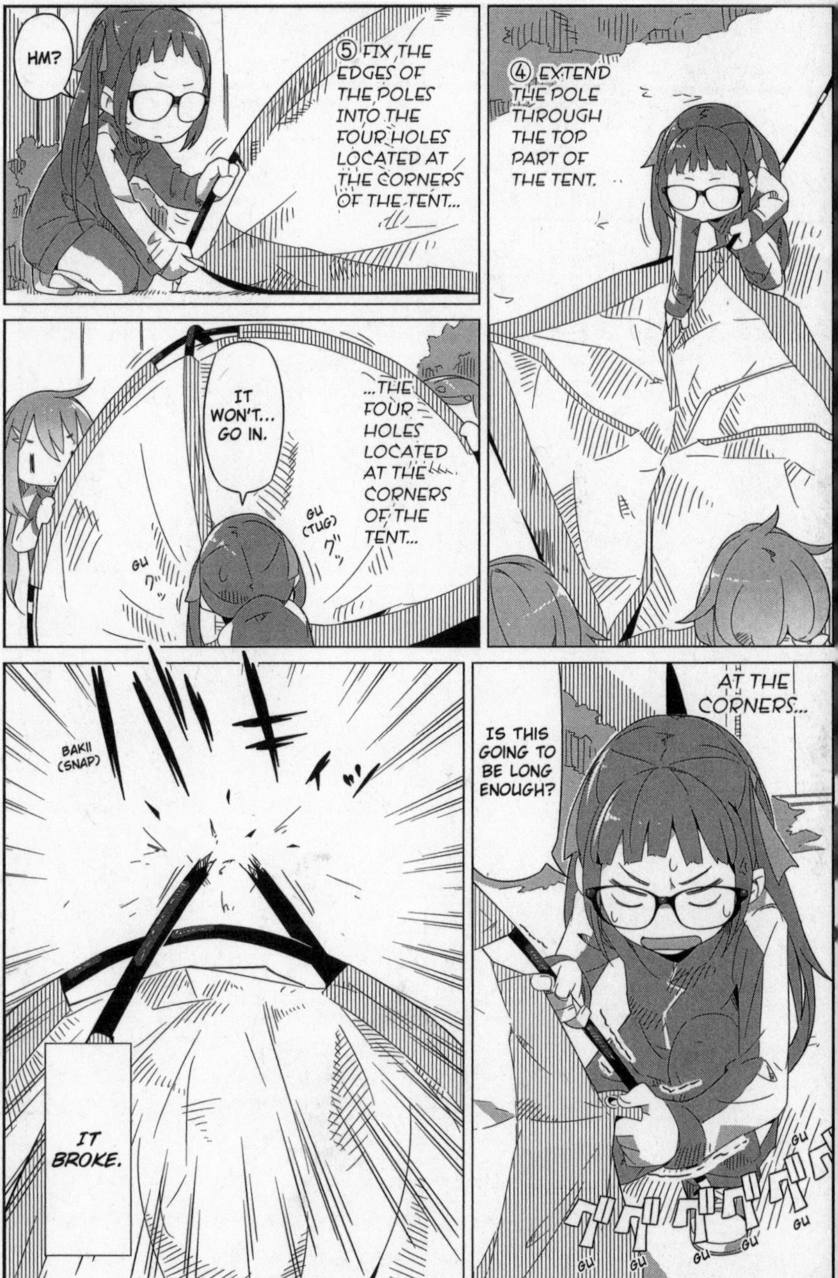
④ EXTEND THE POLE THROUGH THE TOP PART OF THE TENT.
⑤ FIX THE EDGES OF THE POLES INTO THE FOUR HOLES LOCATED AT THE CORNERS OF THE TENT...
HM?
...THE FOUR HOLES LOCATED AT THE CORNERS OF THE TENT...
IT WON'T... GO IN.
GU (TUG)
GU
AT THE CORNERS...
IS THIS GOING TO BE LONG ENOUGH?
GU
GU
GU
GU
GU
GU
BAKII (SNAP)
IT BROKE.

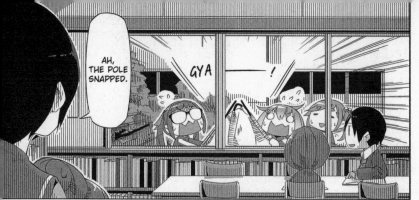

GYA———!
AH, THE POLE SNAPPED.
IF THE POLE BREAKS, WHAT DO THEY DO ABOUT THE TENT? BUY ANOTHER?
WELL... THEY COULD SEND IT BACK TO THE MANUFACTURER.
POLE MAINTENANCE PIPE
BUT IF YOU HAVE SOMETHING LIKE THIS...
WHERE THE POLE BROKE
...YOU CAN DO SOME MAKESHIFT REPAIRS.
WEDGE IT INTO THE PIPE
FIX INTO PLACE WITH TAPE AND ALL DONE!
LIKE THIS?
WHY DO YOU HAVE ONE OF THOSE?
IT WAS IN THAT LOST AND FOUND BOX.
RIN, WHY DON'T YOU TAKE THIS AND GO HELP THEM?
WHOA, THAT'S A REALLY SOUR FACE.

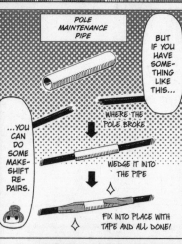

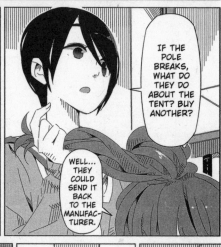

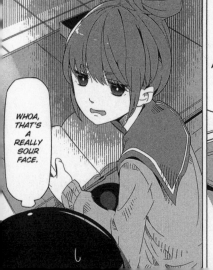

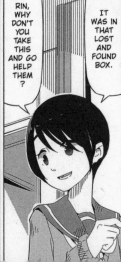

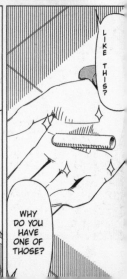

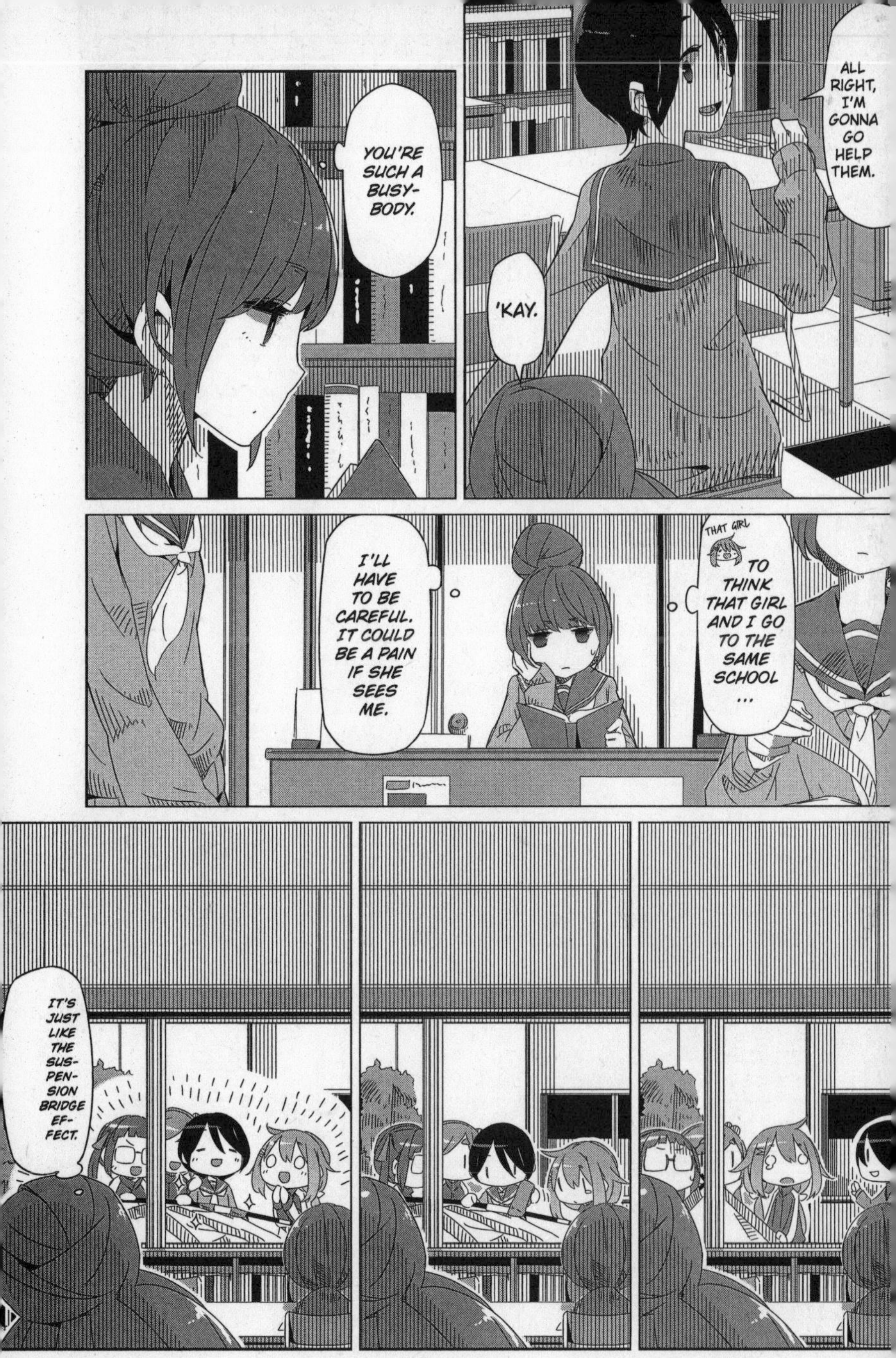
ALL RIGHT, I'M GONNA GO HELP THEM.
'KAY.
YOU'RE SUCH A BUSY-BODY.
THAT GIRL
TO THINK THAT GIRL AND I GO TO THE SAME SCHOOL...
I'LL HAVE TO BE CAREFUL. IT COULD BE A PAIN IF SHE SEES ME.
IT'S JUST LIKE THE SUS-PEN-SION BRIDGE EF-FECT.

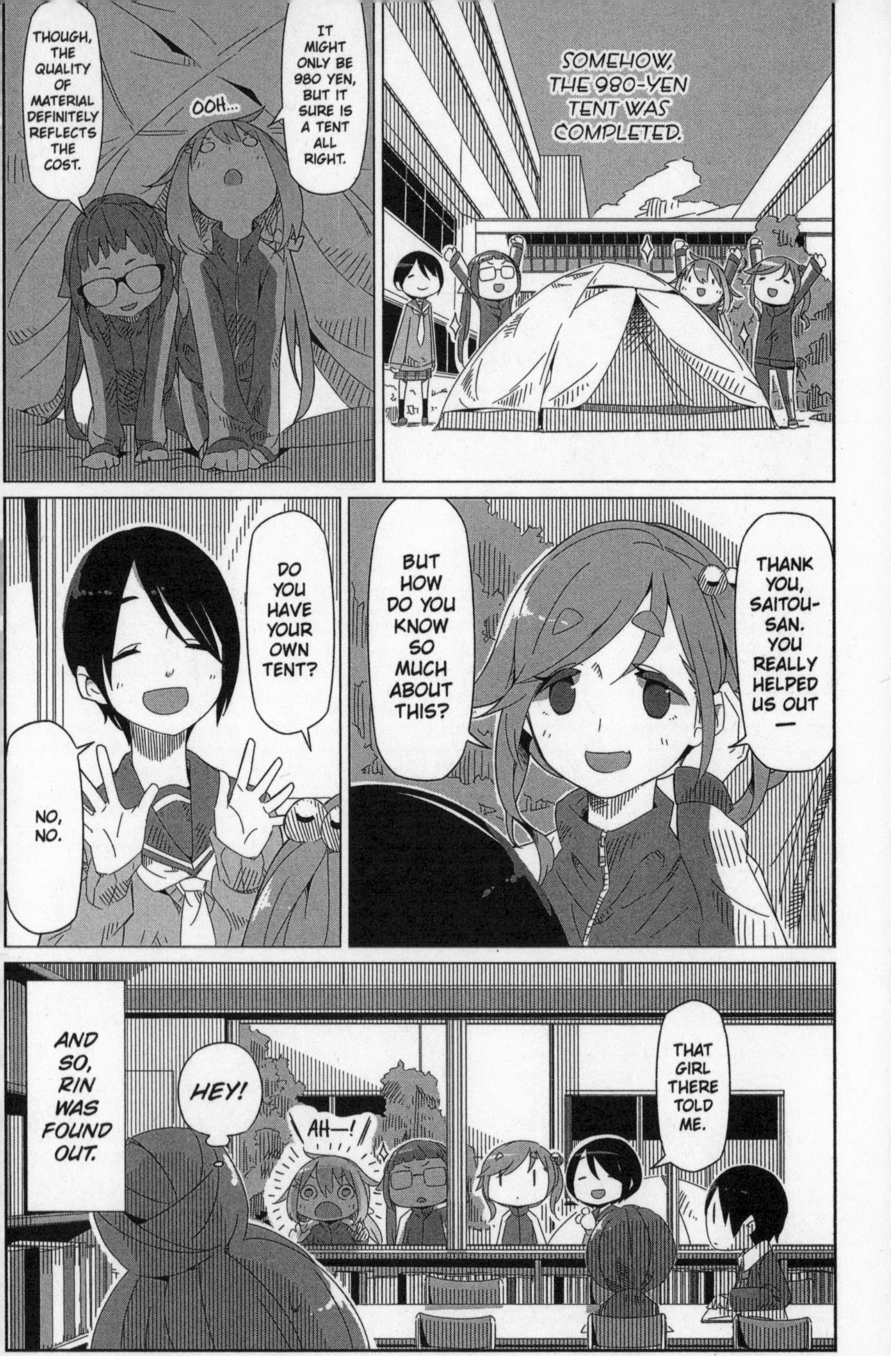
SOMEHOW, THE 980-YEN TENT WAS COMPLETED.
IT MIGHT ONLY BE 980 YEN, BUT IT SURE IS A TENT ALL RIGHT.
OOH...
THOUGH, THE QUALITY OF MATERIAL DEFINITELY REFLECTS THE COST.
THANK YOU, SAITOU-SAN. YOU REALLY HELPED US OUT—
BUT HOW DO YOU KNOW SO MUCH ABOUT THIS?
DO YOU HAVE YOUR OWN TENT?
NO, NO.
THAT GIRL THERE TOLD ME.
AH—!
HEY!
AND SO, RIN WAS FOUND OUT.

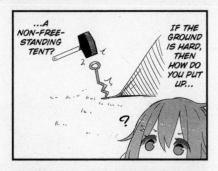

IF THE GROUND IS HARD, THEN HOW DO YOU PUT UP...
...A NON-FREE-STANDING TENT?
?
HF!
HF!
HF!
PIIIN (TAUT)
BA (FWIP)
ばっ
BA
ばっ
FOOD
RIGHT ANSWER
BIG ROCK
TREE
OH, I GUESS THAT WORKS TOO.

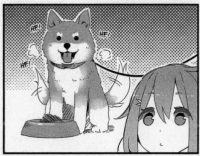

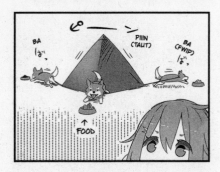

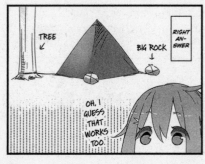

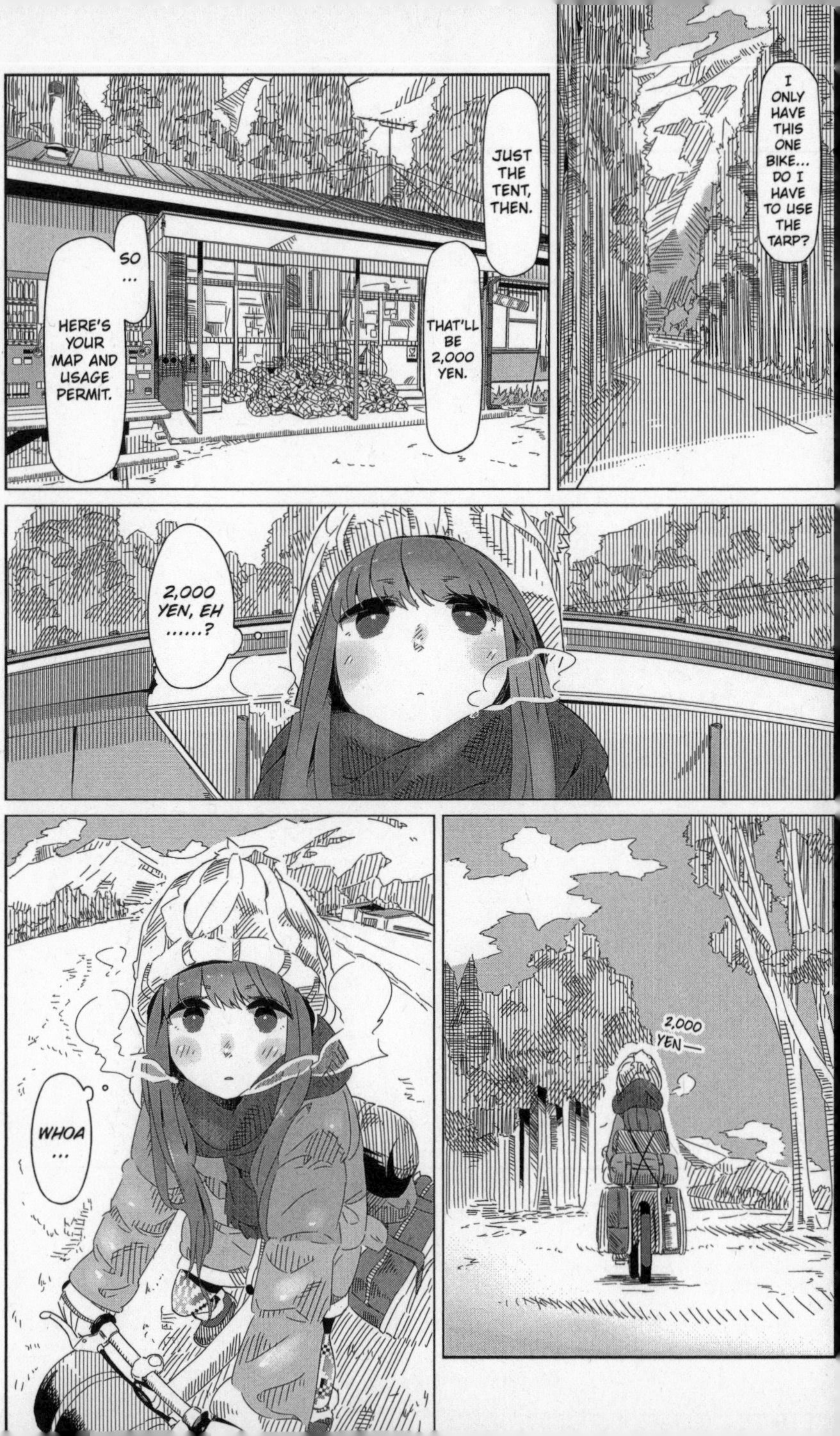
I ONLY HAVE THIS ONE BIKE... DO I HAVE TO USE THE TARP?
JUST THE TENT, THEN.
THAT'LL BE 2,000 YEN.
SO ... HERE'S YOUR MAP AND USAGE PERMIT.
2,000 YEN, EH ......?
2,000 YEN—
WHOA ...

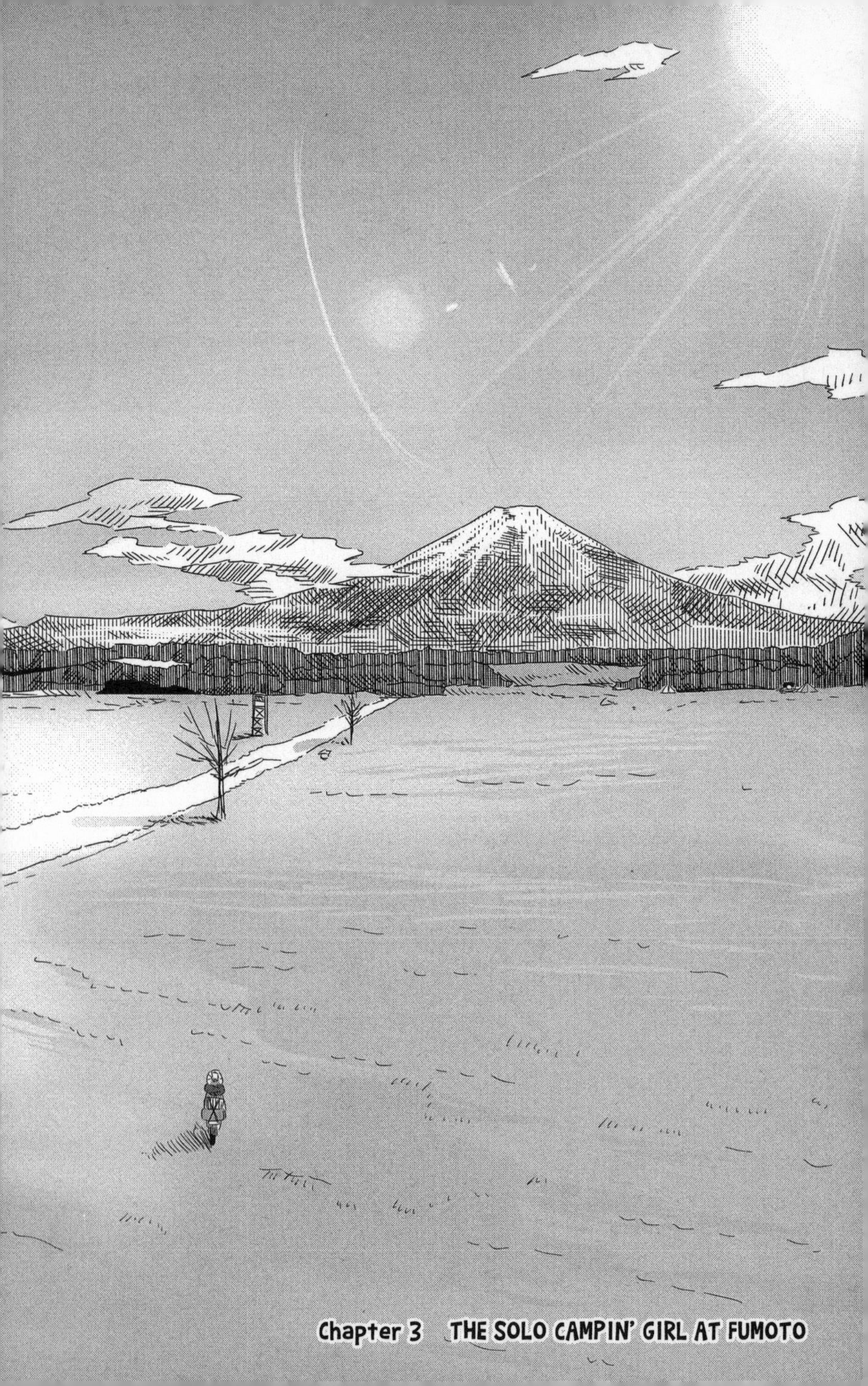

Chapter 3 THE SOLO CAMPIN' GIRL AT FUMOTO

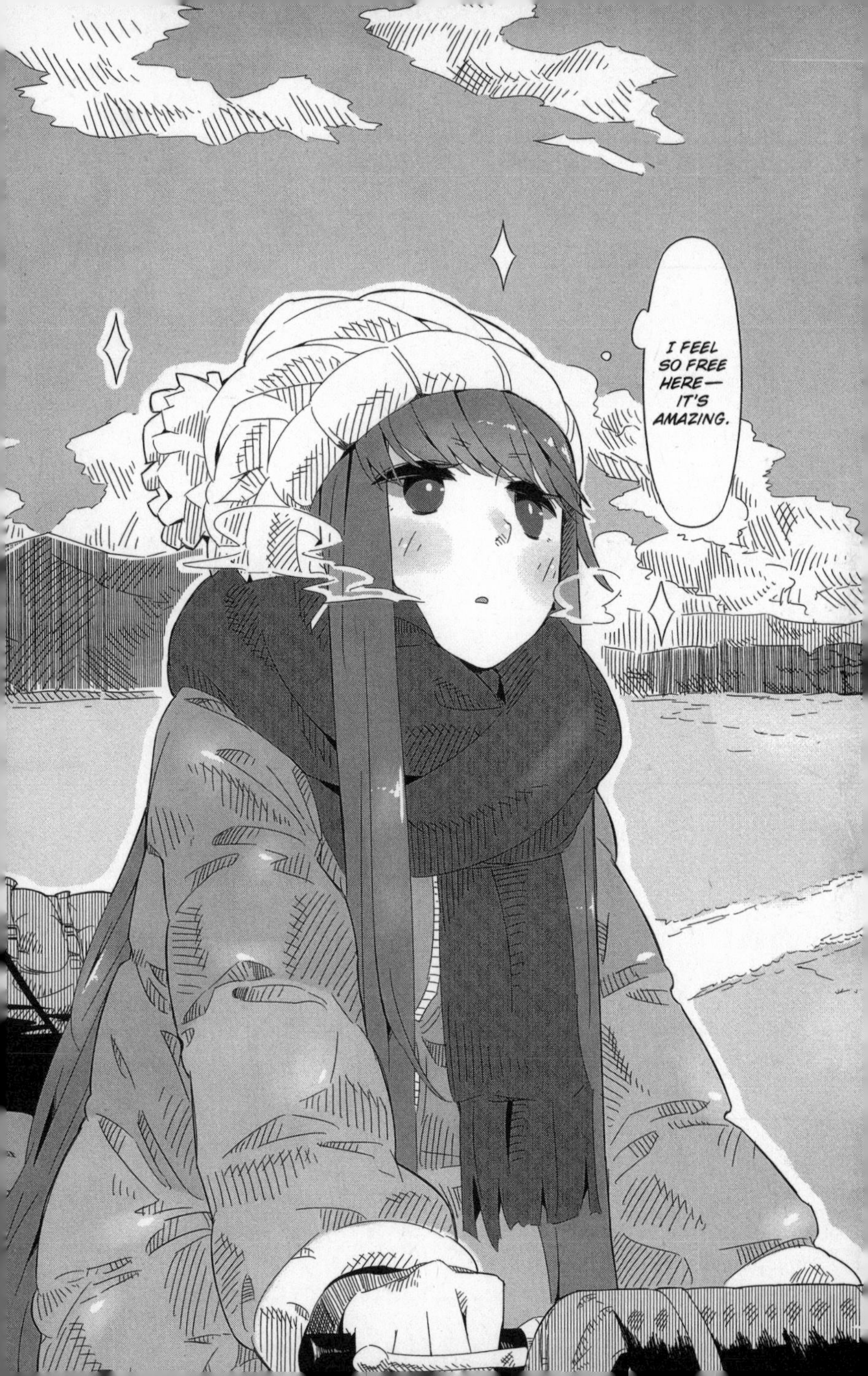
I FEEL SO FREE HERE— IT'S AMAZING.

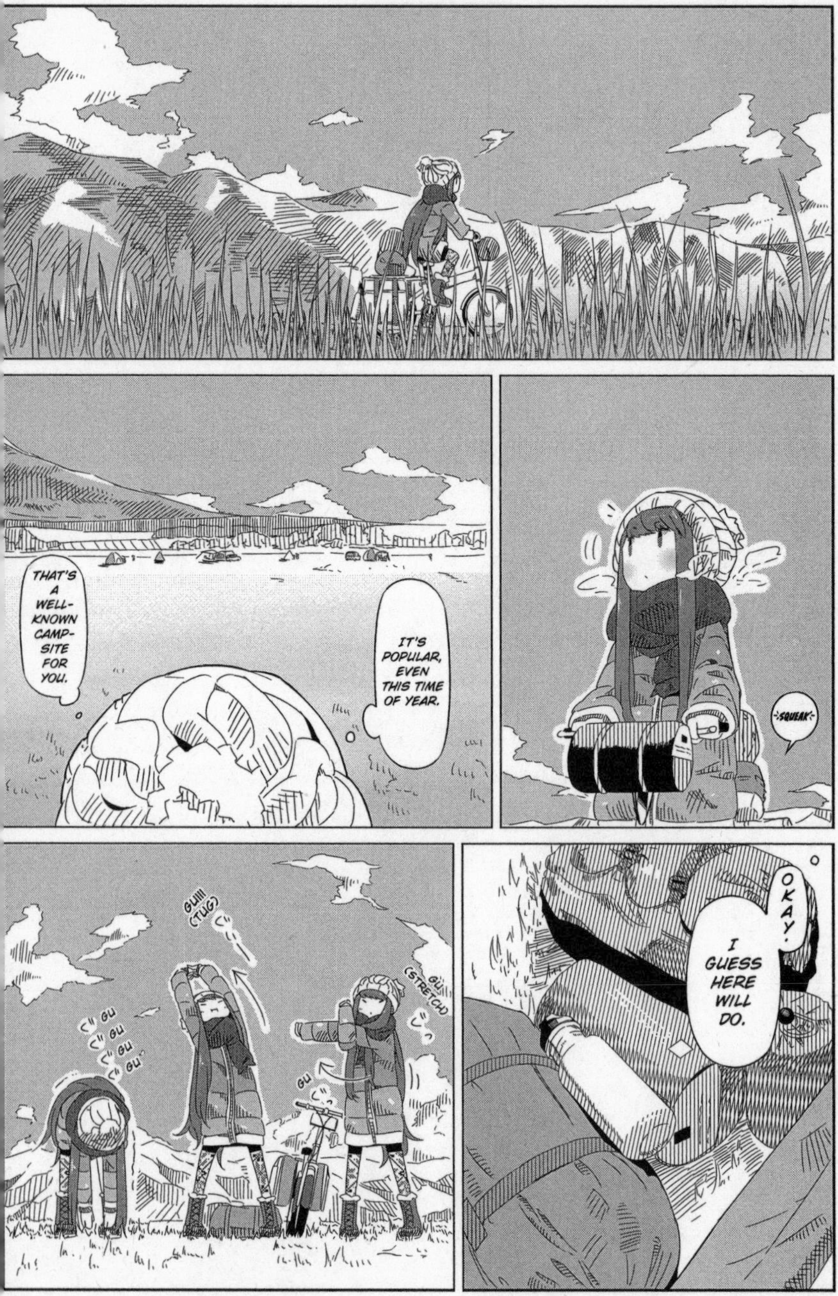
SQUEAK
IT'S POPULAR, EVEN THIS TIME OF YEAR.
THAT'S A WELL-KNOWN CAMP-SITE FOR YOU.
OKAY. I GUESS HERE WILL DO.
GU (STRETCH)
GU
GUIII (TUG)
GU GU GU GU

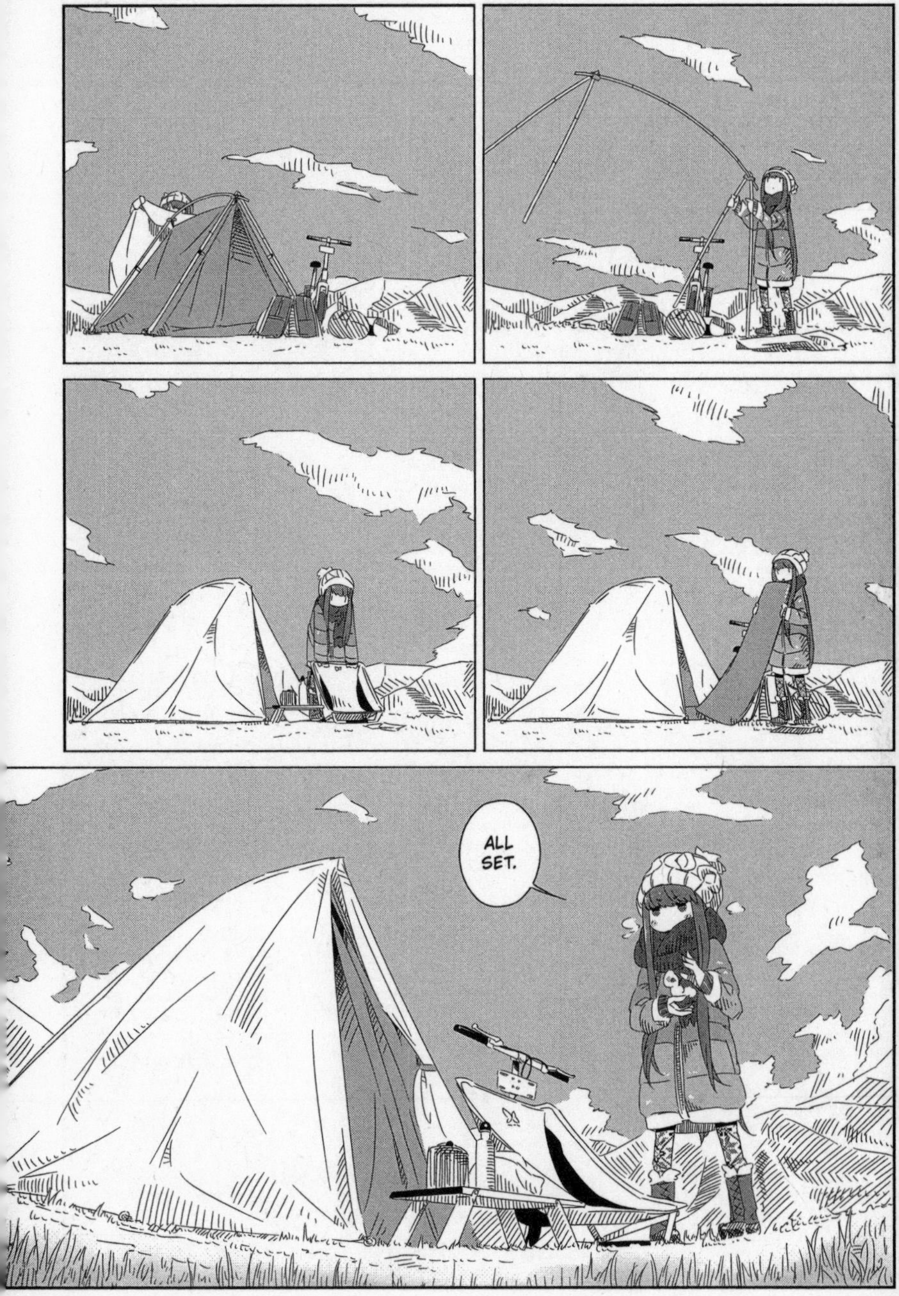
ALL SET.

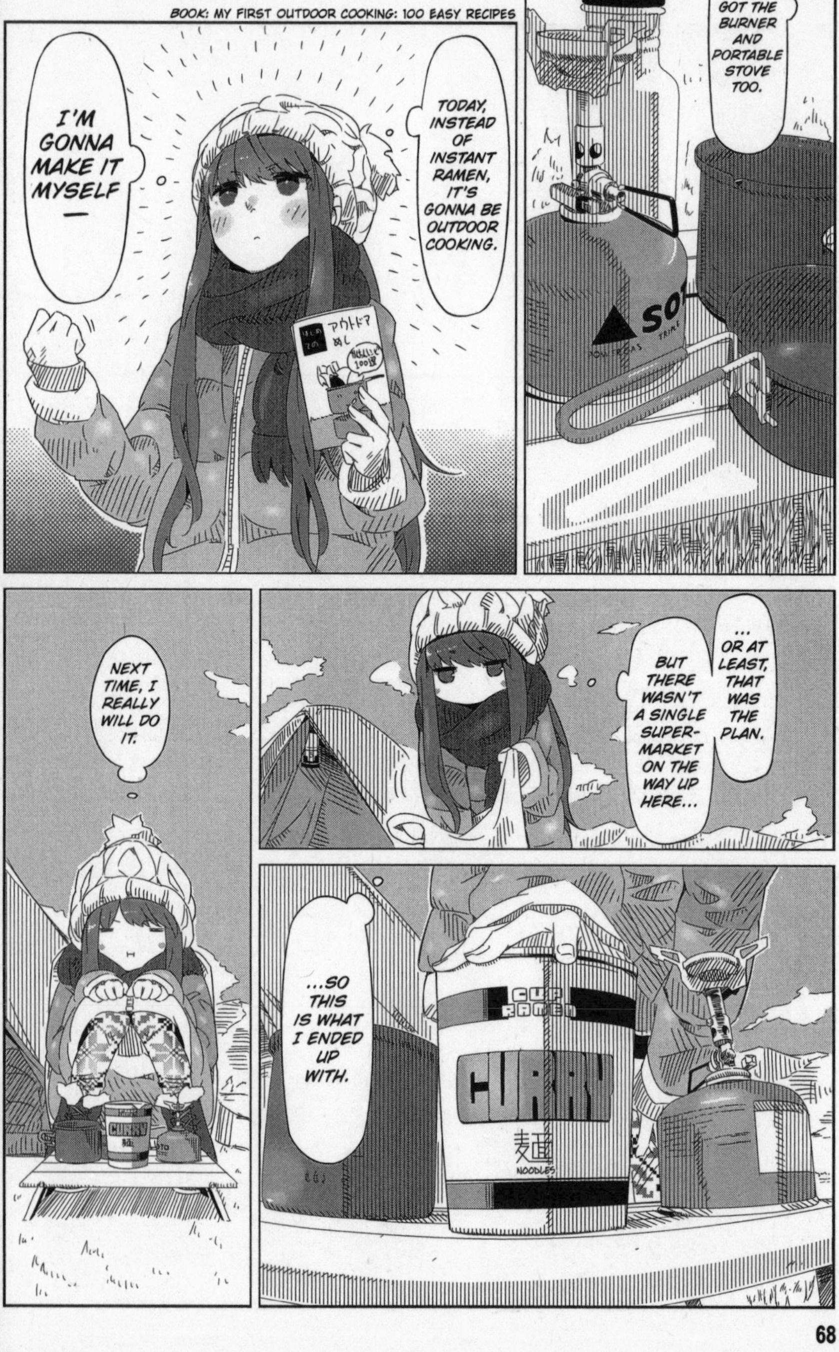
BOOK: MY FIRST OUTDOOR COOKING: 100 EASY RECIPES
GOT THE BURNER AND PORTABLE STOVE TOO.
TODAY, INSTEAD OF INSTANT RAMEN, IT'S GONNA BE OUTDOOR COOKING.
I'M GONNA MAKE IT MYSELF—
... OR AT LEAST, THAT WAS THE PLAN.
BUT THERE WASN'T A SINGLE SUPER-MARKET ON THE WAY UP HERE...
...SO THIS IS WHAT I ENDED UP WITH.
CUP RAMEN
CURRY
麺
NOODLES
NEXT TIME, I REALLY WILL DO IT.

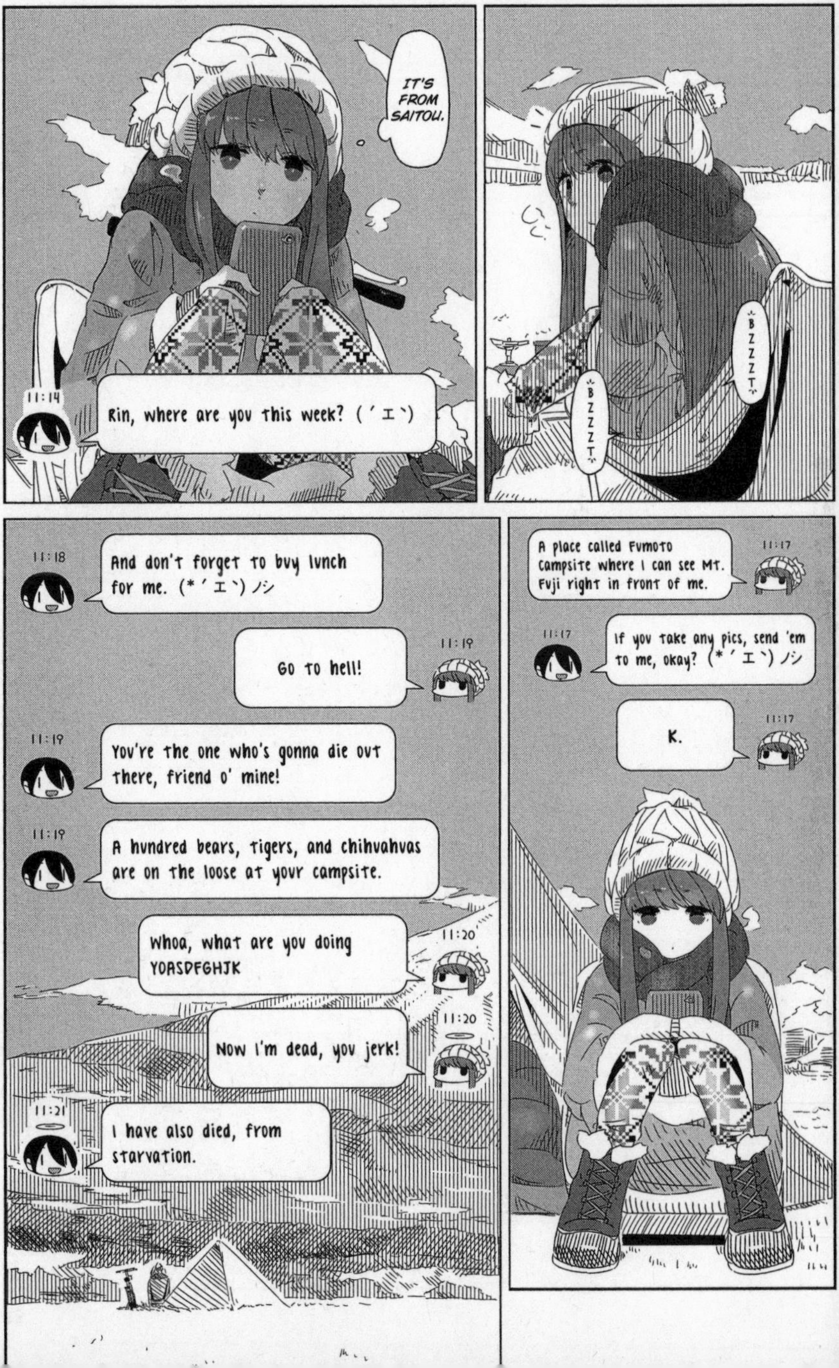
BZZZT
BZZZT
IT'S FROM SAITOU.
11:14
Rin, where are you this week? (´エ`)
11:17
A place called Fumoto Campsite where I can see Mt. Fuji right in front of me.
11:17
If you take any pics, send 'em to me, okay? (*´エ`)ノシ
11:17
K.
11:18
And don't forget to buy lunch for me. (*´エ`)ノシ
11:19
Go to hell!
11:19
You're the one who's gonna die out there, friend o' mine!
11:19
A hundred bears, tigers, and chihuahuas are on the loose at your campsite.
11:20
Whoa, what are you doing YOASDFGHJK
11:20
Now I'm dead, you jerk!
11:21
I have also died, from starvation.

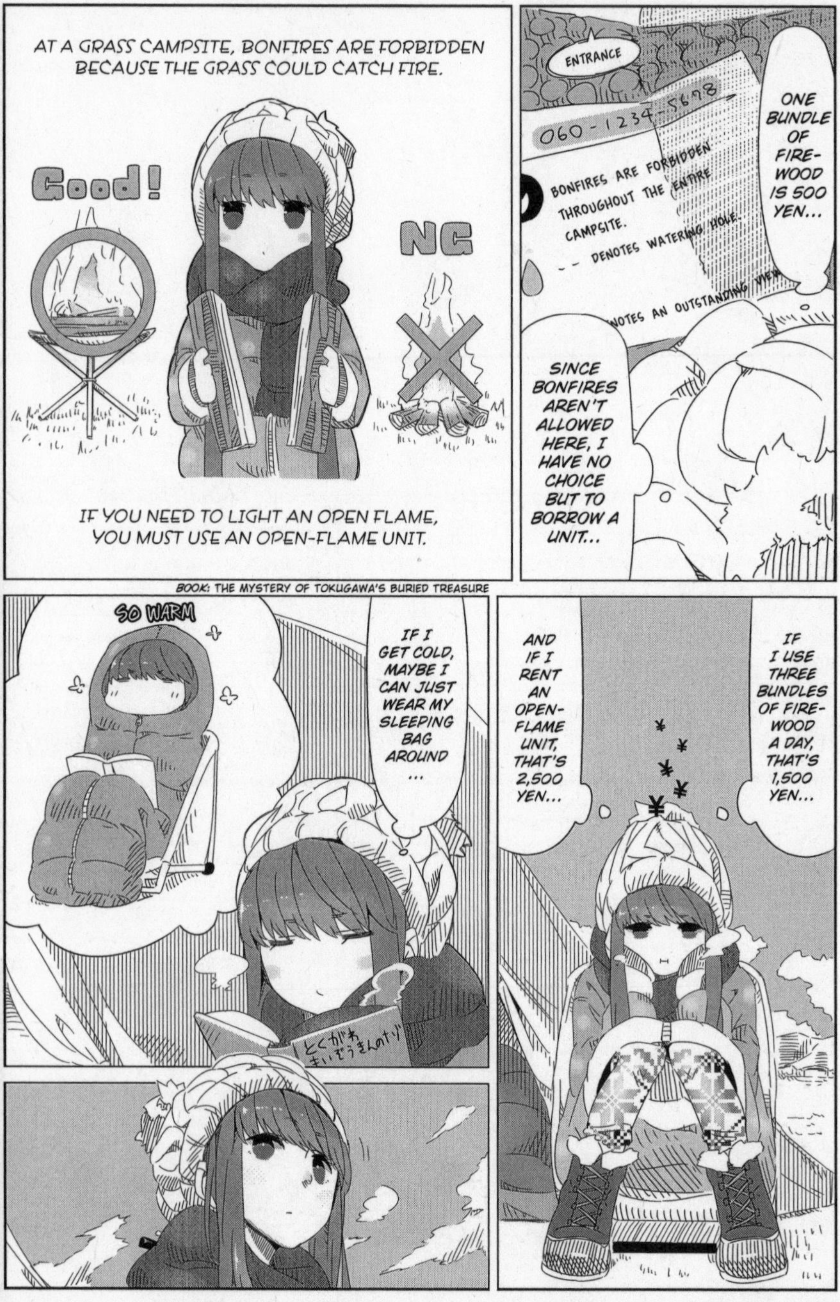
ENTRANCE
060-1234-5678
BONFIRES ARE FORBIDDEN THROUGHOUT THE ENTIRE CAMPSITE.
-- DENOTES WATERING HOLE.
NOTES AN OUTSTANDING VIEW
ONE BUNDLE OF FIRE-WOOD IS 500 YEN...
SINCE BONFIRES AREN'T ALLOWED HERE, I HAVE NO CHOICE BUT TO BORROW A UNIT...
AT A GRASS CAMPSITE, BONFIRES ARE FORBIDDEN BECAUSE THE GRASS COULD CATCH FIRE.
Good!
NG
IF YOU NEED TO LIGHT AN OPEN FLAME, YOU MUST USE AN OPEN-FLAME UNIT.
BOOK: THE MYSTERY OF TOKUGAWA'S BURIED TREASURE
IF I USE THREE BUNDLES OF FIRE-WOOD A DAY, THAT'S 1,500 YEN...
AND IF I RENT AN OPEN-FLAME UNIT, THAT'S 2,500 YEN...
¥ ¥ ¥ ¥ ¥
IF I GET COLD, MAYBE I CAN JUST WEAR MY SLEEPING BAG AROUND...
SO WARM
とくがわ まいぞうきんのナゾ

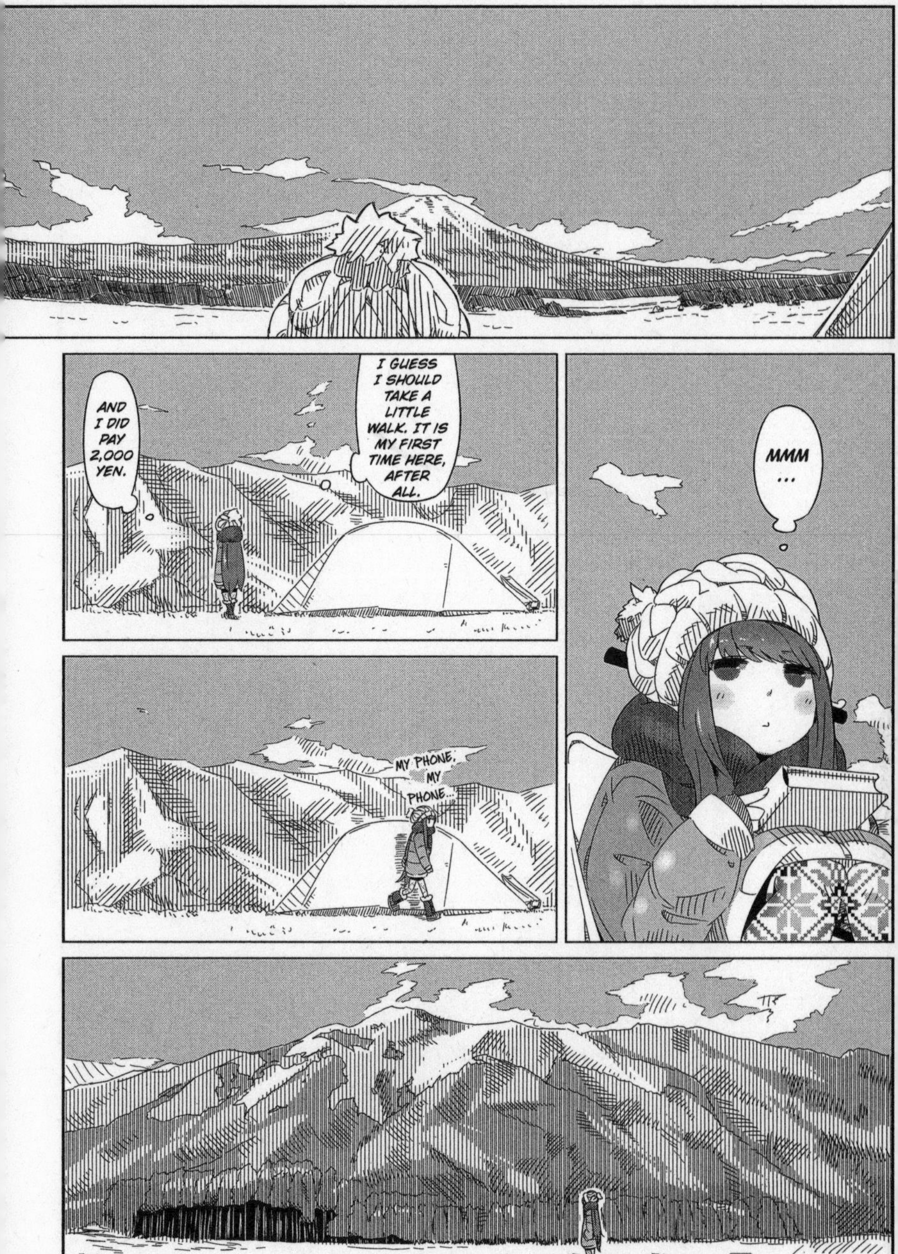
MMM ...
I GUESS I SHOULD TAKE A LITTLE WALK. IT IS MY FIRST TIME HERE, AFTER ALL.
AND I DID PAY 2,000 YEN.
MY PHONE, MY PHONE...

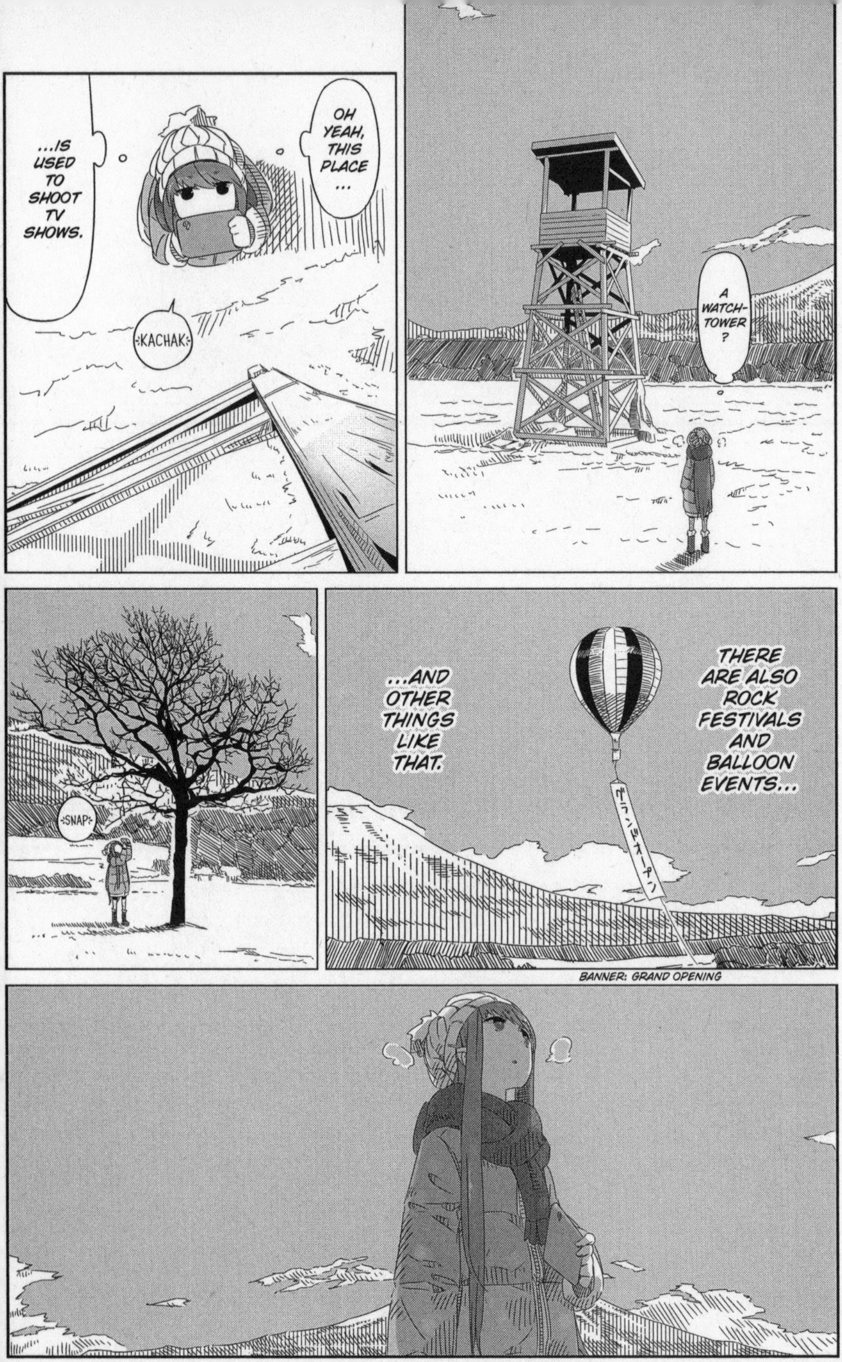
A WATCH-TOWER?
OH YEAH, THIS PLACE...
...IS USED TO SHOOT TV SHOWS.
KACHAK
THERE ARE ALSO ROCK FESTIVALS AND BALLOON EVENTS...
...AND OTHER THINGS LIKE THAT.
グランドオープン
BANNER: GRAND OPENING
SNAP

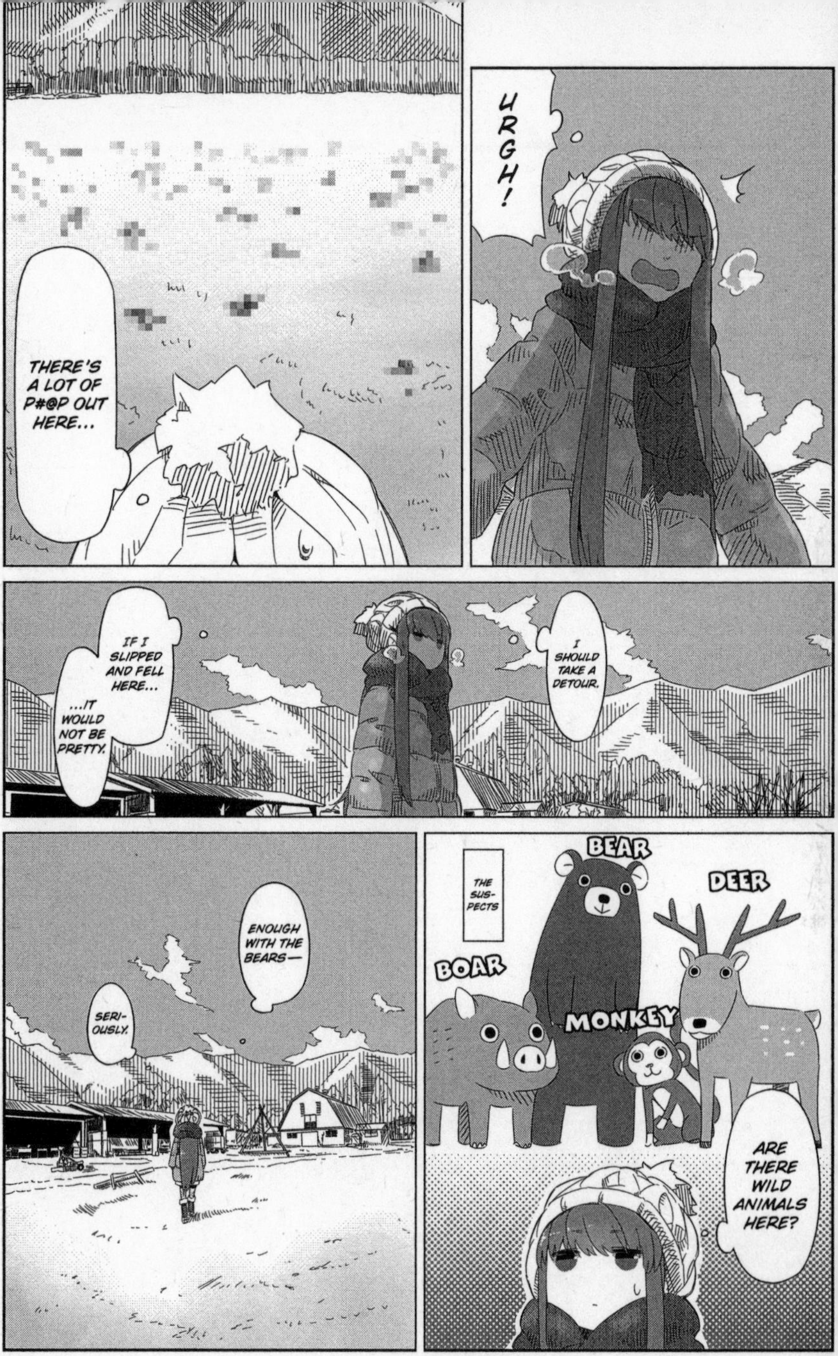
URGH!
THERE'S A LOT OF P#@P OUT HERE...
I SHOULD TAKE A DETOUR.
IF I SLIPPED AND FELL HERE...
...IT WOULD NOT BE PRETTY.
THE SUS-PECTS
BEAR
DEER
BOAR
MONKEY
ARE THERE WILD ANIMALS HERE?
ENOUGH WITH THE BEARS—
SERI-OUSLY.

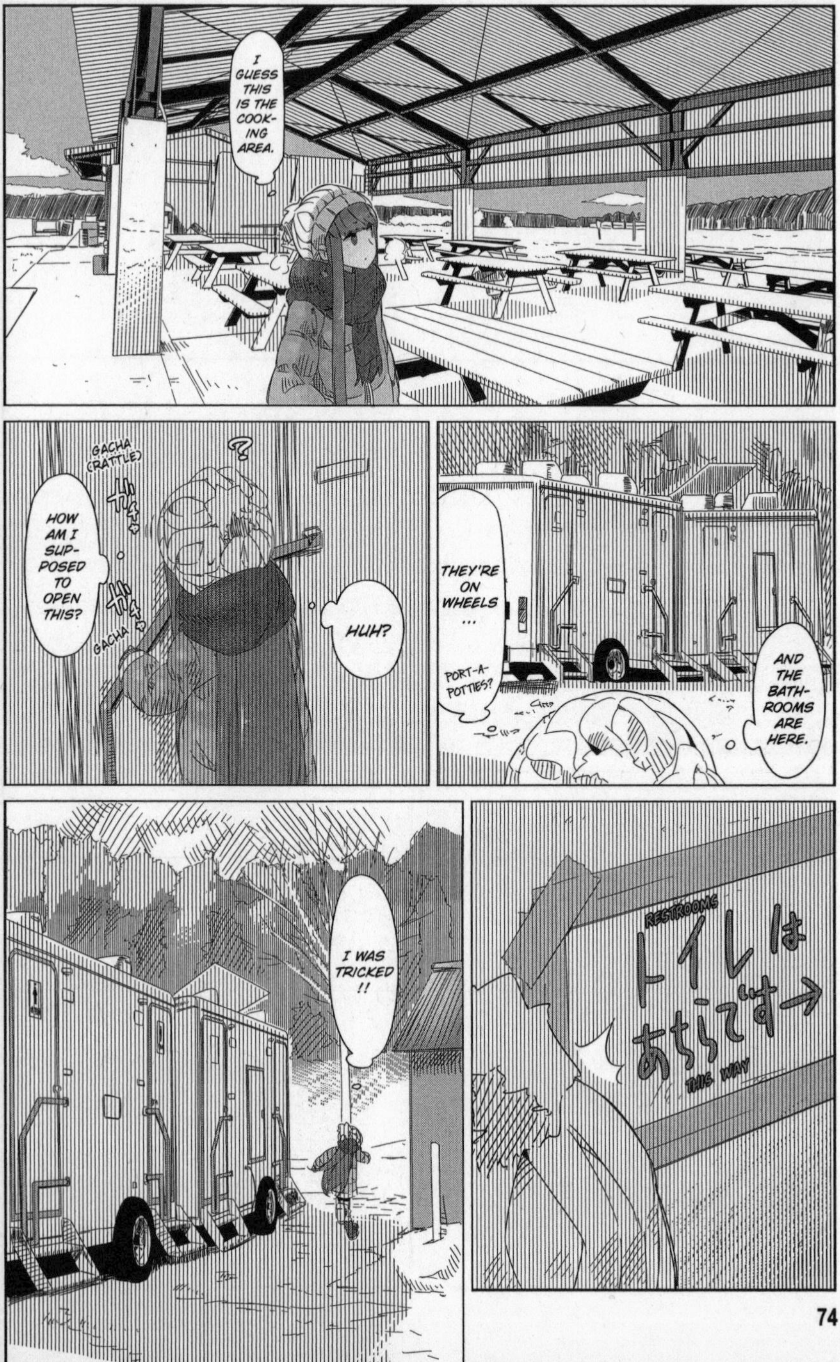
I GUESS THIS IS THE COOKING AREA.
AND THE BATHROOMS ARE HERE.
THEY'RE ON WHEELS...
PORT-A-POTTIES?
HUH?
GACHA (RATTLE)
HOW AM I SUPPOSED TO OPEN THIS?
GACHA
RESTROOMS
トイレはあちらです→
THIS WAY
I WAS TRICKED!!

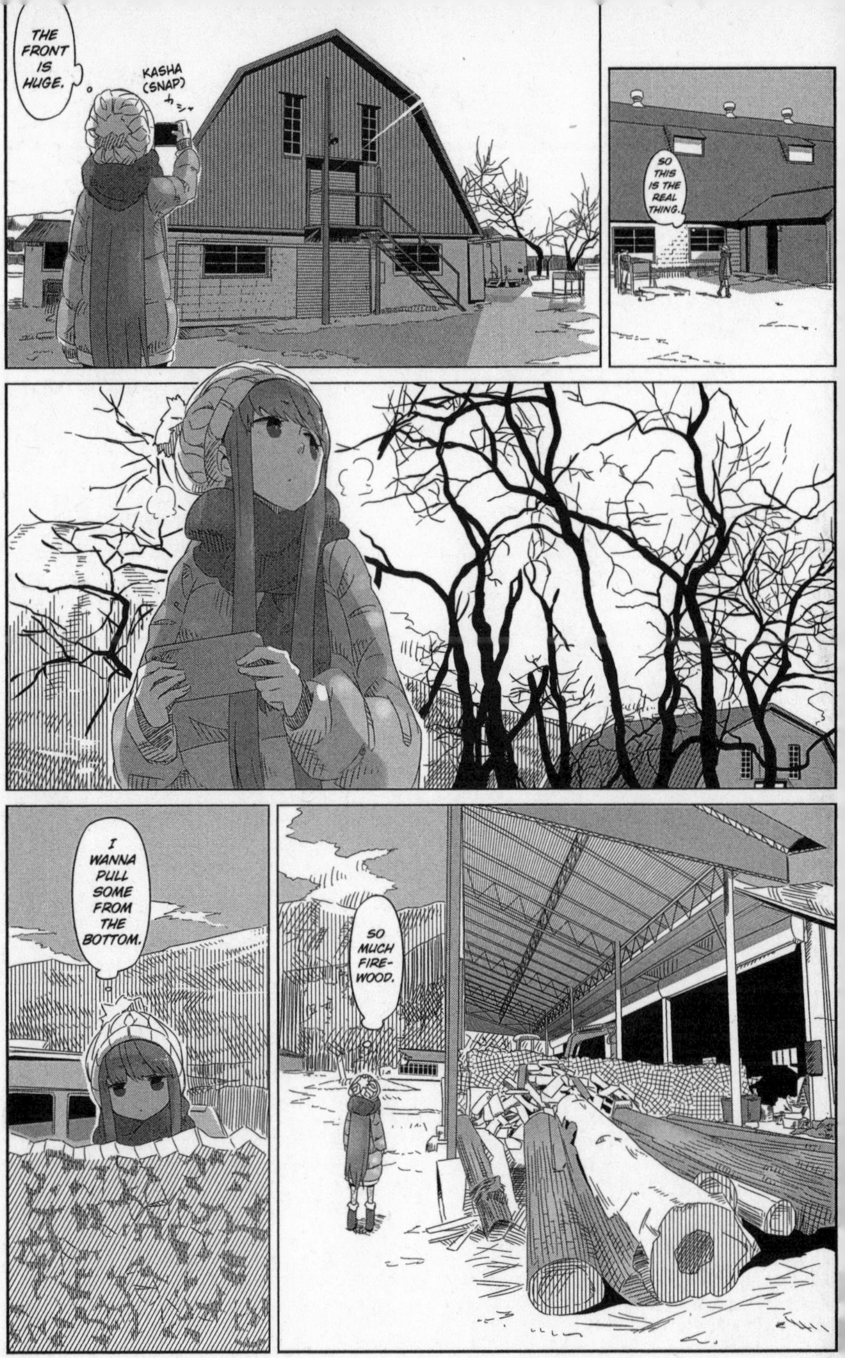
SO THIS IS THE REAL THING.
THE FRONT IS HUGE.
KASHA (SNAP)
SO MUCH FIRE-WOOD.
I WANNA PULL SOME FROM THE BOTTOM.

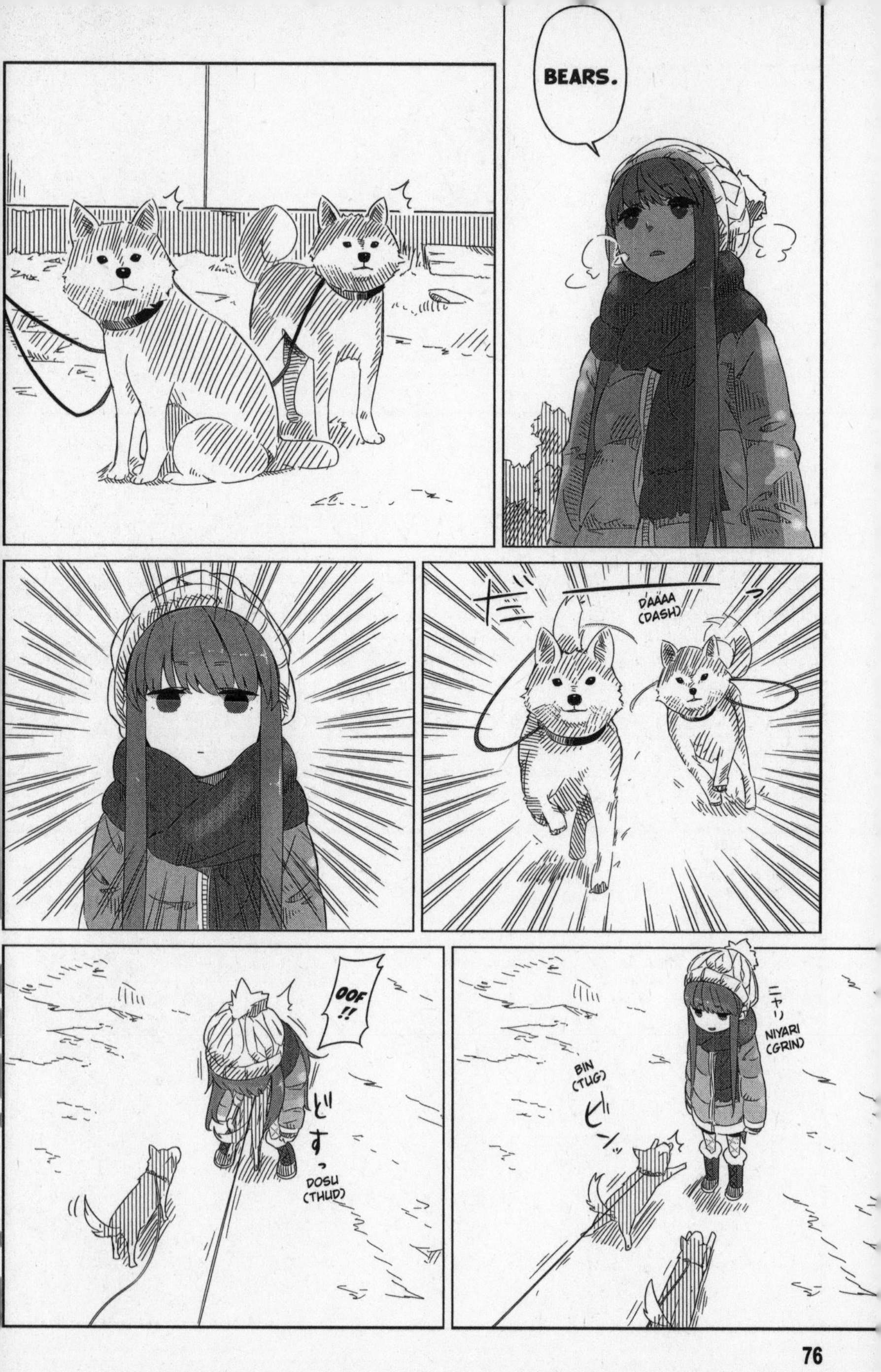

BEARS.
ダーッ
D'AAAA (DASH)
ニヤリ
NIYARI (GRIN)
BIN (TUG)
ビンッ
OOF!!
どすっ
DOSU (THUD)

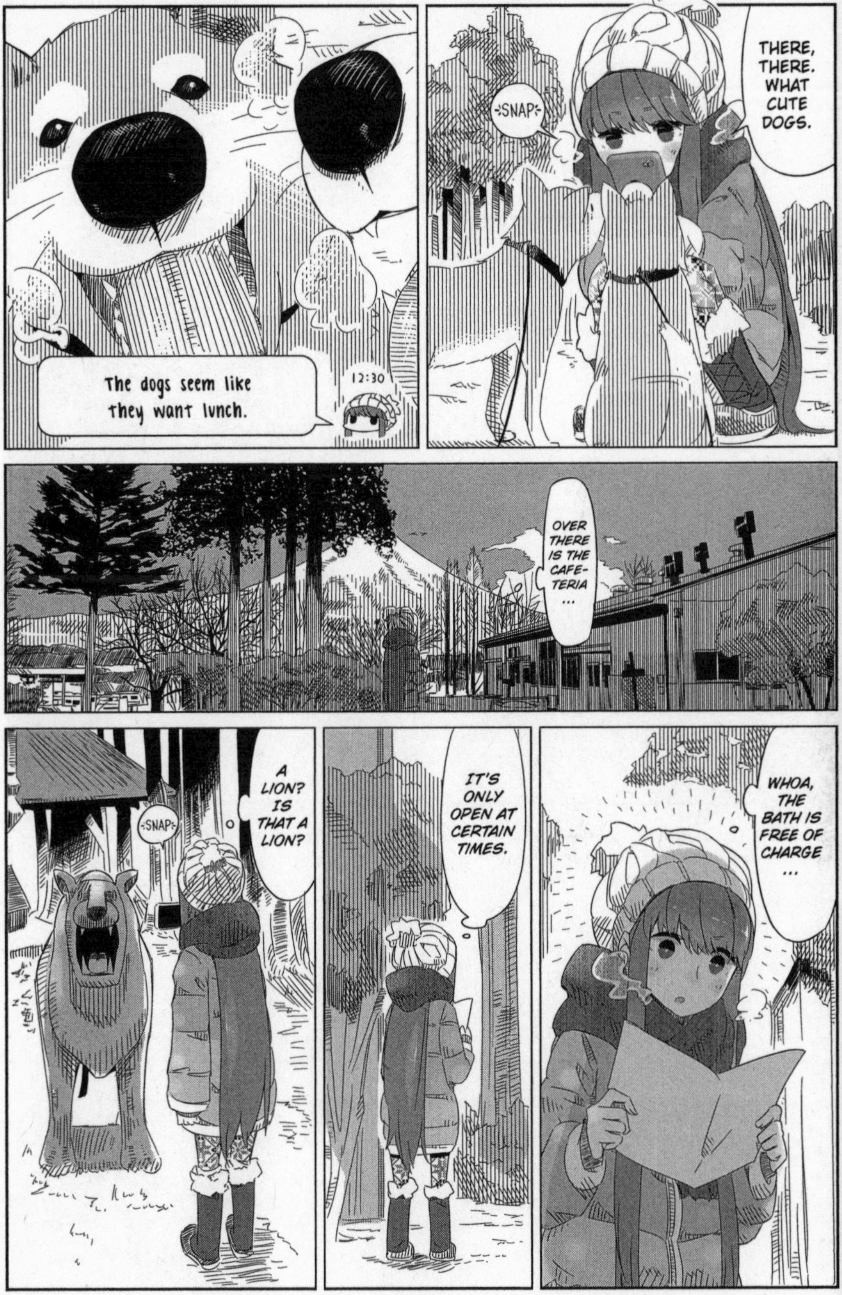
THERE, THERE. WHAT CUTE DOGS.
SNAP
The dogs seem like they want lunch.
12:30
OVER THERE IS THE CAFETERIA...
WHOA, THE BATH IS FREE OF CHARGE...
IT'S ONLY OPEN AT CERTAIN TIMES.
A LION? IS THAT A LION?
SNAP

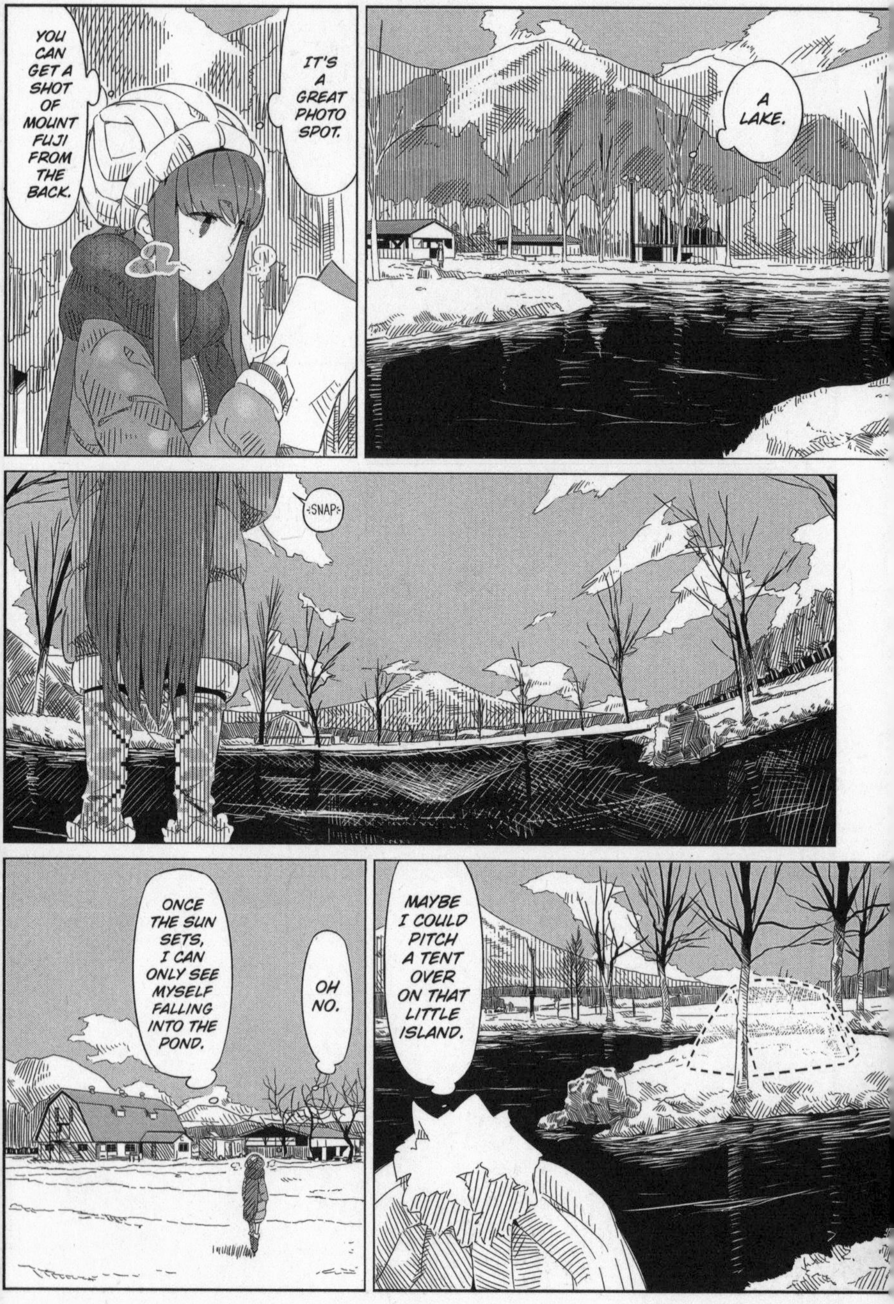

A LAKE.
IT'S A GREAT PHOTO SPOT.
YOU CAN GET A SHOT OF MOUNT FUJI FROM THE BACK.
SNAP
MAYBE I COULD PITCH A TENT OVER ON THAT LITTLE ISLAND.
ONCE THE SUN SETS, I CAN ONLY SEE MYSELF FALLING INTO THE POND.
OH NO.

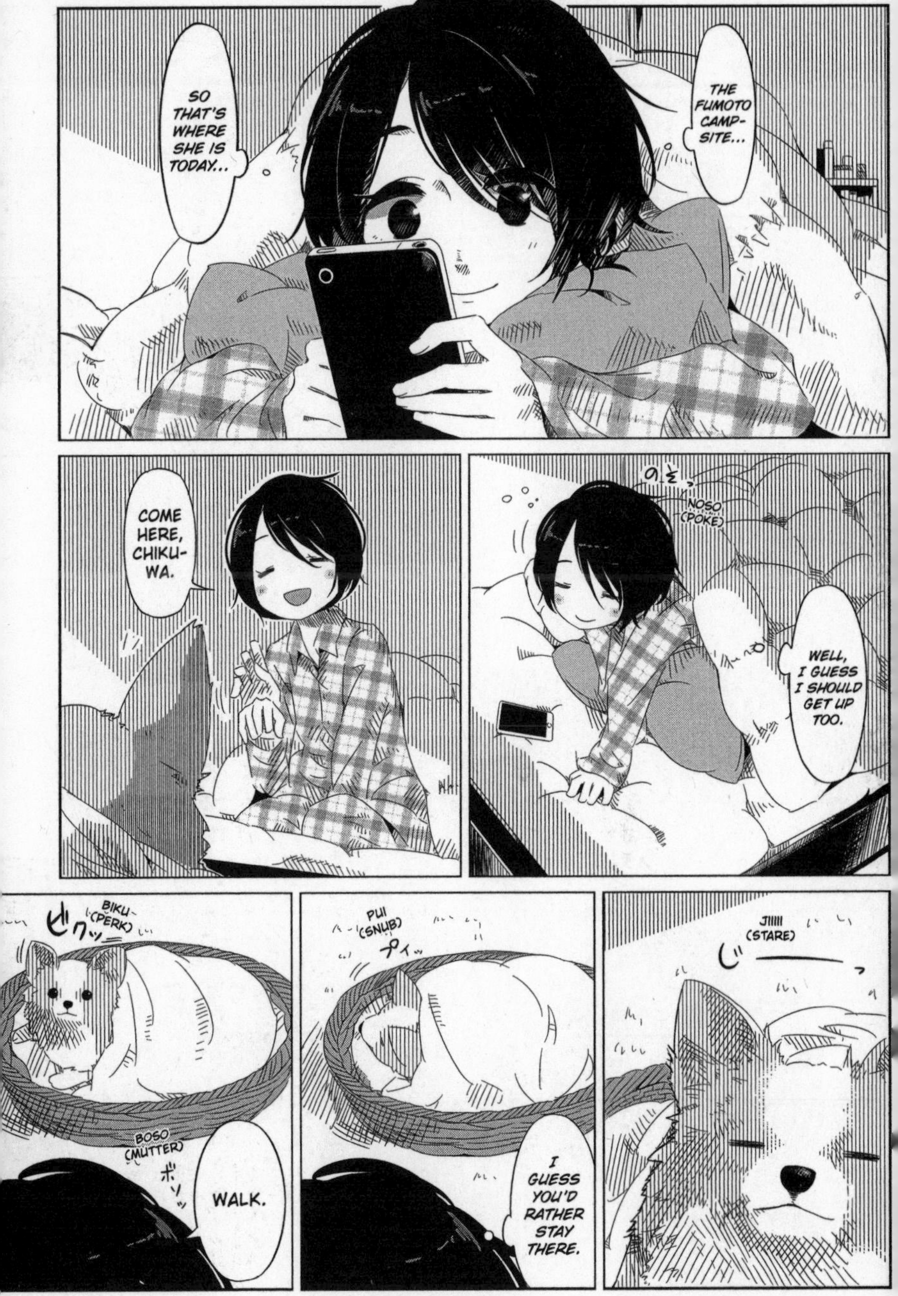
THE FUMOTO CAMP-SITE...
SO THAT'S WHERE SHE IS TODAY...
のそ
NOSO (POKE)
WELL, I GUESS I SHOULD GET UP TOO.
COME HERE, CHIKUWA.
JIIII (STARE)
じーー
PUI (SNUB)
プイッ
I GUESS YOU'D RATHER STAY THERE.
BIKU- (PERK)
ビクッ
BOSO (MUTTER)
ボソッ
WALK.

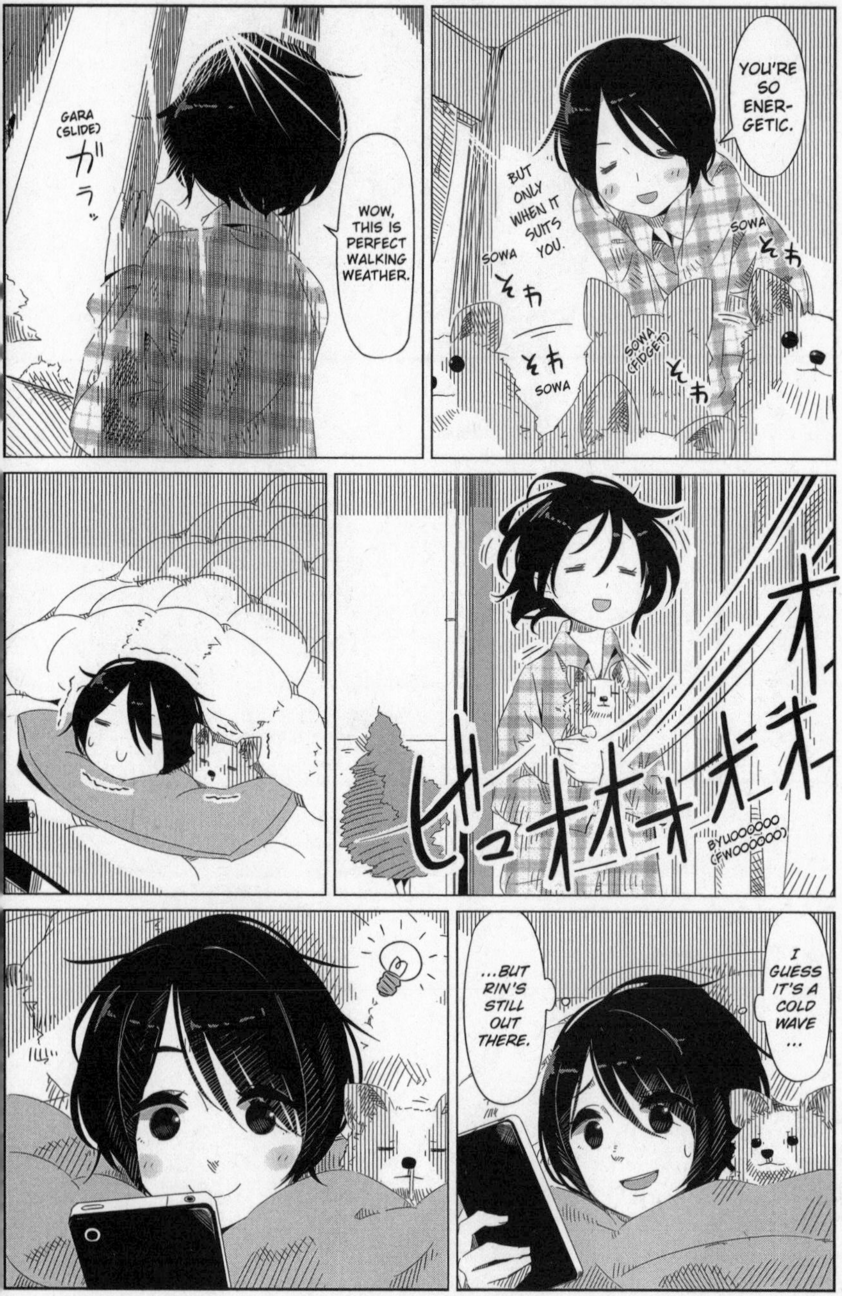
YOU'RE SO ENERGETIC.
BUT ONLY WHEN IT SUITS YOU.
SOWA
そわ
SOWA
そわ
SOWA (FIDGET)
そわ
そわ
SOWA
GARA (SLIDE)
ガラッ
WOW, THIS IS PERFECT WALKING WEATHER.
ビュオオオオオー
BYUOOOOOO (FWOOOOOO)
I GUESS IT'S A COLD WAVE...
...BUT RIN'S STILL OUT THERE.

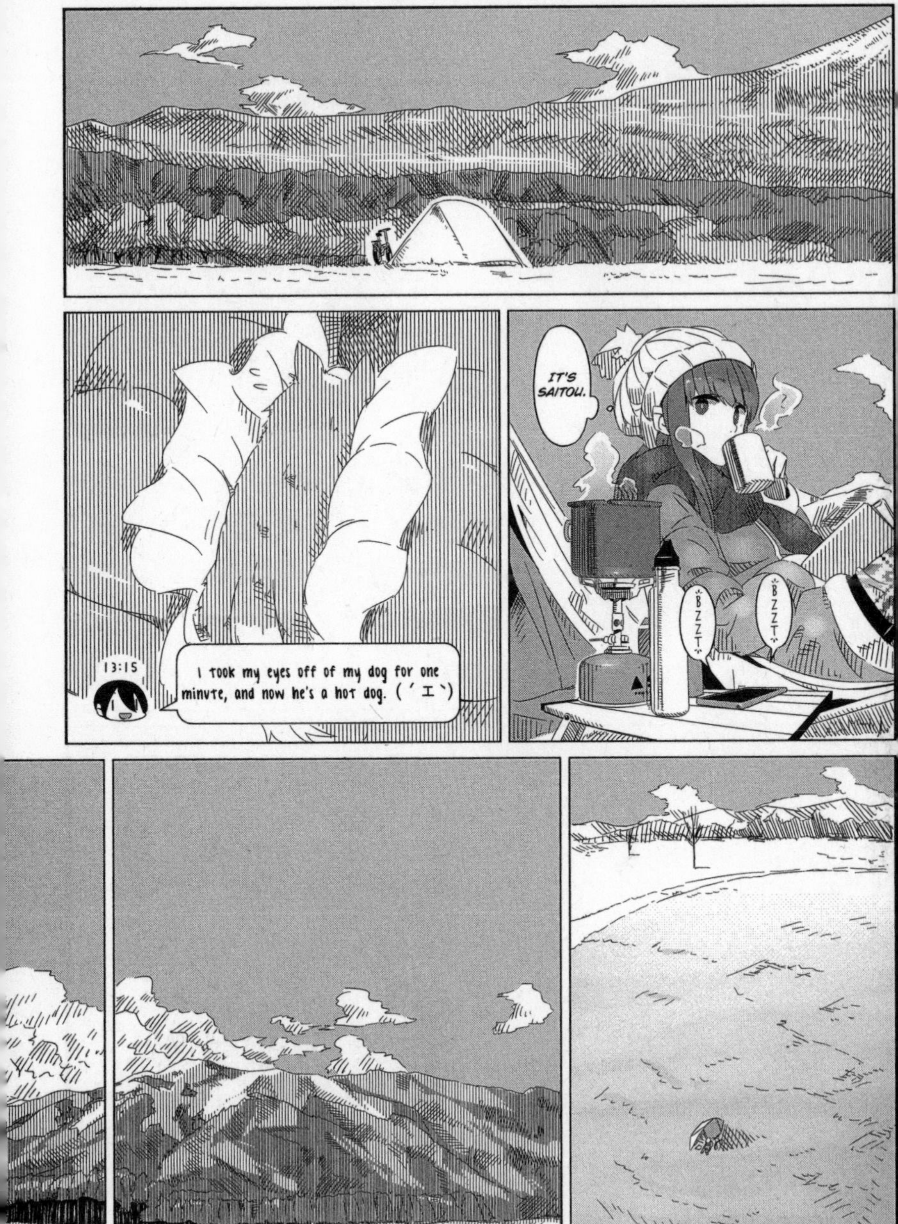
IT'S SAITOU.
BZZT
BZZT
13:15
I took my eyes off of my dog for one minute, and now he's a hot dog. (´エ`)

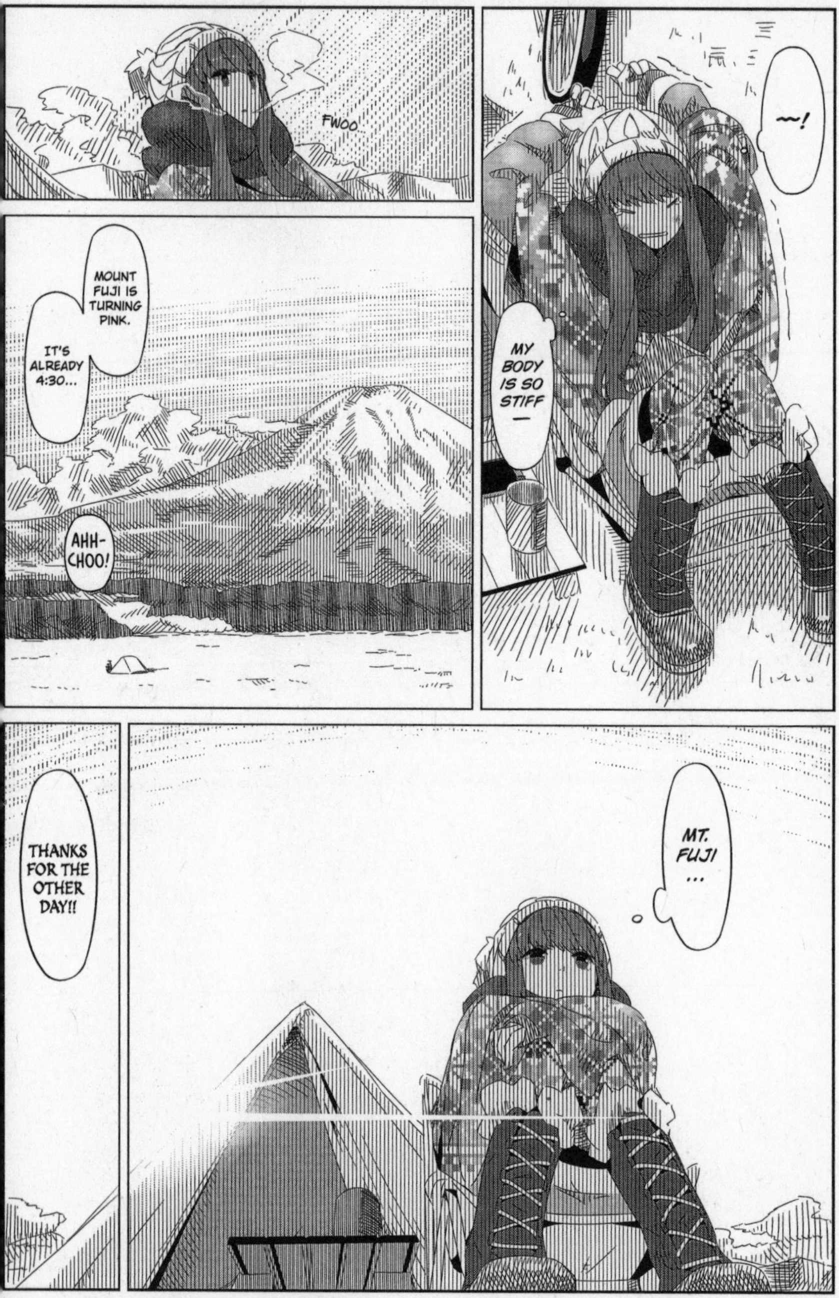
~~!
MY BODY IS SO STIFF—
FWOO
MOUNT FUJI IS TURNING PINK.
IT'S ALREADY 4:30...
AHH-CHOO!
MT. FUJI ...
THANKS FOR THE OTHER DAY!!

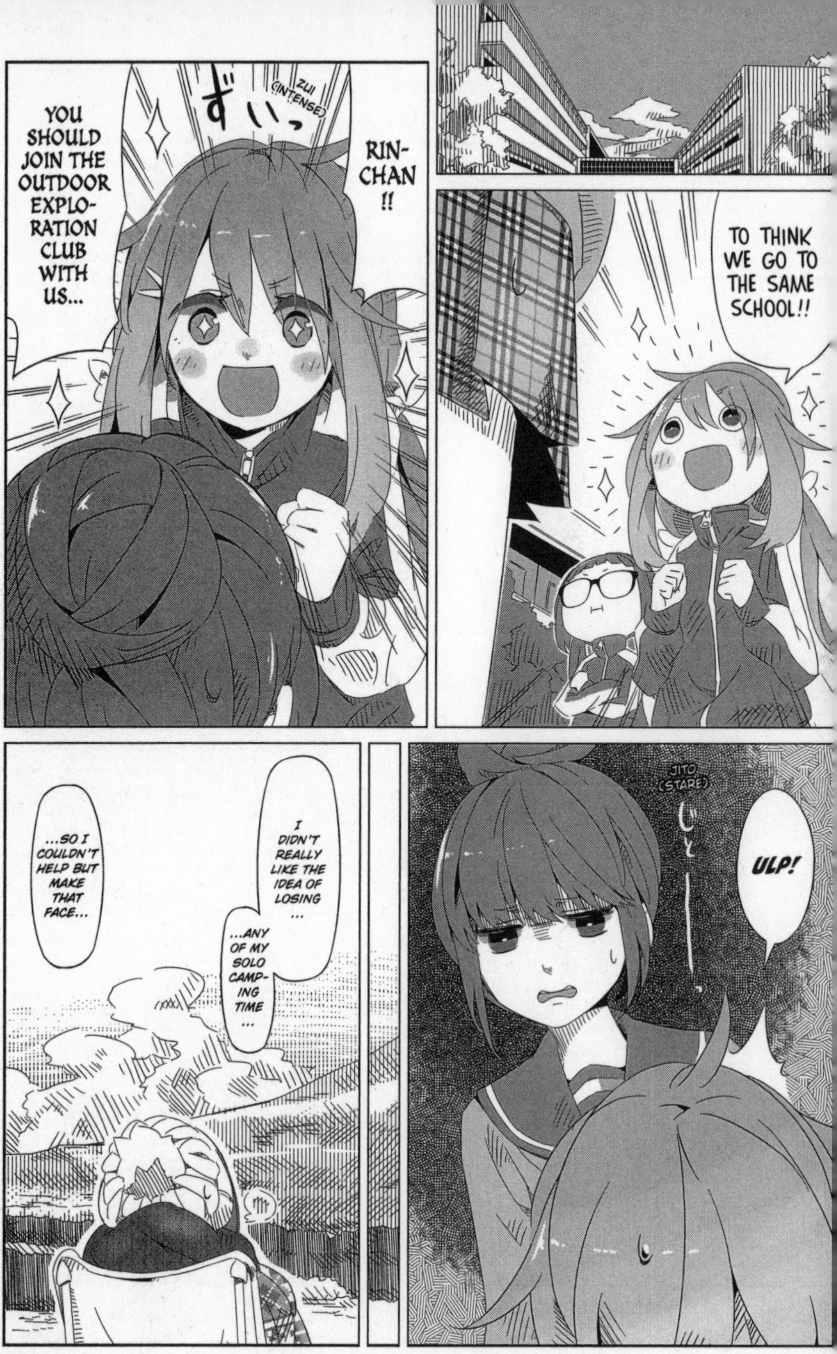
TO THINK WE GO TO THE SAME SCHOOL!!
RIN-CHAN!!
ずいっ
ZUI (INTENSE)
YOU SHOULD JOIN THE OUTDOOR EXPLORATION CLUB WITH US...
JITO (STARE)
じと
ULP!
I DIDN'T REALLY LIKE THE IDEA OF LOSING...
...ANY OF MY SOLO CAMPING TIME...
...SO I COULDN'T HELP BUT MAKE THAT FACE...

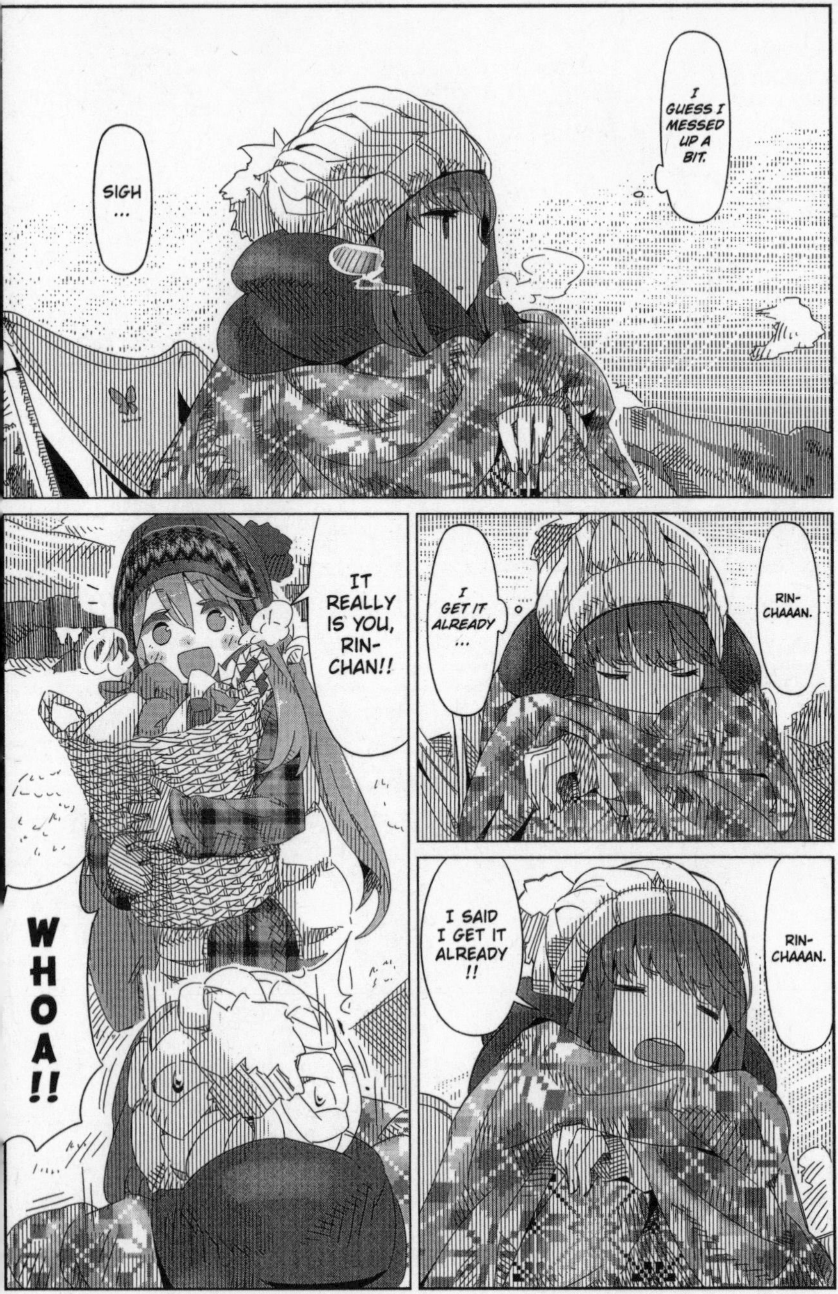
I GUESS I MESSED UP A BIT.
SIGH ...
RIN-CHAAAN.
I GET IT ALREADY ...
RIN-CHAAAN.
I SAID I GET IT ALREADY !!
IT REALLY IS YOU, RIN-CHAN!!
WHOA!!

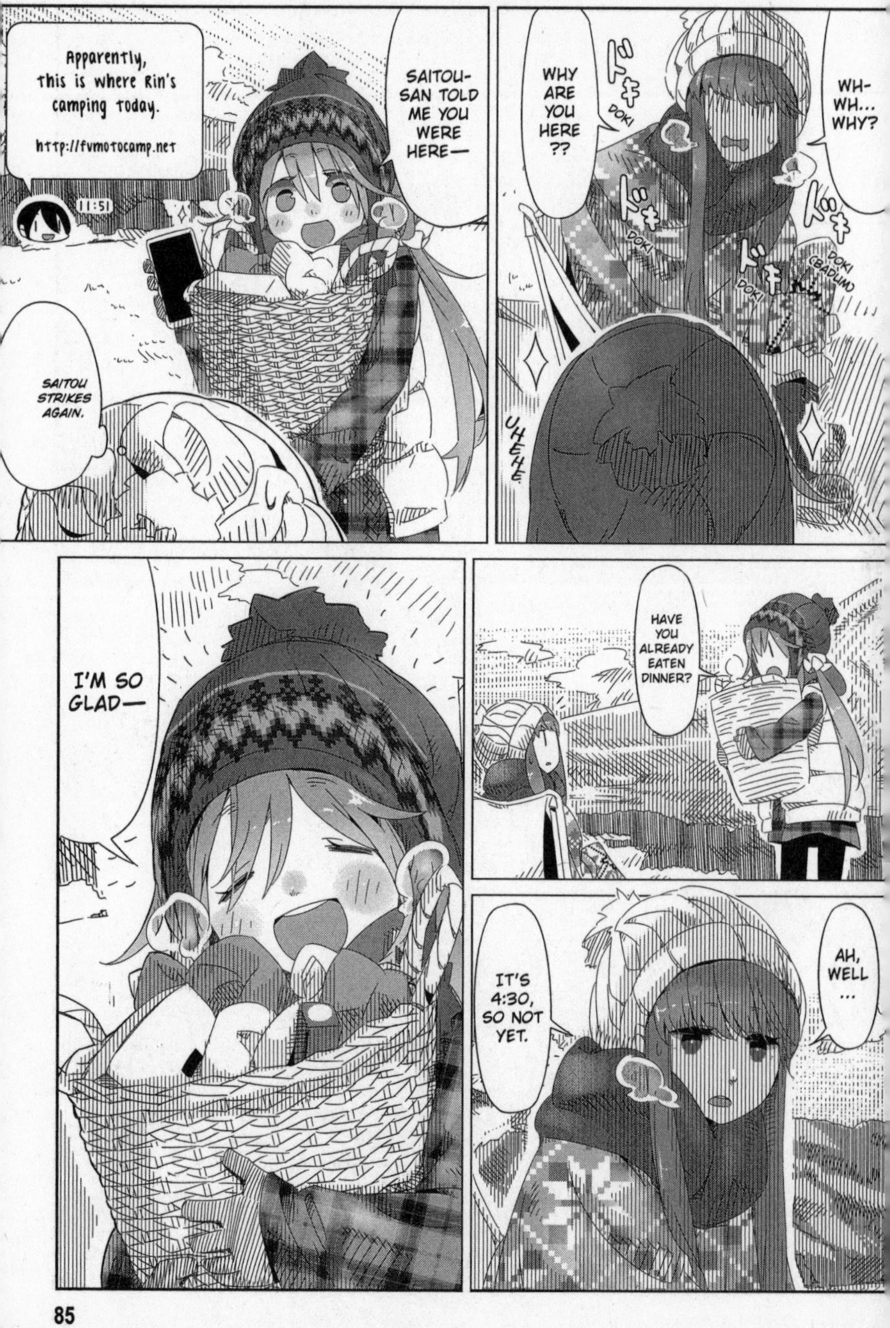
WH-WH... WHY?
WHY ARE YOU HERE??
ドキ DOKI
ドキ DOKI
ドキ DOKI
ドキ DOKI (BADUM)
UHEHE.
SAITOU-SAN TOLD ME YOU WERE HERE—
Apparently, this is where Rin's camping today.
http://fumotocamp.net
11:51
SAITOU STRIKES AGAIN.
HAVE YOU ALREADY EATEN DINNER?
AH, WELL ...
IT'S 4:30, SO NOT YET.
I'M SO GLAD—

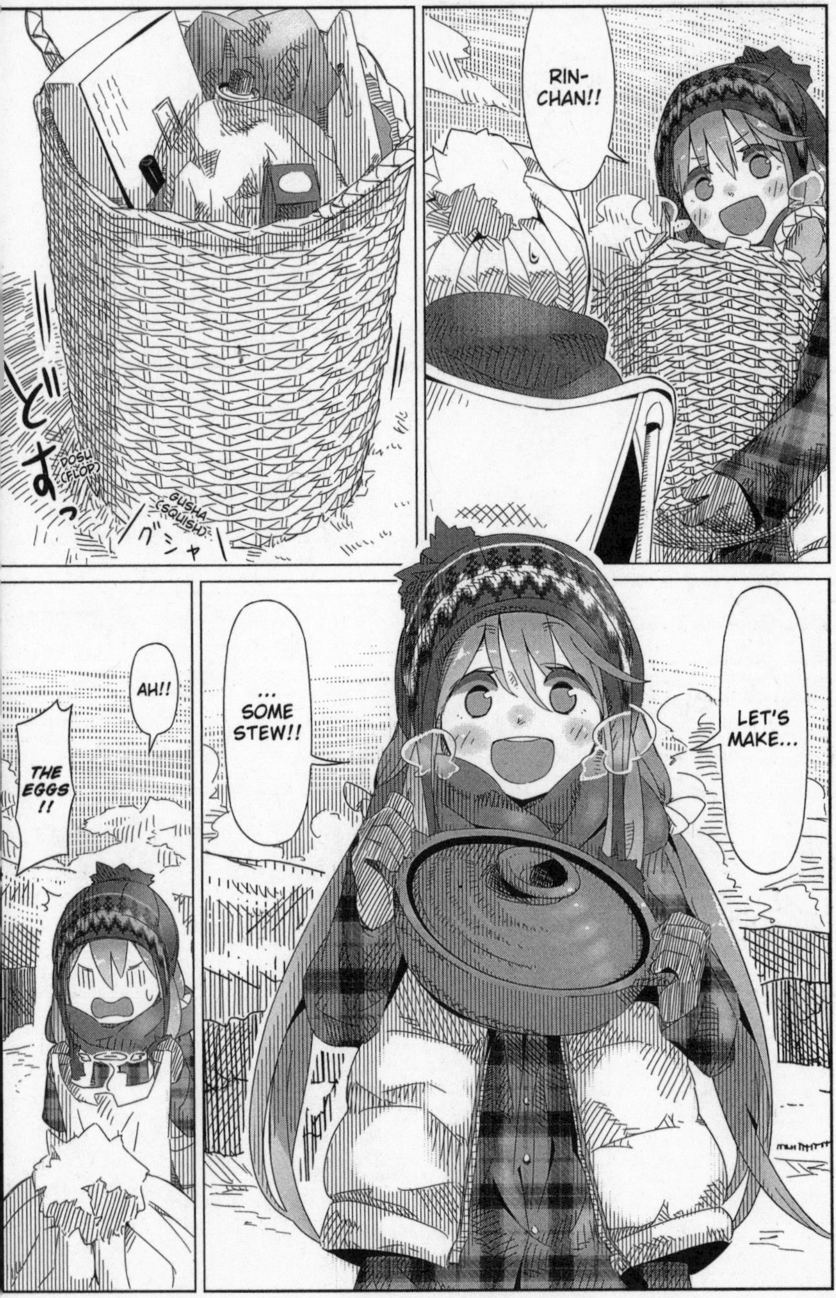
RIN-CHAN!!
どすっ
DOSH (FLOP)
グシャ
GUSHA (SQUISH)
LET'S MAKE...
... SOME STEW!!
AH!!
THE EGGS !!

AH!
SHIBA INU!!
さ
SA (SHFF)

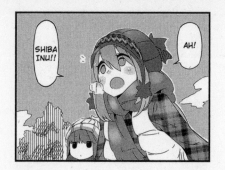

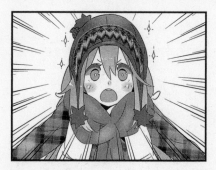

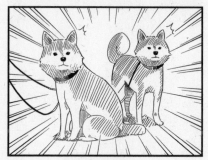

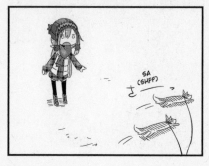

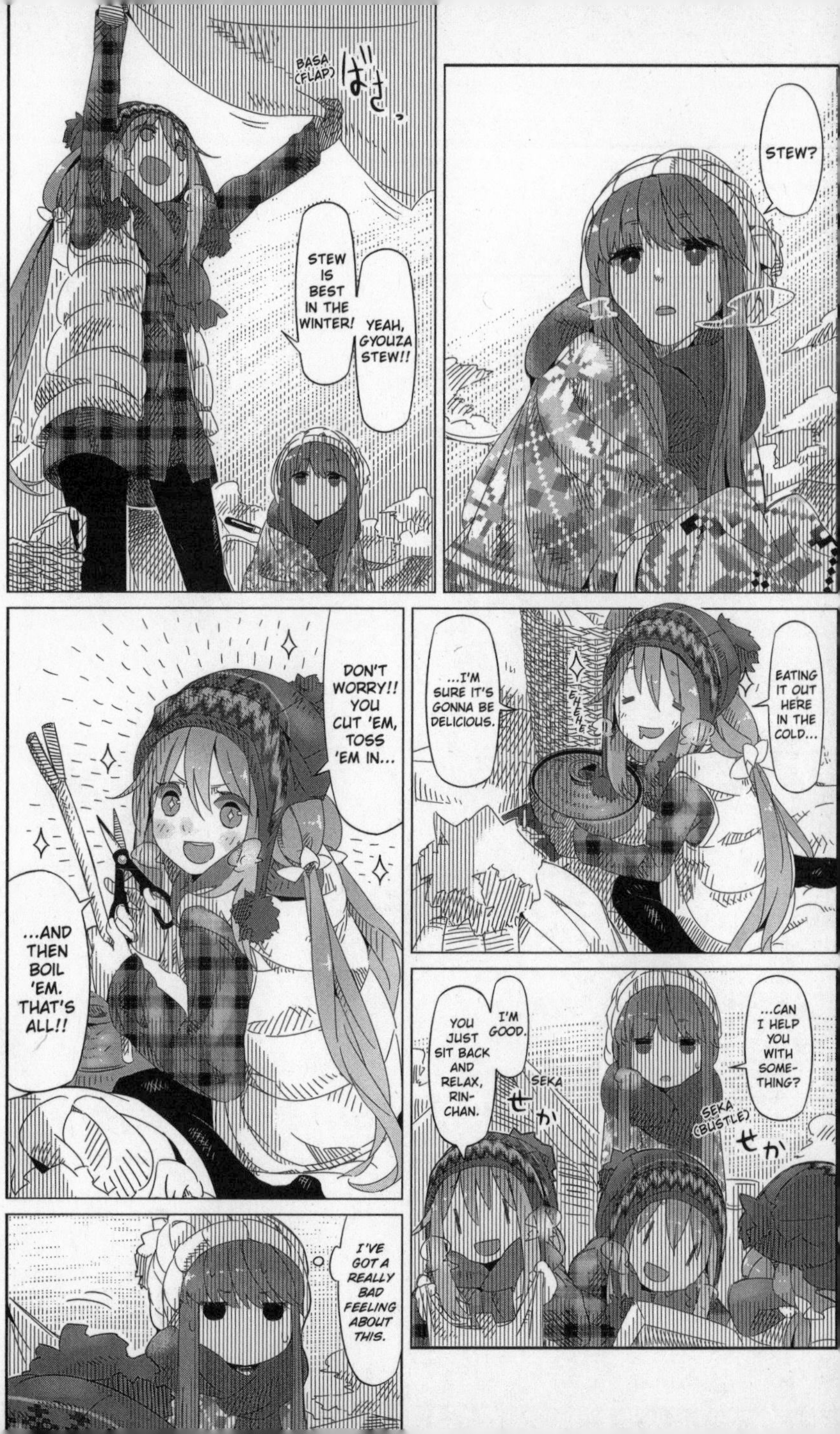
STEW?
BASA (FLAP)
ばさっ
YEAH, GYOUZA STEW!!
STEW IS BEST IN THE WINTER!
EATING IT OUT HERE IN THE COLD...
EHEHE
...I'M SURE IT'S GONNA BE DELICIOUS.
...CAN I HELP YOU WITH SOME-THING?
SEKA (BUSTLE)
せか
SEKA
せか
I'M GOOD.
YOU JUST SIT BACK AND RELAX, RIN-CHAN.
DON'T WORRY!! YOU CUT 'EM, TOSS 'EM IN...
...AND THEN BOIL 'EM. THAT'S ALL!!
I'VE GOT A REALLY BAD FEELING ABOUT THIS.

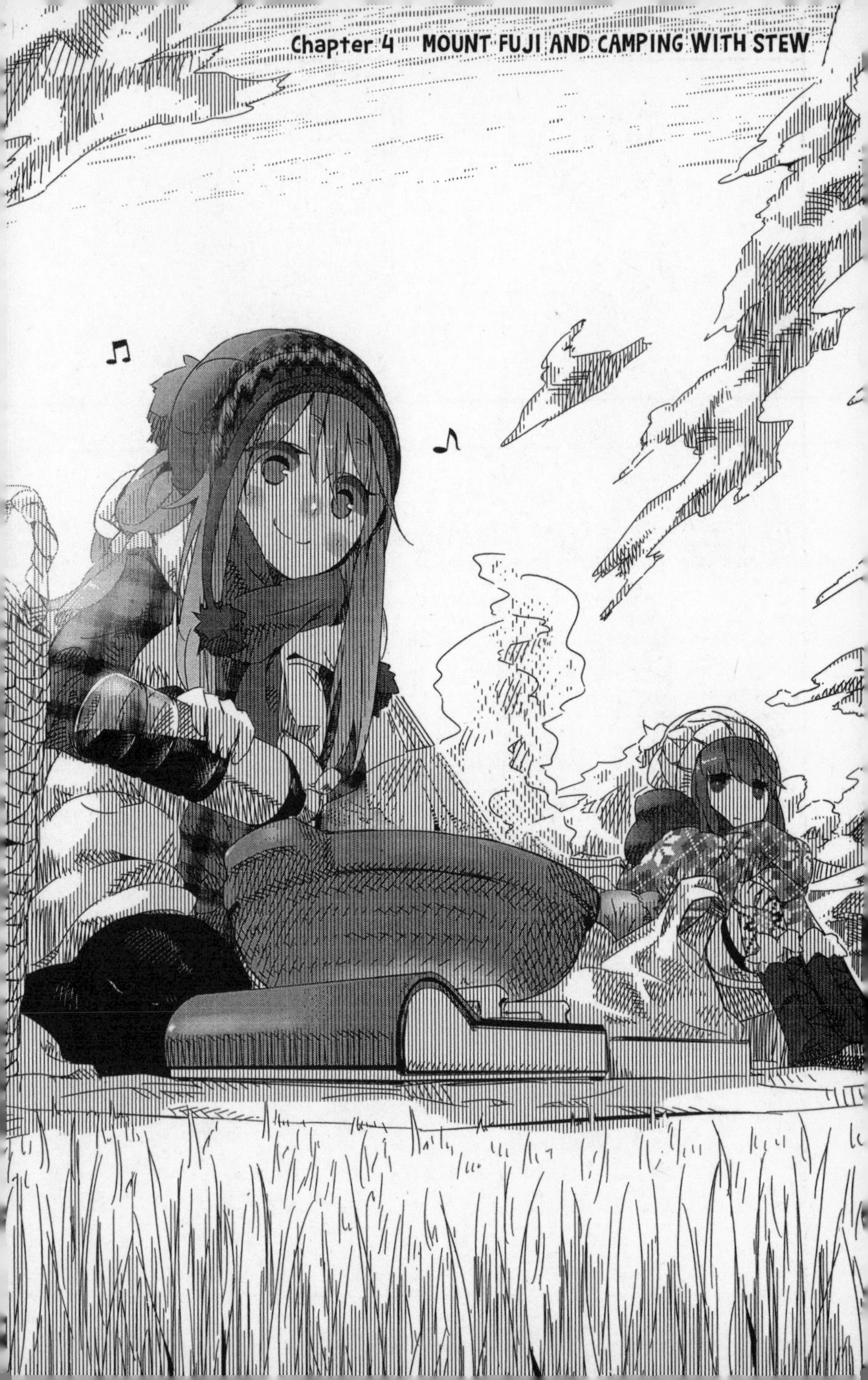
Chapter 4 MOUNT FUJI AND CAMPING WITH STEW

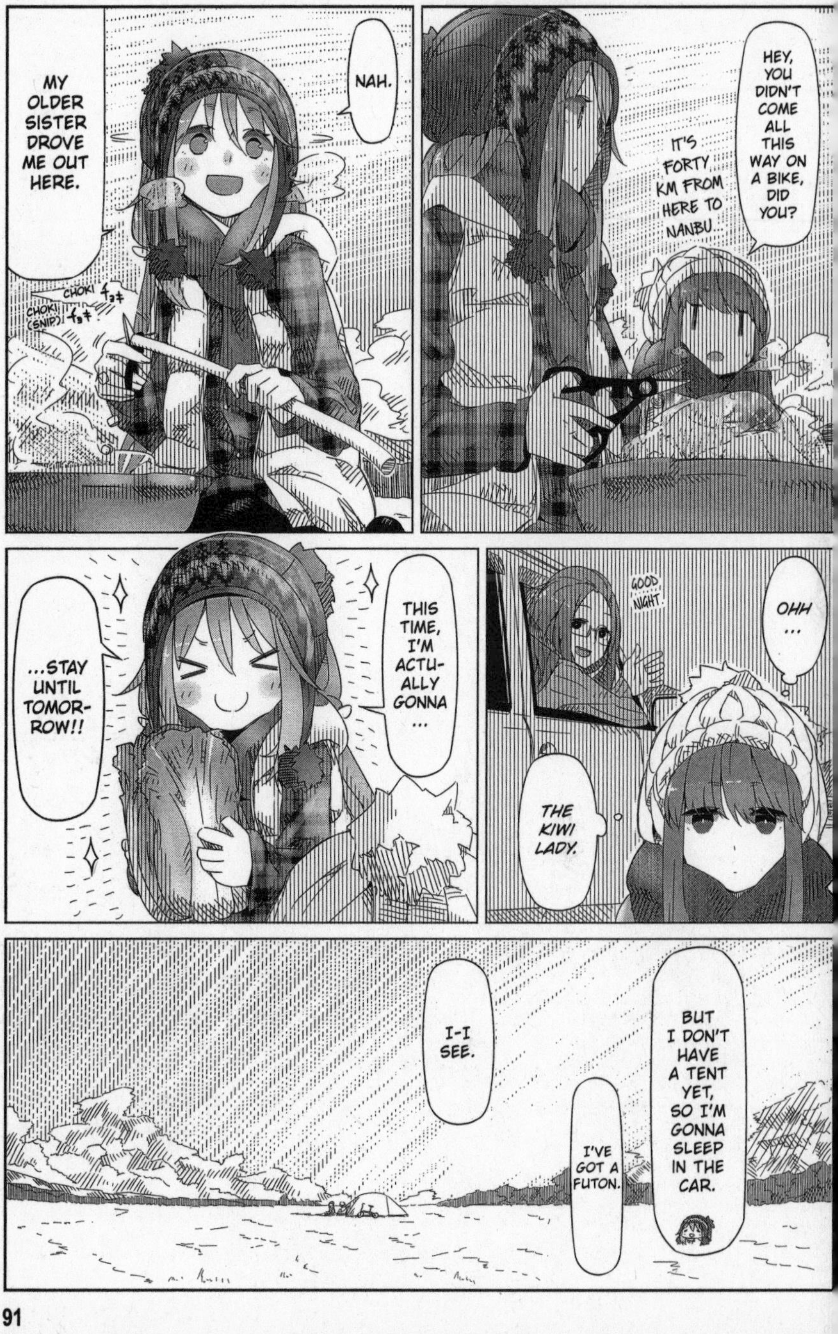
HEY, YOU DIDN'T COME ALL THIS WAY ON A BIKE, DID YOU?
IT'S FORTY KM FROM HERE TO NANBU...
NAH.
MY OLDER SISTER DROVE ME OUT HERE.
CHOKI チョキ
CHOKI (SNIP) チョキ
OHH...
GOOD NIGHT.
THE KIWI LADY.
THIS TIME, I'M ACTU-ALLY GONNA...
...STAY UNTIL TOMOR-ROW!!
BUT I DON'T HAVE A TENT YET, SO I'M GONNA SLEEP IN THE CAR.
I'VE GOT A FUTON.
I-I SEE.

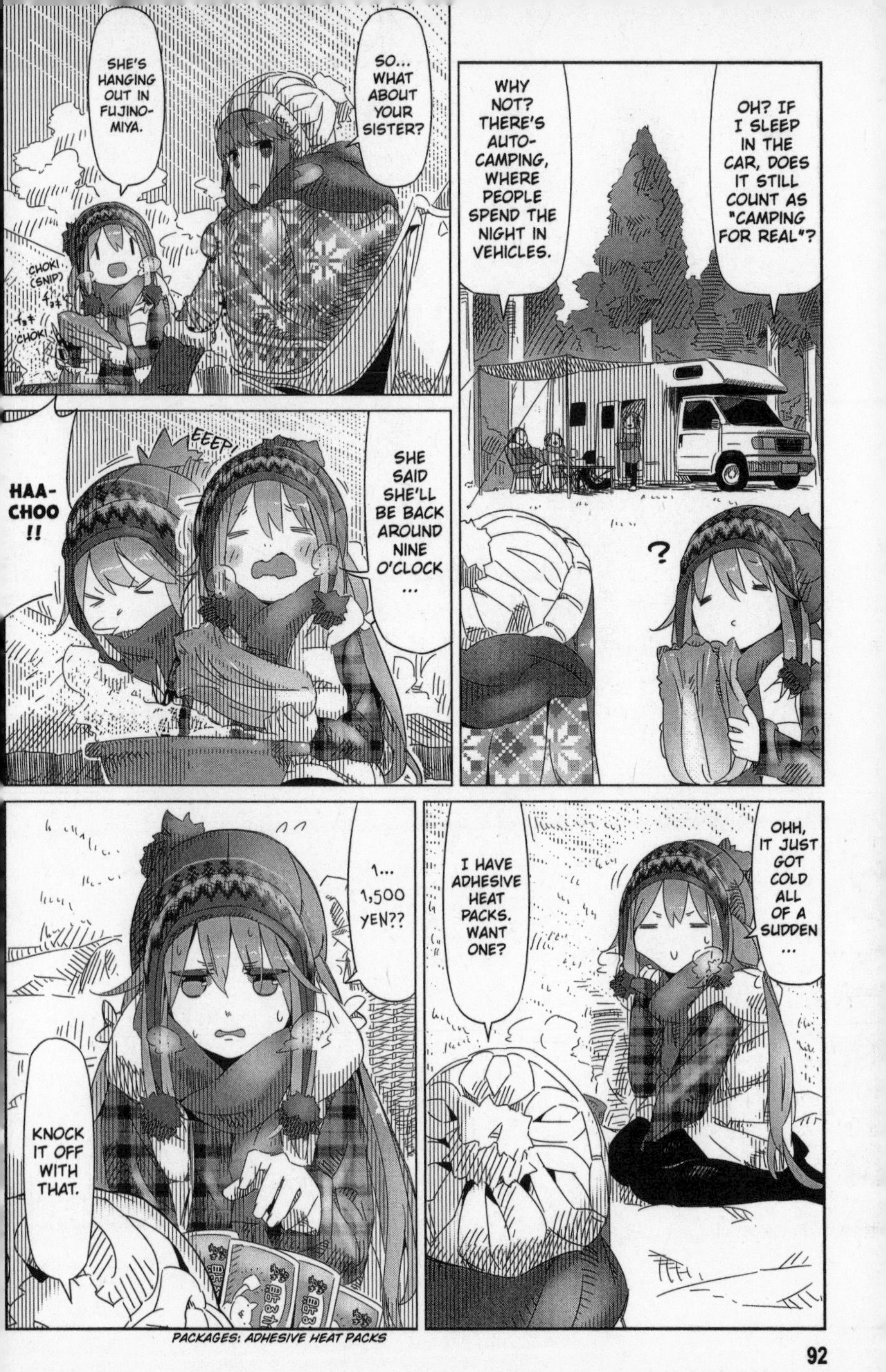
OH? IF I SLEEP IN THE CAR, DOES IT STILL COUNT AS "CAMPING FOR REAL"?
WHY NOT? THERE'S AUTO-CAMPING, WHERE PEOPLE SPEND THE NIGHT IN VEHICLES.
?
SO... WHAT ABOUT YOUR SISTER?
SHE'S HANGING OUT IN FUJINO-MIYA.
CHOKI (SNIP)
CHOKI
SHE SAID SHE'LL BE BACK AROUND NINE O'CLOCK ...
EEEP!
HAA-CHOO !!
OHH, IT JUST GOT COLD ALL OF A SUDDEN ...
I HAVE ADHESIVE HEAT PACKS. WANT ONE?
1... 1,500 YEN??
KNOCK IT OFF WITH THAT.
PACKAGES: ADHESIVE HEAT PACKS

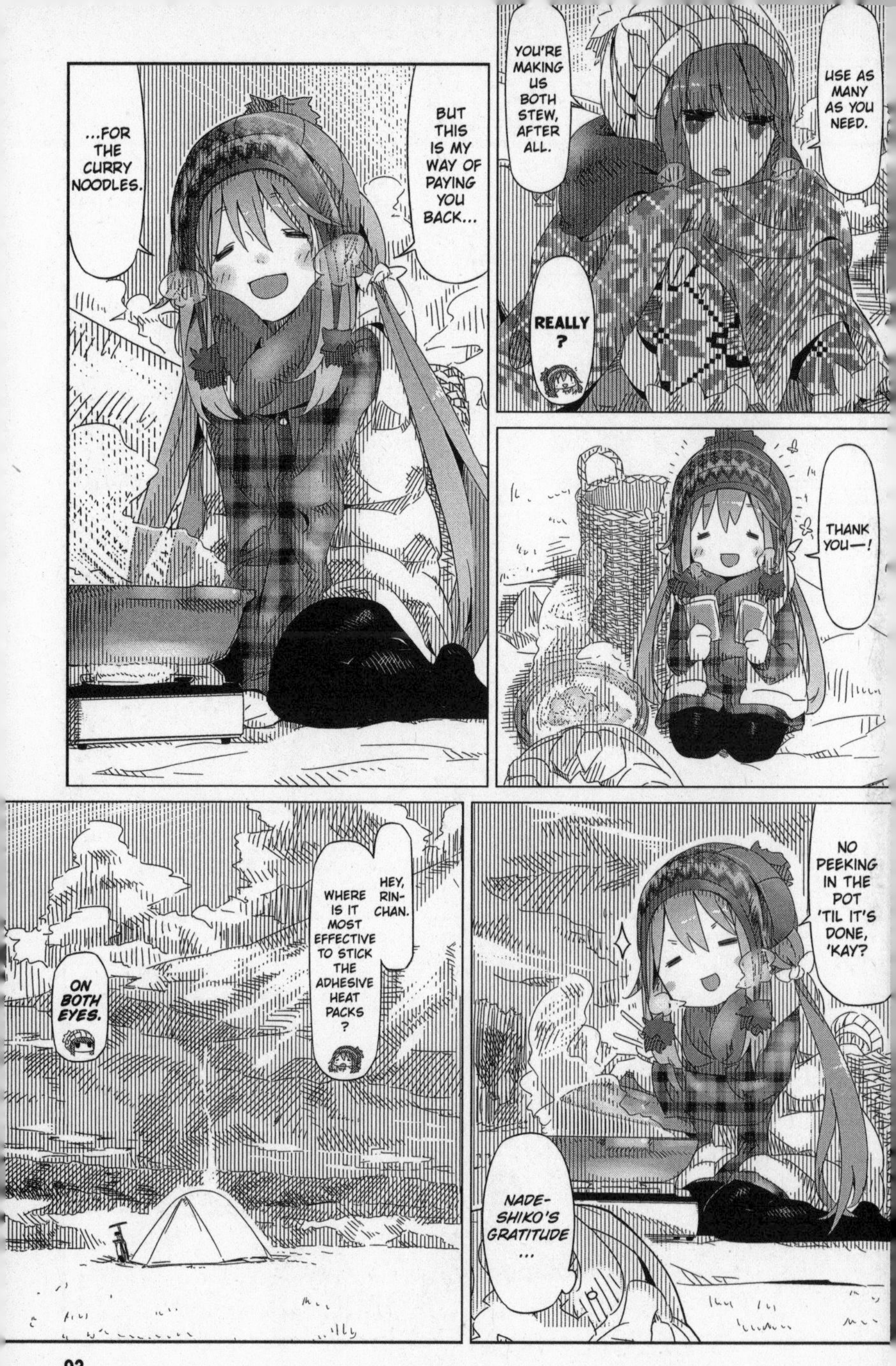
USE AS MANY AS YOU NEED.
YOU'RE MAKING US BOTH STEW, AFTER ALL.
REALLY?
THANK YOU—!
BUT THIS IS MY WAY OF PAYING YOU BACK...
...FOR THE CURRY NOODLES.
NO PEEKING IN THE POT 'TIL IT'S DONE, 'KAY?
NADE-SHIKO'S GRATITUDE...
HEY, RIN-CHAN.
WHERE IS IT MOST EFFECTIVE TO STICK THE ADHESIVE HEAT PACKS?
ON BOTH EYES.

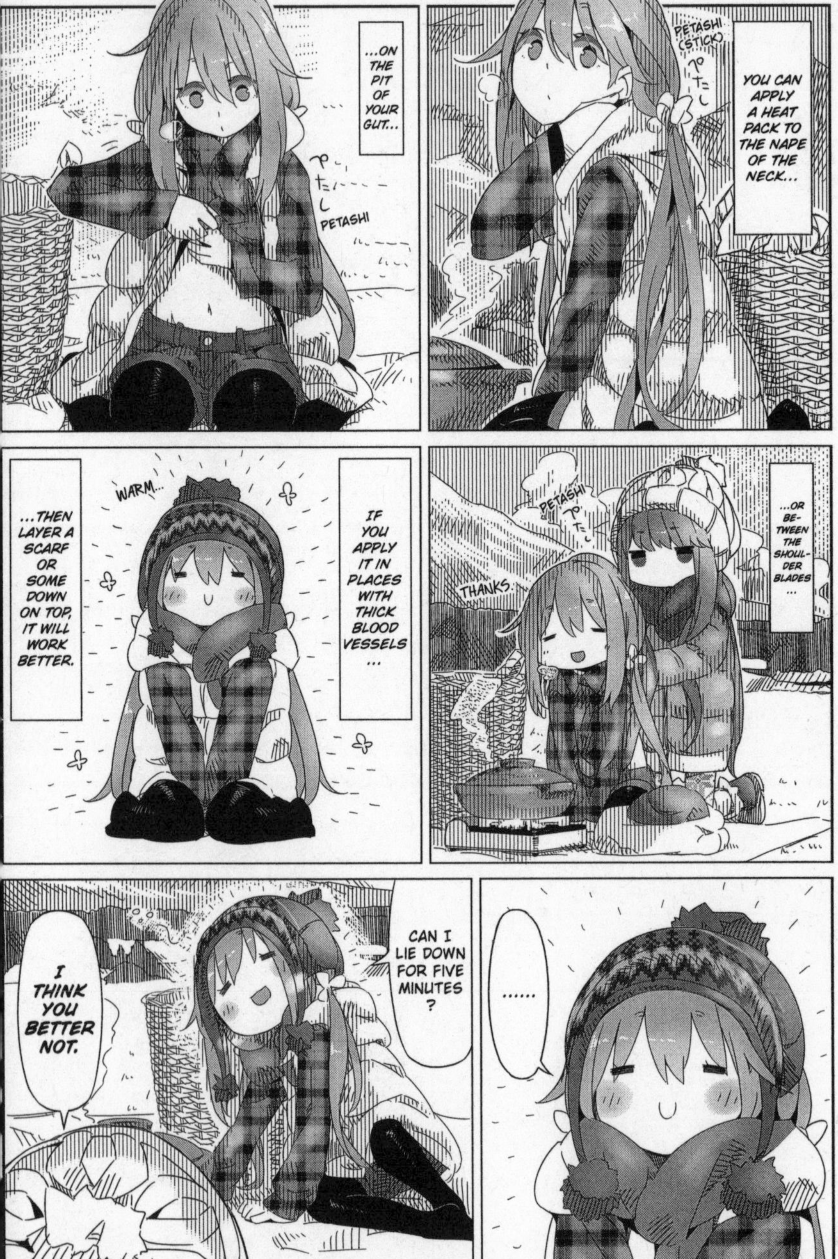
PETASHI (STICK)
ぺたし
YOU CAN APPLY A HEAT PACK TO THE NAPE OF THE NECK...
...ON THE PIT OF YOUR GUT...
ぺたし
PETASHI
...OR BE-TWEEN THE SHOUL-DER BLADES ...
PETASHI
ぺたし
THANKS.
IF YOU APPLY IT IN PLACES WITH THICK BLOOD VESSELS ...
...THEN LAYER A SCARF OR SOME DOWN ON TOP, IT WILL WORK BETTER.
WARM...
......
CAN I LIE DOWN FOR FIVE MINUTES ?
I THINK YOU BETTER NOT.

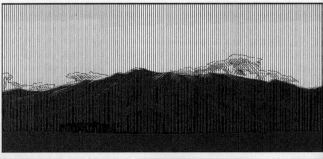

ボワ
BOWA
(POF)

THINK IT SHOULD BE READY?

GUTSU

GUTSU
(BUBBLE)

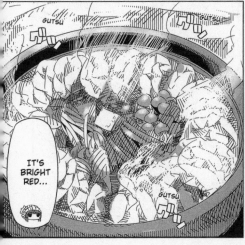

GUTSU

GUTSU

IT'S BRIGHT RED...

GUTSU

UH...

95

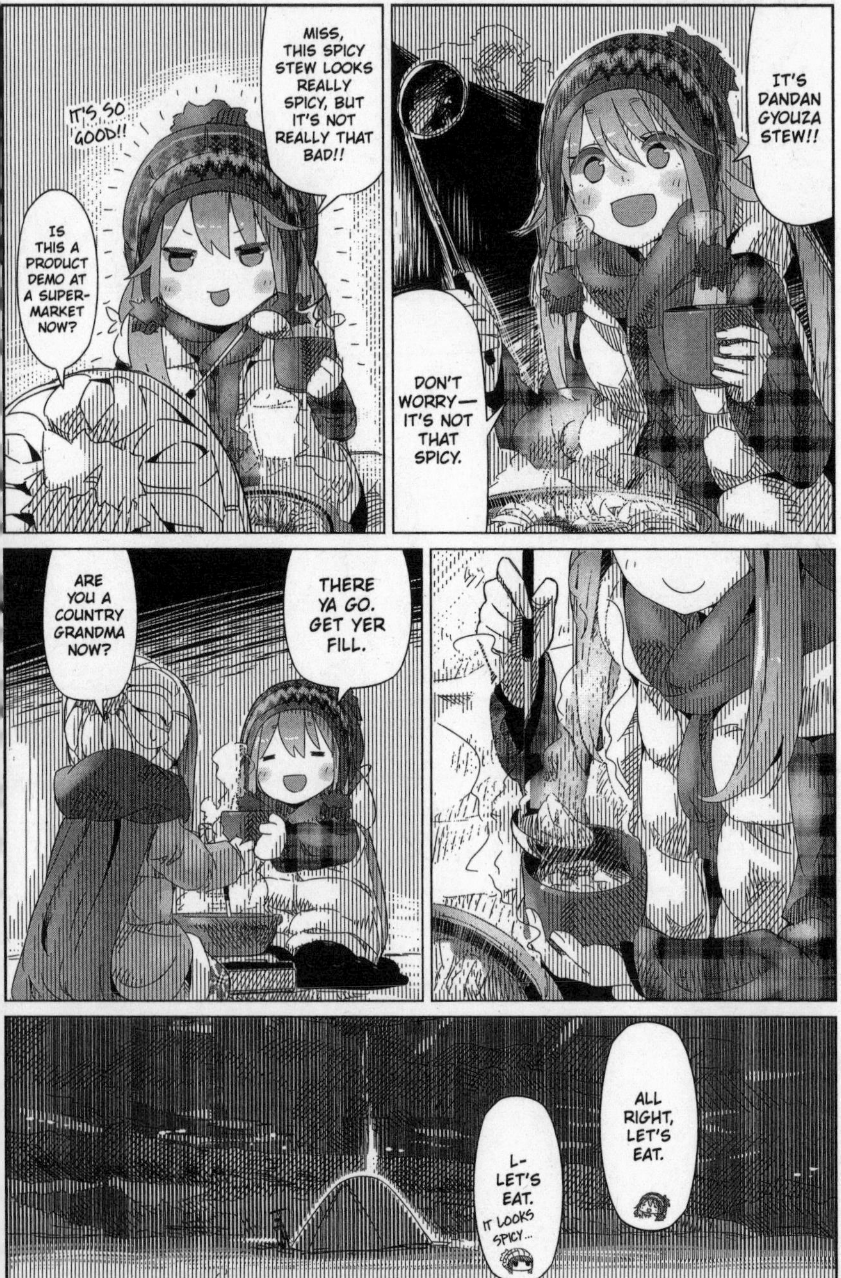
IT'S DANDAN GYOUZA STEW!!
DON'T WORRY— IT'S NOT THAT SPICY.
MISS, THIS SPICY STEW LOOKS REALLY SPICY, BUT IT'S NOT REALLY THAT BAD!!
IT'S SO GOOD!!
IS THIS A PRODUCT DEMO AT A SUPER-MARKET NOW?
THERE YA GO. GET YER FILL.
ARE YOU A COUNTRY GRANDMA NOW?
ALL RIGHT, LET'S EAT.
L- LET'S EAT.
IT LOOKS SPICY...

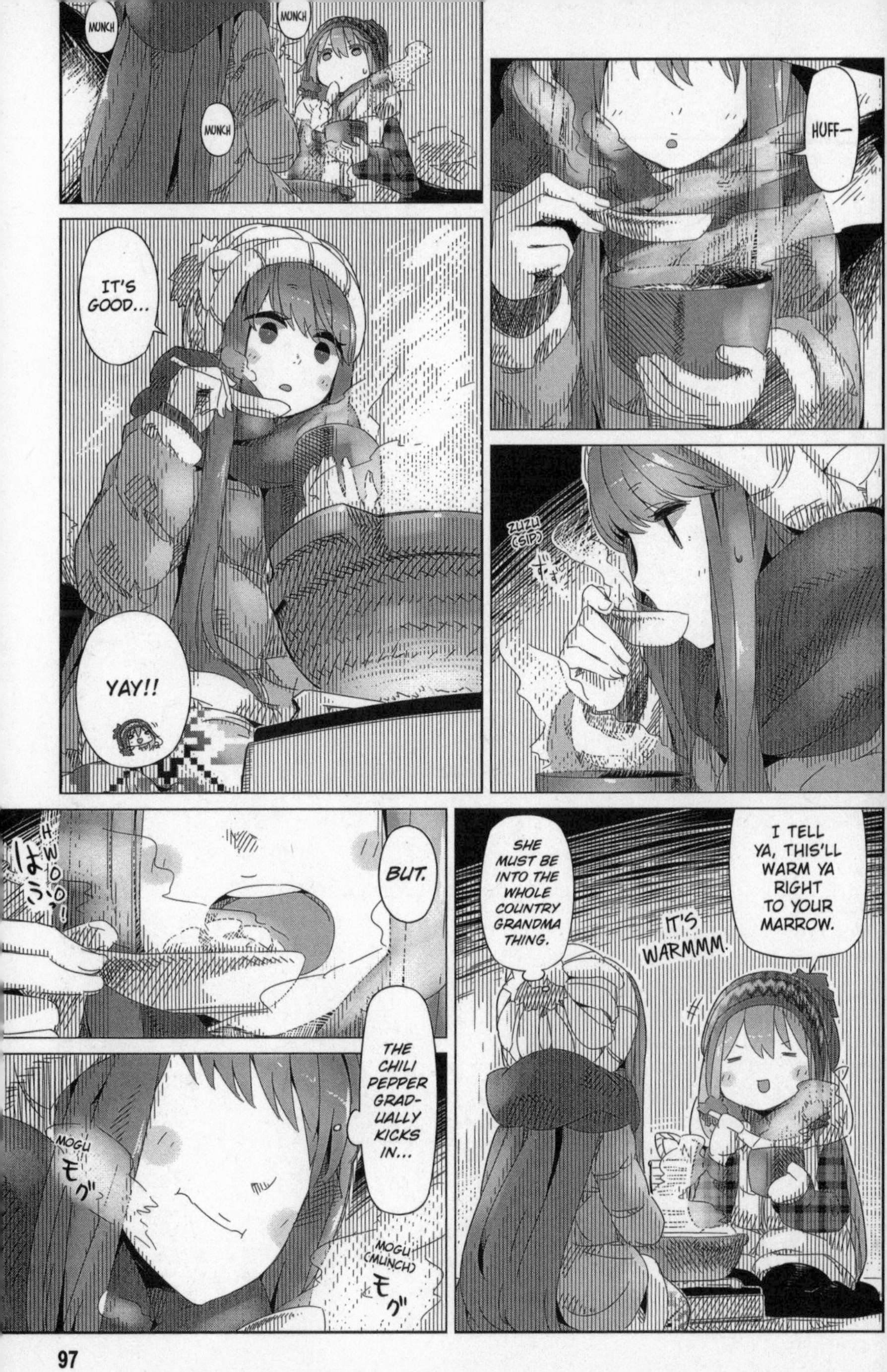
HUFF—
MUNCH
MUNCH
MUNCH
ZUZU (SIP)
IT'S GOOD...
YAY!!
I TELL YA, THIS'LL WARM YA RIGHT TO YOUR MARROW.
IT'S WARMMM.
SHE MUST BE INTO THE WHOLE COUNTRY GRANDMA THING.
BUT.
HWOO!
THE CHILI PEPPER GRAD-UALLY KICKS IN...
MOGU
モグ
MOGU (MUNCH)
モグ

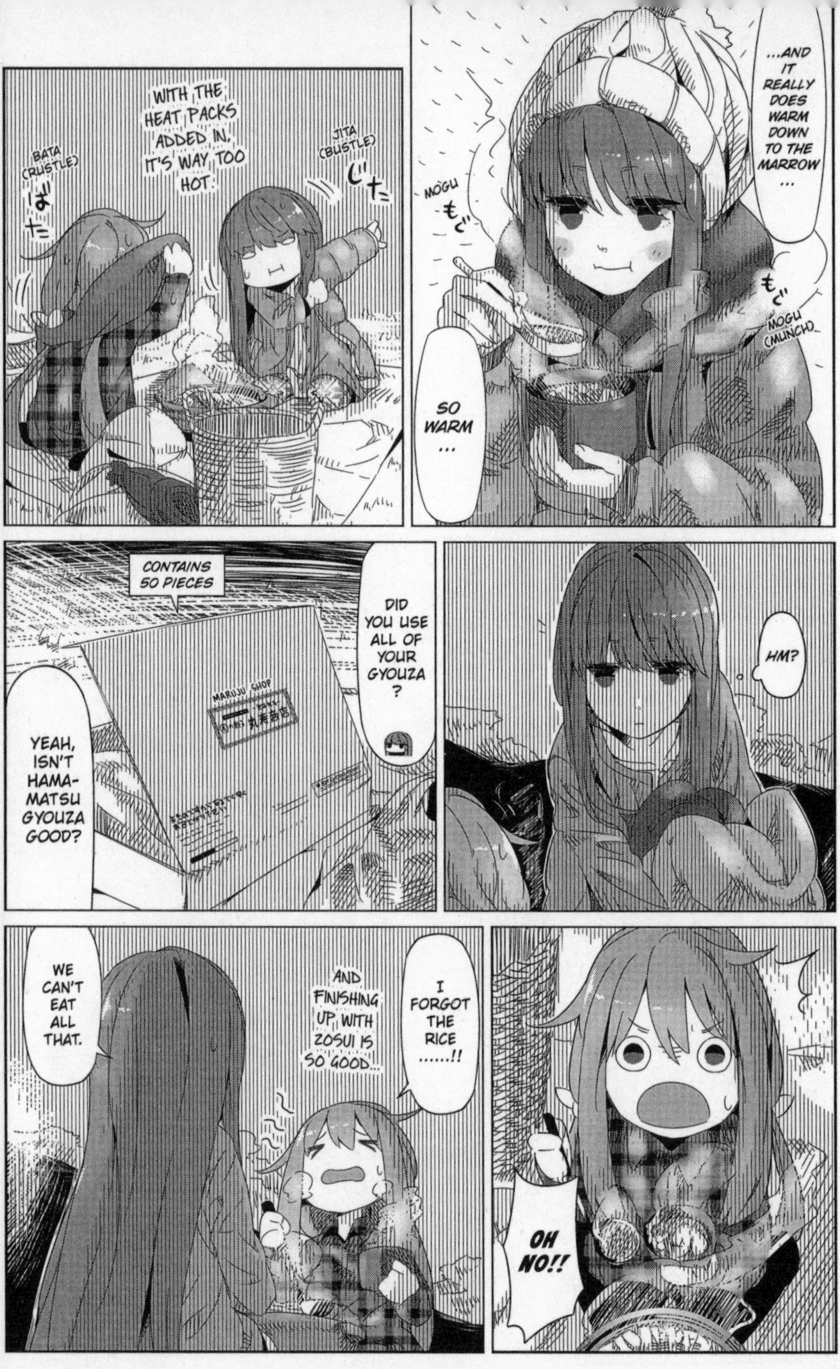
...AND IT REALLY DOES WARM DOWN TO THE MARROW...
MOGU
もぐ
もぐ
MOGU (MUNCH)
SO WARM...
WITH THE HEAT PACKS ADDED IN, IT'S WAY TOO HOT.
JITA (BUSTLE)
じた
BATA (RUSTLE)
ばた
HM?
DID YOU USE ALL OF YOUR GYOUZA?
CONTAINS 50 PIECES
MARUJU SHOP
丸寿商店
YEAH, ISN'T HAMAMATSU GYOUZA GOOD?
OH NO!!
I FORGOT THE RICE......!!
AND FINISHING UP WITH ZOSUI IS SO GOOD...
WE CAN'T EAT ALL THAT.

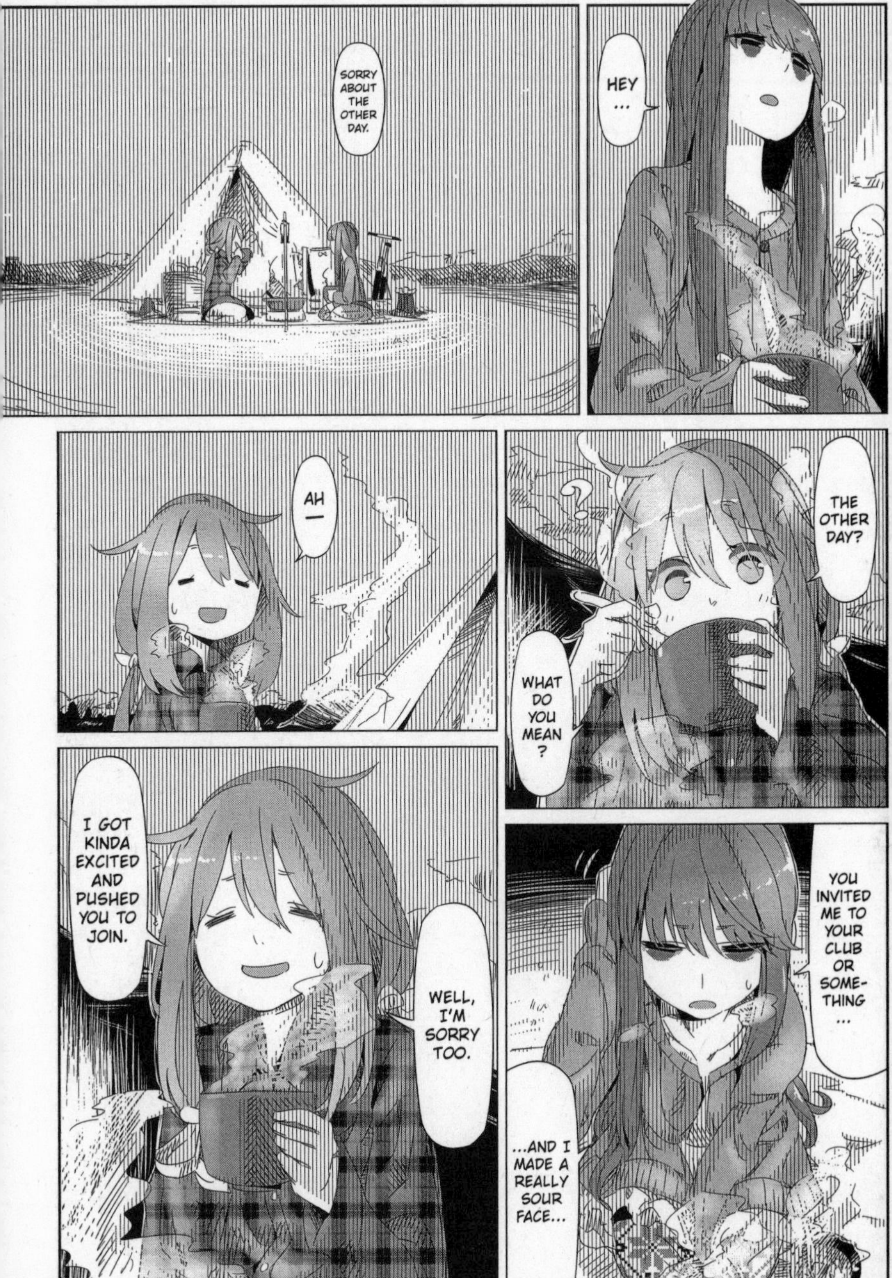
HEY ...
SORRY ABOUT THE OTHER DAY.
THE OTHER DAY?
WHAT DO YOU MEAN?
AH —
YOU INVITED ME TO YOUR CLUB OR SOME-THING ...
...AND I MADE A REALLY SOUR FACE...
WELL, I'M SORRY TOO.
I GOT KINDA EXCITED AND PUSHED YOU TO JOIN.

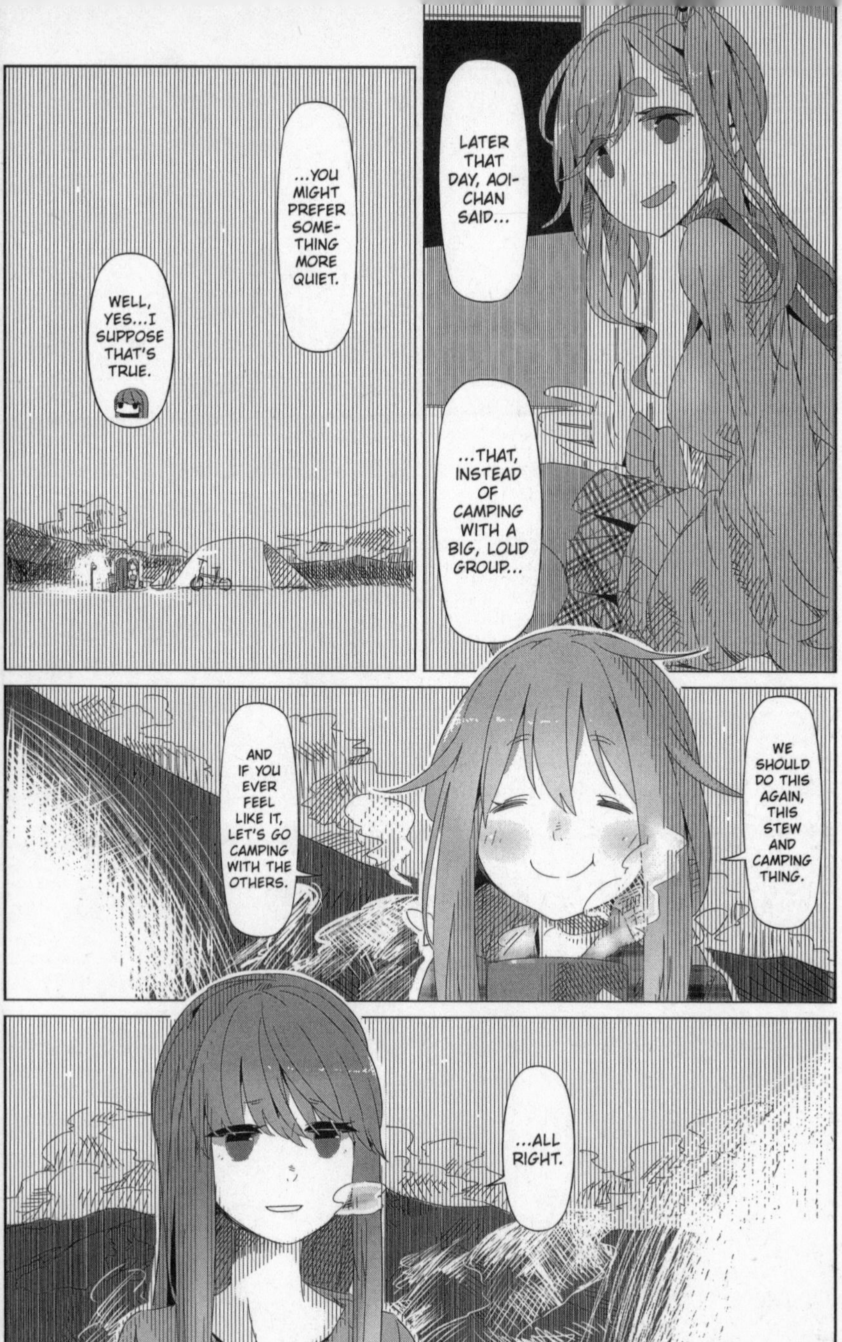
LATER THAT DAY, AOI-CHAN SAID...
...THAT, INSTEAD OF CAMPING WITH A BIG, LOUD GROUP...
...YOU MIGHT PREFER SOME-THING MORE QUIET.
WELL, YES...I SUPPOSE THAT'S TRUE.
WE SHOULD DO THIS AGAIN, THIS STEW AND CAMPING THING.
AND IF YOU EVER FEEL LIKE IT, LET'S GO CAMPING WITH THE OTHERS.
...ALL RIGHT.

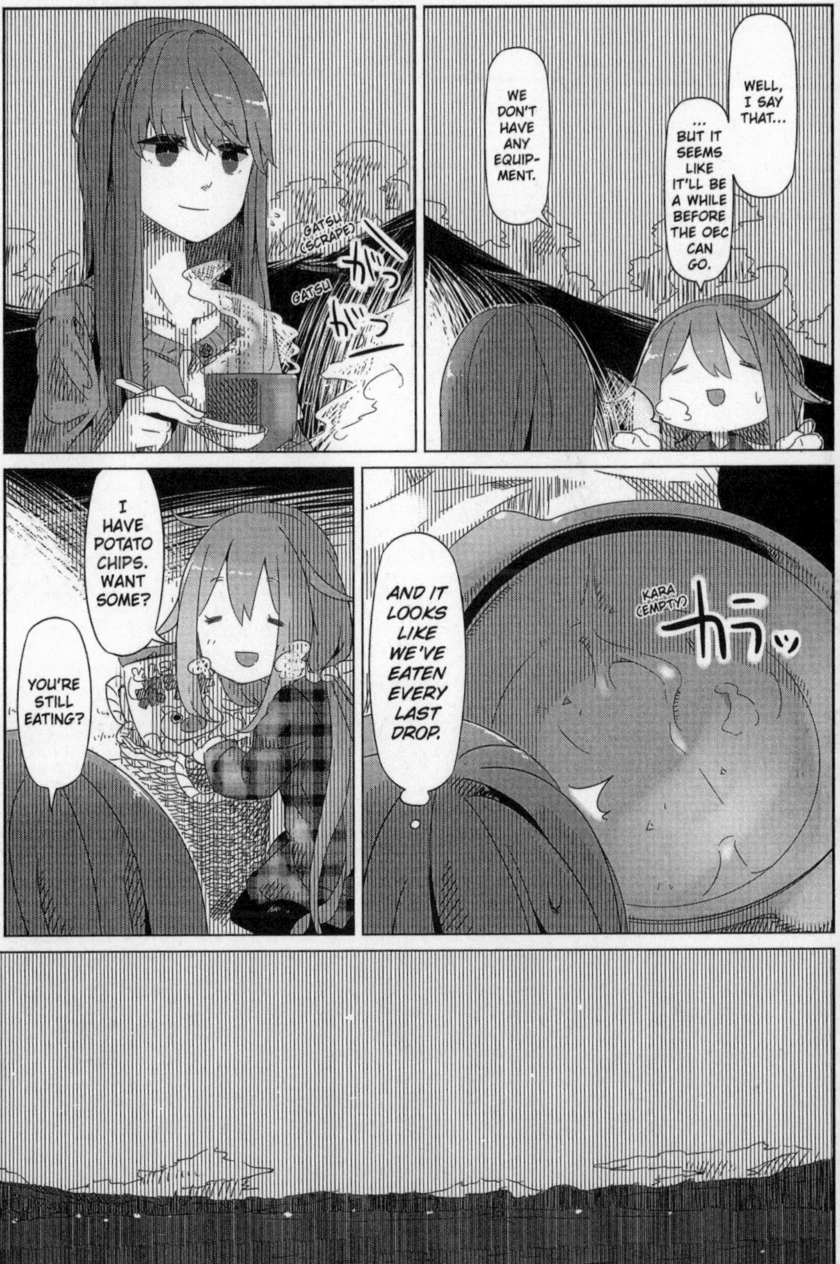
WELL, I SAY THAT...
...BUT IT SEEMS LIKE IT'LL BE A WHILE BEFORE THE OEC CAN GO.
WE DON'T HAVE ANY EQUIPMENT.
GATSU (SCRAPE)
ガッ
GATSU
ガッ
KARA (EMPTY)
カラッ
AND IT LOOKS LIKE WE'VE EATEN EVERY LAST DROP.
I HAVE POTATO CHIPS. WANT SOME?
YOU'RE STILL EATING?

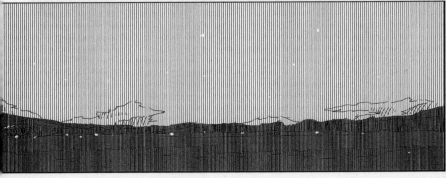

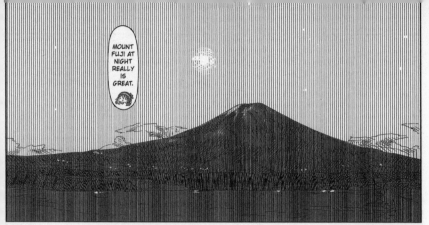

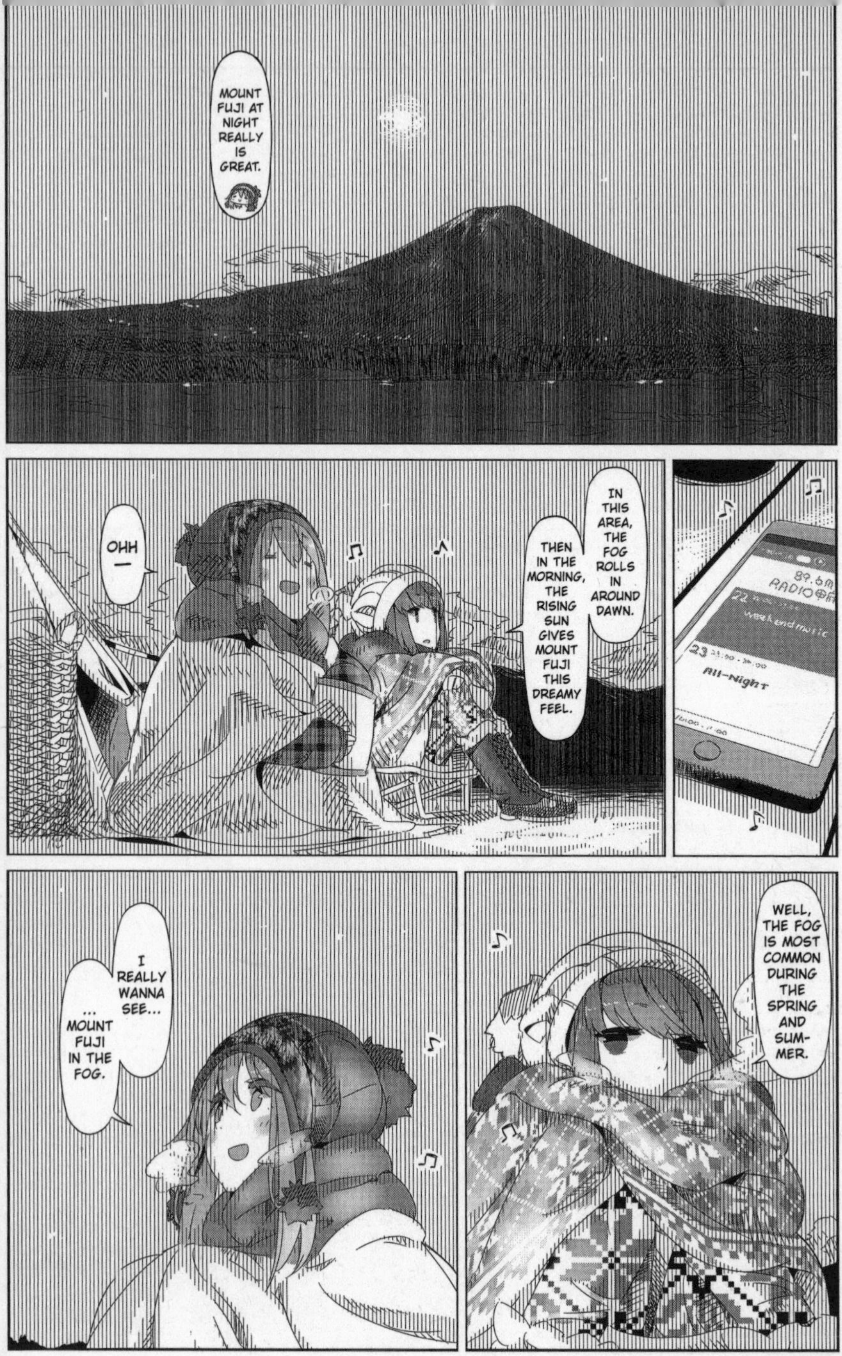
MOUNT FUJI AT NIGHT REALLY IS GREAT.
All-Night
IN THIS AREA, THE FOG ROLLS IN AROUND DAWN.
THEN IN THE MORNING, THE RISING SUN GIVES MOUNT FUJI THIS DREAMY FEEL.
OHH—
WELL, THE FOG IS MOST COMMON DURING THE SPRING AND SUMMER.
I REALLY WANNA SEE...
...MOUNT FUJI IN THE FOG.

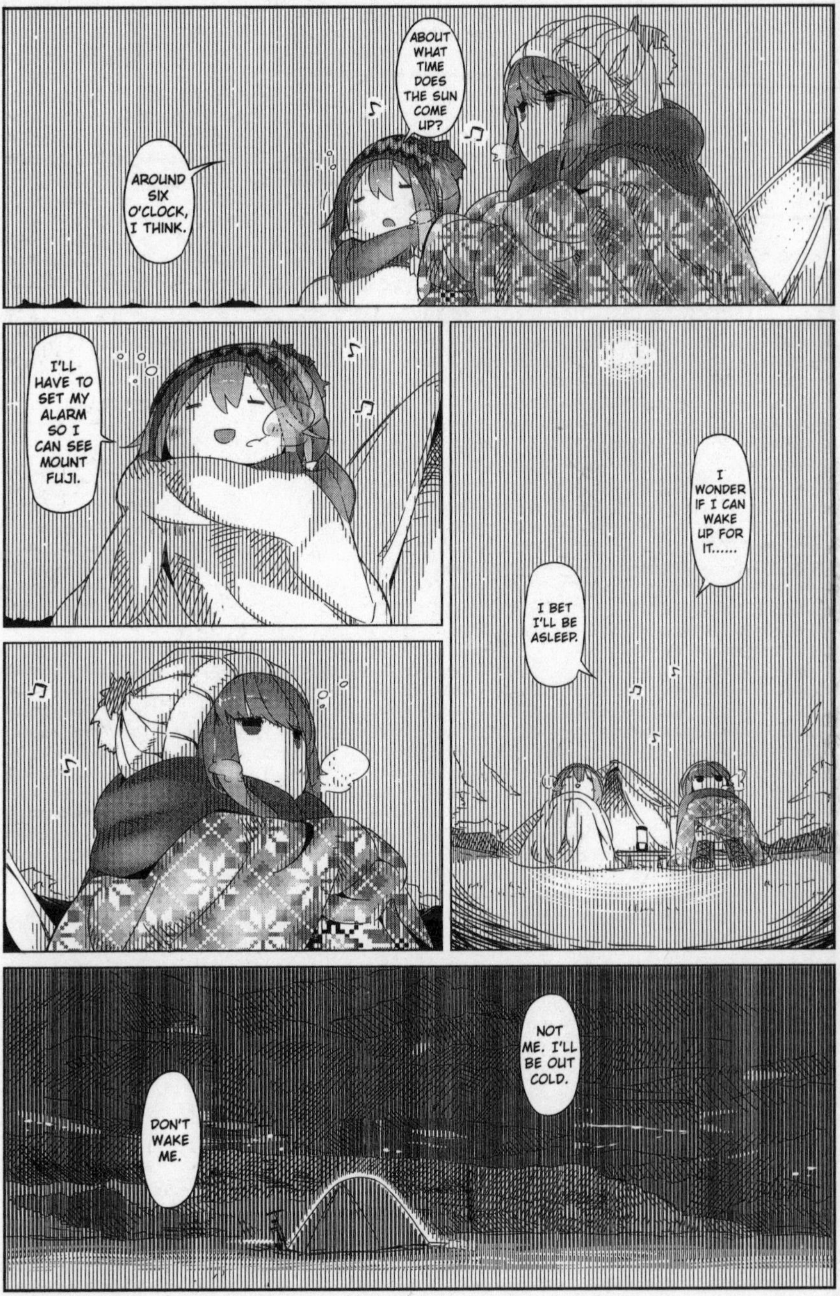
ABOUT WHAT TIME DOES THE SUN COME UP?
AROUND SIX O'CLOCK, I THINK.
I WONDER IF I CAN WAKE UP FOR IT......
I BET I'LL BE ASLEEP.
I'LL HAVE TO SET MY ALARM SO I CAN SEE MOUNT FUJI.
NOT ME. I'LL BE OUT COLD.
DON'T WAKE ME.

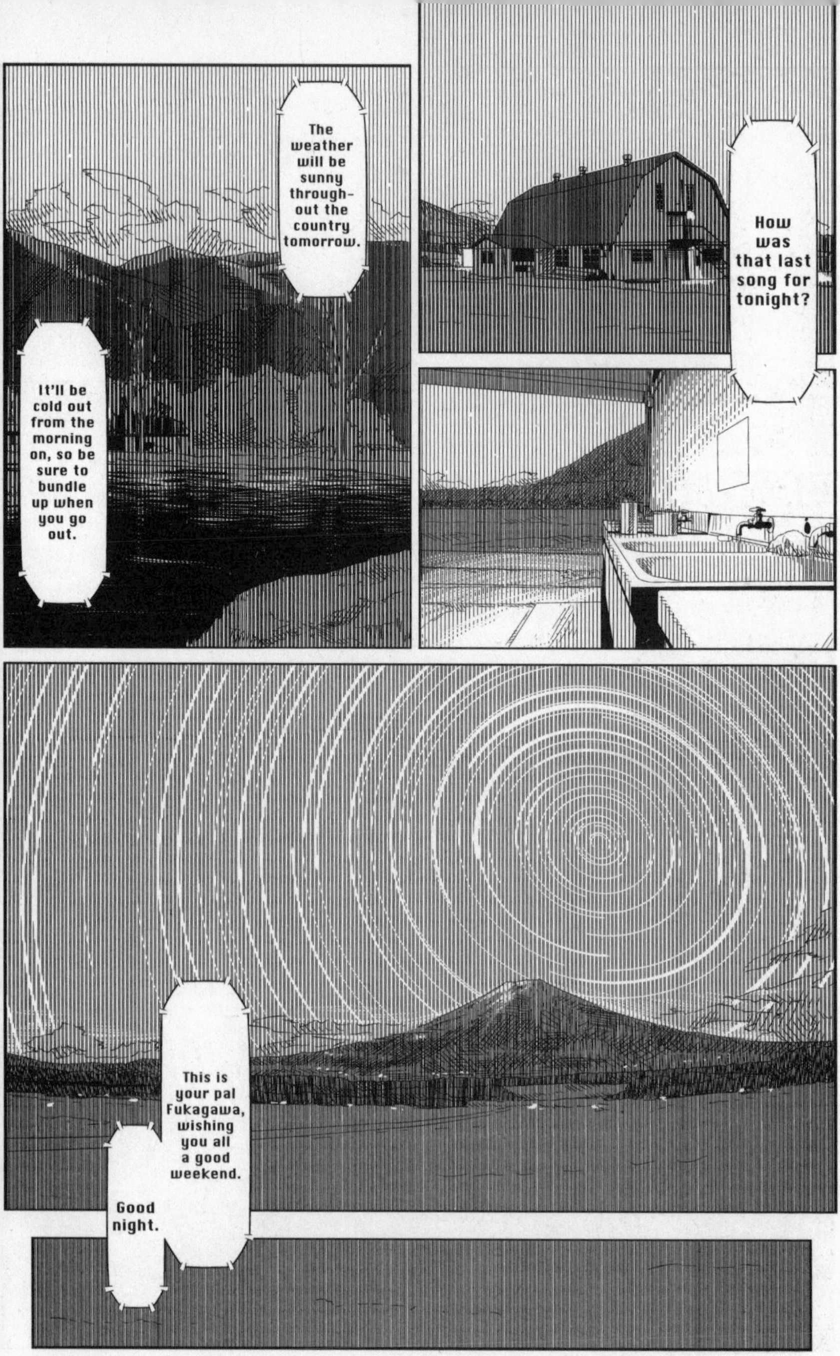
How was that last song for tonight?
The weather will be sunny through-out the country tomorrow.
It'll be cold out from the morning on, so be sure to bundle up when you go out.
This is your pal Fukagawa, wishing you all a good weekend.
Good night.

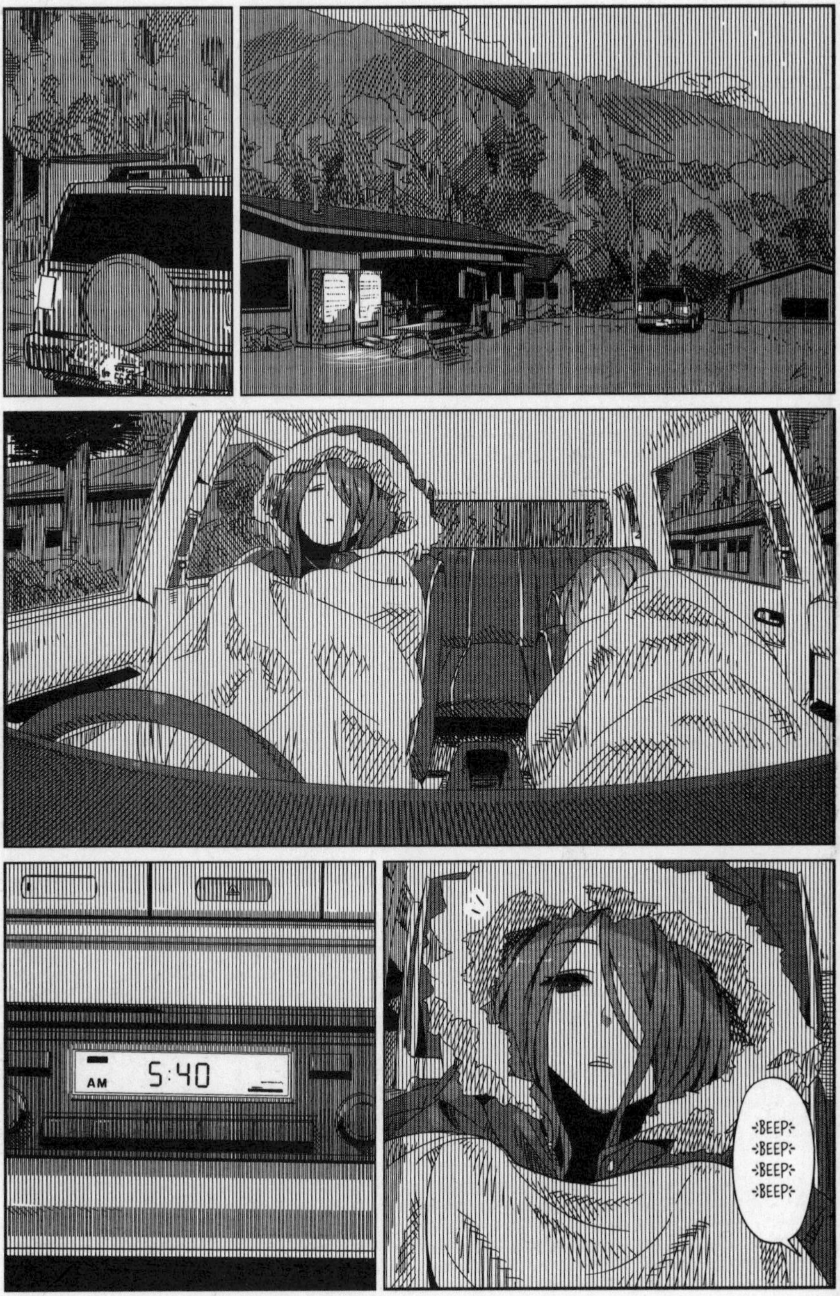
AM 5:40
!
BEEP BEEP BEEP BEEP

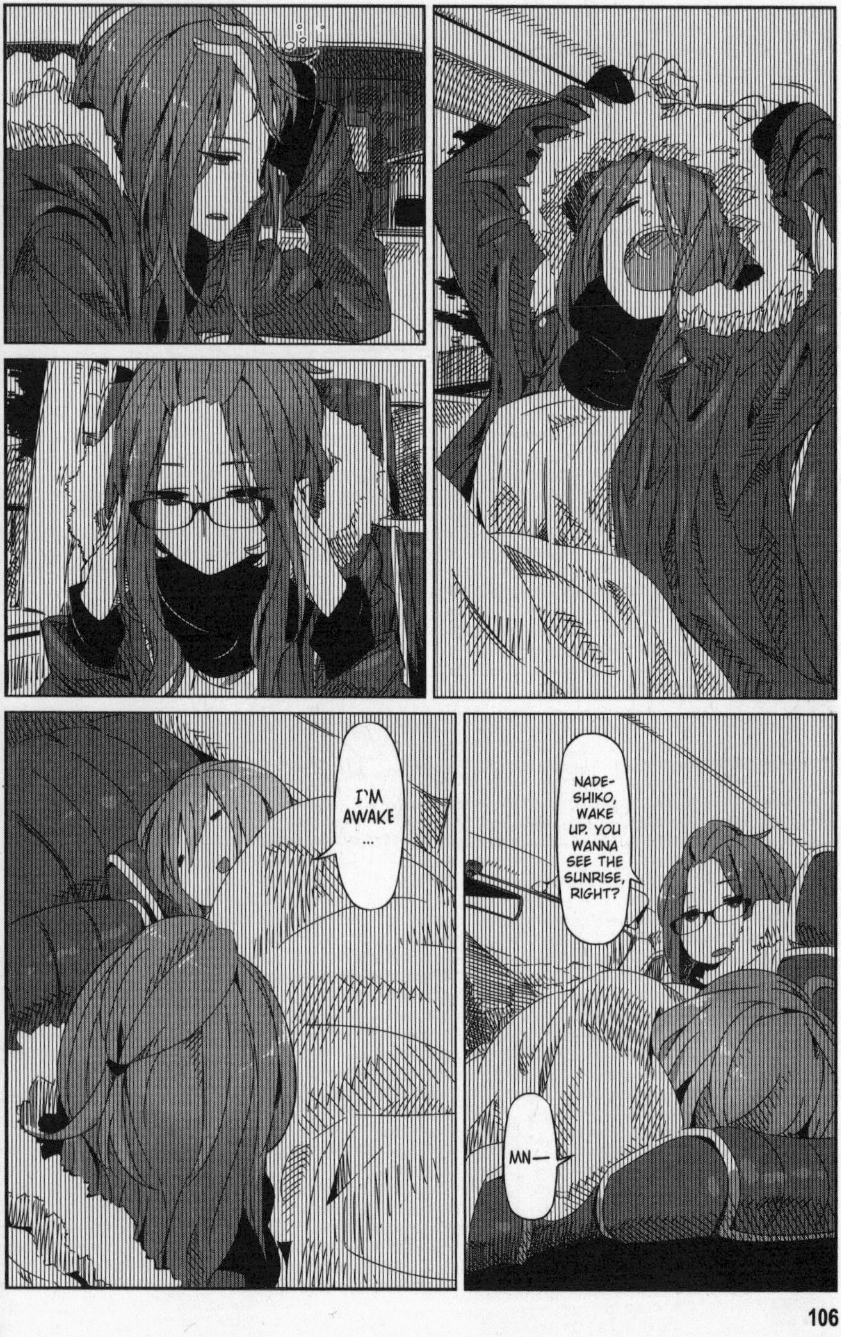
NADE-SHIKO, WAKE UP. YOU WANNA SEE THE SUNRISE, RIGHT?
MN—
I'M AWAKE ...

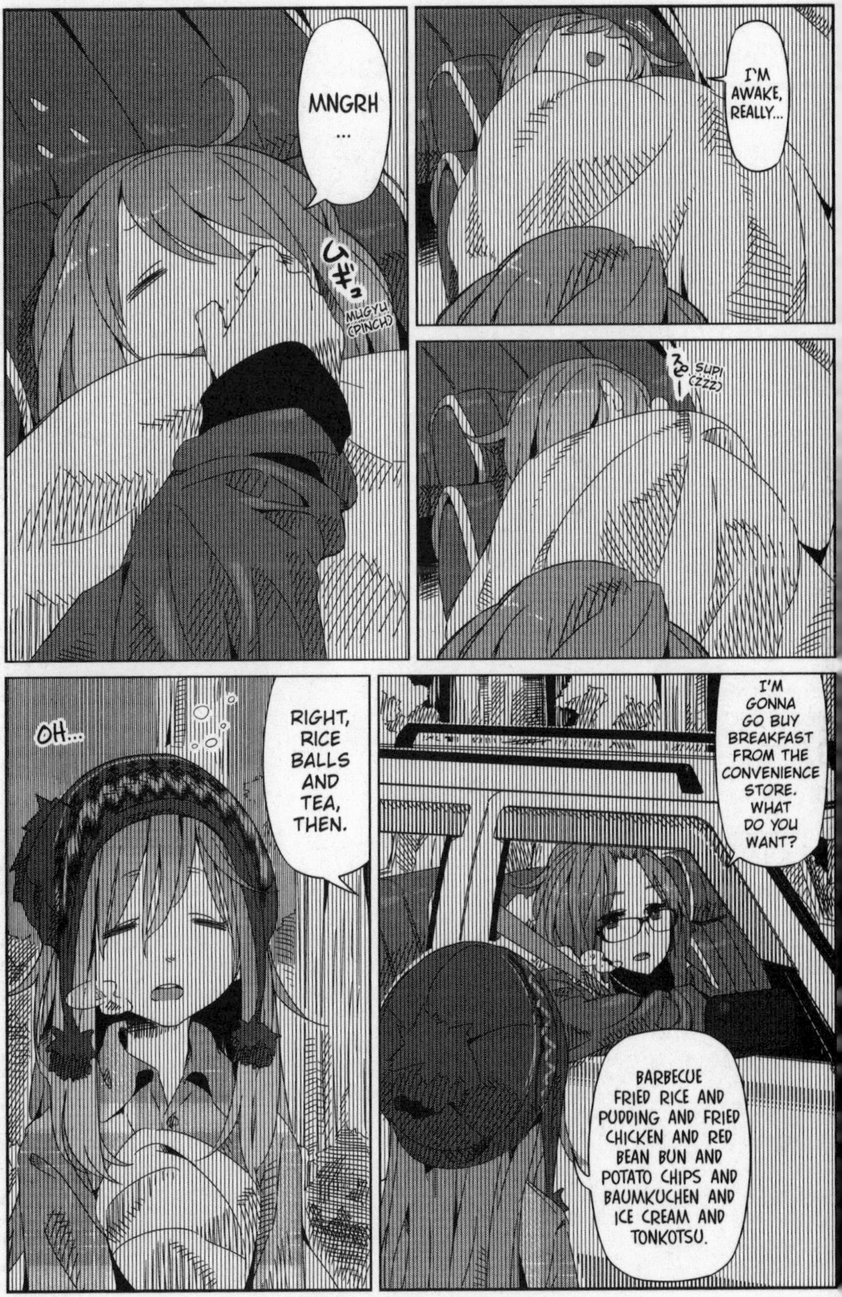
I'M AWAKE, REALLY...
すぴー
SUPI (ZZZ)
MNGRH ...
ムギュ
MUGYU (PINCH)
I'M GONNA GO BUY BREAKFAST FROM THE CONVENIENCE STORE. WHAT DO YOU WANT?
BARBECUE FRIED RICE AND PUDDING AND FRIED CHICKEN AND RED BEAN BUN AND POTATO CHIPS AND BAUMKUCHEN AND ICE CREAM AND TONKOTSU.
RIGHT, RICE BALLS AND TEA, THEN.
OH...

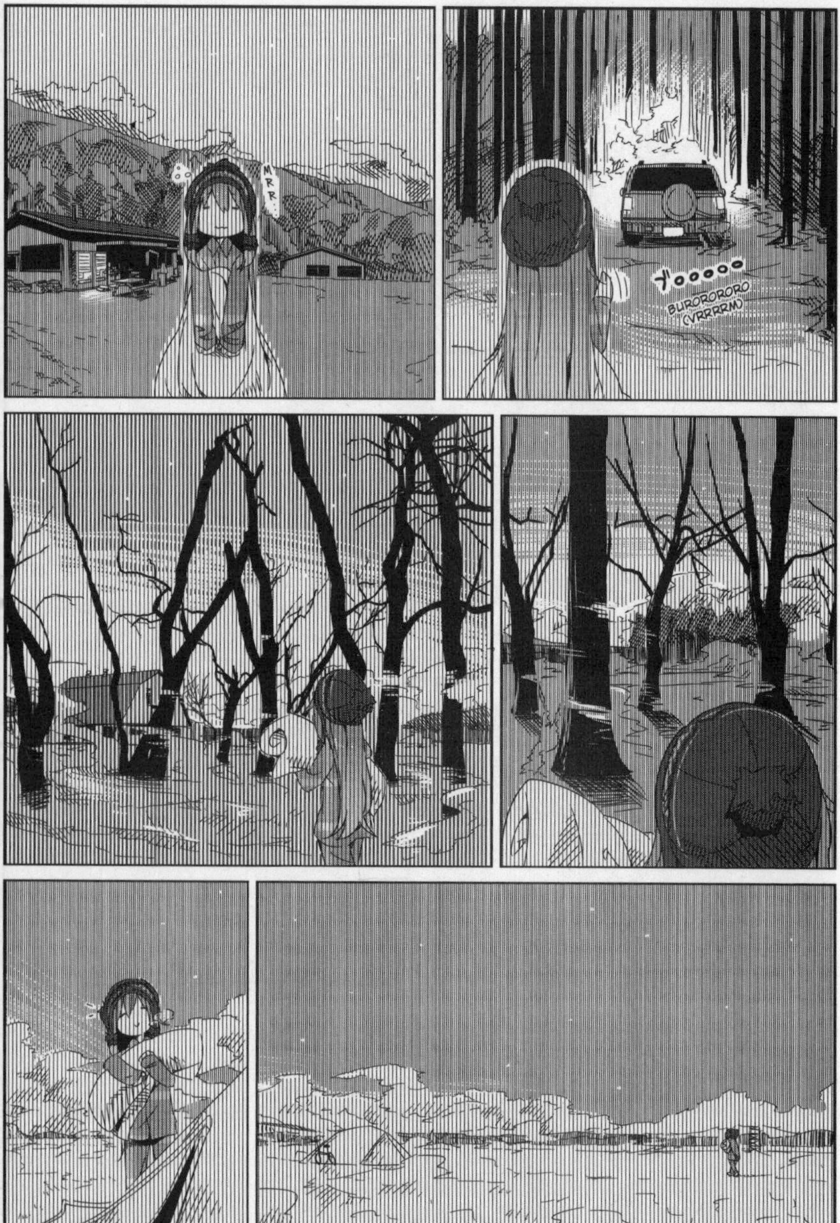
ブooooo
BURORORORO (VRRRRM)
MRR...

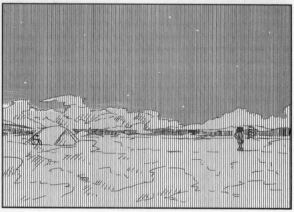

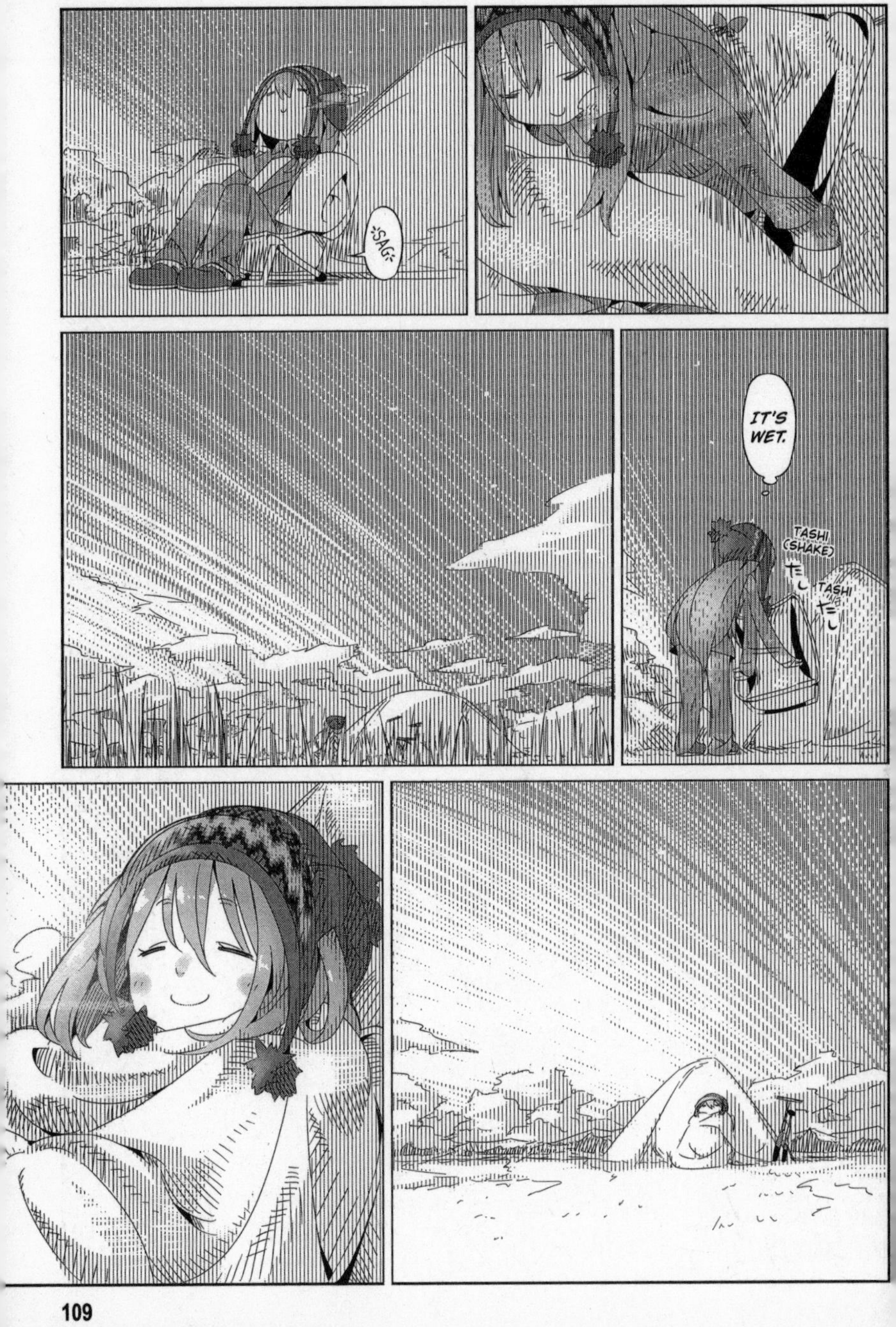
SAG
IT'S WET.
TASHI (SHAKE)
たし
TASHI
たし

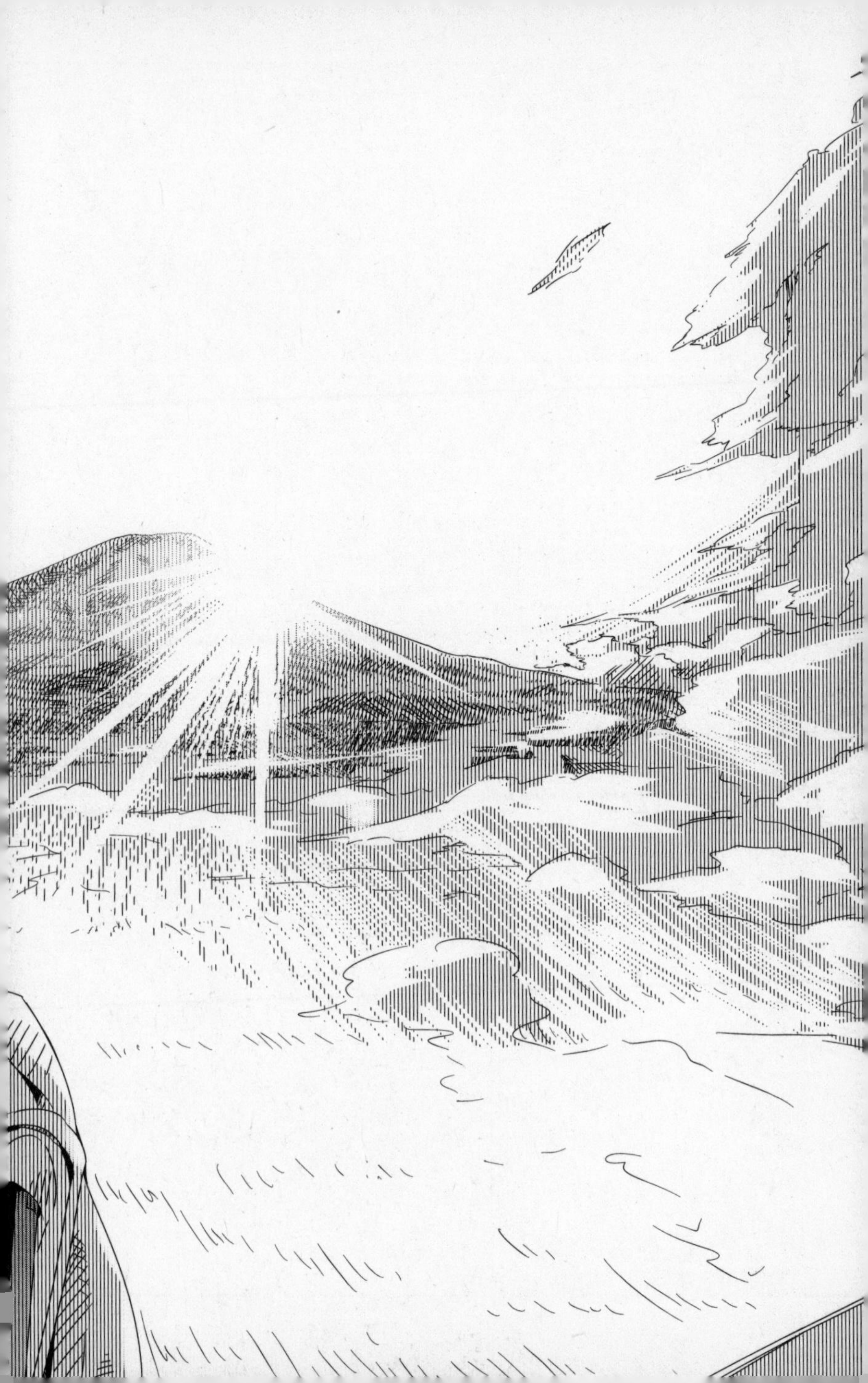

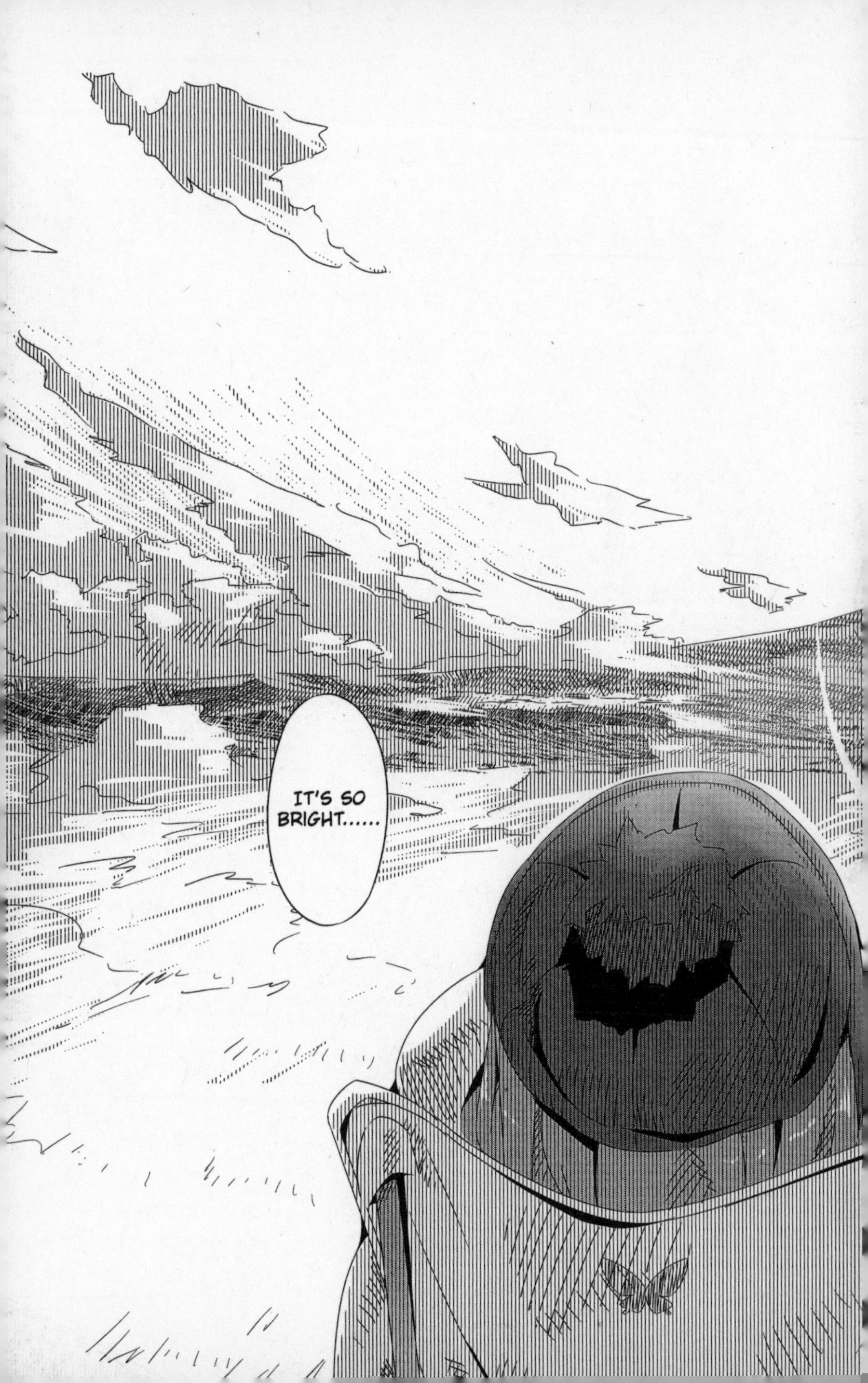
IT'S SO BRIGHT......

?

ゴソ
GOSO
(RUSTLE)

ゴソ
GOSO

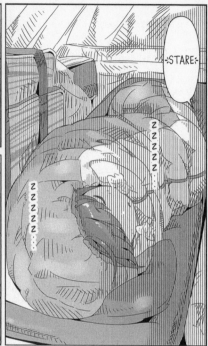

-:STARE:-

ZZZZZ....

ZZZZZ....

AH,
WHAT-
EVER.

ZZZZ... ZZZZ...
SHE'S NOT WAKING UP.
LET'S JUST PACK UP.
ZZZZ...
ZZZZ...
SHE'S NOT WAK-ING UP.
MM-HM.
ZZZ...

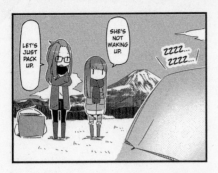

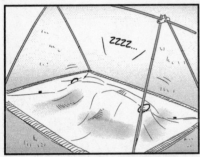

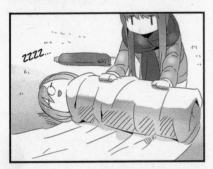

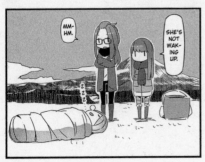

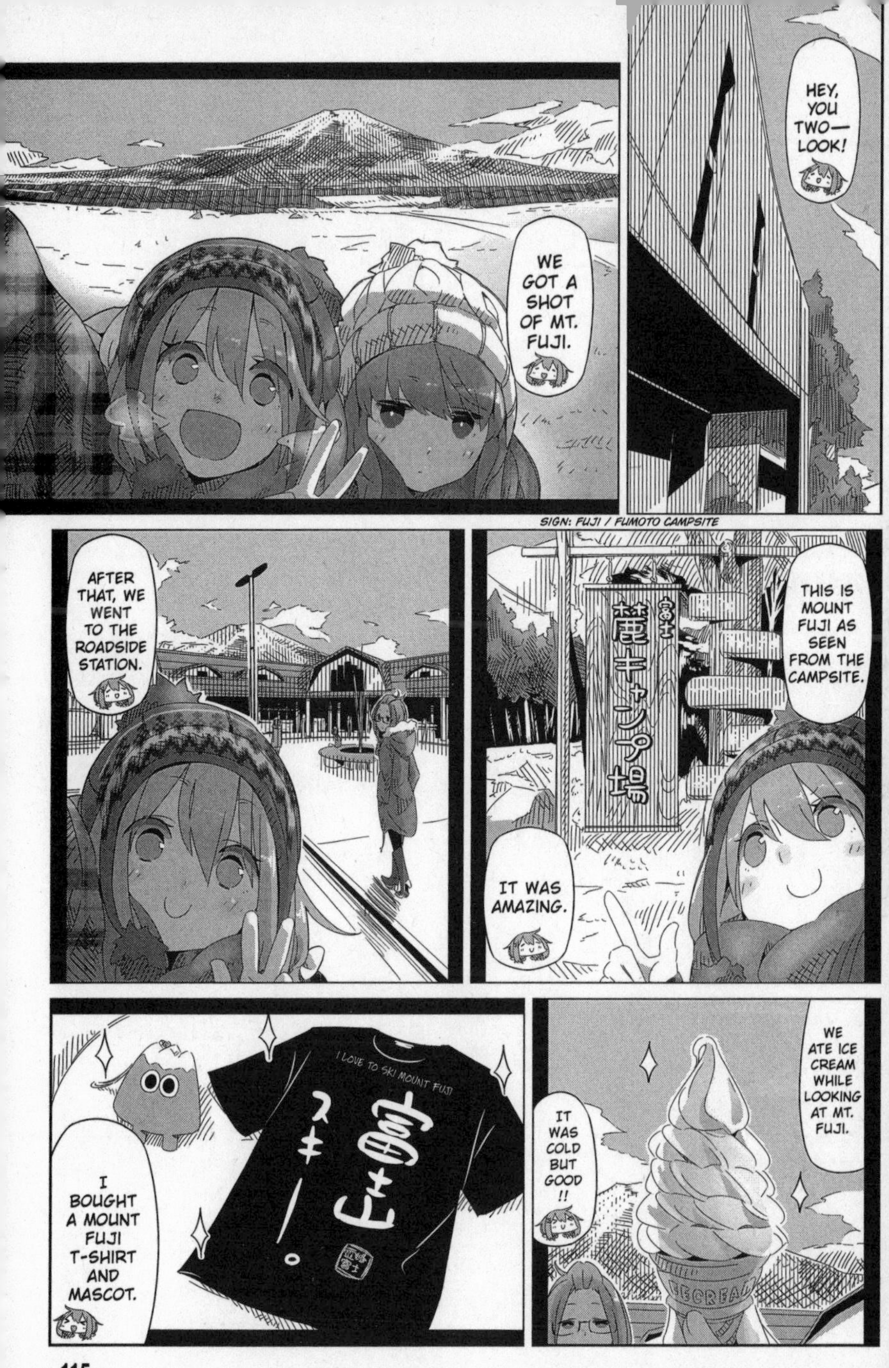
HEY, YOU TWO—LOOK!
WE GOT A SHOT OF MT. FUJI.
SIGN: FUJI / FUMOTO CAMPSITE
富士
麓キャンプ場
THIS IS MOUNT FUJI AS SEEN FROM THE CAMPSITE.
IT WAS AMAZING.
AFTER THAT, WE WENT TO THE ROADSIDE STATION.
WE ATE ICE CREAM WHILE LOOKING AT MT. FUJI.
IT WAS COLD BUT GOOD!!
I LOVE TO SKI MOUNT FUJI
I BOUGHT A MOUNT FUJI T-SHIRT AND MASCOT.

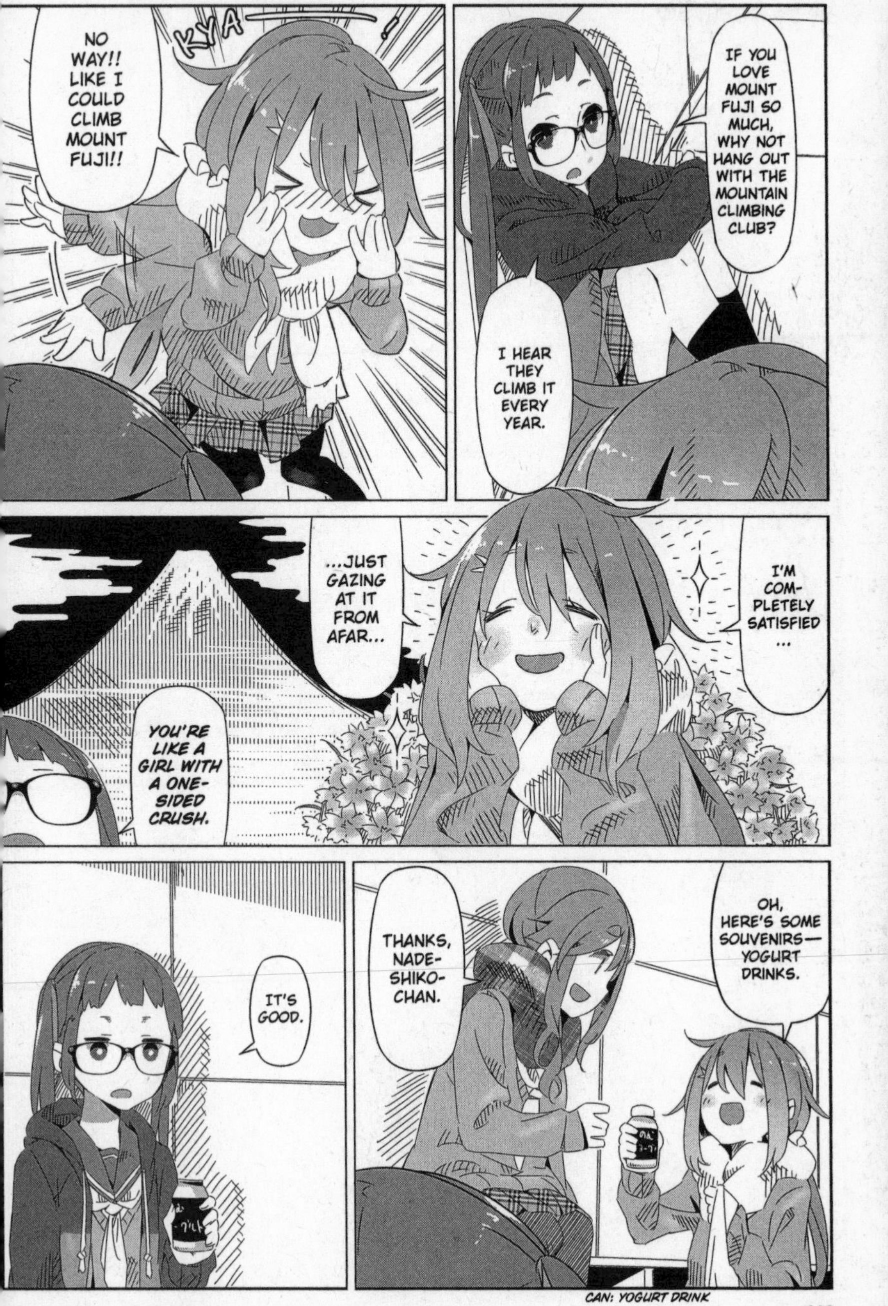
IF YOU LOVE MOUNT FUJI SO MUCH, WHY NOT HANG OUT WITH THE MOUNTAIN CLIMBING CLUB?
I HEAR THEY CLIMB IT EVERY YEAR.
KYA
NO WAY!! LIKE I COULD CLIMB MOUNT FUJI!!
I'M COM-PLETELY SATISFIED ...
...JUST GAZING AT IT FROM AFAR...
YOU'RE LIKE A GIRL WITH A ONE-SIDED CRUSH.
OH, HERE'S SOME SOUVENIRS—YOGURT DRINKS.
THANKS, NADE-SHIKO-CHAN.
IT'S GOOD.

CAN: YOGURT DRINK

Chapter 5 YOU CAN ONLY GO CAMPING ONCE YOU'VE GOT YOUR GEAR

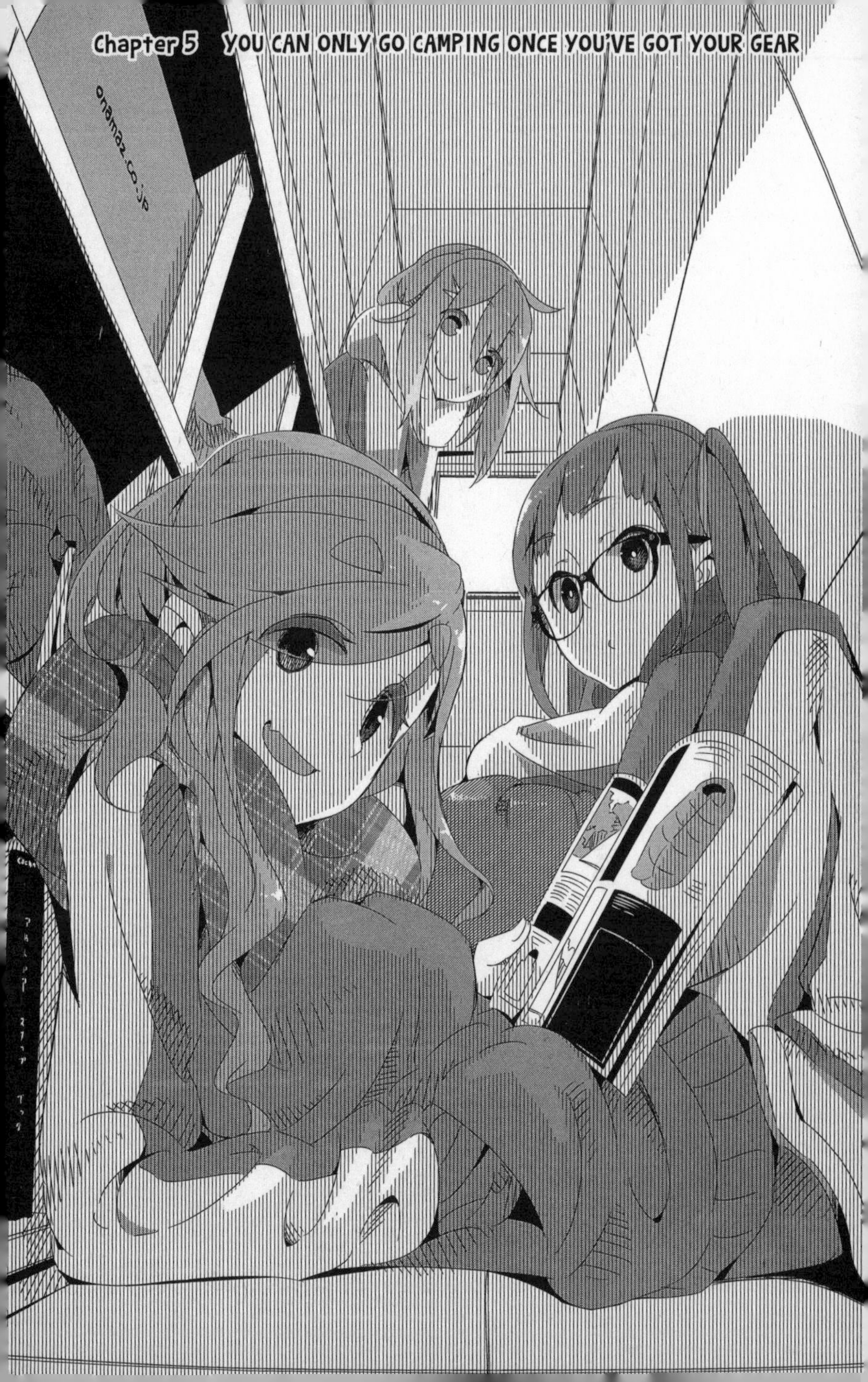
onamaz.co.jp

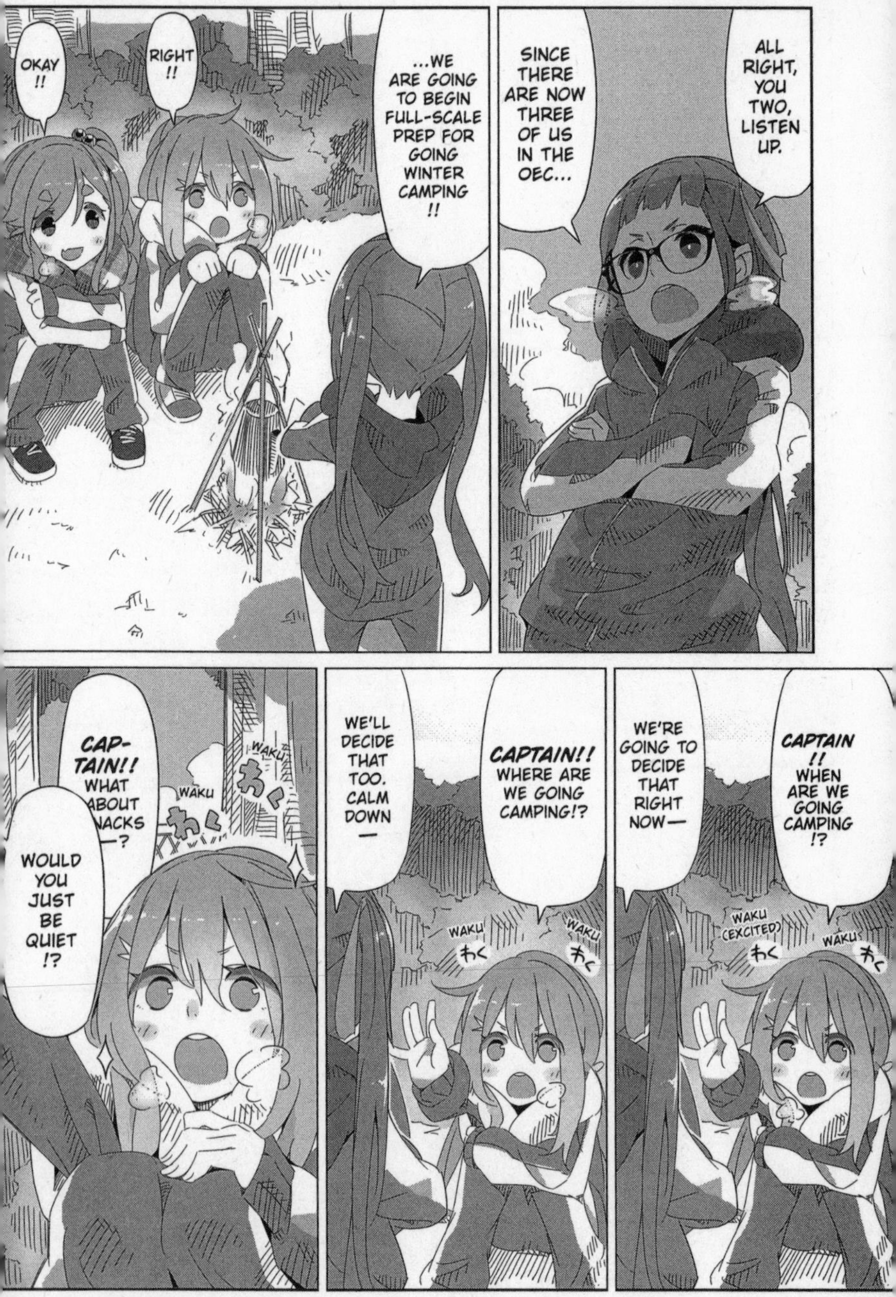
ALL RIGHT, YOU TWO, LISTEN UP.
SINCE THERE ARE NOW THREE OF US IN THE OEC...
...WE ARE GOING TO BEGIN FULL-SCALE PREP FOR GOING WINTER CAMPING!!
RIGHT!!
OKAY!!
CAPTAIN!! WHEN ARE WE GOING CAMPING!?
WE'RE GOING TO DECIDE THAT RIGHT NOW—
WAKU わく
WAKU (EXCITED) わく
CAPTAIN!! WHERE ARE WE GOING CAMPING!?
WE'LL DECIDE THAT TOO. CALM DOWN—
WAKU わく
WAKU わく
CAP-TAIN!! WHAT ABOUT NACKS—?
WAKU わく
WAKU わく
WOULD YOU JUST BE QUIET!?

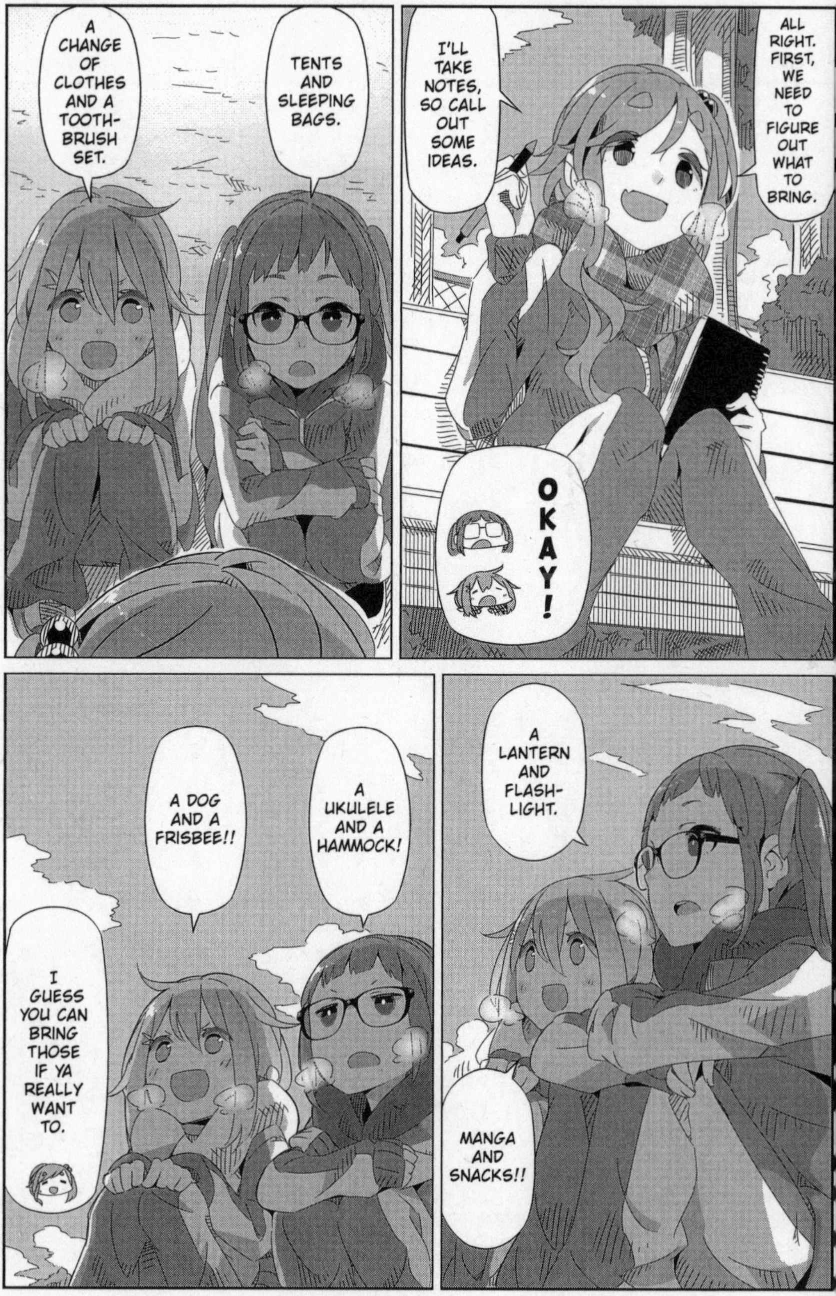
ALL RIGHT. FIRST, WE NEED TO FIGURE OUT WHAT TO BRING.
I'LL TAKE NOTES, SO CALL OUT SOME IDEAS.
OKAY!
TENTS AND SLEEPING BAGS.
A CHANGE OF CLOTHES AND A TOOTH-BRUSH SET.
A LANTERN AND FLASH-LIGHT.
MANGA AND SNACKS!!
A UKULELE AND A HAMMOCK!
A DOG AND A FRISBEE!!
I GUESS YOU CAN BRING THOSE IF YA REALLY WANT TO.

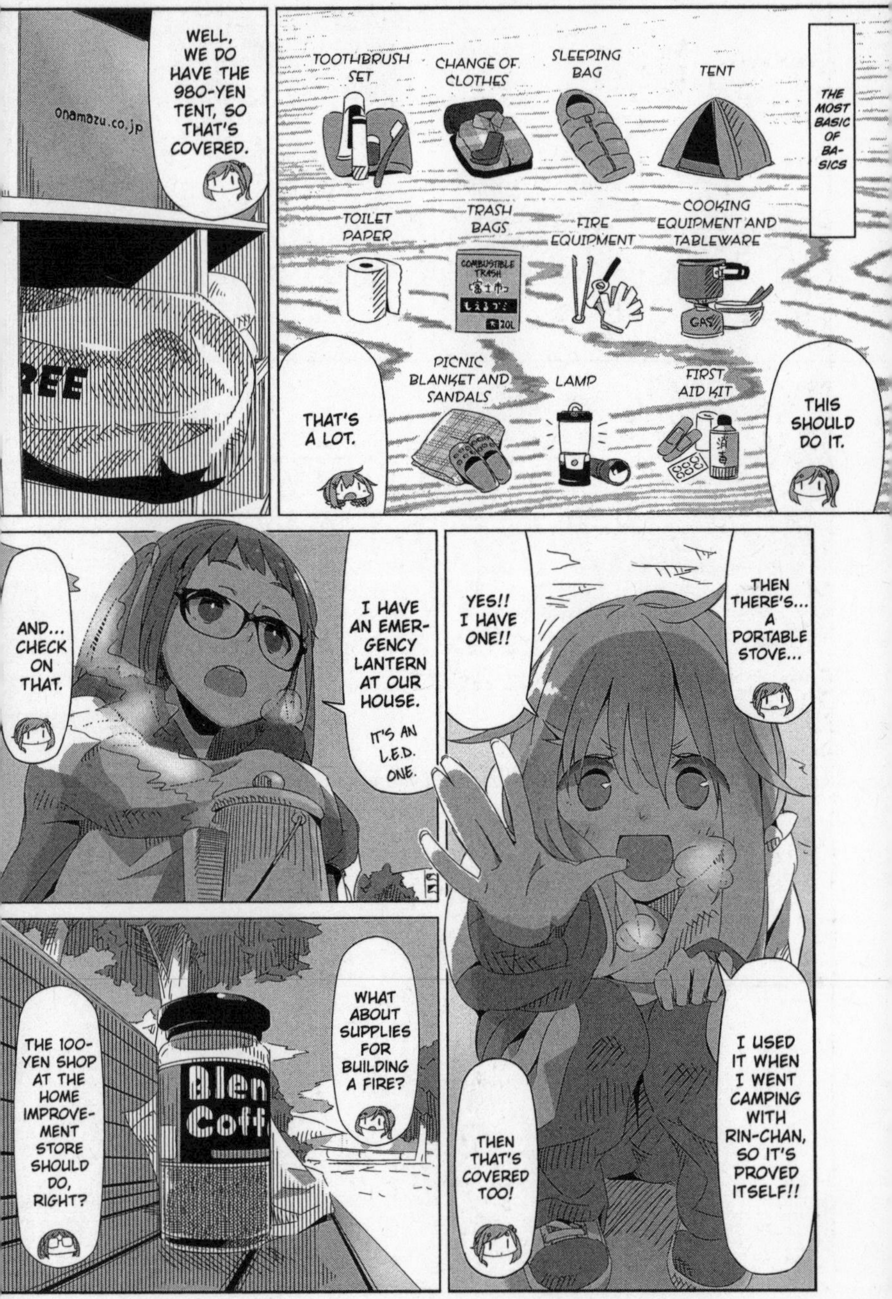
THE MOST BASIC OF BA-SICS
TENT
SLEEPING BAG
CHANGE OF CLOTHES
TOOTHBRUSH SET
COOKING EQUIPMENT AND TABLEWARE
GAS
FIRE EQUIPMENT
TRASH BAGS
COMBUSTIBLE TRASH
20L
TOILET PAPER
FIRST AID KIT
LAMP
PICNIC BLANKET AND SANDALS
THIS SHOULD DO IT.
THAT'S A LOT.
WELL, WE DO HAVE THE 980-YEN TENT, SO THAT'S COVERED.
onamazu.co.jp
THEN THERE'S... A PORTABLE STOVE...
YES!! I HAVE ONE!!
I USED IT WHEN I WENT CAMPING WITH RIN-CHAN, SO IT'S PROVED ITSELF!!
THEN THAT'S COVERED TOO!
I HAVE AN EMERGENCY LANTERN AT OUR HOUSE.
IT'S AN L.E.D. ONE.
AND... CHECK ON THAT.
WHAT ABOUT SUPPLIES FOR BUILDING A FIRE?
THE 100-YEN SHOP AT THE HOME IMPROVEMENT STORE SHOULD DO, RIGHT?

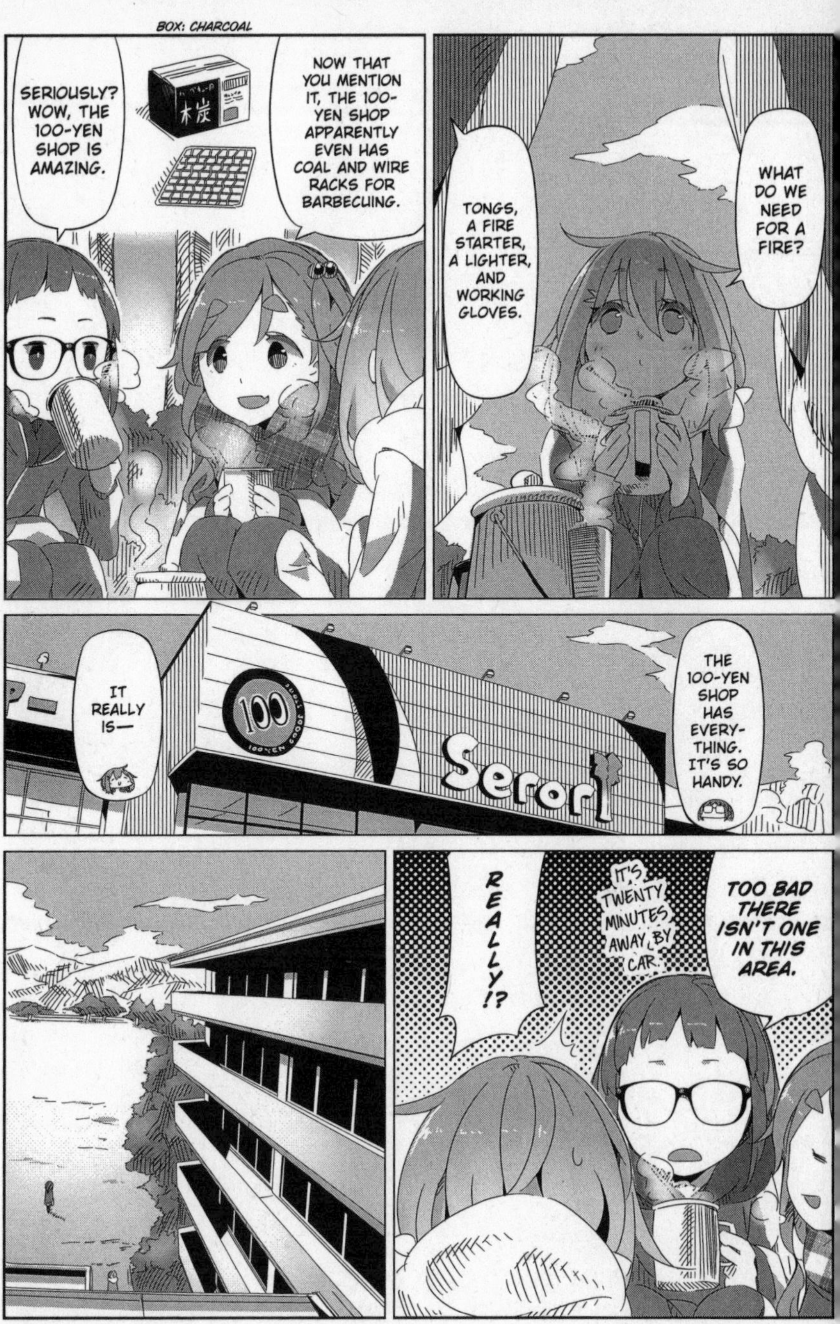
WHAT DO WE NEED FOR A FIRE?
TONGS, A FIRE STARTER, A LIGHTER, AND WORKING GLOVES.
BOX: CHARCOAL
NOW THAT YOU MENTION IT, THE 100-YEN SHOP APPARENTLY EVEN HAS COAL AND WIRE RACKS FOR BARBECUING.
SERIOUSLY? WOW, THE 100-YEN SHOP IS AMAZING.
THE 100-YEN SHOP HAS EVERY-THING. IT'S SO HANDY.
IT REALLY IS—
100
Serori
TOO BAD THERE ISN'T ONE IN THIS AREA.
IT'S TWENTY MINUTES AWAY, BY CAR.
REALLY!?

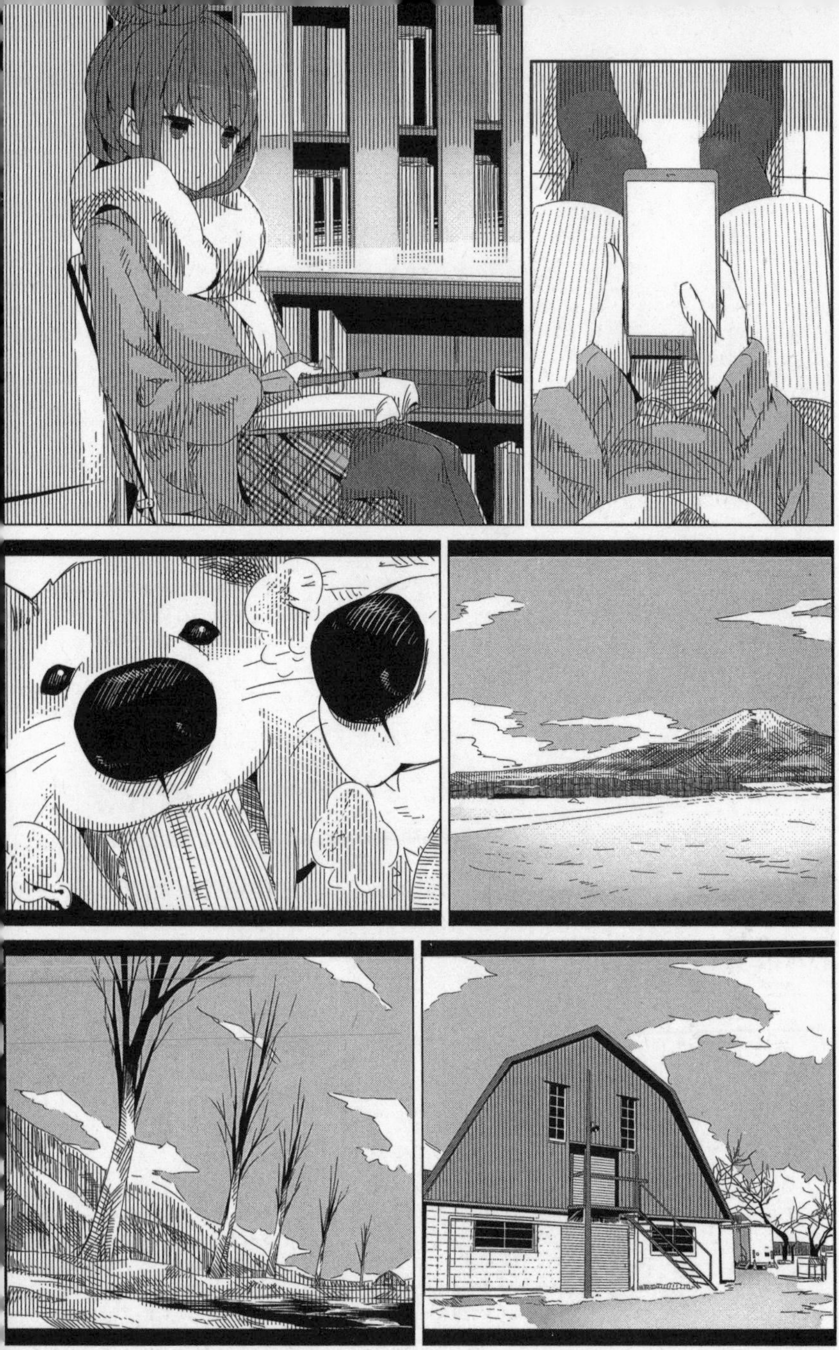

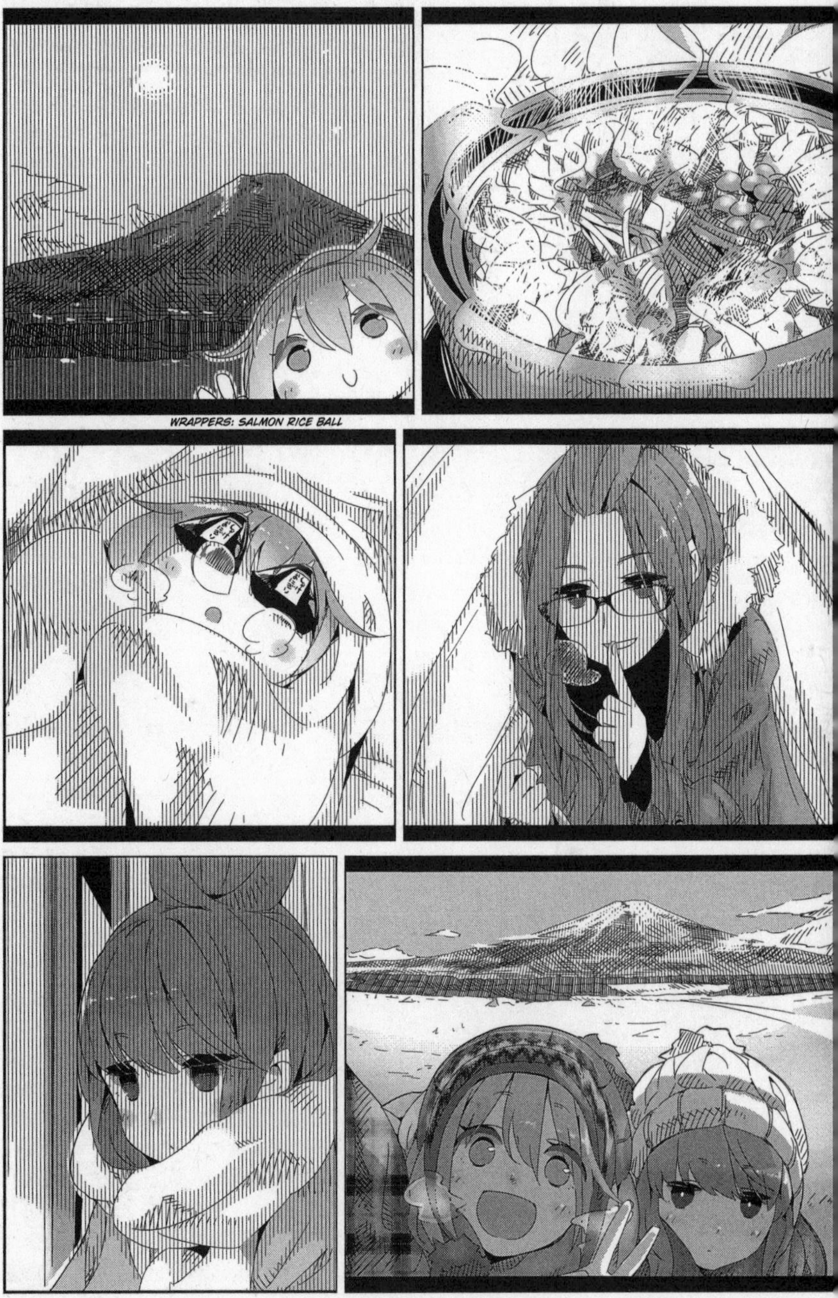
WRAPPERS: SALMON RICE BALL

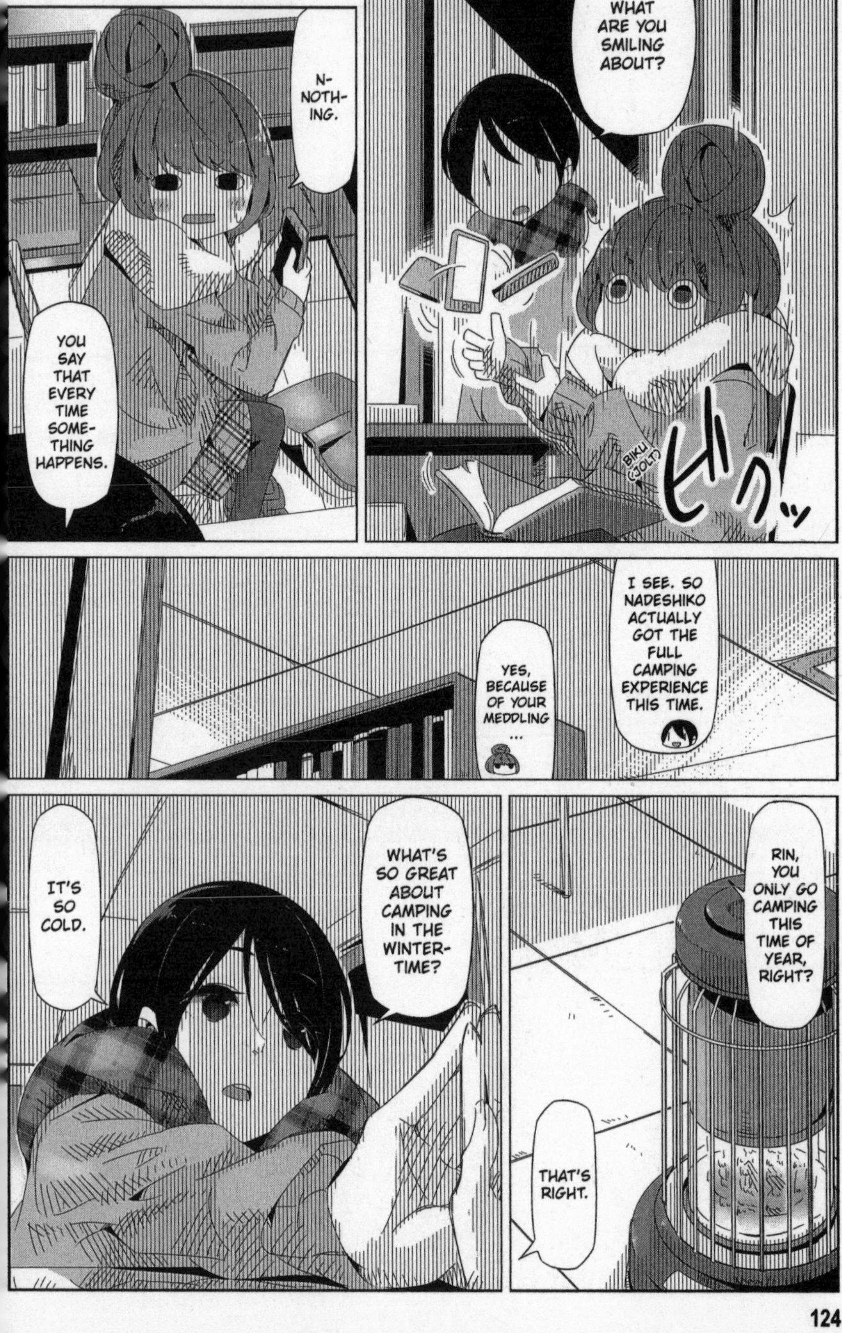
WHAT ARE YOU SMILING ABOUT?
BIKU (JOLT)
ビクッ
N-NOTHING.
YOU SAY THAT EVERY TIME SOMETHING HAPPENS.
I SEE. SO NADESHIKO ACTUALLY GOT THE FULL CAMPING EXPERIENCE THIS TIME.
YES, BECAUSE OF YOUR MEDDLING...
RIN, YOU ONLY GO CAMPING THIS TIME OF YEAR, RIGHT?
THAT'S RIGHT.
WHAT'S SO GREAT ABOUT CAMPING IN THE WINTERTIME?
IT'S SO COLD.

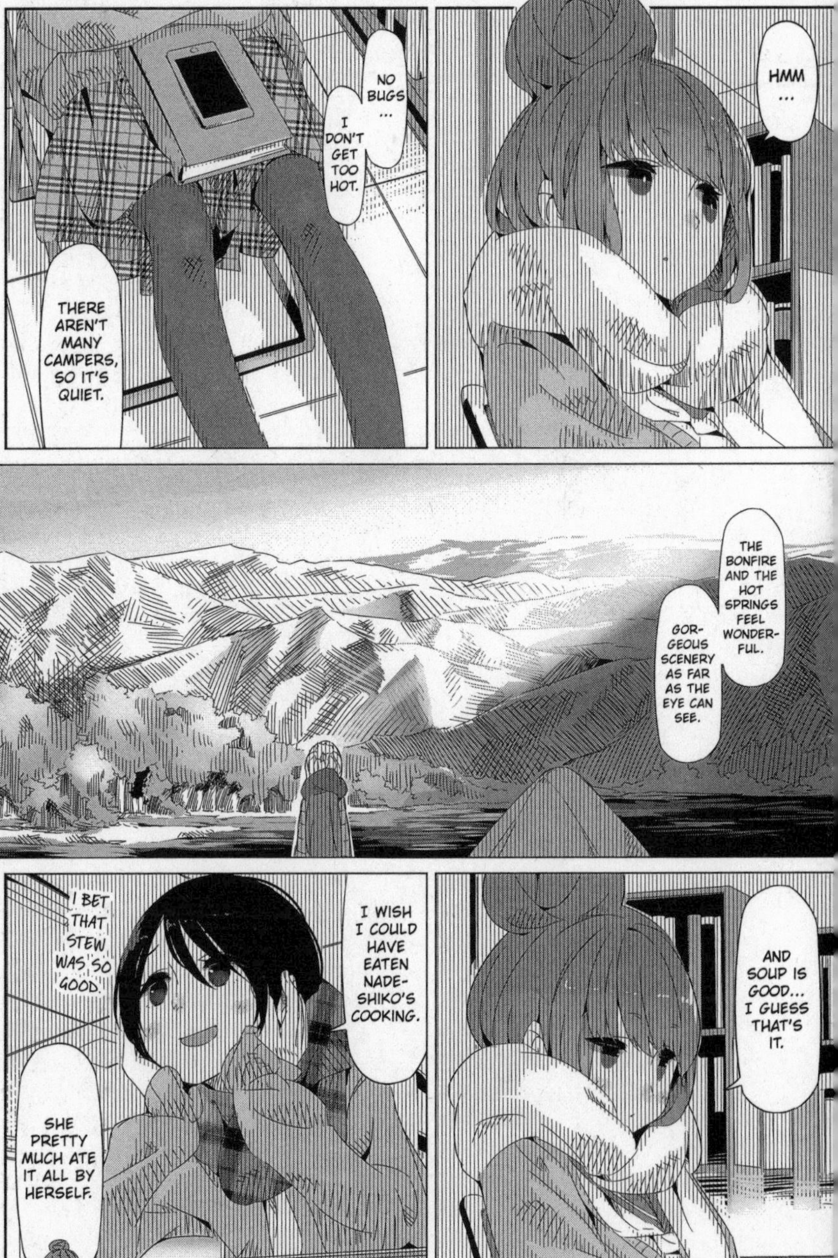
HMM ...
NO BUGS ...
I DON'T GET TOO HOT.
THERE AREN'T MANY CAMPERS, SO IT'S QUIET.
THE BONFIRE AND THE HOT SPRINGS FEEL WONDERFUL.
GORGEOUS SCENERY AS FAR AS THE EYE CAN SEE.
AND SOUP IS GOOD... I GUESS THAT'S IT.
I WISH I COULD HAVE EATEN NADESHIKO'S COOKING.
I BET THAT STEW WAS SO GOOD.
SHE PRETTY MUCH ATE IT ALL BY HERSELF.

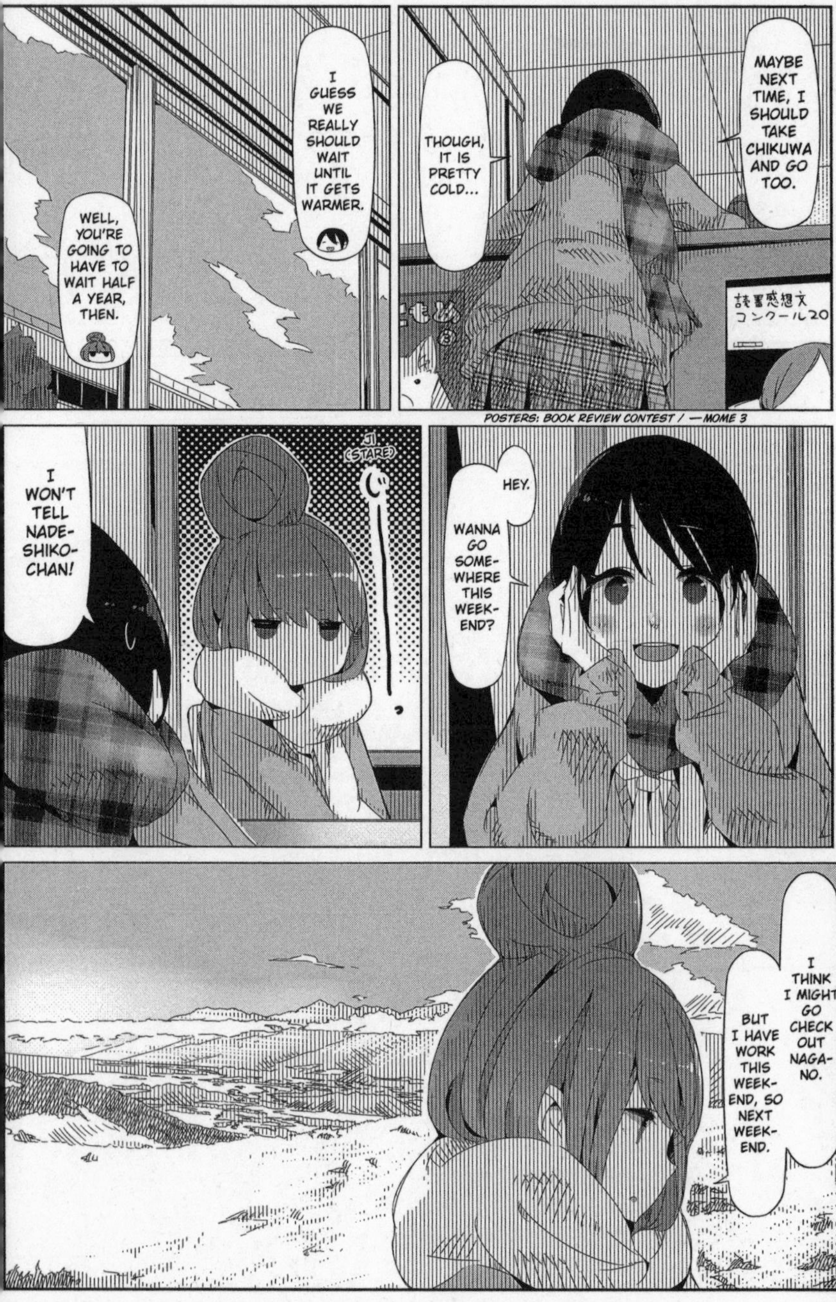
MAYBE NEXT TIME, I SHOULD TAKE CHIKUWA AND GO TOO.
THOUGH, IT IS PRETTY COLD...
読書感想文 コンクール20
I GUESS WE REALLY SHOULD WAIT UNTIL IT GETS WARMER.
WELL, YOU'RE GOING TO HAVE TO WAIT HALF A YEAR, THEN.
POSTERS: BOOK REVIEW CONTEST / —MOME 3
HEY.
WANNA GO SOMEWHERE THIS WEEKEND?
JI (STARE)
I WON'T TELL NADESHIKO-CHAN!
I THINK I MIGHT GO CHECK OUT NAGANO.
BUT I HAVE WORK THIS WEEKEND, SO NEXT WEEKEND.

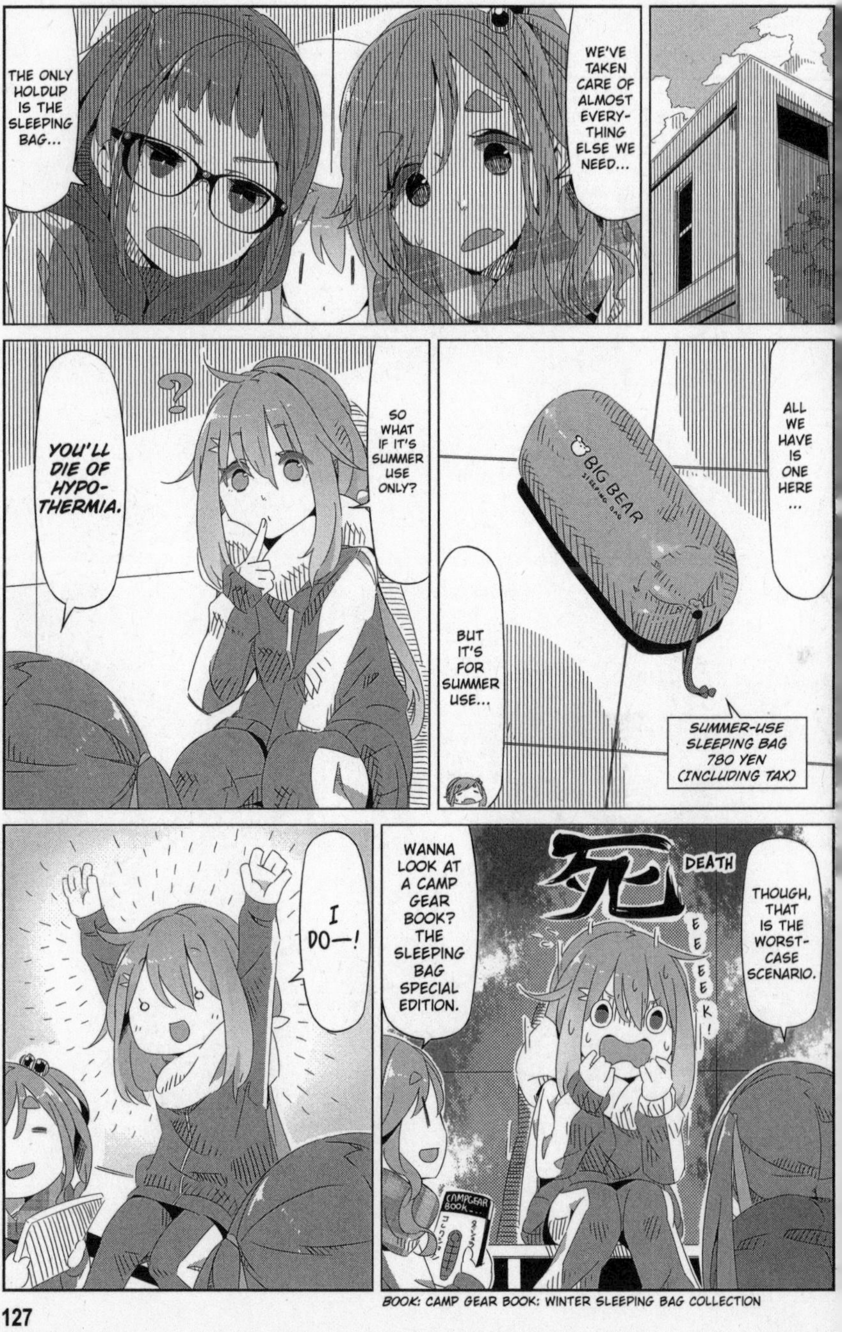
WE'VE TAKEN CARE OF ALMOST EVERYTHING ELSE WE NEED...
THE ONLY HOLDUP IS THE SLEEPING BAG...
ALL WE HAVE IS ONE HERE...
BIG BEAR SLEEPING BAG
BUT IT'S FOR SUMMER USE...
SUMMER-USE SLEEPING BAG 780 YEN (INCLUDING TAX)
SO WHAT IF IT'S SUMMER USE ONLY?
YOU'LL DIE OF HYPOTHERMIA.
THOUGH, THAT IS THE WORST-CASE SCENARIO.
死
DEATH
EEEEK!
WANNA LOOK AT A CAMP GEAR BOOK? THE SLEEPING BAG SPECIAL EDITION.
CAMPGEAR BOOK...
I DO—!

BOOK: CAMP GEAR BOOK: WINTER SLEEPING BAG COLLECTION

BODY-STYLE	MUMMY-STYLE	ENVELOPE-STYLE	TYPES OF SLEEPING BAGS

THE ARMS AND LEGS ARE SEPARATE, SO THE USER CAN FREELY WALK ABOUT.

IT COVERS THE ENTIRE BODY, SO IT'S A GOOD CHOICE FOR WINTER USE.

IT'S A COMMON VARIETY FOR SUMMER USE, SO THE PRICE CAN BE RATHER CHEAP.

WHAT IS THIS!? IT'S SO FUNNY!!

RIN-CHAN'S IS THE MUMMY TYPE.

OURS IS THIS TYPE.

WHETHER OR NOT YOU RUN, THE BEAR WILL BE THE ULTIMATE VICTOR.

BUN

BUN (SHAKE)

BEAR!

GIVE IT A LITTLE MORE THOUGHT, NADE-SHIKO.

THIS MUST BE A GOOD ONE.

IT SAYS, "EVEN IF A BEAR CHASES YOU, YOU CAN STILL RUN AWAY"!!

BEEEEEEEEEAR!

THEY CAN RUN AS FAST AS A BIKE.

STANDARD VELOCITY 60KM/H

128

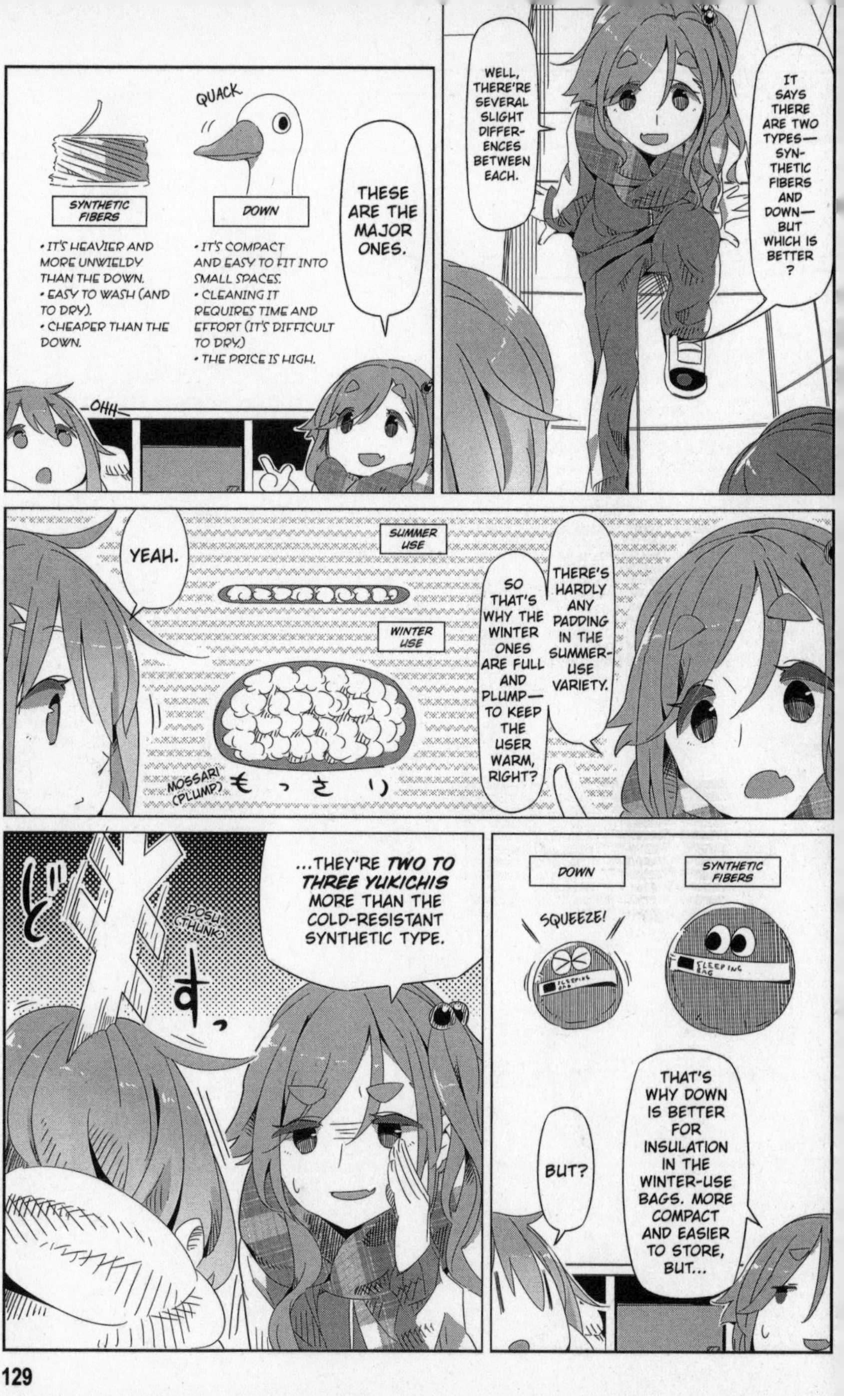
IT SAYS THERE ARE TWO TYPES—SYNTHETIC FIBERS AND DOWN—BUT WHICH IS BETTER?
WELL, THERE'RE SEVERAL SLIGHT DIFFERENCES BETWEEN EACH.
THESE ARE THE MAJOR ONES.
QUACK
DOWN
• IT'S COMPACT AND EASY TO FIT INTO SMALL SPACES.
• CLEANING IT REQUIRES TIME AND EFFORT (IT'S DIFFICULT TO DRY.)
• THE PRICE IS HIGH.
SYNTHETIC FIBERS
• IT'S HEAVIER AND MORE UNWIELDY THAN THE DOWN.
• EASY TO WASH (AND TO DRY).
• CHEAPER THAN THE DOWN.
-OHH-
THERE'S HARDLY ANY PADDING IN THE SUMMER-USE VARIETY.
SO THAT'S WHY THE WINTER ONES ARE FULL AND PLUMP—TO KEEP THE USER WARM, RIGHT?
SUMMER USE
WINTER USE
MOSSARI (PLUMP) もっさり
YEAH.
DOWN
SYNTHETIC FIBERS
SQUEEZE!
SLEEPING BAG
SLEEPING BAG
THAT'S WHY DOWN IS BETTER FOR INSULATION IN THE WINTER-USE BAGS. MORE COMPACT AND EASIER TO STORE, BUT...
BUT?
...THEY'RE TWO TO THREE YUKICHIS MORE THAN THE COLD-RESISTANT SYNTHETIC TYPE.
DOSU (THUNK)
どすっ

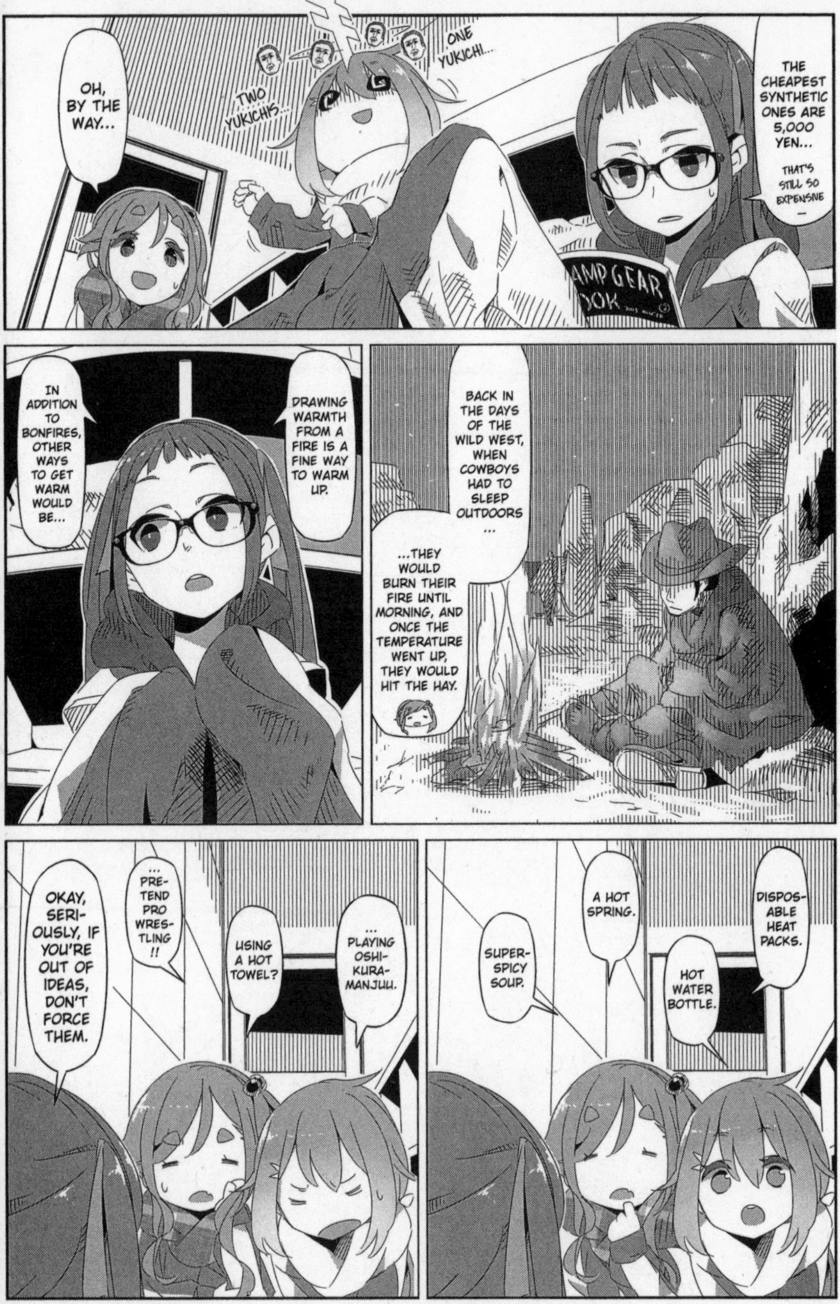
THE CHEAPEST SYNTHETIC ONES ARE 5,000 YEN...
THAT'S STILL SO EXPENSIVE
ONE YUKICHI...
TWO YUKICHIS...
OH, BY THE WAY...
BACK IN THE DAYS OF THE WILD WEST, WHEN COWBOYS HAD TO SLEEP OUTDOORS ...
...THEY WOULD BURN THEIR FIRE UNTIL MORNING, AND ONCE THE TEMPERATURE WENT UP, THEY WOULD HIT THE HAY.
....
DRAWING WARMTH FROM A FIRE IS A FINE WAY TO WARM UP.
IN ADDITION TO BONFIRES, OTHER WAYS TO GET WARM WOULD BE...
DISPOSABLE HEAT PACKS.
HOT WATER BOTTLE.
A HOT SPRING.
SUPER-SPICY SOUP.
...PLAYING OSHI-KURA-MANJUU.
USING A HOT TOWEL?
...PRETEND PRO WRESTLING!!
OKAY, SERIOUSLY, IF YOU'RE OUT OF IDEAS, DON'T FORCE THEM.

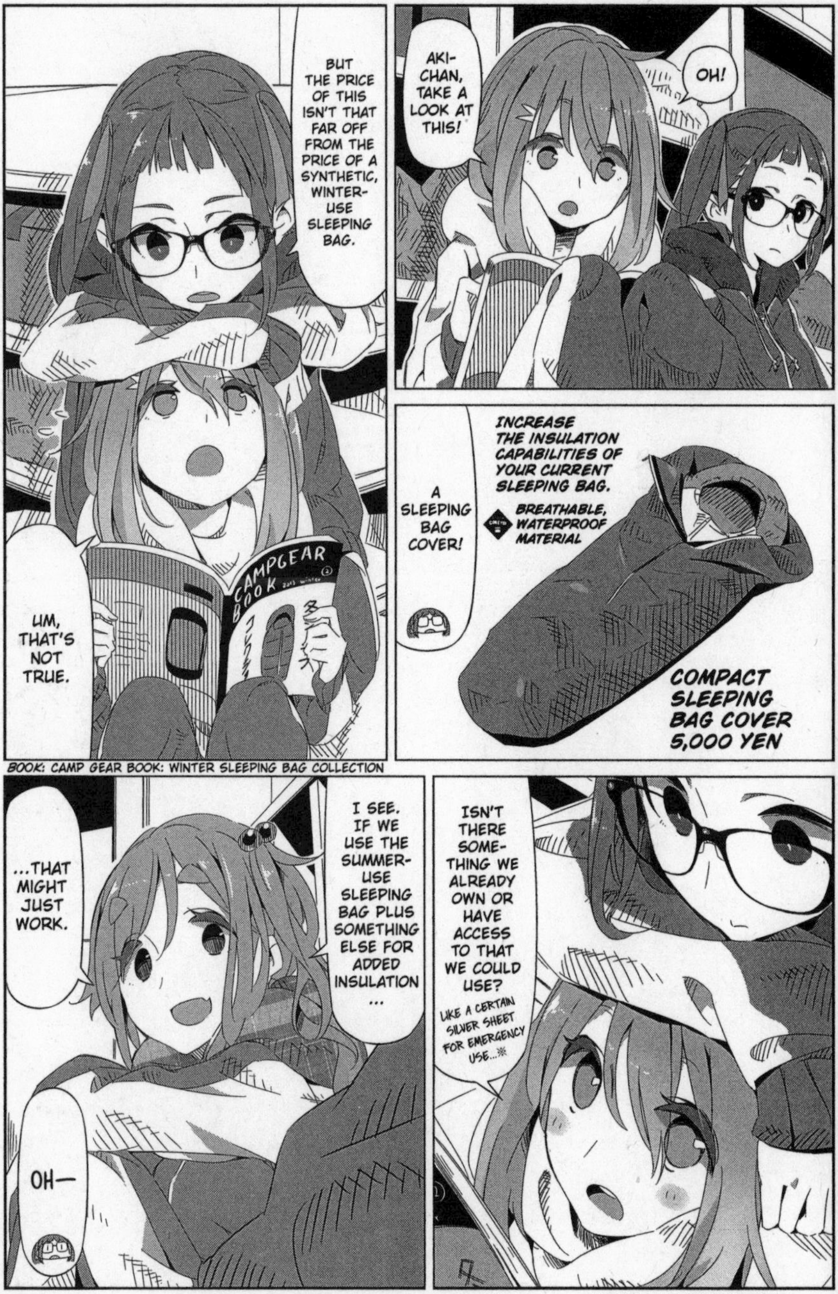
AKI-CHAN, TAKE A LOOK AT THIS!
OH!
INCREASE THE INSULATION CAPABILITIES OF YOUR CURRENT SLEEPING BAG.
BREATHABLE, WATERPROOF MATERIAL
A SLEEPING BAG COVER!
COMPACT SLEEPING BAG COVER 5,000 YEN
BUT THE PRICE OF THIS ISN'T THAT FAR OFF FROM THE PRICE OF A SYNTHETIC, WINTER-USE SLEEPING BAG.
UM, THAT'S NOT TRUE.
CAMPGEAR BOOK
BOOK: CAMP GEAR BOOK: WINTER SLEEPING BAG COLLECTION
ISN'T THERE SOMETHING WE ALREADY OWN OR HAVE ACCESS TO THAT WE COULD USE?
LIKE A CERTAIN SILVER SHEET FOR EMERGENCY USE...※
I SEE. IF WE USE THE SUMMER-USE SLEEPING BAG PLUS SOMETHING ELSE FOR ADDED INSULATION...
...THAT MIGHT JUST WORK.
OH—

※EMERGENCY MYLAR BLANKET

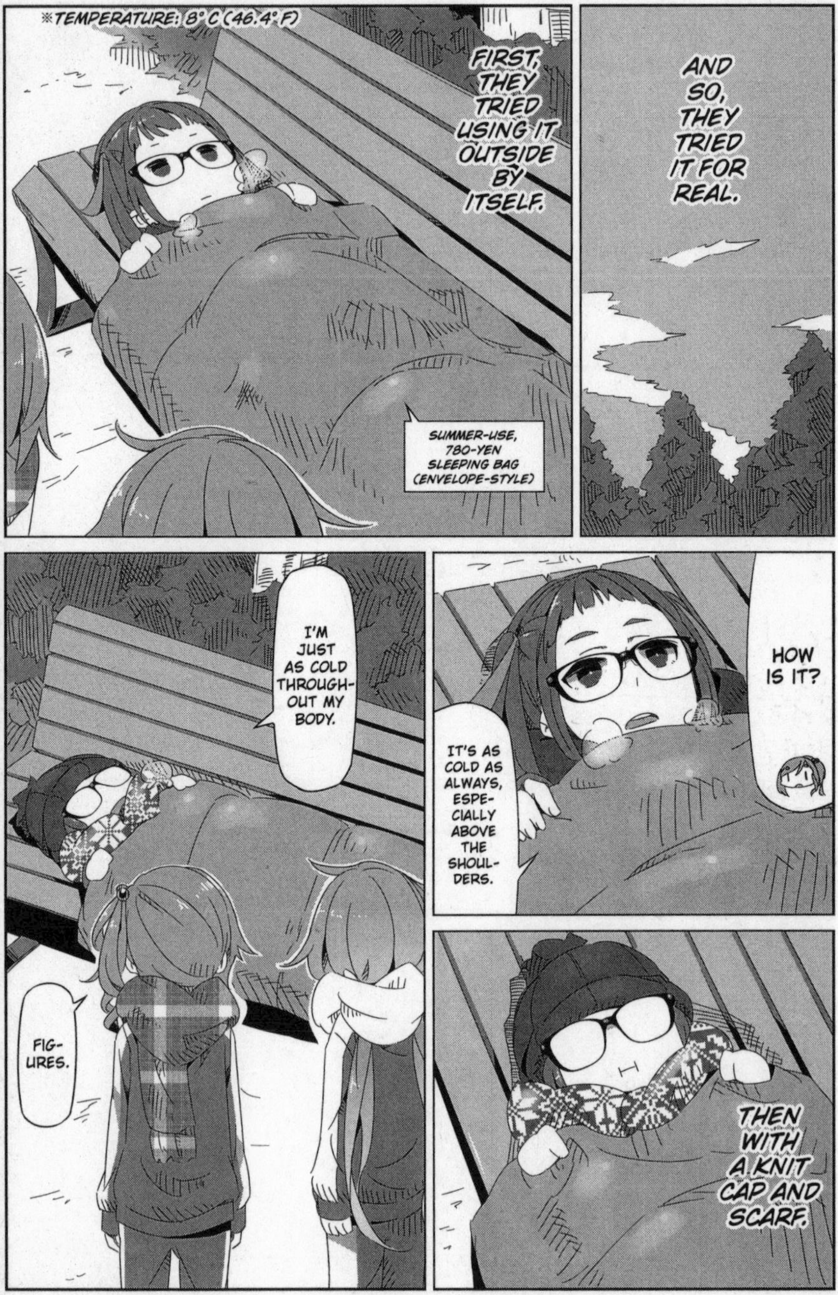
AND SO, THEY TRIED IT FOR REAL.
※TEMPERATURE: 8° C (46.4° F)
FIRST, THEY TRIED USING IT OUTSIDE BY ITSELF.
SUMMER-USE, 780-YEN SLEEPING BAG (ENVELOPE-STYLE)
HOW IS IT?
IT'S AS COLD AS ALWAYS, ESPE-CIALLY ABOVE THE SHOUL-DERS.
THEN WITH A KNIT CAP AND SCARF.
I'M JUST AS COLD THROUGH-OUT MY BODY.
FIG-URES.

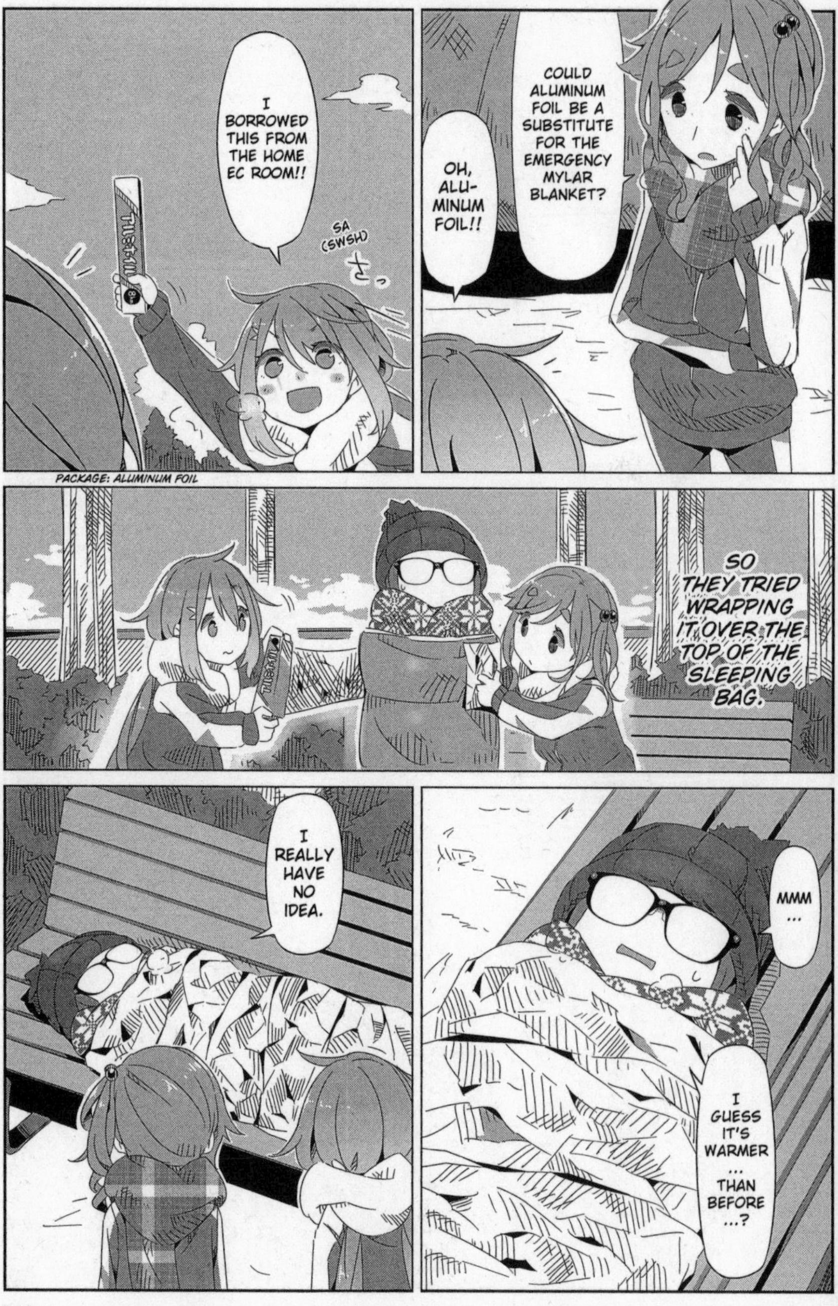
COULD ALUMINUM FOIL BE A SUBSTITUTE FOR THE EMERGENCY MYLAR BLANKET?
OH, ALU-MINUM FOIL!!
I BORROWED THIS FROM THE HOME EC ROOM!!
SA (SWSH)
PACKAGE: ALUMINUM FOIL
SO THEY TRIED WRAPPING IT OVER THE TOP OF THE SLEEPING BAG.
MMM ...
I GUESS IT'S WARMER ... THAN BEFORE ...?
I REALLY HAVE NO IDEA.

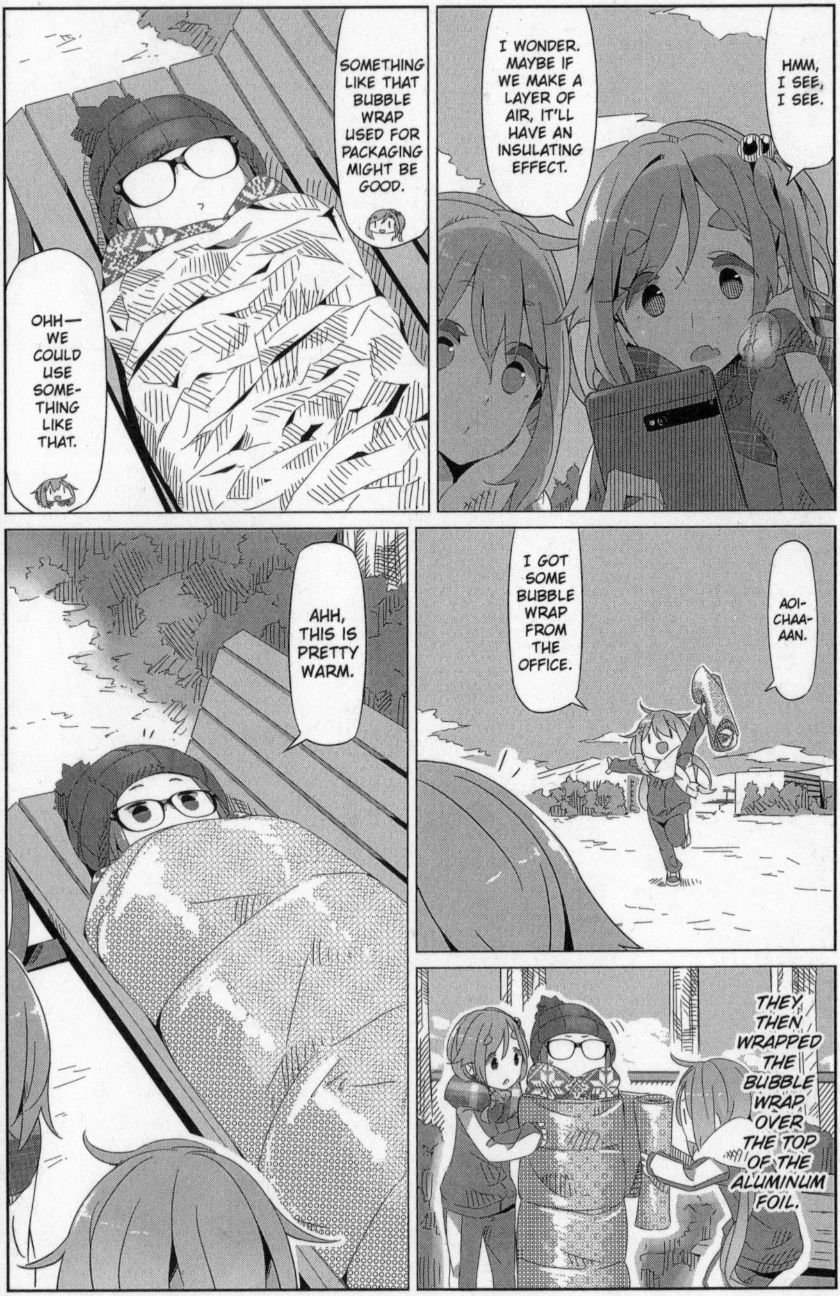
HMM, I SEE, I SEE.
I WONDER. MAYBE IF WE MAKE A LAYER OF AIR, IT'LL HAVE AN INSULATING EFFECT.
SOMETHING LIKE THAT BUBBLE WRAP USED FOR PACKAGING MIGHT BE GOOD.
OHH— WE COULD USE SOME-THING LIKE THAT.
AOI-CHAA-AAN.
I GOT SOME BUBBLE WRAP FROM THE OFFICE.
THEY THEN WRAPPED THE BUBBLE WRAP OVER THE TOP OF THE ALUMINUM FOIL.
AHH, THIS IS PRETTY WARM.

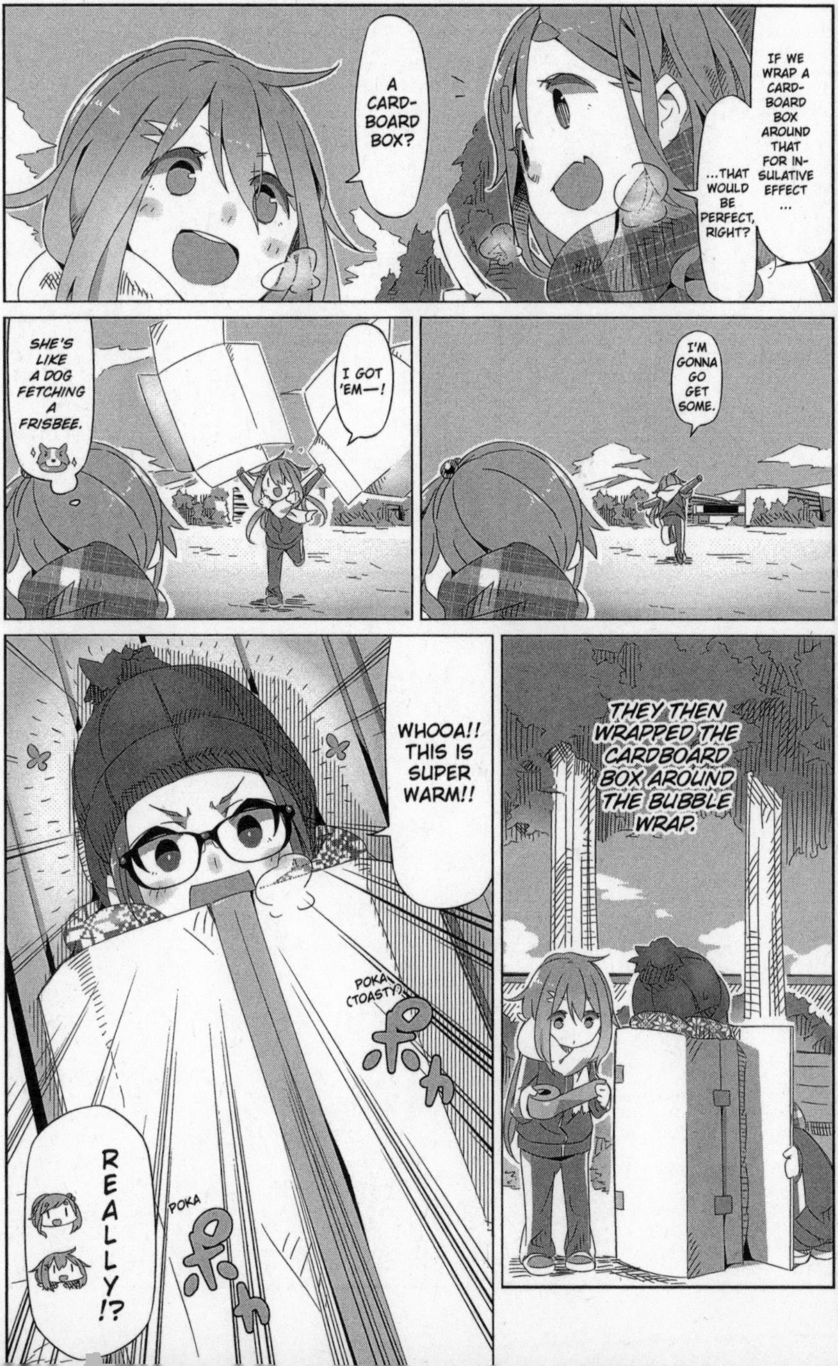
IF WE WRAP A CARDBOARD BOX AROUND THAT FOR INSULATIVE EFFECT...
...THAT WOULD BE PERFECT, RIGHT?
A CARDBOARD BOX?
I'M GONNA GO GET SOME.
I GOT 'EM—!
SHE'S LIKE A DOG FETCHING A FRISBEE.
THEY THEN WRAPPED THE CARDBOARD BOX AROUND THE BUBBLE WRAP.
WHOOA!! THIS IS SUPER WARM!!
POKA (TOASTY)
REALLY!?
POKA

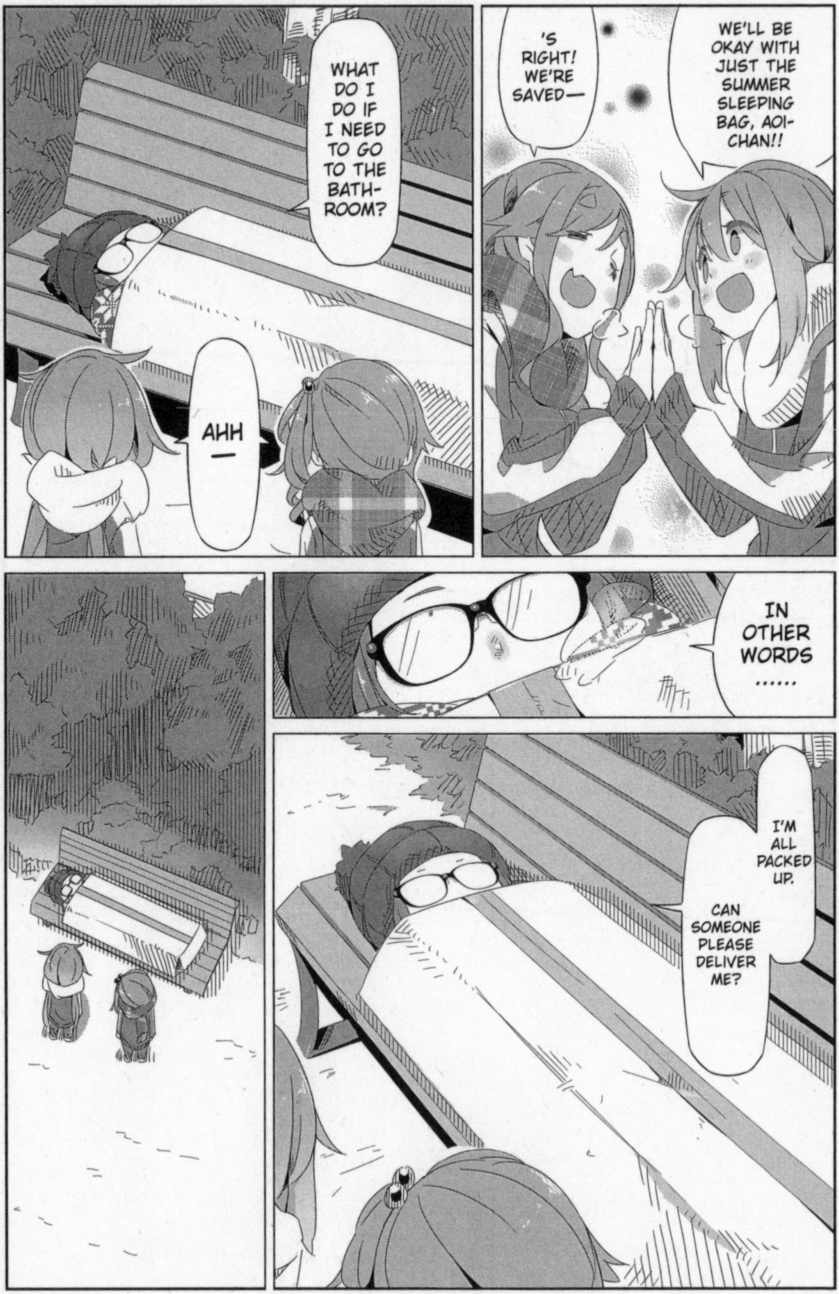
WE'LL BE OKAY WITH JUST THE SUMMER SLEEPING BAG, AOI-CHAN!!
'S RIGHT! WE'RE SAVED—
WHAT DO I DO IF I NEED TO GO TO THE BATH-ROOM?
AHH—
IN OTHER WORDS......
I'M ALL PACKED UP.
CAN SOMEONE PLEASE DELIVER ME?

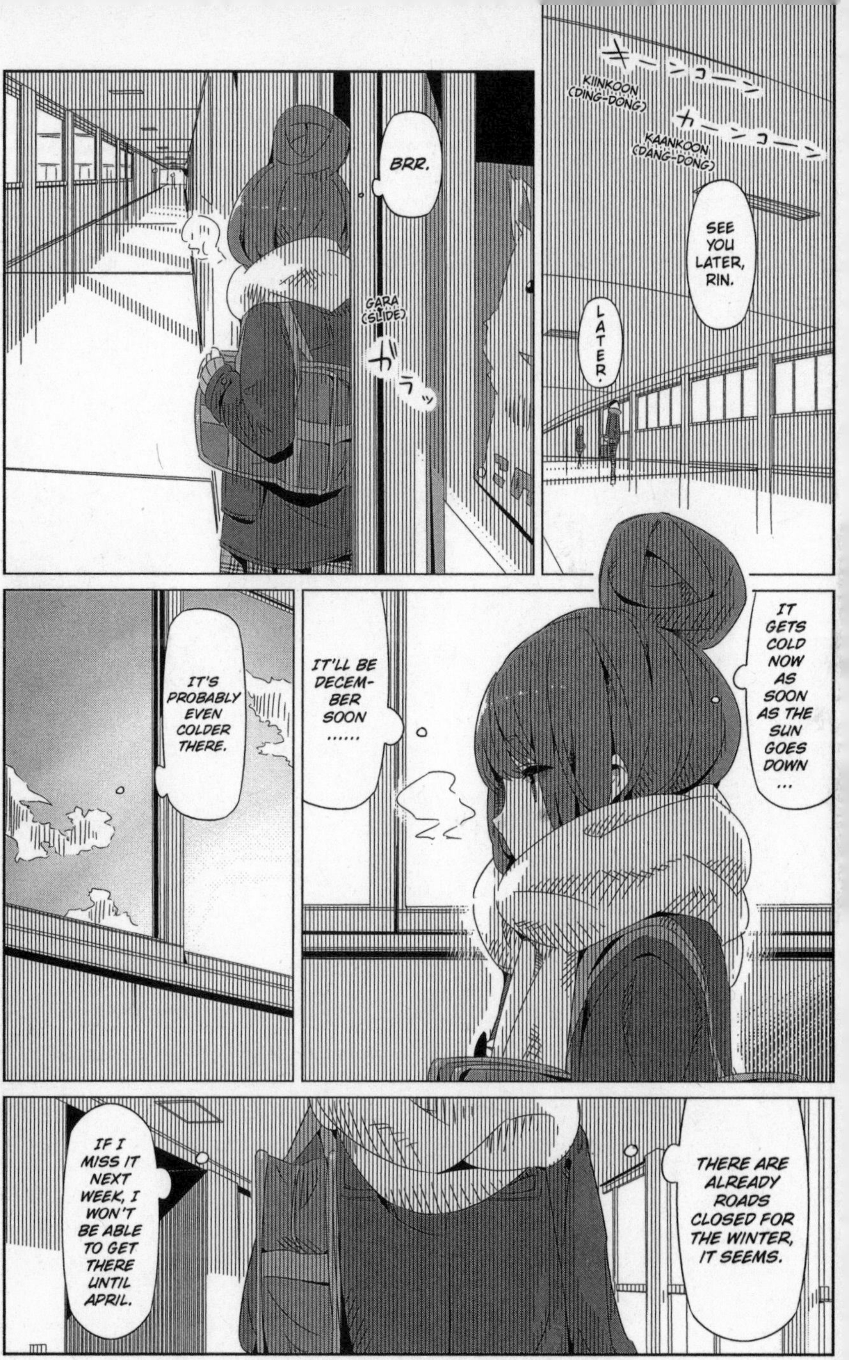
キーンコーン
KIINKOON (DING-DONG)
カーンコーン
KAANKOON (DANG-DONG)
SEE YOU LATER, RIN.
LATER.
BRR.
GARA (SLIDE)
ガラッ
IT GETS COLD NOW AS SOON AS THE SUN GOES DOWN...
IT'LL BE DECEMBER SOON......
IT'S PROBABLY EVEN COLDER THERE.
THERE ARE ALREADY ROADS CLOSED FOR THE WINTER, IT SEEMS.
IF I MISS IT NEXT WEEK, I WON'T BE ABLE TO GET THERE UNTIL APRIL.

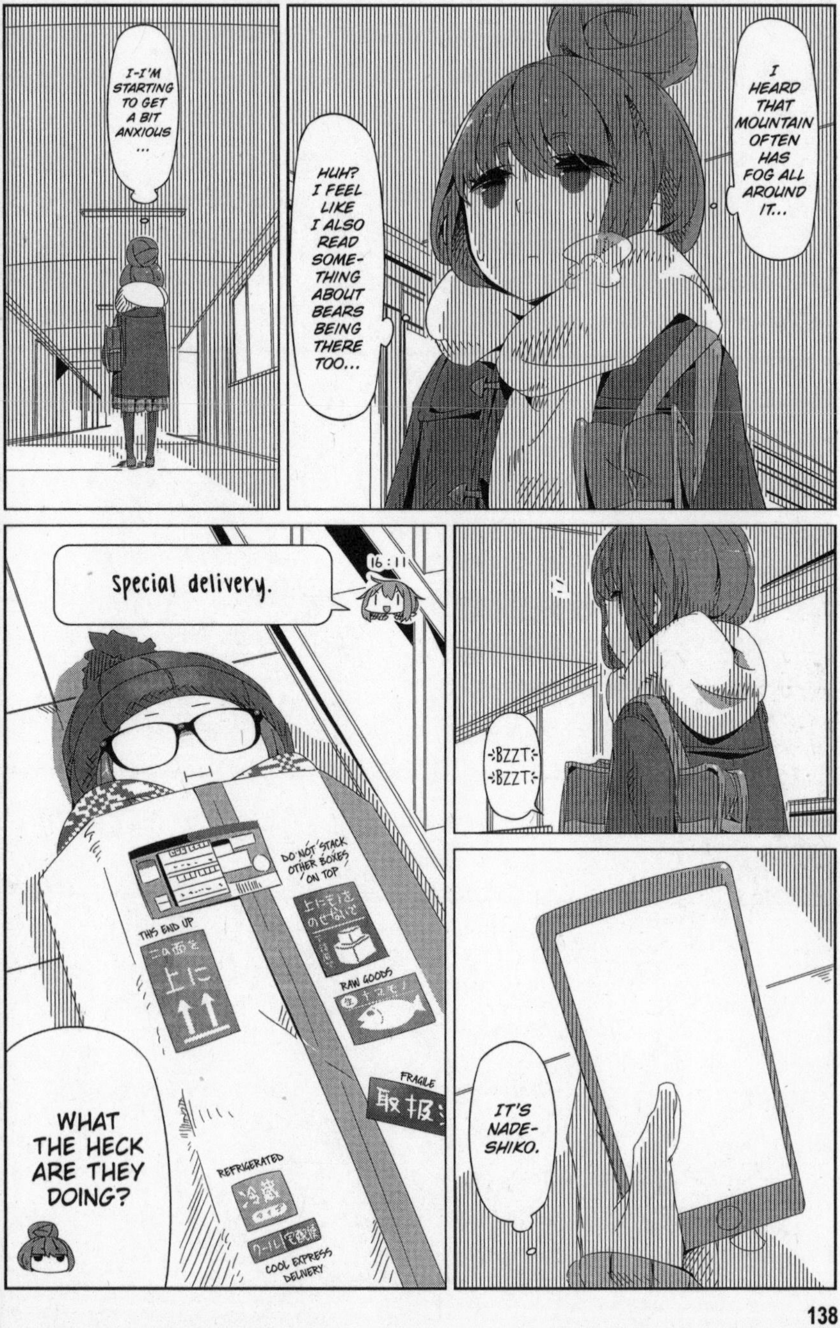
I HEARD THAT MOUNTAIN OFTEN HAS FOG ALL AROUND IT...
HUH? I FEEL LIKE I ALSO READ SOME-THING ABOUT BEARS BEING THERE TOO...
I-I'M STARTING TO GET A BIT ANXIOUS ...
BZZT BZZT
IT'S NADE-SHIKO.
16:11
Special delivery.
DO NOT STACK OTHER BOXES ON TOP
THIS END UP
この面を
上に
RAW GOODS
FRAGILE
REFRIGERATED
冷蔵
COOL EXPRESS DELIVERY
WHAT THE HECK ARE THEY DOING?

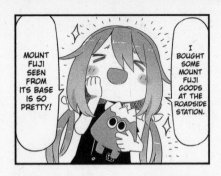

I BOUGHT SOME MOUNT FUJI GOODS AT THE ROADSIDE STATION.
MOUNT FUJI SEEN FROM ITS BASE IS SO PRETTY!
YOU JUST WON'T SHUT UP ABOUT MOUNT FUJI, SO STARTING TODAY, YOU'LL BE KNOWN AS "FUJIKO."
SHIRT: I LOVE TO SKI MOUNT FUJI
I LIKE IT!!
REALLY?

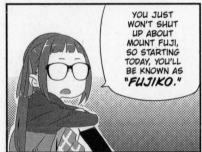

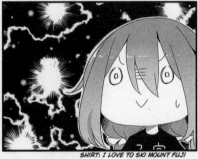

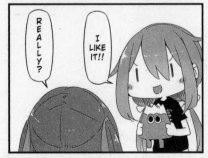

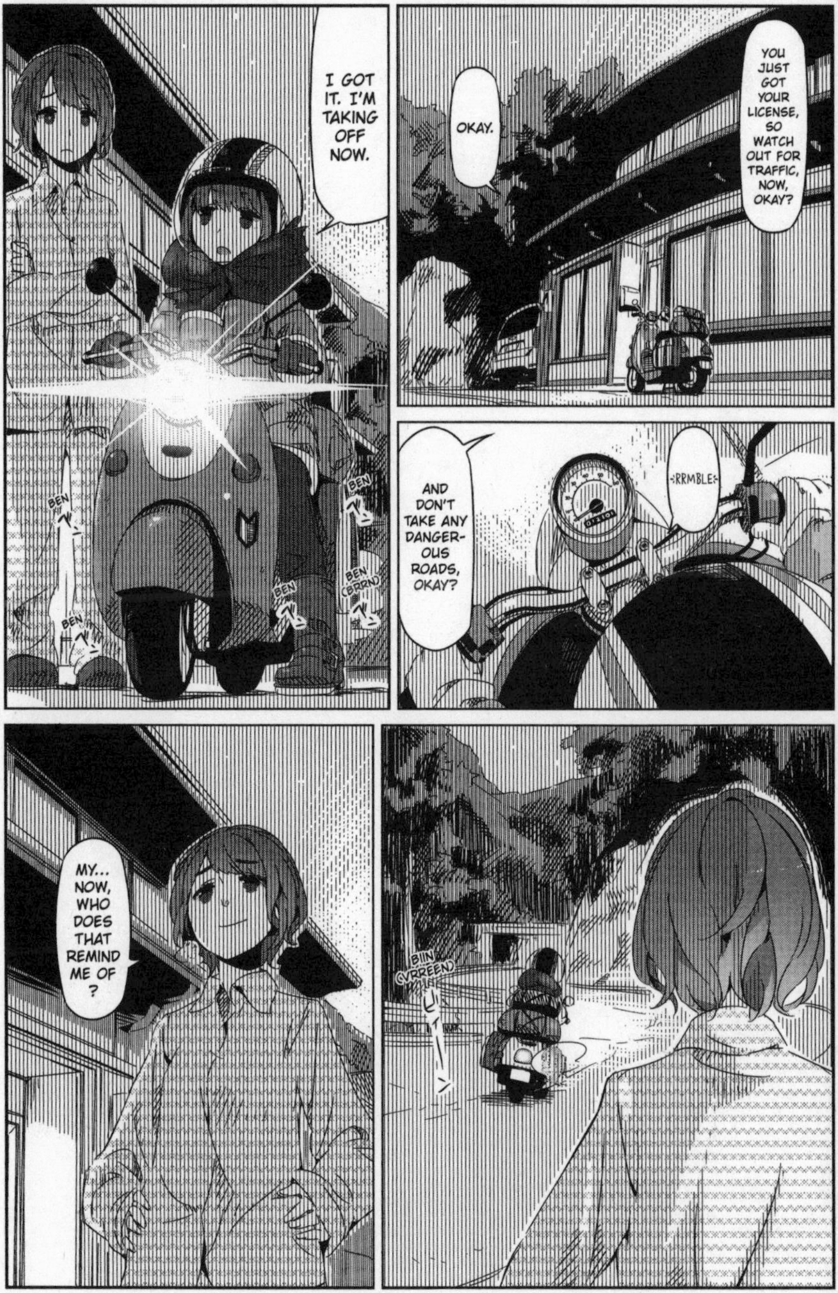
YOU JUST GOT YOUR LICENSE, SO WATCH OUT FOR TRAFFIC, NOW, OKAY?
OKAY.
AND DON'T TAKE ANY DANGER-OUS ROADS, OKAY?
RRRMBLE
I GOT IT. I'M TAKING OFF NOW.
BEN
BEN (BRRN)
BEN
BEN
BEN
BIIN (VRREEN)
MY... NOW, WHO DOES THAT REMIND ME OF?

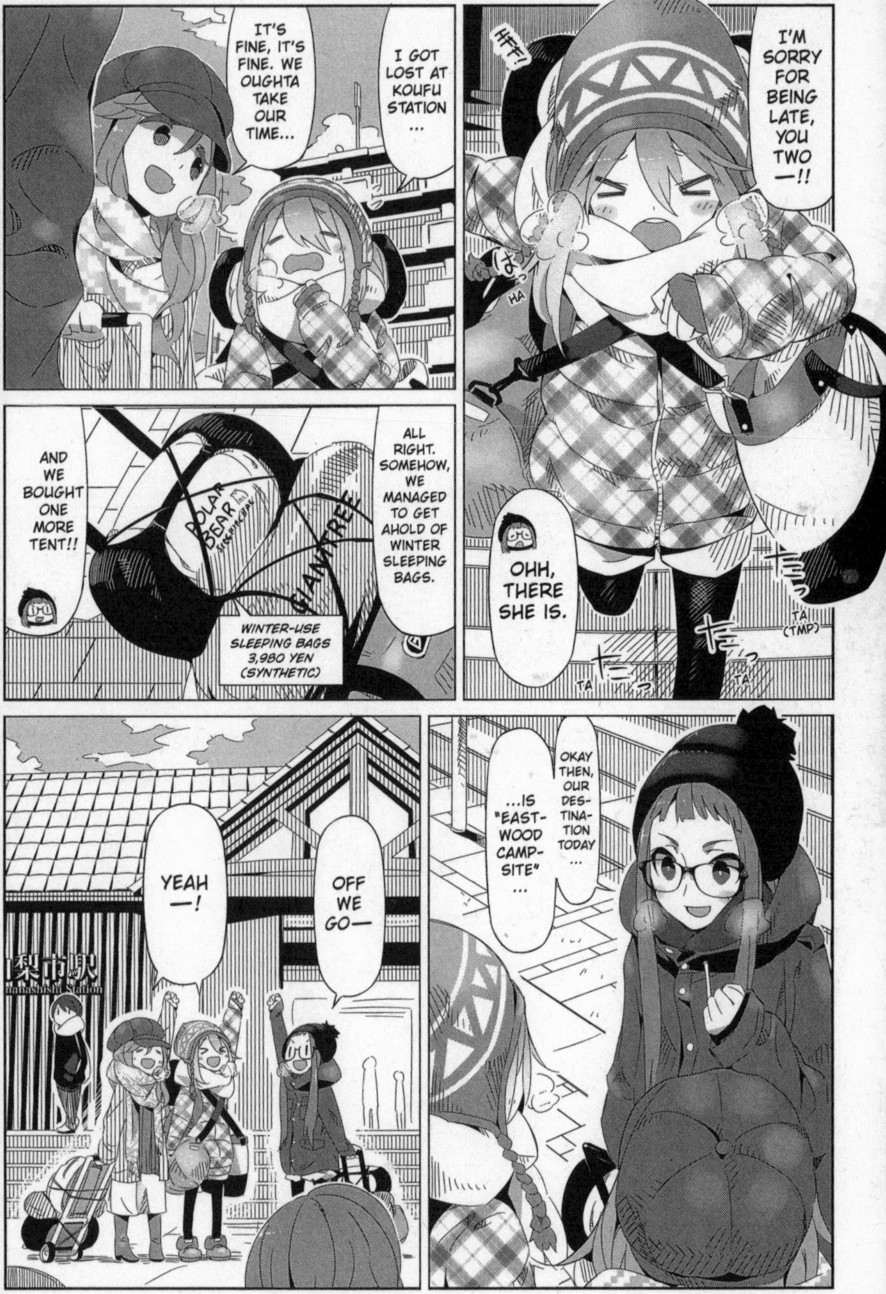
I'M SORRY FOR BEING LATE, YOU TWO—!!
HA
OHH, THERE SHE IS.
TA (TMP)
TA
TA
I GOT LOST AT KOUFU STATION ...
IT'S FINE, IT'S FINE. WE OUGHTA TAKE OUR TIME...
ALL RIGHT. SOMEHOW, WE MANAGED TO GET AHOLD OF WINTER SLEEPING BAGS.
POLAR BEAR
GIANTREE
WINTER-USE SLEEPING BAGS 3,980 YEN (SYNTHETIC)
AND WE BOUGHT ONE MORE TENT!!
OKAY THEN, OUR DESTINATION TODAY ...
...IS "EASTWOOD CAMPSITE" ...
OFF WE GO—
YEAH—!
梨市駅

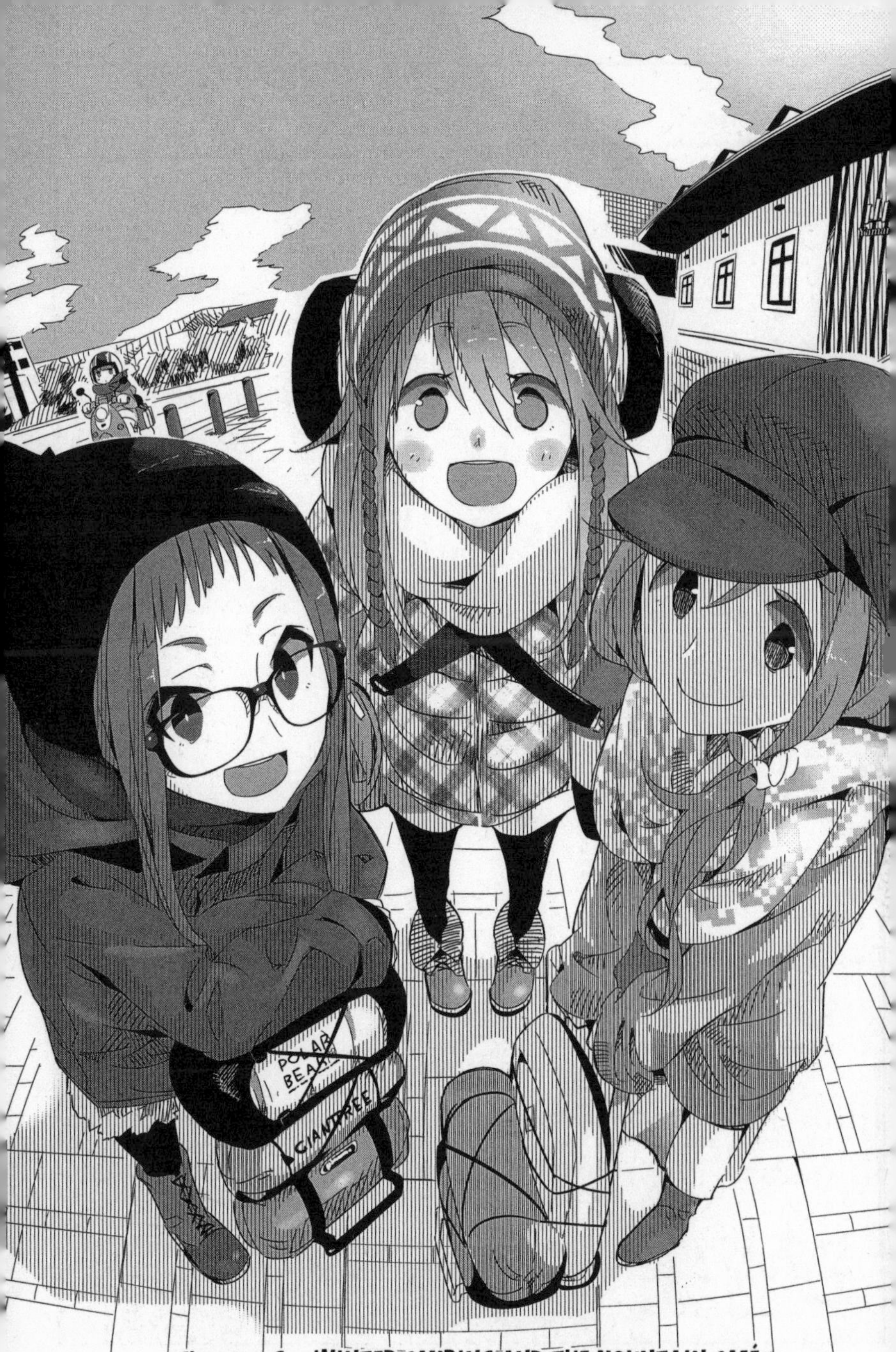
GIANTREE

Chapter 6 WINTER CAMPING AND THE MOUNTAIN CAFÉ

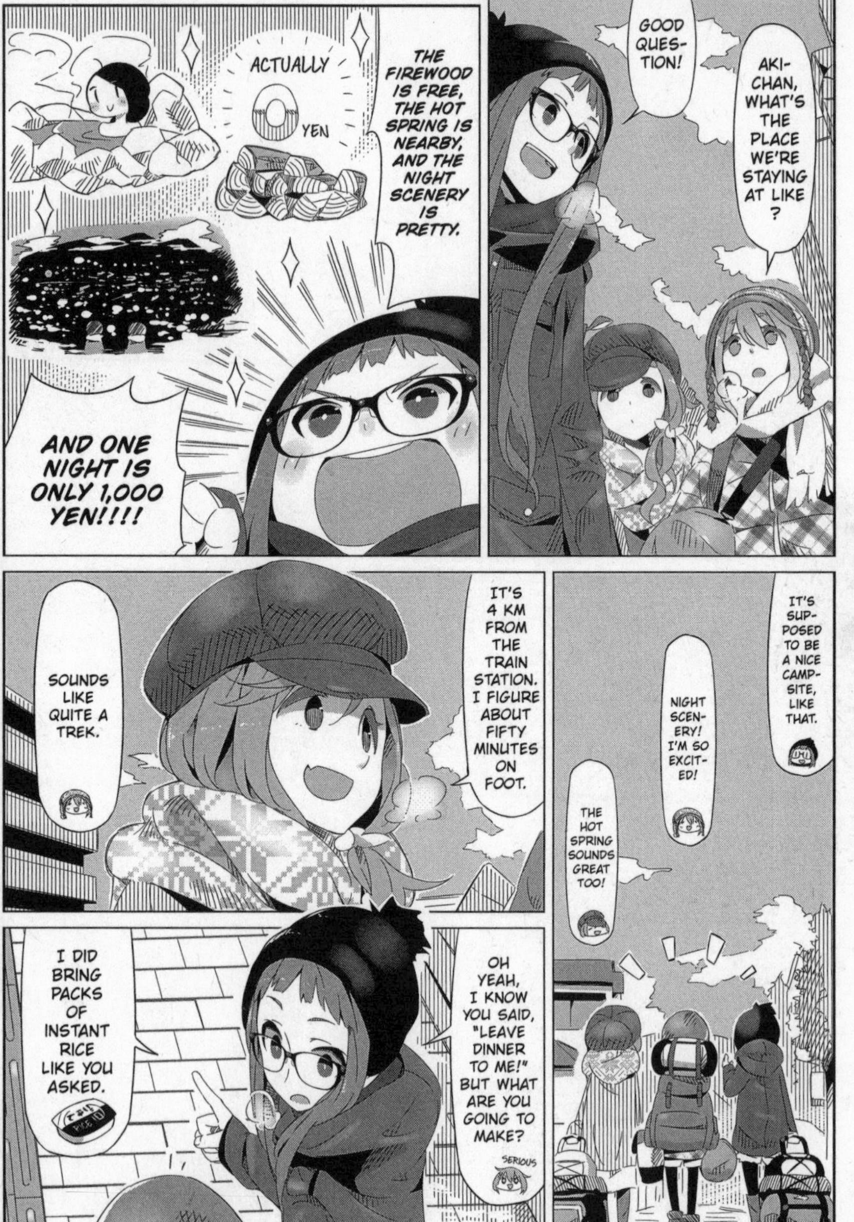
AKI-CHAN, WHAT'S THE PLACE WE'RE STAYING AT LIKE?
GOOD QUESTION!
THE FIREWOOD IS FREE, THE HOT SPRING IS NEARBY, AND THE NIGHT SCENERY IS PRETTY.
ACTUALLY
0
YEN
AND ONE NIGHT IS ONLY 1,000 YEN!!!!
IT'S SUPPOSED TO BE A NICE CAMPSITE, LIKE THAT.
NIGHT SCENERY! I'M SO EXCITED!
THE HOT SPRING SOUNDS GREAT TOO!
IT'S 4 KM FROM THE TRAIN STATION. I FIGURE ABOUT FIFTY MINUTES ON FOOT.
SOUNDS LIKE QUITE A TREK.
OH YEAH, I KNOW YOU SAID, "LEAVE DINNER TO ME!" BUT WHAT ARE YOU GOING TO MAKE?
SERIOUS
I DID BRING PACKS OF INSTANT RICE LIKE YOU ASKED.

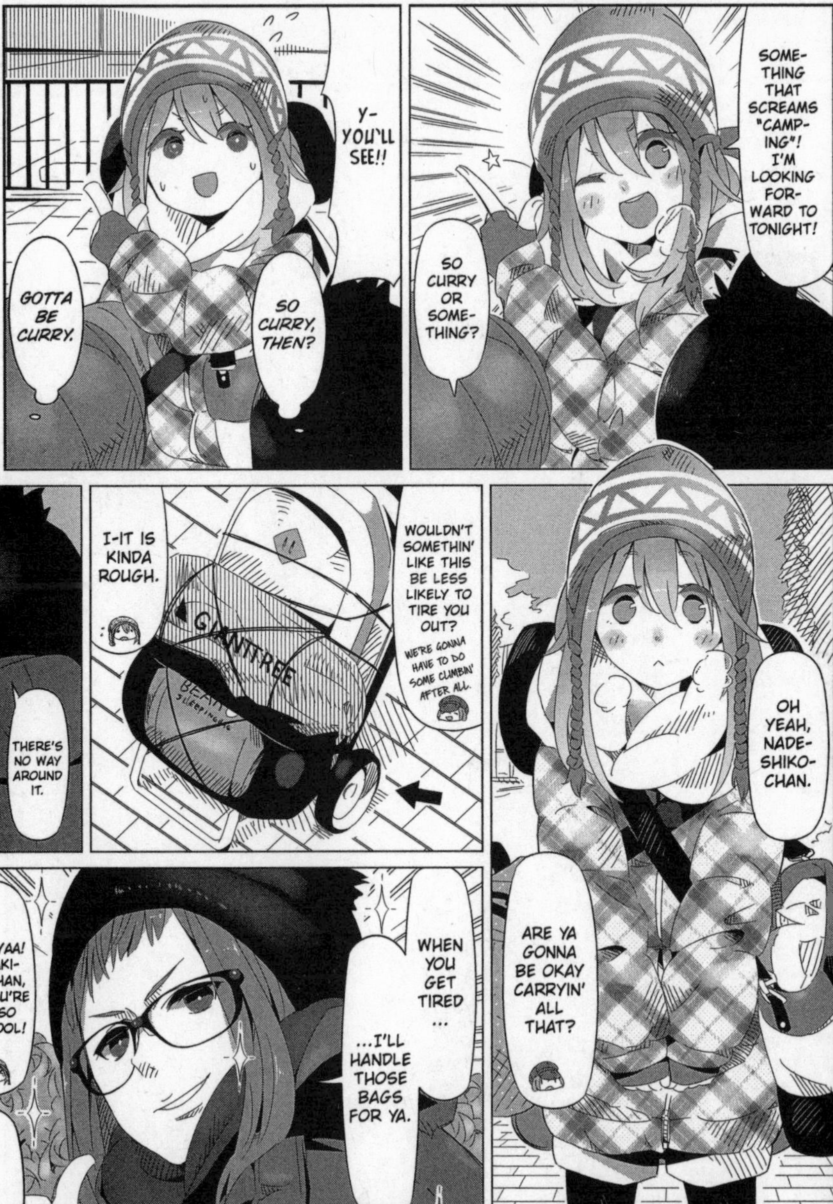
SOMETHING THAT SCREAMS "CAMPING"! I'M LOOKING FORWARD TO TONIGHT!
SO CURRY OR SOMETHING?
Y-YOU'LL SEE!!
SO CURRY, THEN?
GOTTA BE CURRY.
OH YEAH, NADESHIKO-CHAN.
ARE YA GONNA BE OKAY CARRYIN' ALL THAT?
WOULDN'T SOMETHIN' LIKE THIS BE LESS LIKELY TO TIRE YOU OUT?
WE'RE GONNA HAVE TO DO SOME CLIMBIN' AFTER ALL.
GIANTTREE
I-IT IS KINDA ROUGH.
THERE'S NO WAY AROUND IT.
WHEN YOU GET TIRED...
...I'LL HANDLE THOSE BAGS FOR YA.
KYAA! AKI-CHAN, YOU'RE SO COOL!
KYA!

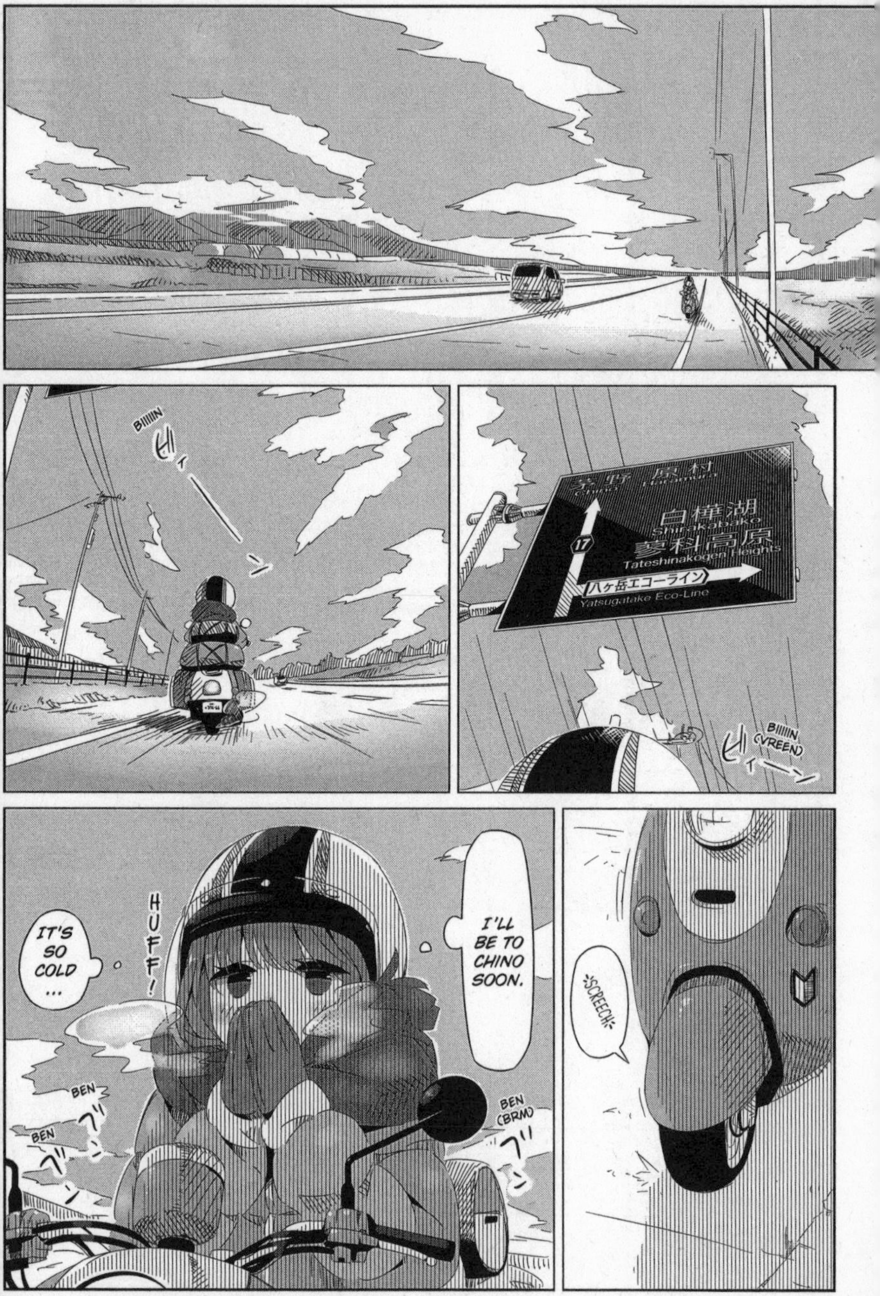

原村
Haramura
白樺湖
Shirakabako
蓼科高原
Tateshinakogen Heights
17
八ヶ岳エコーライン
Yatsugatake Eco-Line
BIIIIIN (VREEN)
ビィーン
BIIIIIN
ビィーーン
SCREECH
I'LL BE TO CHINO SOON.
HUFF!
IT'S SO COLD ...
BEN (BRM)
ブン
BEN
ブン
BEN
ブン

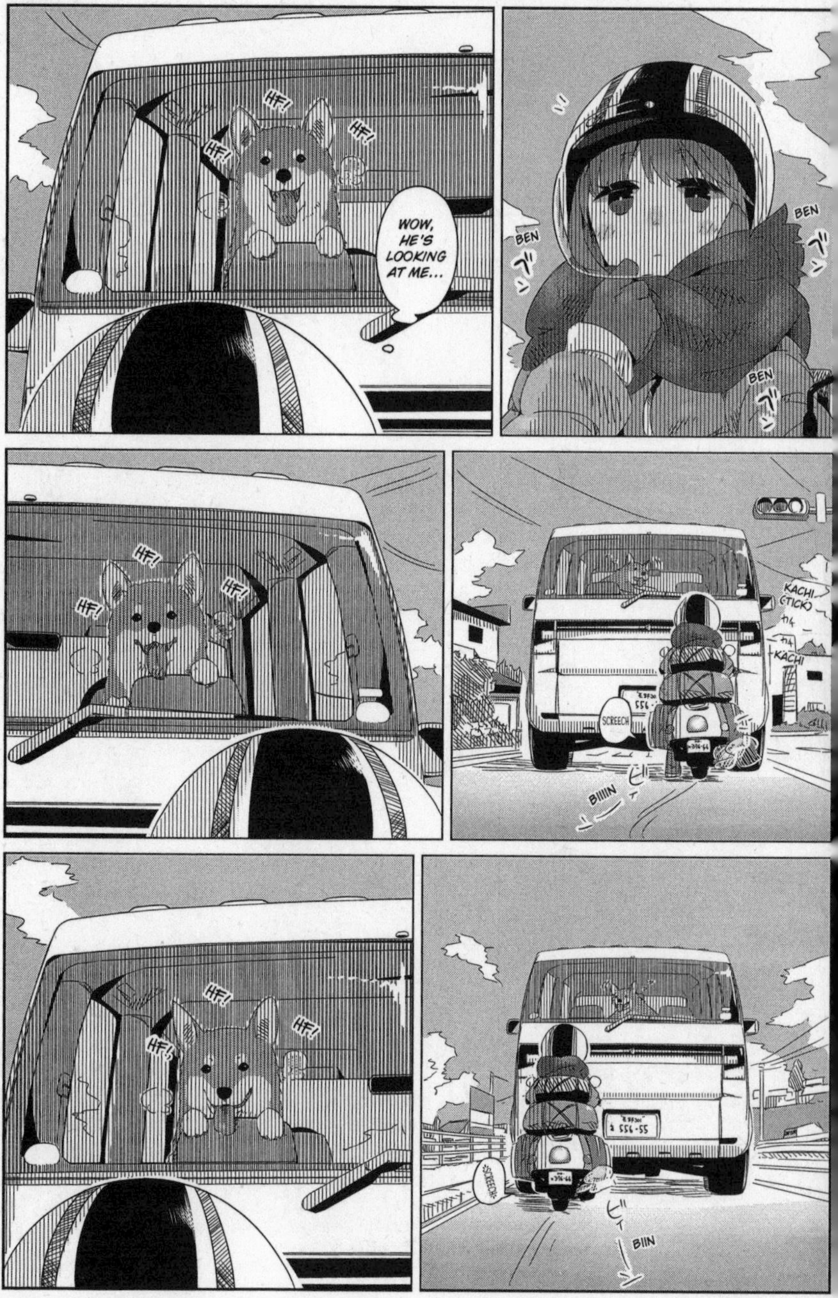
BEN
BEN
BEN
HF!
HF!
HF!
WOW, HE'S LOOKING AT ME...
KACHI (TICK)
KACHI
SCREECH
BIIIIN
HF!
HF!
HF!
SCREECH
BIIN
HF!
HF!
HF!

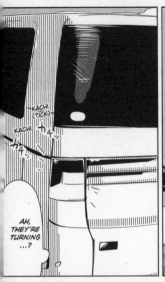

KACHI
(TICK)

AH,
THEY'RE
TURNING
...?

IT'S
SO CUTE
......

BEN

BEN
(IDLE)

BURORORORO
(VRRRROOOM)

HF

BYE-
BYE.

BEN

BEN

BEN

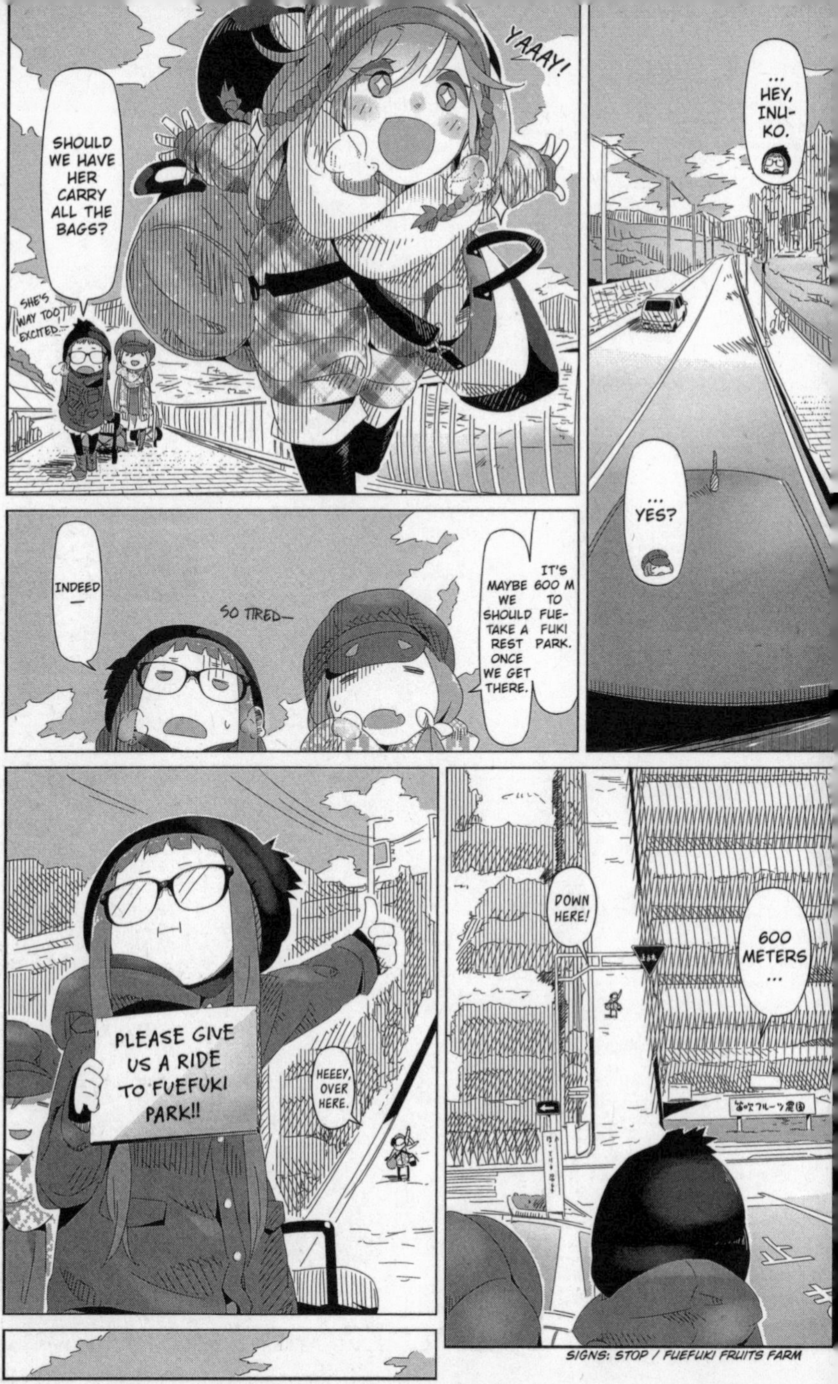
... HEY, INUKO.
... YES?
YAAAY!
SHOULD WE HAVE HER CARRY ALL THE BAGS?
SHE'S WAY TOO EXCITED...
IT'S 600 M TO FUEFUKI PARK. MAYBE WE SHOULD TAKE A REST ONCE WE GET THERE.
SO TIRED—
INDEED—
600 METERS...
DOWN HERE!
HEEEY, OVER HERE.
PLEASE GIVE US A RIDE TO FUEFUKI PARK!!

SIGNS: STOP / FUEFUKI FRUITS FARM

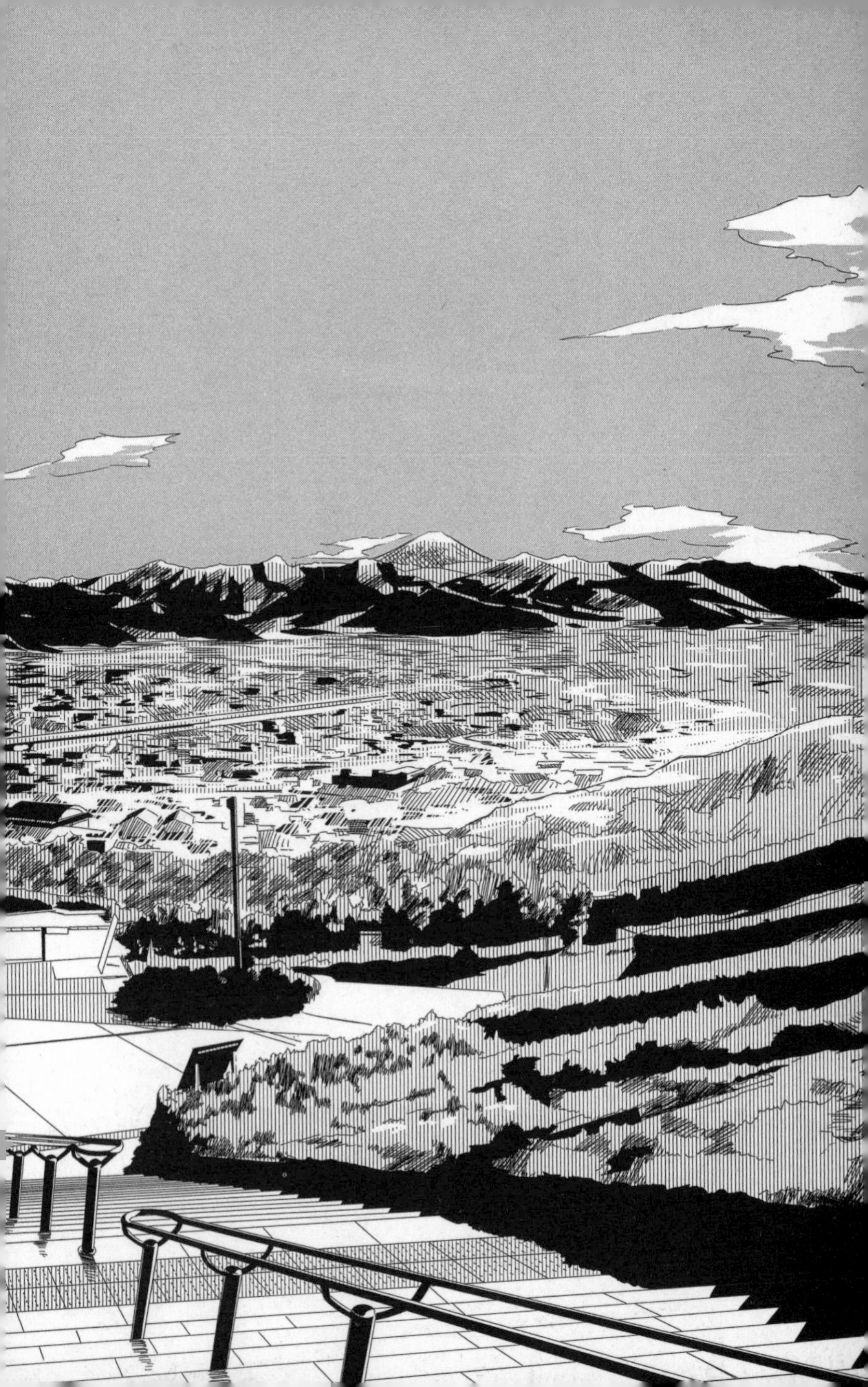

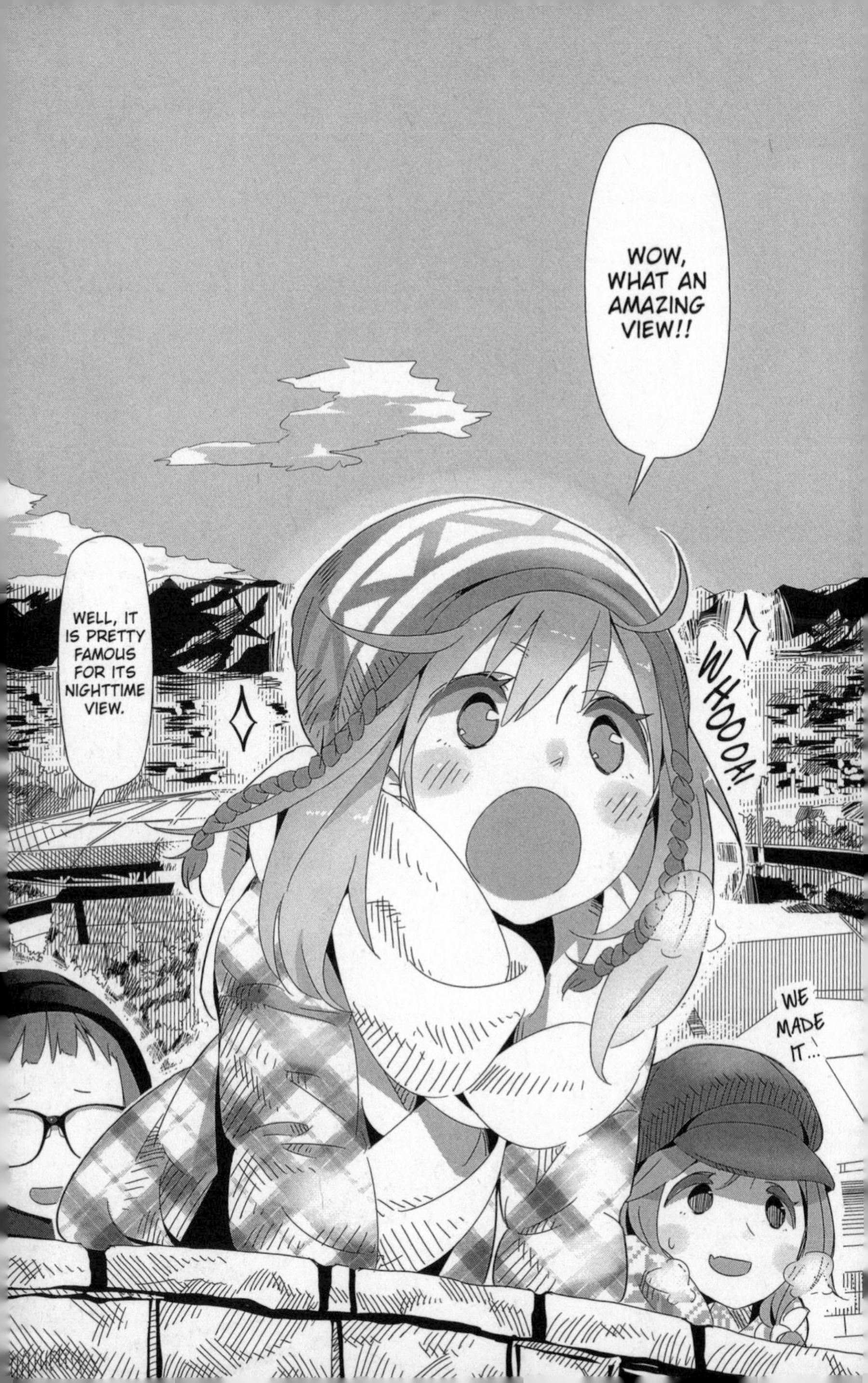
WOW, WHAT AN AMAZING VIEW!!
WHOOOA!
WELL, IT IS PRETTY FAMOUS FOR ITS NIGHTTIME VIEW.
WE MADE IT...

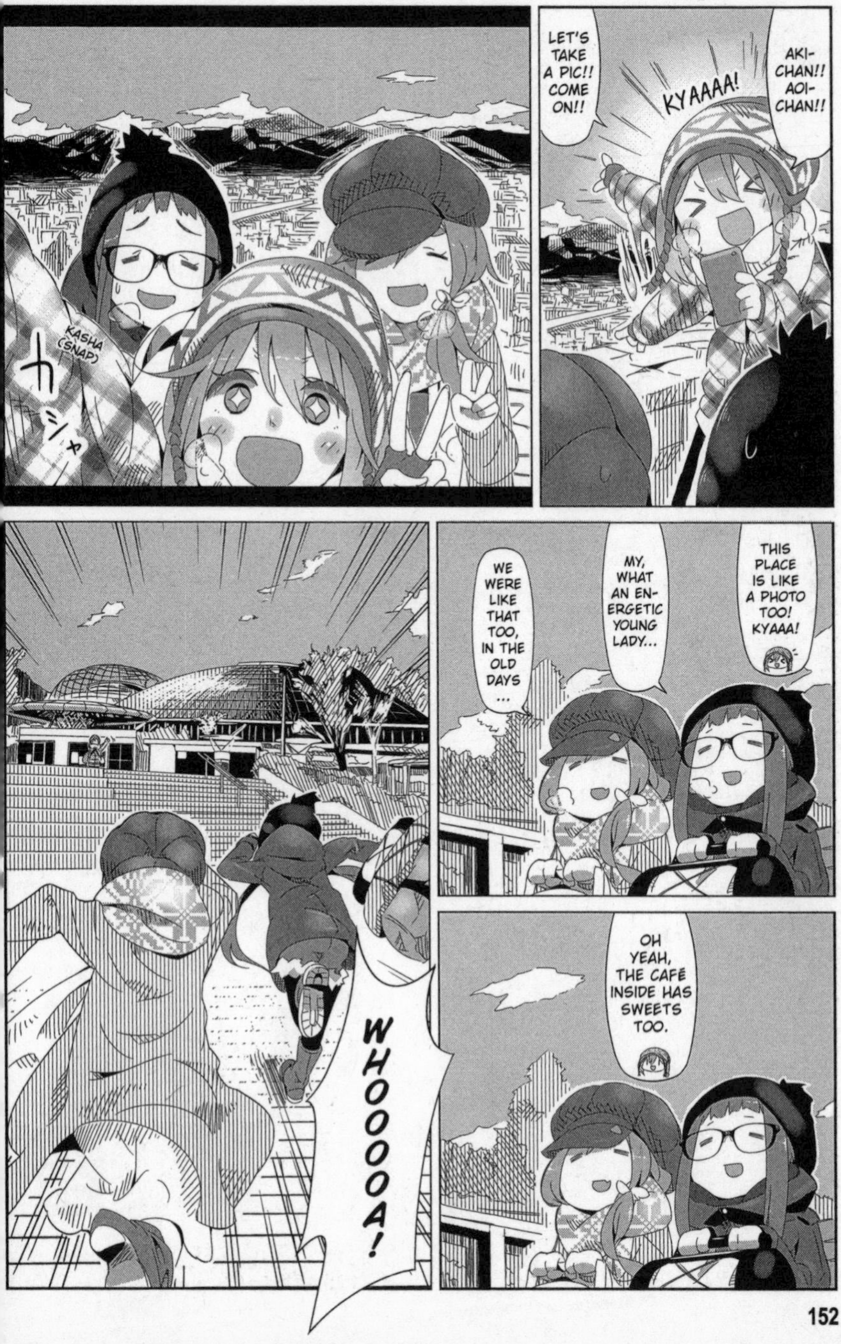
AKI-CHAN!! AOI-CHAN!!
KYAAAA!
LET'S TAKE A PIC!! COME ON!!
KASHA (SNAP)
カシャ
THIS PLACE IS LIKE A PHOTO TOO! KYAAA!
MY, WHAT AN ENERGETIC YOUNG LADY...
WE WERE LIKE THAT TOO, IN THE OLD DAYS ...
OH YEAH, THE CAFÉ INSIDE HAS SWEETS TOO.
WHOOOOOA!

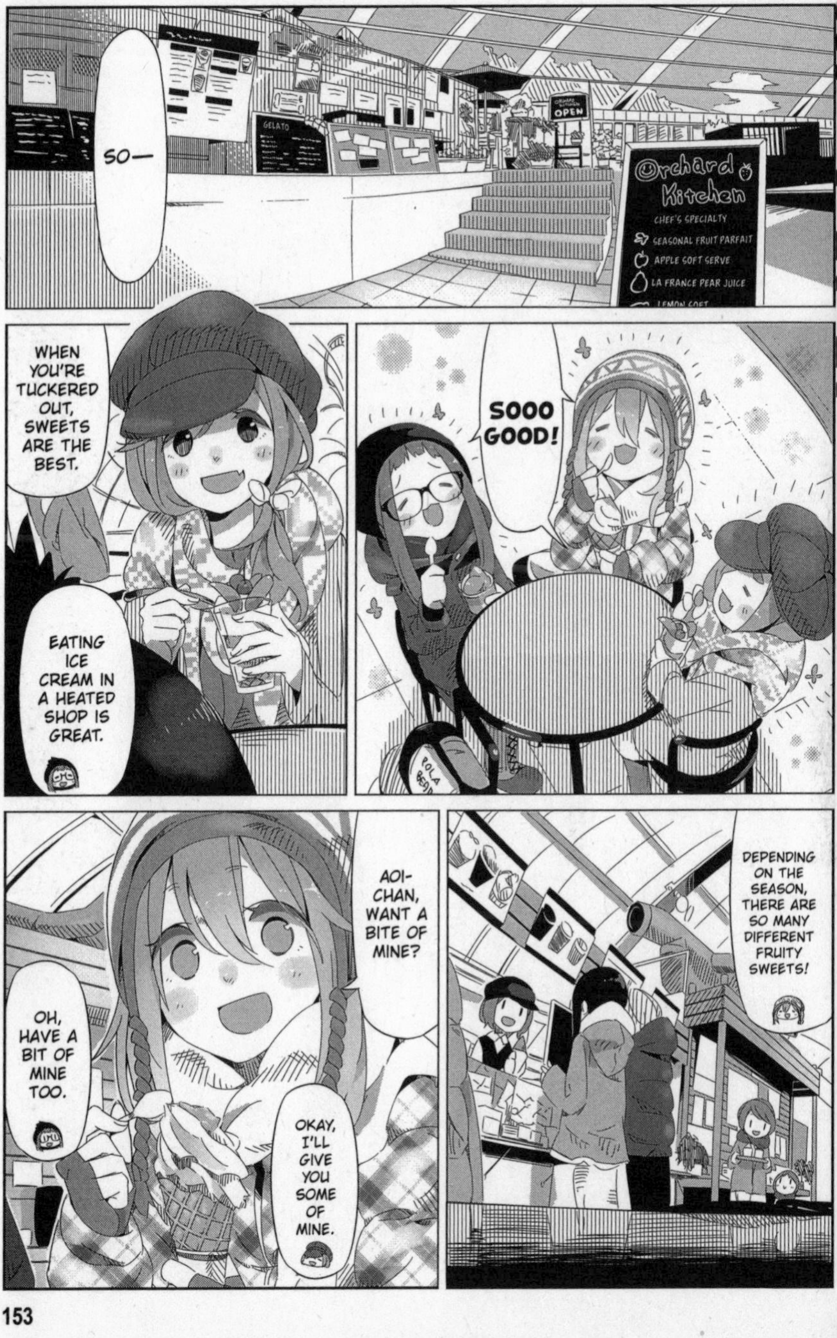
SO—
GELATO
OPEN
Orchard Kitchen
CHEF'S SPECIALTY
SEASONAL FRUIT PARFAIT
APPLE SOFT SERVE
LA FRANCE PEAR JUICE
SOOO GOOD!
WHEN YOU'RE TUCKERED OUT, SWEETS ARE THE BEST.
EATING ICE CREAM IN A HEATED SHOP IS GREAT.
DEPENDING ON THE SEASON, THERE ARE SO MANY DIFFERENT FRUITY SWEETS!
AOI-CHAN, WANT A BITE OF MINE?
OKAY, I'LL GIVE YOU SOME OF MINE.
OH, HAVE A BIT OF MINE TOO.

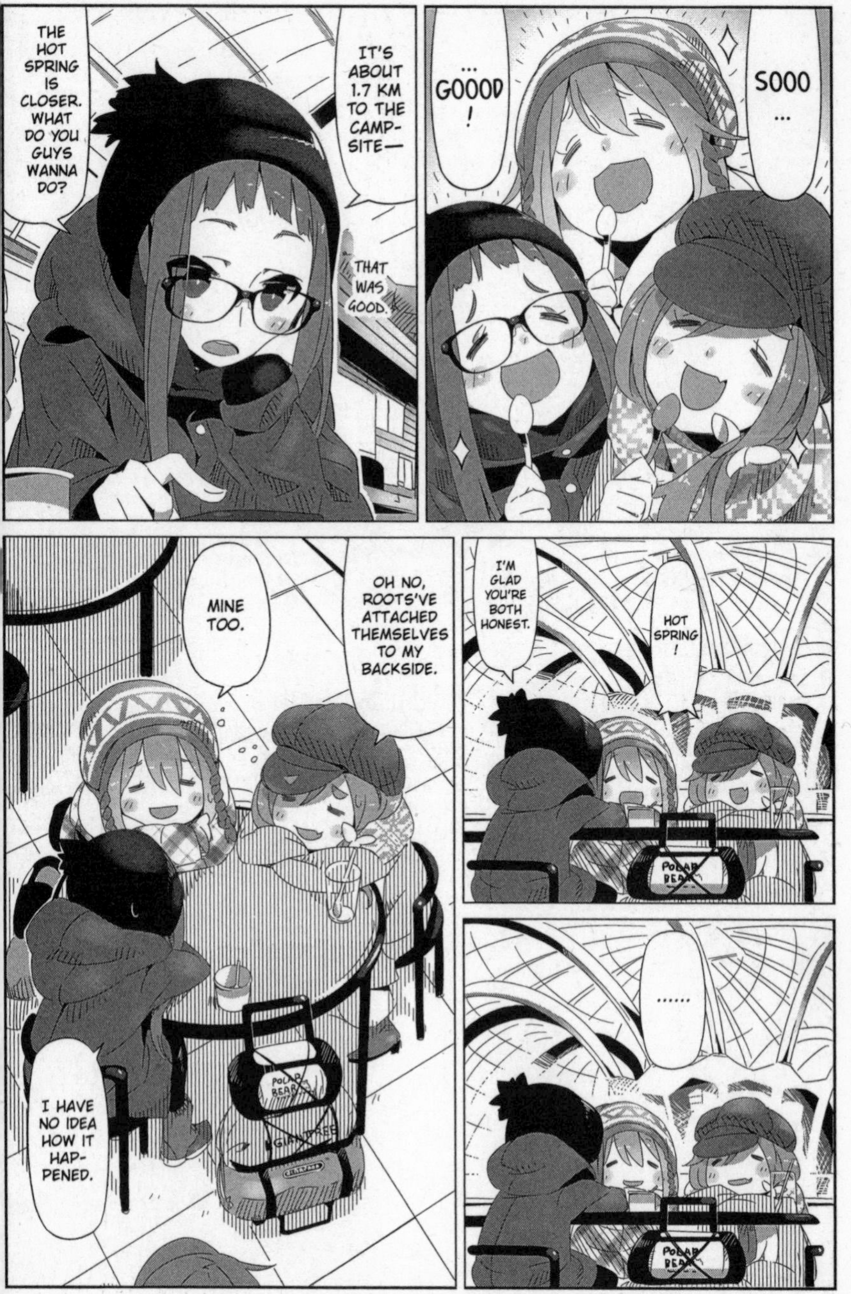
SOOO ...
... GOOOD !
IT'S ABOUT 1.7 KM TO THE CAMP-SITE—
THE HOT SPRING IS CLOSER. WHAT DO YOU GUYS WANNA DO?
THAT WAS GOOD.
HOT SPRING !
I'M GLAD YOU'RE BOTH HONEST.
POLAR BEAR
......
POLAR BEAR
OH NO, ROOTS'VE ATTACHED THEMSELVES TO MY BACKSIDE.
MINE TOO.
POLAR BEAR
GIANT TREE
I HAVE NO IDEA HOW IT HAP-PENED.

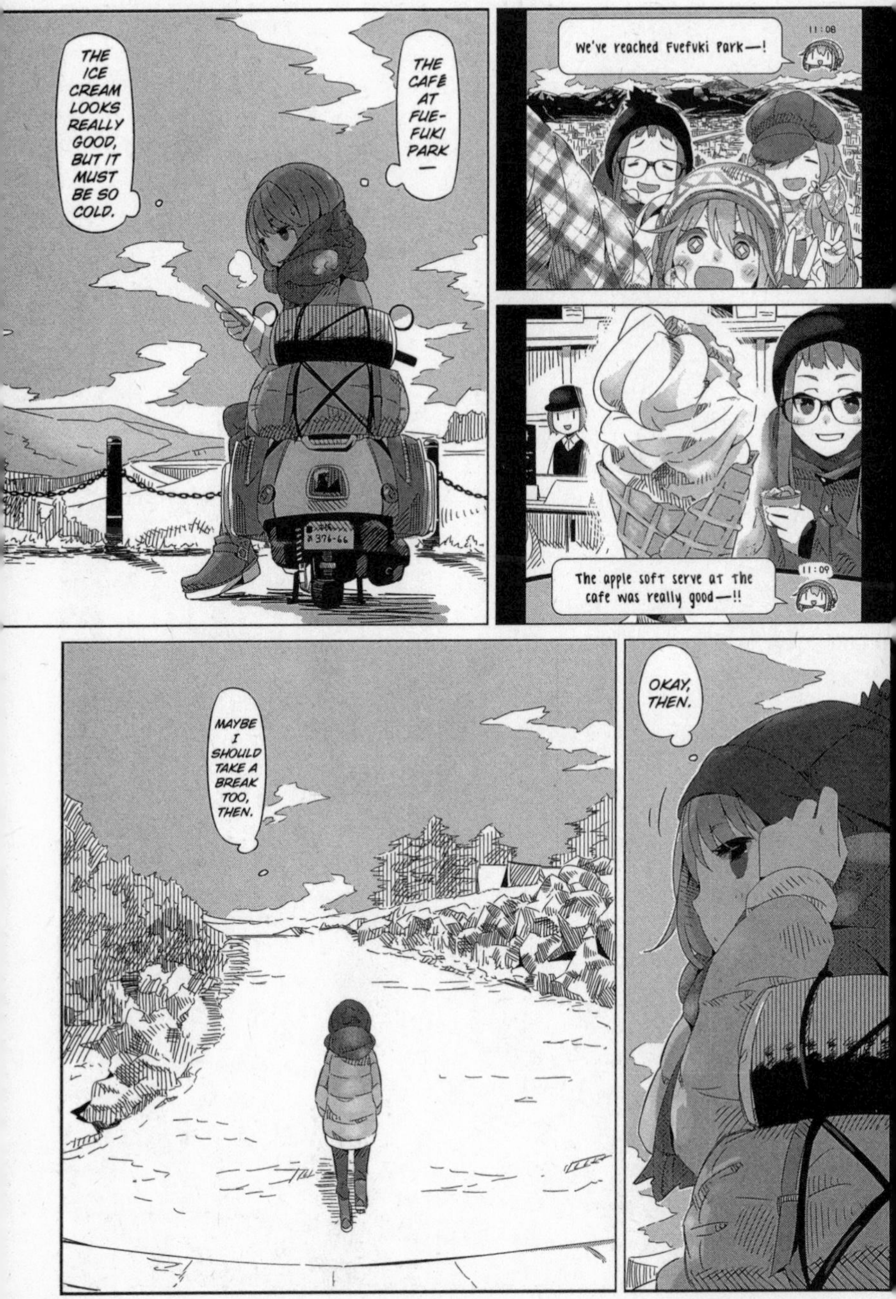
11:08
We've reached Fuefuki Park—!
The apple soft serve at the cafe was really good—!!
11:09
THE CAFÉ AT FUE-FUKI PARK—
THE ICE CREAM LOOKS REALLY GOOD, BUT IT MUST BE SO COLD.
OKAY, THEN.
MAYBE I SHOULD TAKE A BREAK TOO, THEN.

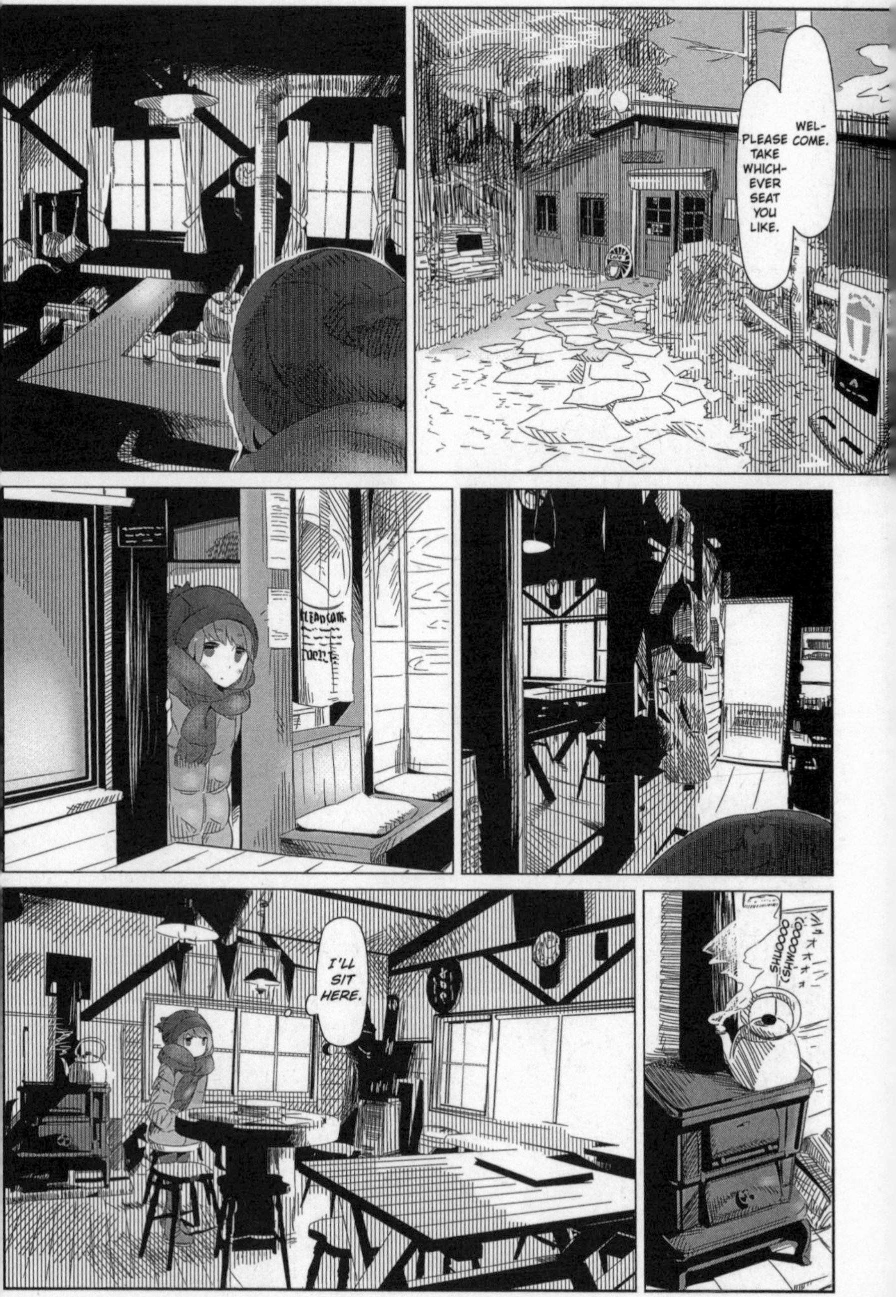
WEL-COME. PLEASE TAKE WHICH-EVER SEAT YOU LIKE.
(SHWOOOOO)
SHUOOOOO
I'LL SIT HERE.

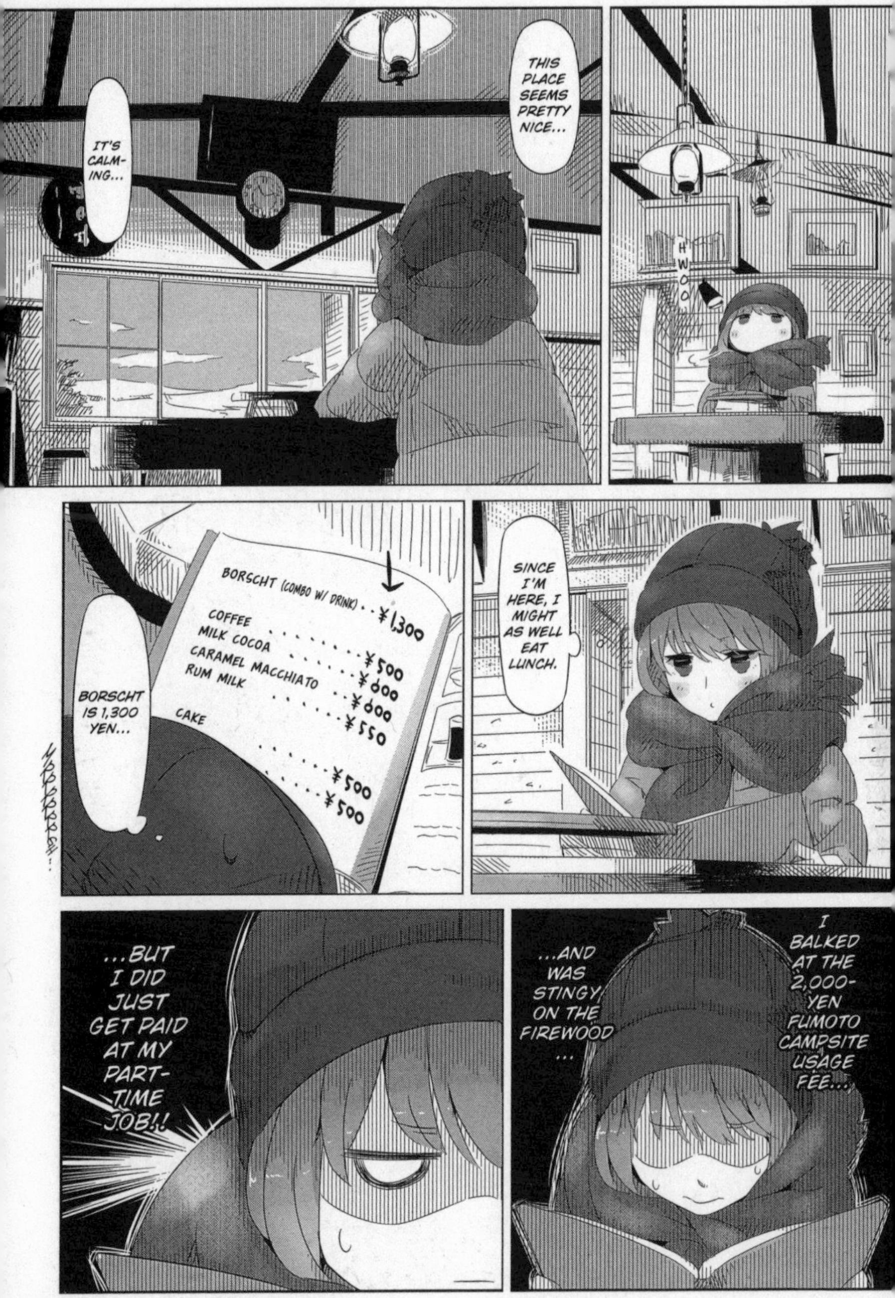
HWOO
THIS PLACE SEEMS PRETTY NICE...
IT'S CALMING...
SINCE I'M HERE, I MIGHT AS WELL EAT LUNCH.
BORSCHT (COMBO W/ DRINK) · · ¥1,300
COFFEE · · · · · · · ¥500
MILK COCOA · · · ¥600
CARAMEL MACCHIATO · · ¥600
RUM MILK · · · ¥550
CAKE · · · · · · ¥500
· · · ¥500
BORSCHT IS 1,300 YEN...
MRRRRRGH...
I BALKED AT THE 2,000-YEN FUMOTO CAMPSITE USAGE FEE...
...AND WAS STINGY ON THE FIREWOOD...
...BUT I DID JUST GET PAID AT MY PART-TIME JOB!!

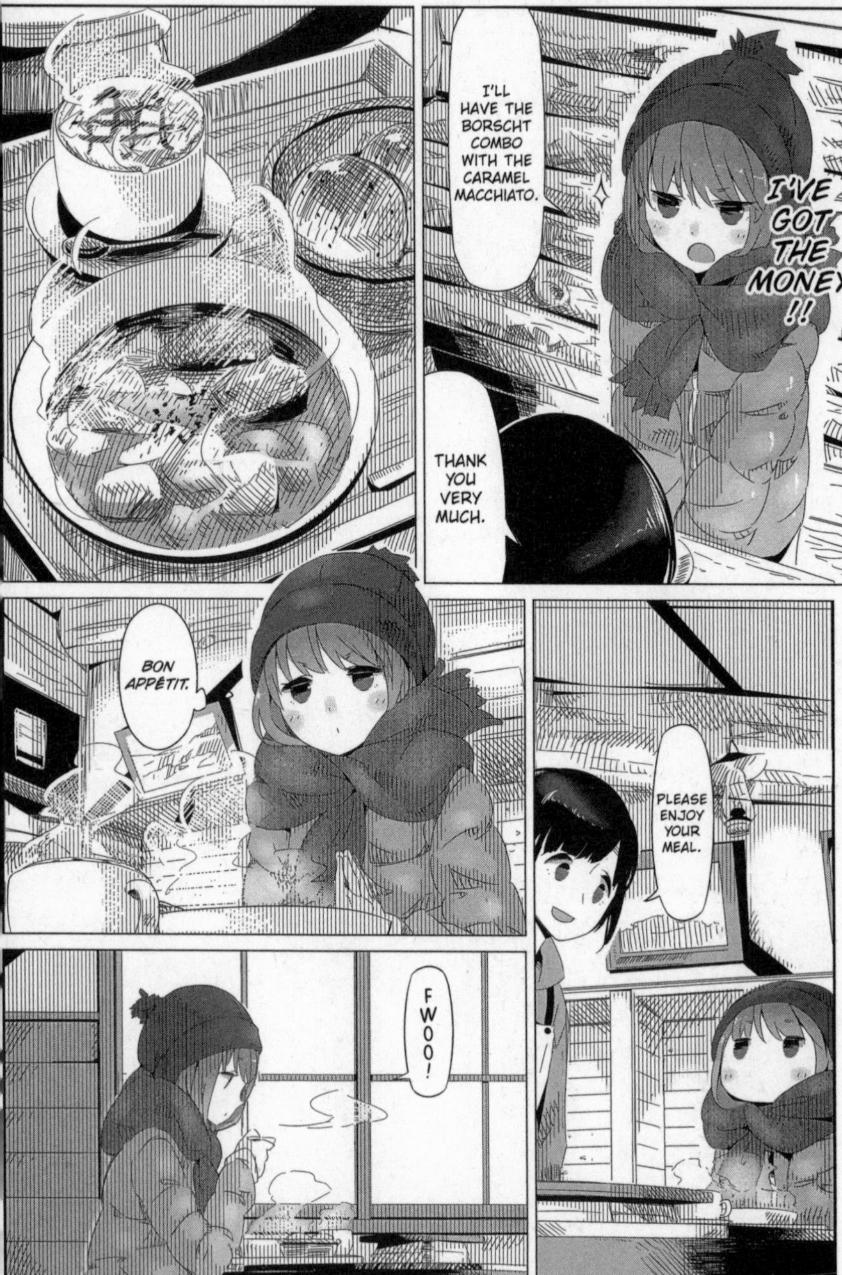
I'LL HAVE THE BORSCHT COMBO WITH THE CARAMEL MACCHIATO.
I'VE GOT THE MONEY!!
THANK YOU VERY MUCH.
PLEASE ENJOY YOUR MEAL.
BON APPÉTIT.
FWOO!

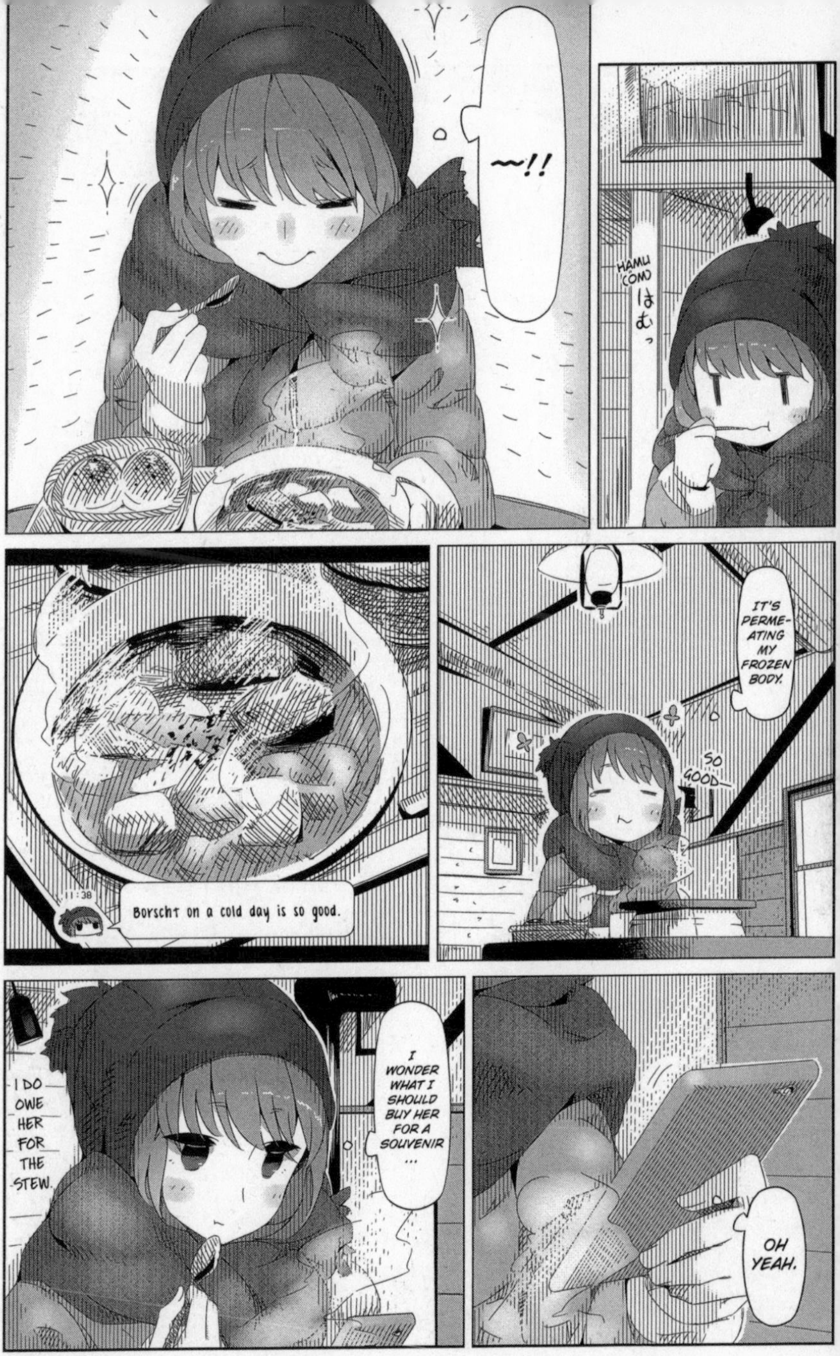
HAMU (OM)
はむっ
~!!
IT'S PERMEATING MY FROZEN BODY.
SO GOOD
11:38
Borscht on a cold day is so good.
OH YEAH.
I WONDER WHAT I SHOULD BUY HER FOR A SOUVENIR...
I DO OWE HER FOR THE STEW.

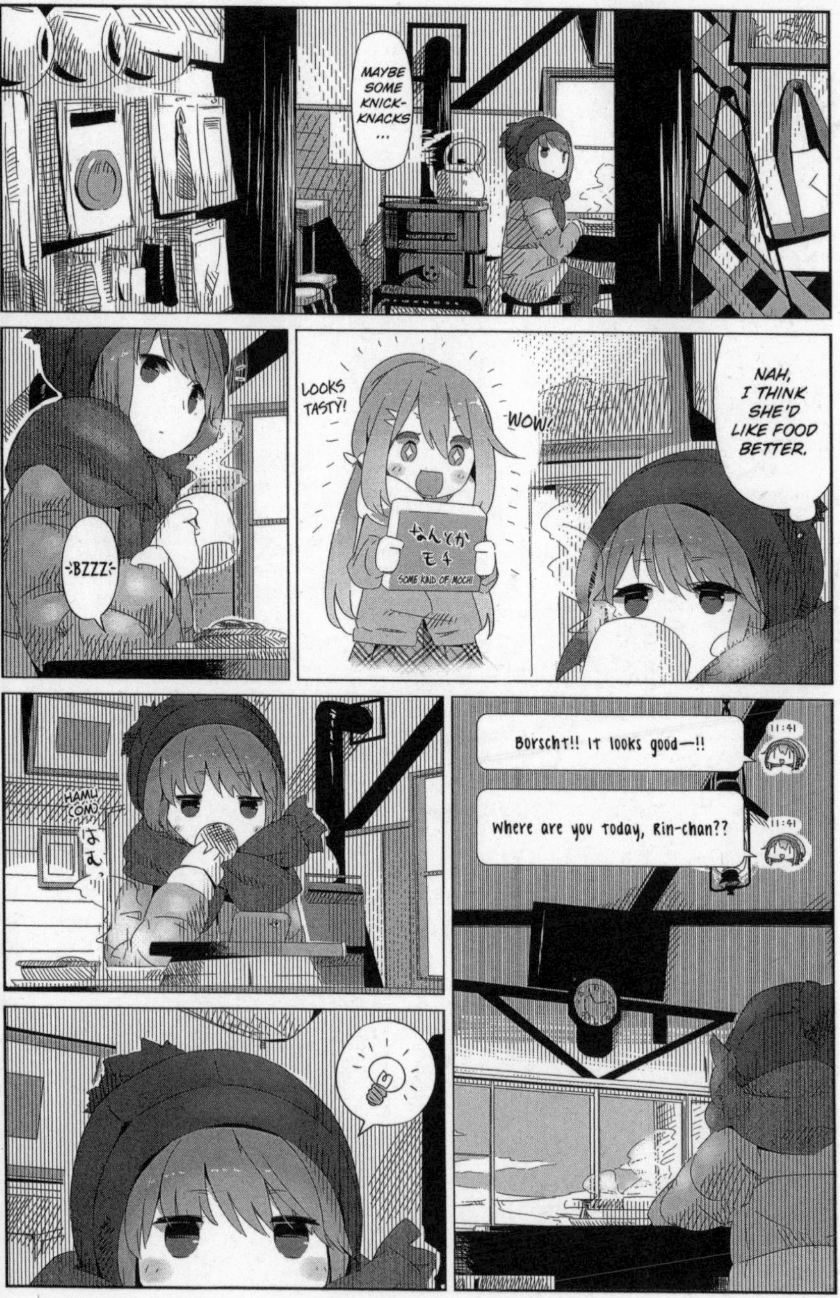
MAYBE SOME KNICK-KNACKS...
NAH, I THINK SHE'D LIKE FOOD BETTER.
LOOKS TASTY!
WOW!
なんとかモチ
SOME KIND OF MOCHI
-BZZZ-
Borscht!! It looks good—!!
11:41
Where are you today, Rin-chan??
11:41
HAMU (OM)
はむっ

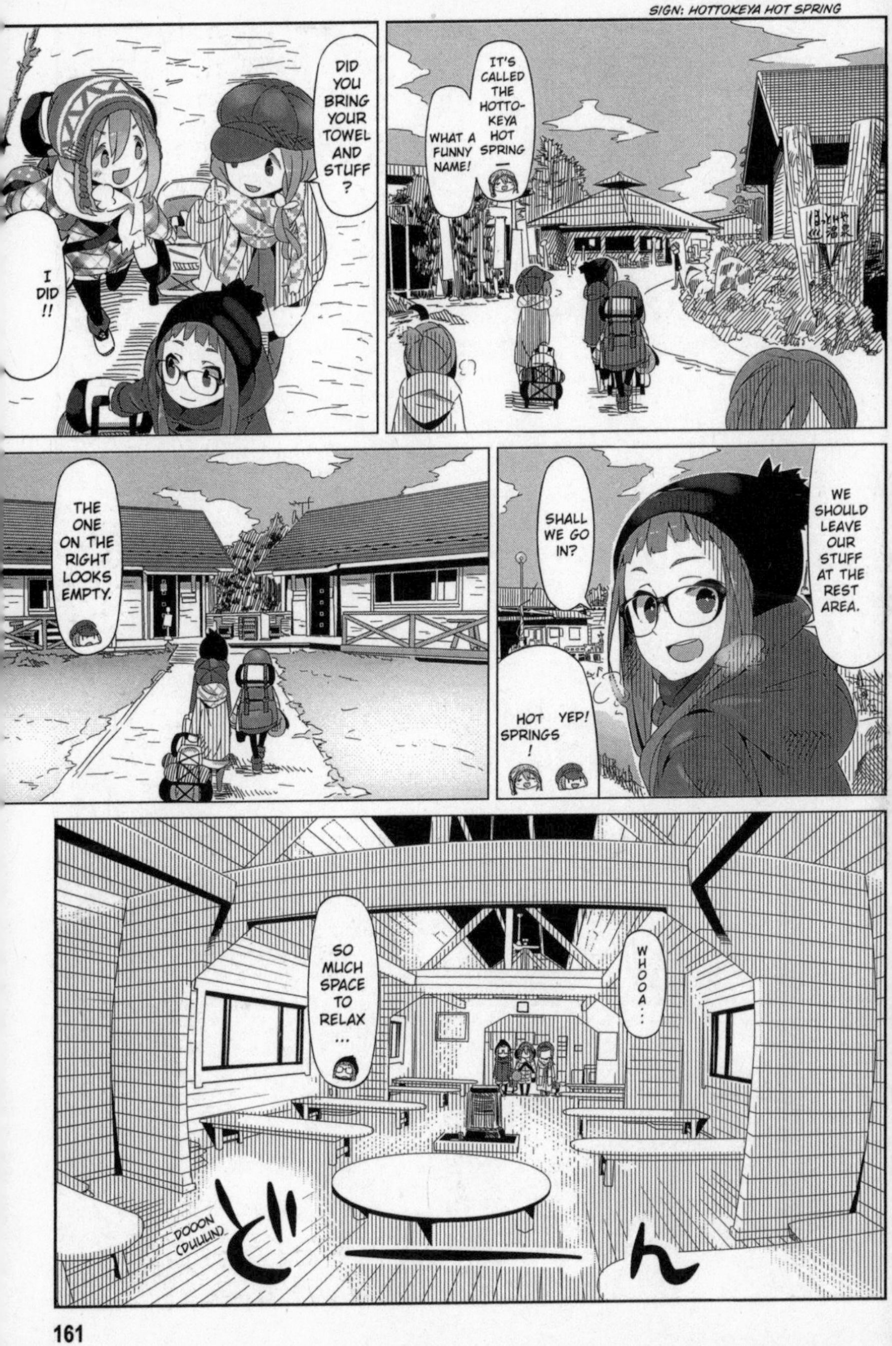
IT'S CALLED THE HOTTO-KEYA HOT SPRING
WHAT A FUNNY NAME!
DID YOU BRING YOUR TOWEL AND STUFF?
I DID!!
WE SHOULD LEAVE OUR STUFF AT THE REST AREA.
SHALL WE GO IN?
YEP!
HOT SPRINGS!
THE ONE ON THE RIGHT LOOKS EMPTY.
WHOOA...
SO MUCH SPACE TO RELAX...
DOOON (DUUUN)

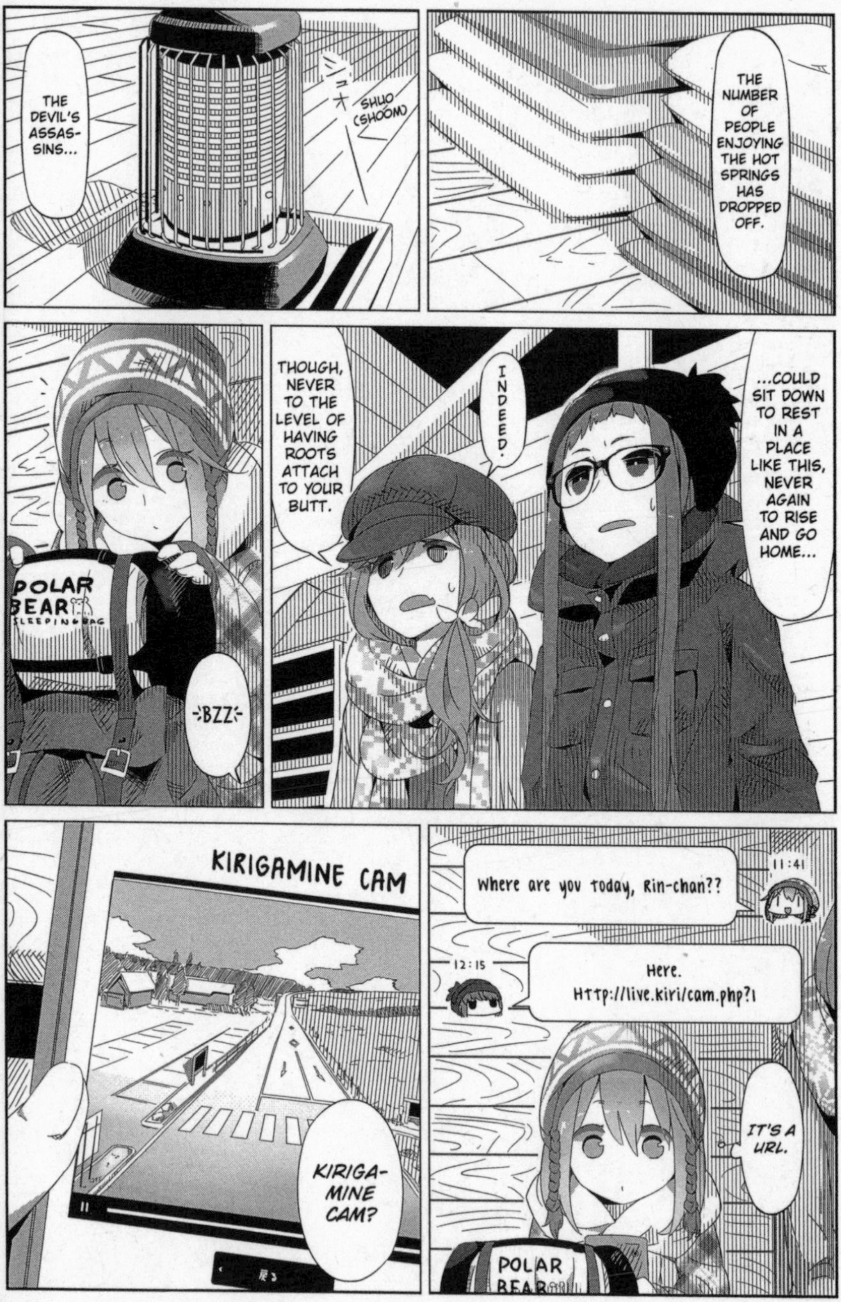
THE NUMBER OF PEOPLE ENJOYING THE HOT SPRINGS HAS DROPPED OFF.
THE DEVIL'S ASSAS-SINS...
シュオ
SHUO (SHOOM)
...COULD SIT DOWN TO REST IN A PLACE LIKE THIS, NEVER AGAIN TO RISE AND GO HOME...
INDEED.
THOUGH, NEVER TO THE LEVEL OF HAVING ROOTS ATTACH TO YOUR BUTT.
POLAR BEAR SLEEPING BAG
BZZ
11:41
Where are you today, Rin-chan??
12:15
Here.
Http://live.kiri/cam.php?1
IT'S A URL.
POLAR BEAR
KIRIGAMINE CAM
KIRIGA-MINE CAM?

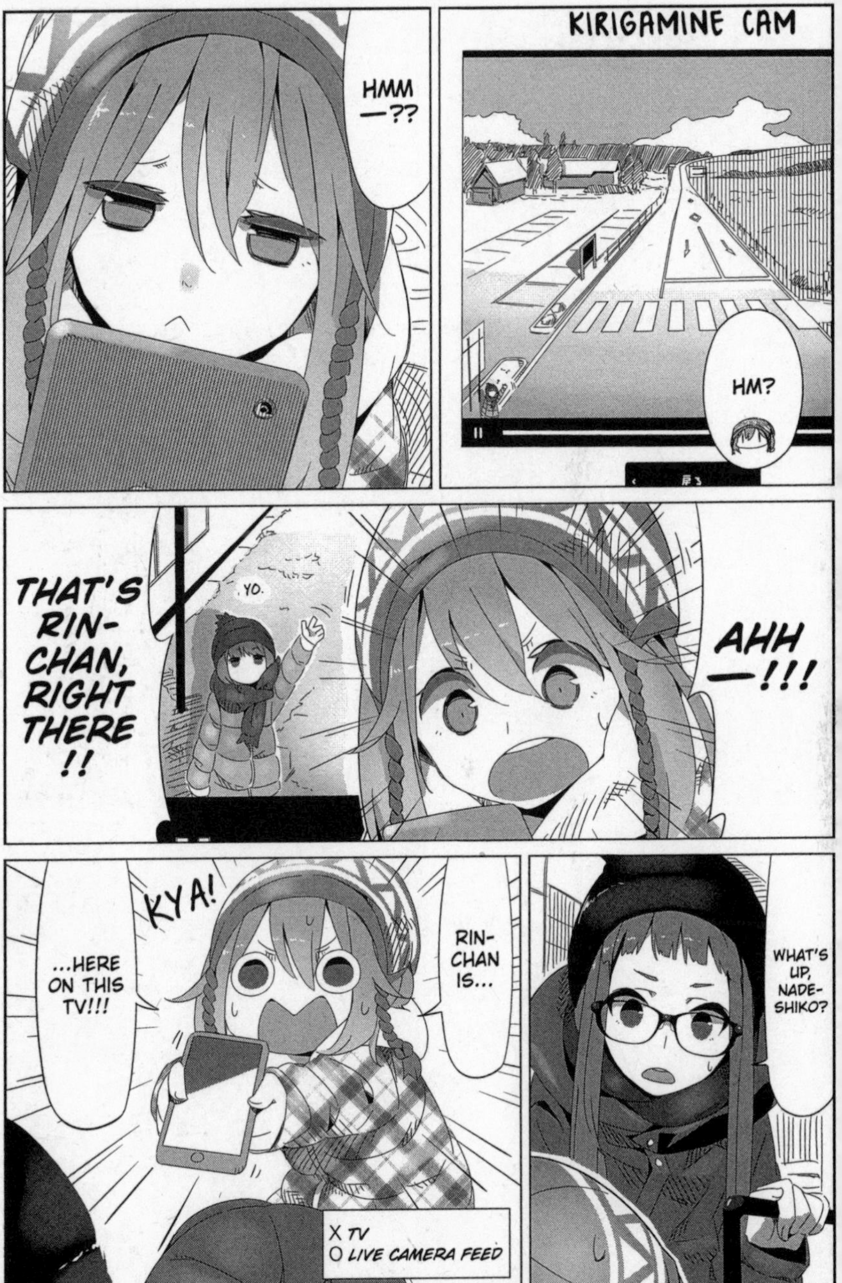
KIRIGAMINE CAM
HM?
HMM —??
AHH —!!!
YO.
THAT'S RIN-CHAN, RIGHT THERE!!
WHAT'S UP, NADE-SHIKO?
RIN-CHAN IS...
KYA!
...HERE ON THIS TV!!!
X TV
O LIVE CAMERA FEED

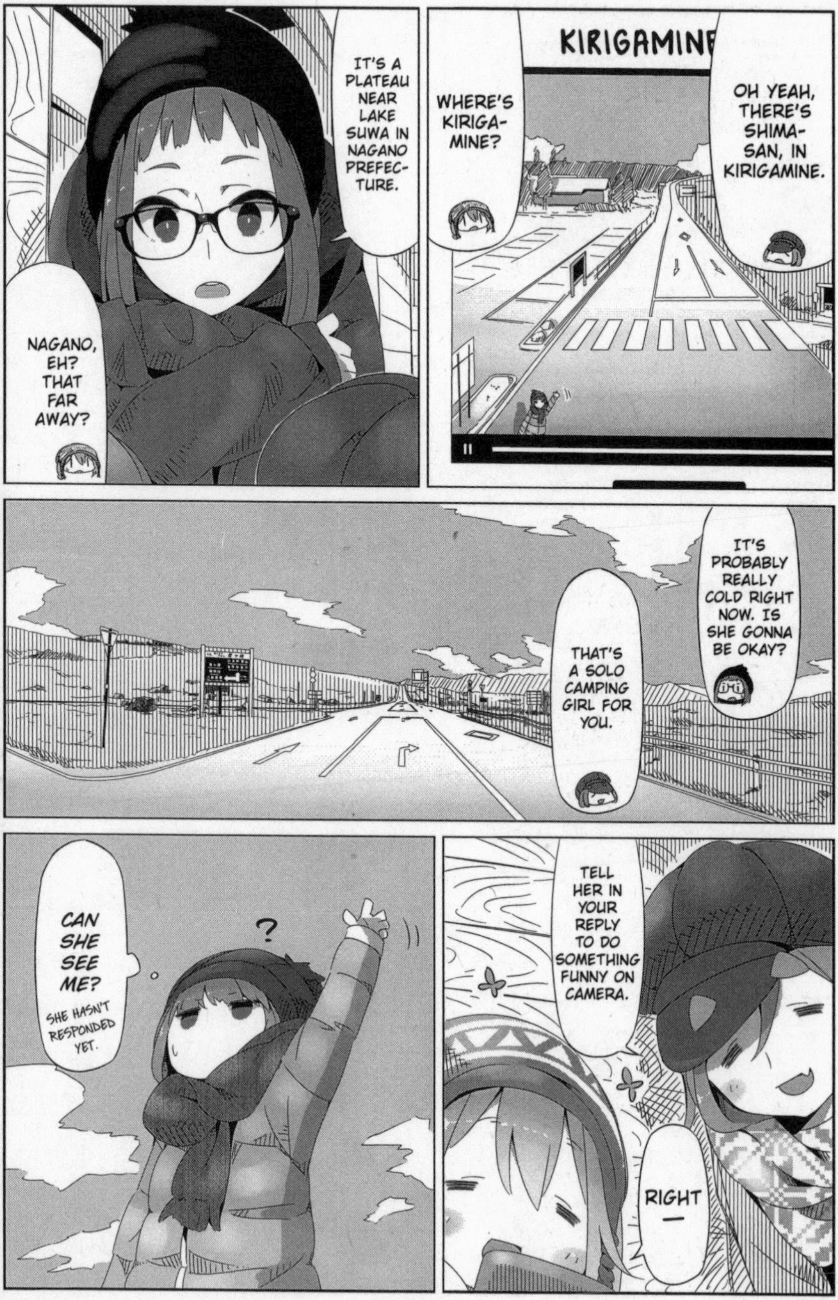
KIRIGAMINE
OH YEAH, THERE'S SHIMA-SAN, IN KIRIGAMINE.
WHERE'S KIRIGA-MINE?
IT'S A PLATEAU NEAR LAKE SUWA IN NAGANO PREFEC-TURE.
NAGANO, EH? THAT FAR AWAY?
IT'S PROBABLY REALLY COLD RIGHT NOW. IS SHE GONNA BE OKAY?
THAT'S A SOLO CAMPING GIRL FOR YOU.
TELL HER IN YOUR REPLY TO DO SOMETHING FUNNY ON CAMERA.
RIGHT—
CAN SHE SEE ME?
SHE HASN'T RESPONDED YET.

TELL HER IN YOUR REPLY TO DO SOME-THING FUNNY ON CAMERA.
RIGHT —
LOOK AT HER WAVE! RIN-CHAN'S SURE FULL OF PEP!
THAT'S FOR SURE — EVEN WITH IT THIS COLD.
WAIT, WE OUGHTA WRITE HER BACK.
OH.
TH-THAT'S SO TRUE.
AH!! A CAR'S COMING FROM BEHIND!!
WHOA!! RIN-CHAN, MOVE!!

<—THE SIDE STORY THAT BEGINS ON THE NEXT PAGE TOOK PLACE A SHORT TIME BEFORE CHAPTER 6...

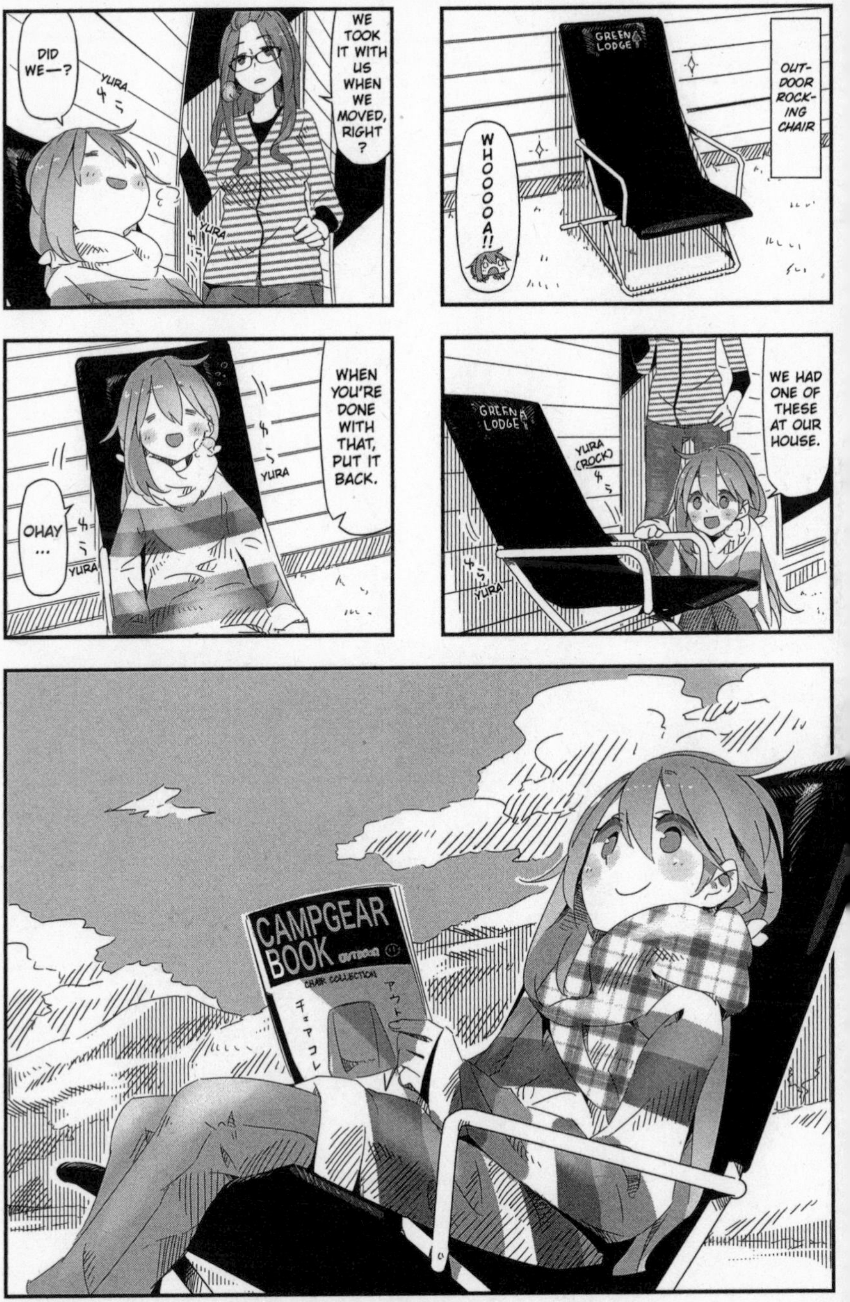
OUT-DOOR ROCK-ING CHAIR
GREEN LODGE
WHOOOOOA!!
WE TOOK IT WITH US WHEN WE MOVED, RIGHT?
DID WE—?
YURA
YURA
WE HAD ONE OF THESE AT OUR HOUSE.
GREEN LODGE
YURA (ROCK)
YURA
WHEN YOU'RE DONE WITH THAT, PUT IT BACK.
YURA
OHAY...
YURA
CAMPGEAR BOOK
CHAIR COLLECTION

Side Story SUNDAY AND THE ROCKING CHAIR

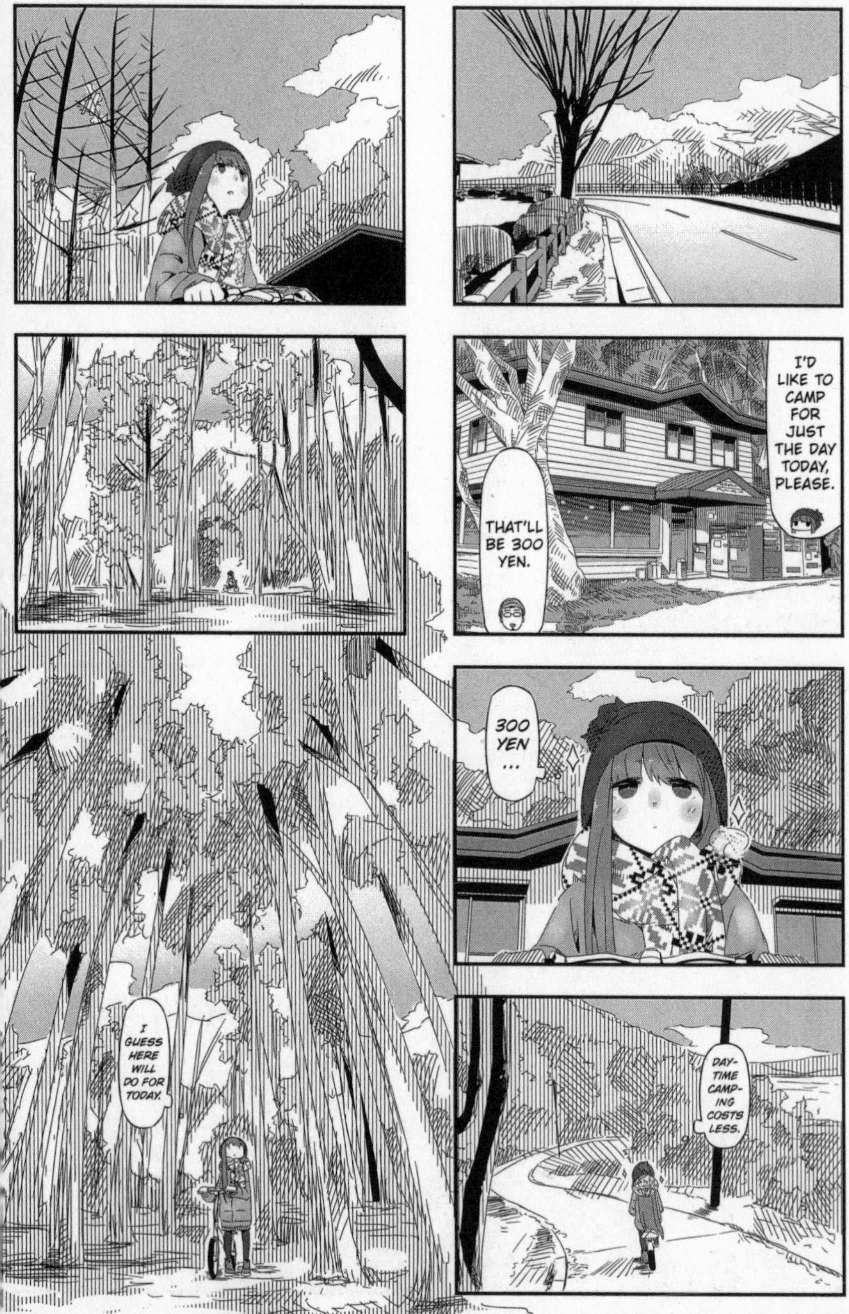
I'D LIKE TO CAMP FOR JUST THE DAY TODAY, PLEASE.
THAT'LL BE 300 YEN.
300 YEN...
DAY-TIME CAMP-ING COSTS LESS.
I GUESS HERE WILL DO FOR TODAY.

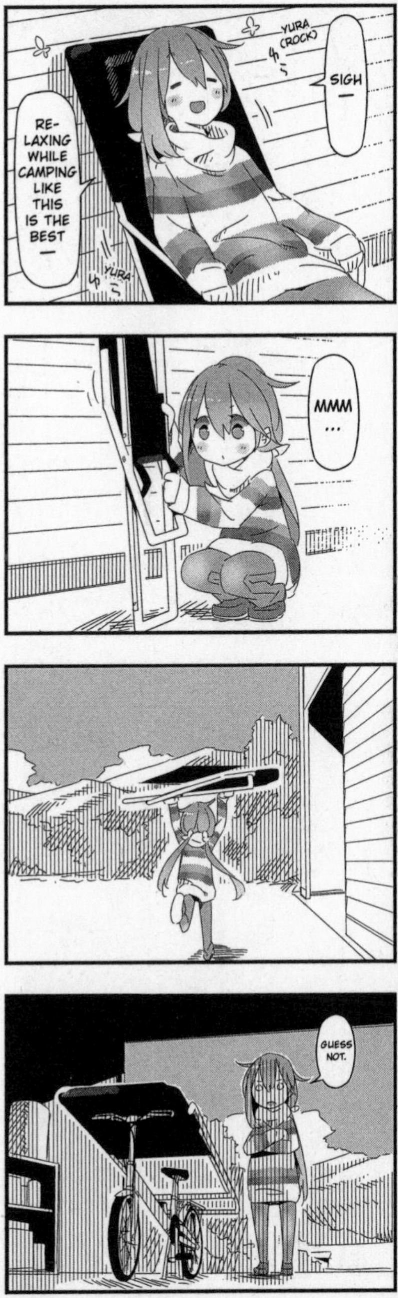
YURA (ROCK)
SIGH—
RE-LAXING WHILE CAMPING LIKE THIS IS THE BEST—
YURA
MMM...
GUESS NOT.

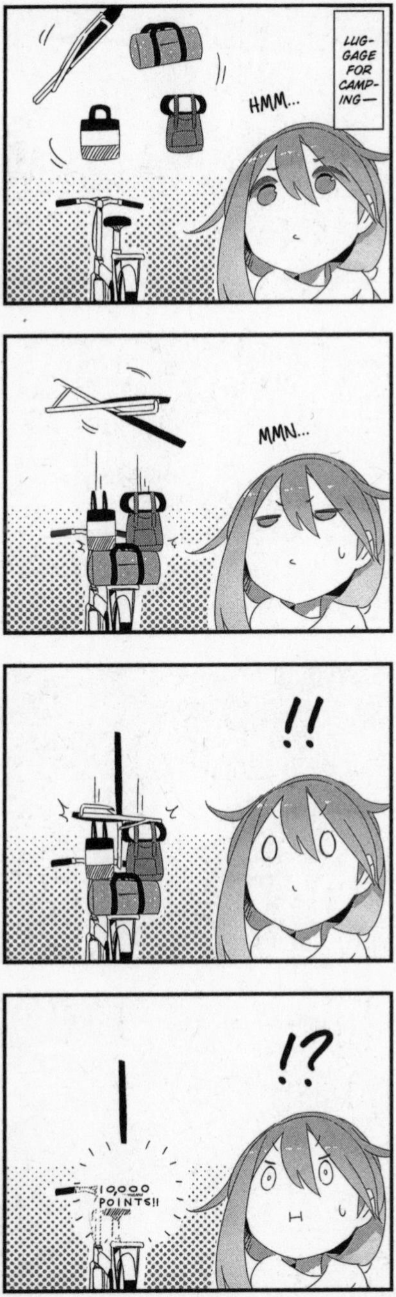
LUG-GAGE FOR CAMP-ING—
HMM...
MMN...
!!
!?
10,000 POINTS!!

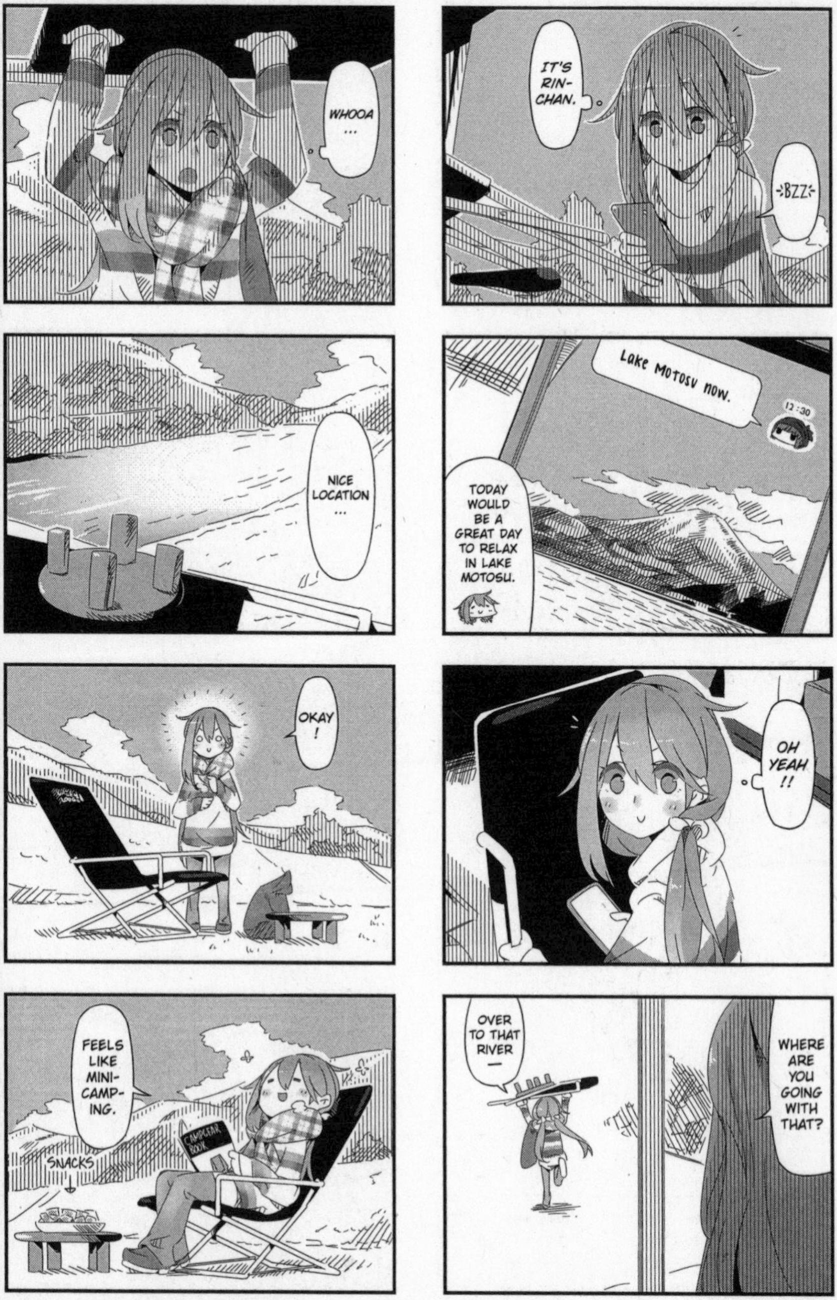

IT'S RIN-CHAN.
BZZ
WHOOA...
Lake Motosv now.
12:30
TODAY WOULD BE A GREAT DAY TO RELAX IN LAKE MOTOSU.
NICE LOCATION...
OH YEAH!!
OKAY!
WHERE ARE YOU GOING WITH THAT?
OVER TO THAT RIVER—
FEELS LIKE MINI-CAMPING.
CAMPGEAR BOOK
SNACKS

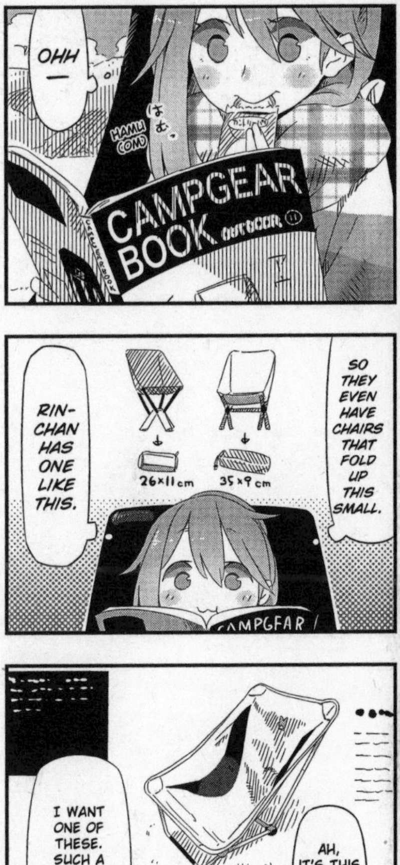
OHH—
HAMU (OM)
CAMPGEAR BOOK
SO THEY EVEN HAVE CHAIRS THAT FOLD UP THIS SMALL.
RIN-CHAN HAS ONE LIKE THIS.
26×11 cm
35×9 cm
AH, IT'S THIS ONE, THIS ONE.
I WANT ONE OF THESE. SUCH A COMFORTABLE CHAIR— ...
¥13,000 (TAX EXCLUDED)
THAT'S SO MUCH!!

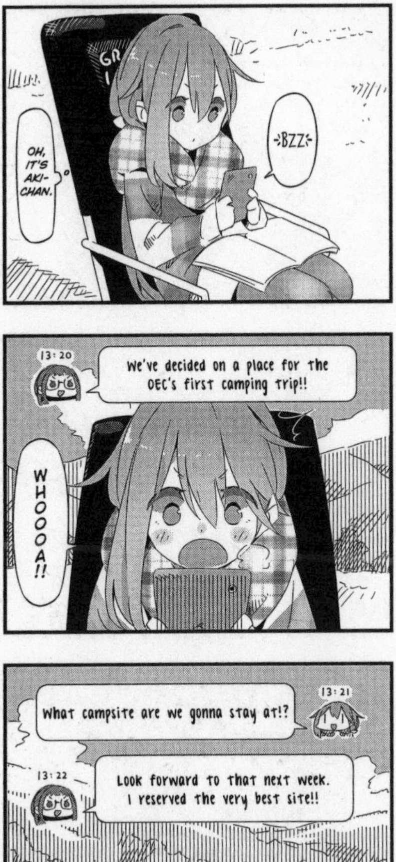
BZZ
OH, IT'S AKI-CHAN.
13:20
We've decided on a place for the OEC's first camping trip!!
WHOOOOA!!
13:21
What campsite are we gonna stay at!?
13:22
Look forward to that next week. I reserved the very best site!!
13:22
That's our Aki-chan!! (>V<)
13:23
Keh-keh...Like taking candy from a baby!!

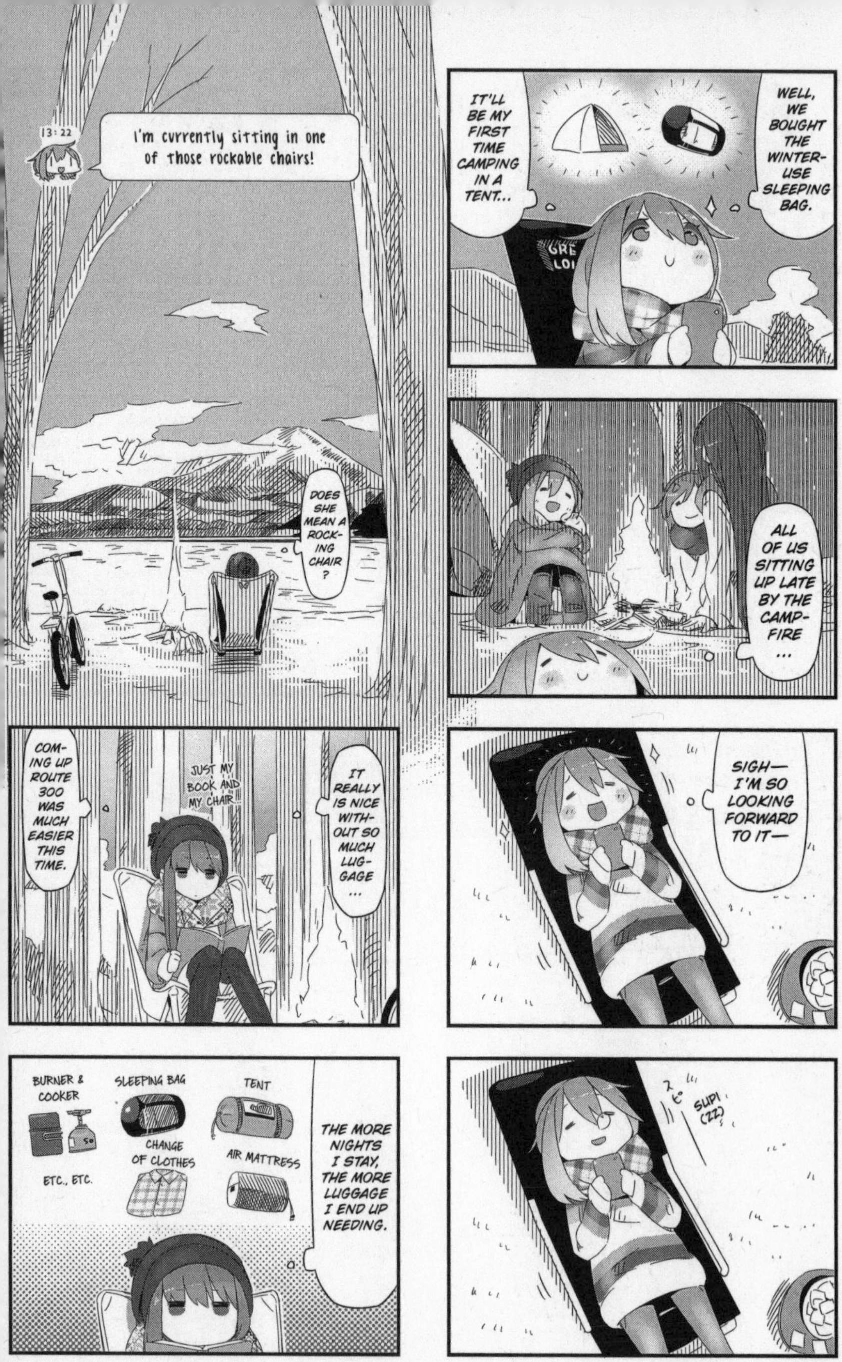
WELL, WE BOUGHT THE WINTER-USE SLEEPING BAG.
IT'LL BE MY FIRST TIME CAMPING IN A TENT...
GRE
LOI
ALL OF US SITTING UP LATE BY THE CAMP-FIRE...
SIGH— I'M SO LOOKING FORWARD TO IT—
SUPI (ZZZ)
13:22
I'm currently sitting in one of those rockable chairs!
DOES SHE MEAN A ROCK-ING CHAIR?
IT REALLY IS NICE WITH-OUT SO MUCH LUG-GAGE...
JUST MY BOOK AND MY CHAIR.
COM-ING UP ROUTE 300 WAS MUCH EASIER THIS TIME.
THE MORE NIGHTS I STAY, THE MORE LUGGAGE I END UP NEEDING.
BURNER & COOKER
SLEEPING BAG
TENT
CHANGE OF CLOTHES
AIR MATTRESS
ETC., ETC.

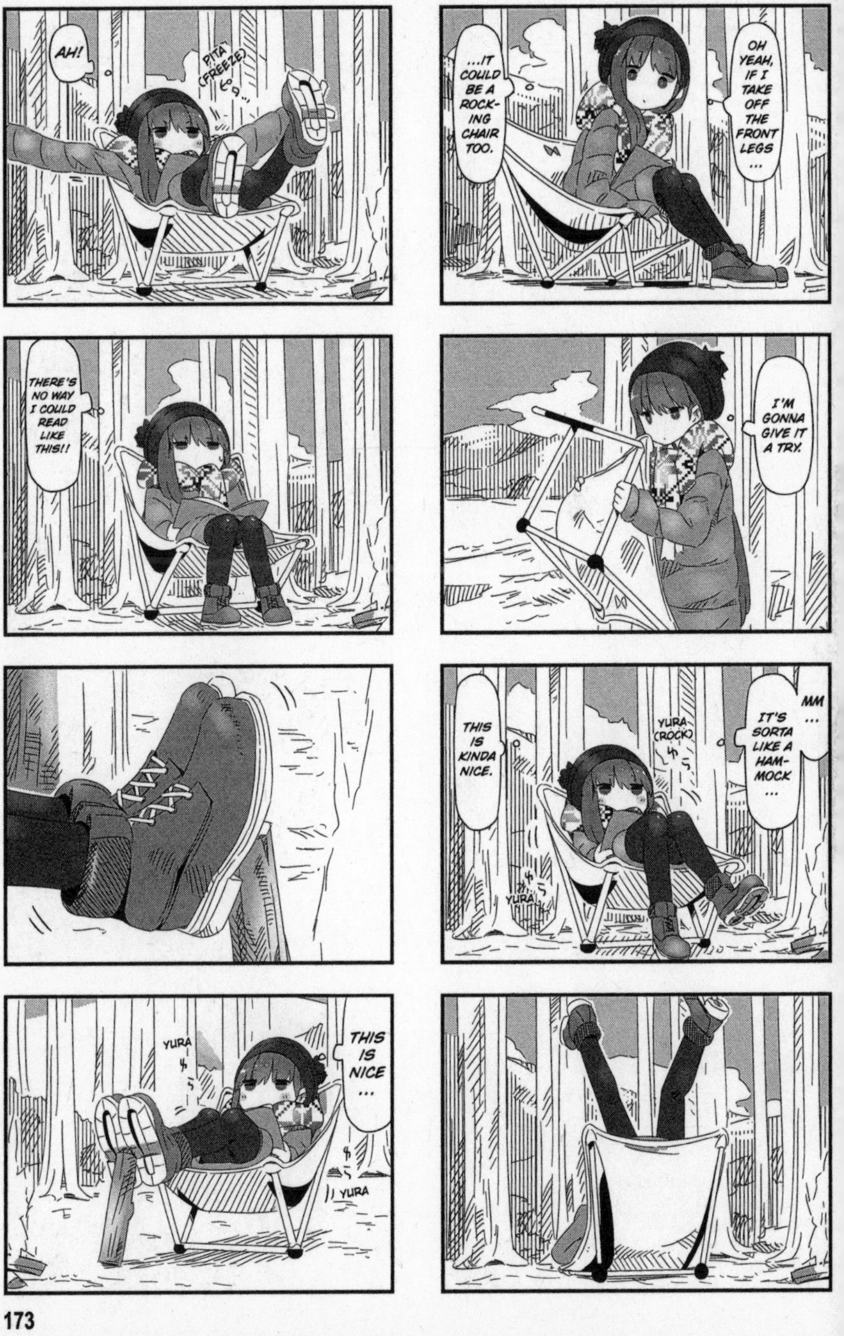
OH YEAH, IF I TAKE OFF THE FRONT LEGS ...
...IT COULD BE A ROCK-ING CHAIR TOO.
AH!
PITA (FREEZE)
I'M GONNA GIVE IT A TRY.
THERE'S NO WAY I COULD READ LIKE THIS!!
MM ...
IT'S SORTA LIKE A HAM-MOCK ...
YURA (ROCK)
THIS IS KINDA NICE.
YURA
THIS IS NICE ...
YURA
YURA

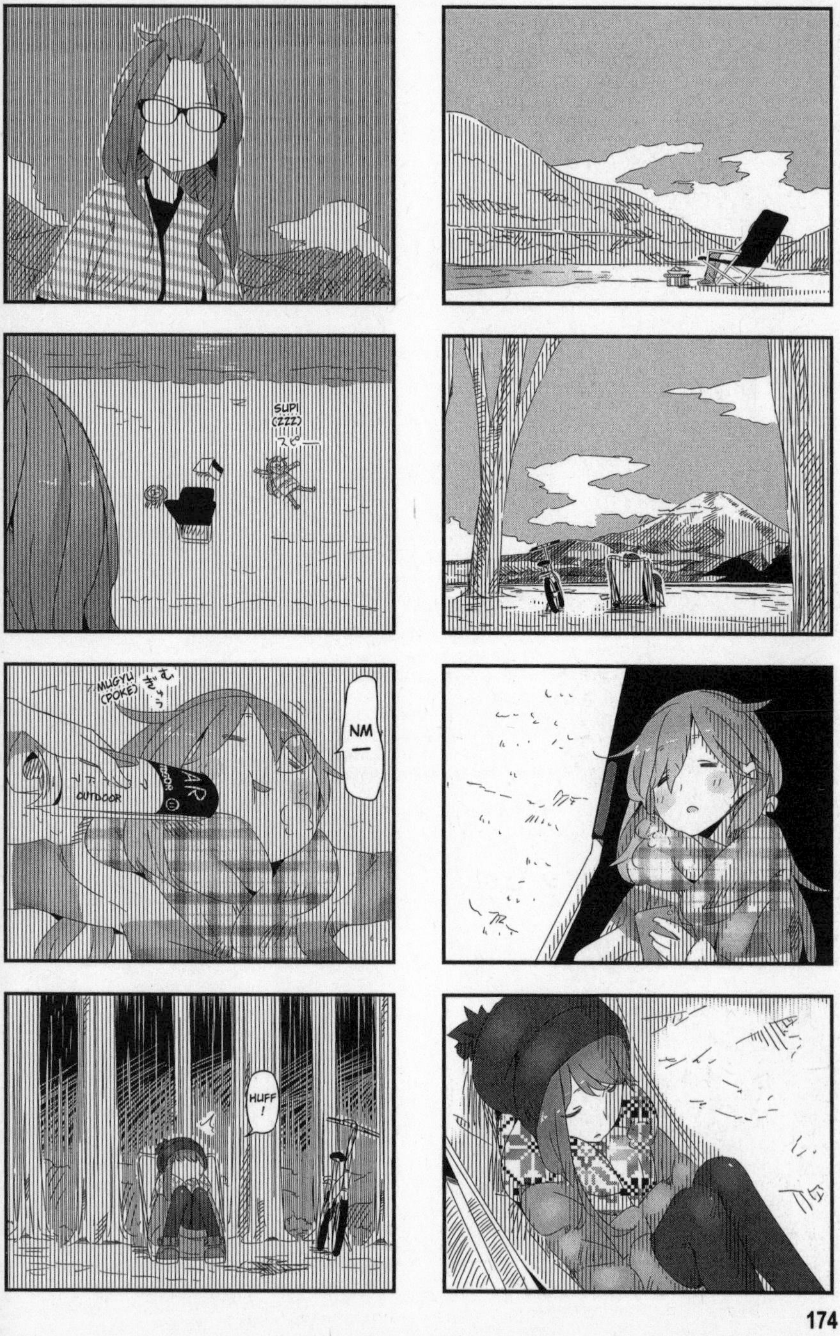
SUPI (ZZZ)
スピー
MUGYU (POKE)
むぎゅう
NM—
OUTDOOR
HUFF!

ピカ——— PIKAAA (FLASH)
THIS LIGHT LOOKS LIKE THE TYPE A FACTORY WORKER WOULD WEAR.
SO THEY HAVE THINGS LIKE THIS TOO.
UL-L.E.D. HEADLIGHT
5,000 YEN + TAX
HANGING THIS FROM THE TOP OF THE TENT, IT COULD WORK LIKE A LAN-TERN.
ピカ——— PIKAAA
WOW! THIS IS SO CON-VENIENT.
HEADLIGHT ...
SO CUTE ...
ピカ——— PIKAAA

TRANSLATION NOTES

COMMON HONORIFICS

no honorific: Indicates familiarity or closeness; if used without permission or reason, addressing someone in this manner would constitute an insult.

-san: The Japanese equivalent of Mr./Mrs./Miss. If a situation calls for politeness, this is the fail-safe honorific.

-kun: Used most often when referring to boys, this indicates affection or familiarity. Occasionally used by older men among their peers, but it may also be used by anyone referring to a person of lower standing.

-chan: An affectionate honorific indicating familiarity used mostly in reference to girls; also used in reference to cute persons or animals of either gender.

-sensei: A respectful term for teachers, artists, or high-level professionals.

(o)nee: Japanese equivalent to "older sis."
(o)nii: Japanese equivalent to "older bro."

100 yen is approximately $1 USD.

PAGE 11

"Cone-nichiwa": A portmanteau of cone and *konnichiwa*, Japanese for "hello."

PAGE 42

"Like an eel's bed": The expression *unagi no nedokoro* is used to described long, narrow spaces.

PAGE 59

Suspension bridge effect: When someone sees another while standing on a suspension bridge and misattributes their heart-pounding fear for the feeling of love.

PAGE 98

Zosui: A rice and vegetable stew, often made from leftover ingredients.

PAGE 118

I Love to Ski Mount Fuji: The Japanese reads *Fuji-san sukiiiii*, a play on words between *suki* (like/love) and *sukii* (skiing).

PAGE 129

"They're two to three Yukichis more": Yukichi Fukuzawa, one of the fathers of modern Japan, is the face of the 10,000-yen note. Yukichi is similar to how the term "Benjamins" refers to $100 bills in the United States.

PAGE 130

Oshikuramanjuu: A game where a group of kids make a circle on the ground, then, standing back-to-back/side to side against one another, arms folded, they try to jostle one another out of the circle without using their arms.

PAGE 161

Hottokeya: "Hottokeya" sounds similar to the Japanese for "leave it alone."

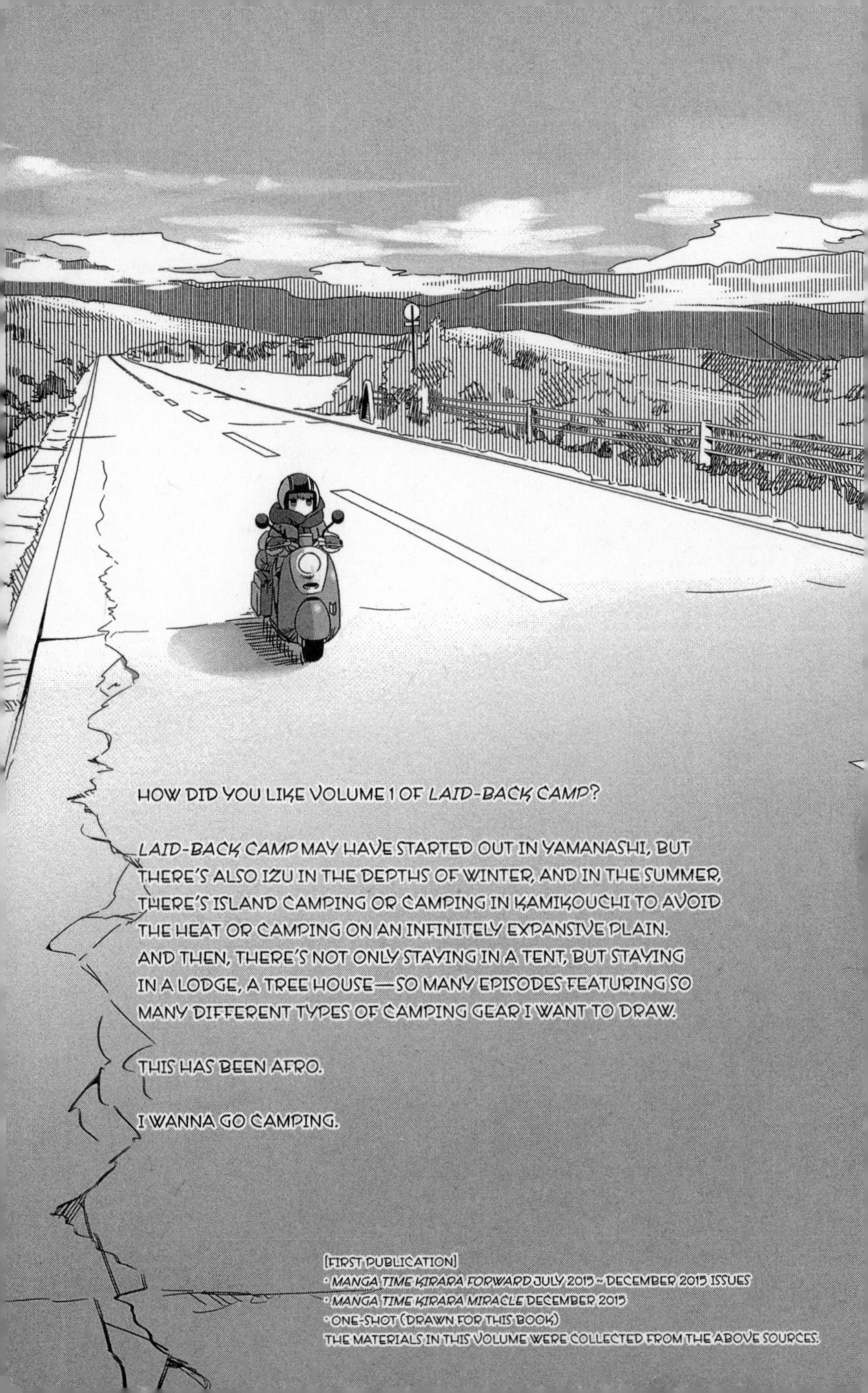

HOW DID YOU LIKE VOLUME 1 OF *LAID-BACK CAMP*?

LAID-BACK CAMP MAY HAVE STARTED OUT IN YAMANASHI, BUT THERE'S ALSO IZU IN THE DEPTHS OF WINTER, AND IN THE SUMMER, THERE'S ISLAND CAMPING OR CAMPING IN KAMIKOUCHI TO AVOID THE HEAT OR CAMPING ON AN INFINITELY EXPANSIVE PLAIN. AND THEN, THERE'S NOT ONLY STAYING IN A TENT, BUT STAYING IN A LODGE, A TREE HOUSE—SO MANY EPISODES FEATURING SO MANY DIFFERENT TYPES OF CAMPING GEAR I WANT TO DRAW.

THIS HAS BEEN AFRO.

I WANNA GO CAMPING.

[FIRST PUBLICATION]
· *MANGA TIME KIRARA FORWARD* JULY 2015 ~ DECEMBER 2015 ISSUES
· *MANGA TIME KIRARA MIRACLE* DECEMBER 2015
· ONE-SHOT (DRAWN FOR THIS BOOK)
THE MATERIALS IN THIS VOLUME WERE COLLECTED FROM THE ABOVE SOURCES.

LAID BACK CAMP 1

Afro

Translation: **Amber Tamosaitis** ✳ Lettering: **Bianca Pistillo**

YURUCAMP Vol. 1
© 2015 Afro. All rights reserved. First published in Japan in 2015 by HOUBUNSHA CO., LTD., Tokyo. English translation rights in United States, Canada, and United Kingdom arranged with HOUBUNSHA CO., LTD. through Tuttle-Mori Agency, Inc., Tokyo.

English translation © 2018 by Yen Press, LLC

Yen Press
1290 Avenue of the Americas
New York, NY 10104

Visit us at yenpress.com
facebook.com/yenpress
twitter.com/yenpress
yenpress.tumblr.com
instagram.com/yenpress

First Yen Press Edition: March 2018

Yen Press is an imprint of Yen Press, LLC.
The Yen Press name and logo are trademarks of Yen Press, LLC.

The publisher is not responsible for websites (or their content) that are not owned by the publisher.

Library of Congress Control Number: 2017959206

ISBNs: 978-0-316-51778-2 (paperback)
       978-0-316-51780-5 (ebook)

10 9 8 7 6 5 4 3 2 1

BVG

Printed in the United States of America